"Get out of my office, Dr. Dwight!"

There was no real anger in Dr. Chris Land's voice, only sudden knowledge of what he must do.

Dr. Dwight's face flushed with rage. "You're forcing me to fight!"

"For your life."

Dwight turned toward the door. Then he spoke. "You might force me to delve into your private life."

"Meaning?"

"Dr. Land, I think the State Commission might be interested to learn that one of the doctors in your clinic is also your mistress!"

A TOUCH OF GLORY
was originally published by
Doubleday & Company, Inc.

Are there paperbound books you want but cannot find in your retail stores?

Frank G. Slaughter

A TOUCH
OF GLORY

PUBLISHED BY POCKET BOOKS NEW YORK

A TOUCH OF GLORY

Doubleday edition published 1945

POCKET BOOK edition published January, 1956

8th printing.....................September, 1975

L

This POCKET BOOK edition includes every word contained
in the original, higher-priced edition. It is printed from
brand-new plates made from completely reset, clear, easy-to-
read type. POCKET BOOK editions are published by POCKET
BOOKS, a division of Simon & Schuster, Inc., 630 Fifth
Avenue, New York, N.Y. 10020. Trademarks registered
in the United States and other countries.

A TOUCH
OF GLORY

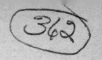

1

HE SAT on the observation platform of the Gulf Coast Limited
with his hands folded on his cane—a tall, rather spare figure
in his faded summer uniform, his eyes searching the curve of
track ahead. The sun (it was low in the west now) etched the
ragged shapes of pines against a copper sky; one of the last
direct rays picked out the caduceus on his lapel and softened
the tanned face above. It was a face gaunt from recent illness,
withdrawn in a sadness of its own; a face that didn't quite
respond to the caress of the Southern evening. But the eyes
lighted when they marked a gash in the pine barrens to the
west. Once the Limited took that curve, Chris Land knew that
he'd breathe the familiar blue tang of the Gulf itself. One
more mile, and the water tower of the Milton switching yard
would make its own silhouette against the sunset. He wondered why he felt no thrill of home-coming.

Two months ago—lying in a hospital in Devon, and fresh
from the slogging grind in Italy—this moment had seemed his
ultimate goal in the war. There had been no afterthought re-
garding his duty, no sense of guilt at leaving war behind.
Certainly he felt conscience-free now. Reposing in the pocket
of his blouse were his official retirement papers; pinned to his
left breast were his campaign ribbons and the ribbon of the
Purple Heart.

No one could ask questions as to the future of Major
Christopher Land, MCAUS. That had been firmly settled
months ago, in a rubble-strewn garden just north of Civita-

vecchia. Pete Barrows, his surgical assistant, had done the settling when he had ripped away a blood-soaked legging to show how thoroughly a rifle bullet can splinter the tibia.

As always, Chris felt his mind jump wildly at the memory. There was the slow, numbing ache, spreading from thigh to brain as Pete whisked him back to the stretcher line. Pete's insistence on surgery then and there—a decision that had saved his leg. Pete's skillful paravertebral blocks to control spasm and allow circulation to reassert itself. The Tobruk splint at the dressing station, combining traction and cast and permitting his immediate evacuation to the air strip. In an hour he'd been on a table at the Ospedale Maggiore. . . . Yes, Pete Barrows had saved his leg, all right. It was ironic that Pete should have been blown to bits just four days later, when the 90th Portable Hospital Unit had moved on to the next big show.

Even now Chris wondered why he couldn't feel Pete's loss more keenly. He had already been flown to a hospital cot in England when they'd brought him the news; in fact, he'd been waiting for the numbing spinal anesthesia to creep higher, for the stretcher that would take him to another operating room.

That was the last installment in the battle to put him on two feet again. The bone graft had taken hours. When he'd come out of his postoperative coma, the weight of the cast enclosing his leg was the only reality. He had tried hard to concentrate on the memory of Pete Barrows, to remind himself that he would never work in a front line again. Thoughts like that wouldn't come real. He couldn't face them now, with his rehabilitation behind him: the long weeks at Walter Reed, the month on a sun deck at Virginia Beach, the painful but definite transition from wheel chair to crutches to cane.

Once again he told himself solemnly that he was free of the job he'd signed on for the duration. Free of regret that he could never return, and of the emptiness of Pete's death. But no compensating emotion had moved into the void. He was numb and waiting, that was all.

Waiting for what? For your first glimpse of home, he told himself sharply. The Limited rumbled over a trestle on the edge of the apron of marsh that fanned out from the pine barrens to meet the Gulf. He had hunted through those green channels as a boy—and camped in the high dunes that fringed the Gulf. Now he got up carefully, reminded himself that he

2

could walk without pain again, and leaned out from the rail of the observation platform. Something's gone wrong out there, he told himself. My feelings have changed—but not half as much as the landscape.

It wasn't an optical illusion: the marsh had vanished when he looked again. Perhaps it hadn't ever existed. Certainly the drowned estuary he had expected was now a high-banked drainage ditch. The land beyond had been reclaimed—for miles, it seemed: a flat monotony of white sand, bulkheaded solidly where Lighthouse Creek had once meandered. The dunes were leveled too. On the horizon the Gulf of Mexico gleamed in the sunset like an endless tranquil millpond. Even the Gulf looked far off and unreal against the raw newness of the fill.

The Limited roared inland as the tracks swept toward a cypress hammock. The trees were yellow ghosts in the evening—tall and grave and blessedly untouched by time or steam shovels. Chris breathed the hot stench of the swamp gratefully. Memory stirred in earnest, bringing back the spindly-legged boy who had shot a bobcat from that same water-logged palmetto—and missed death by inches when a cottonmouth uncoiled in its nest of hyacinth.

He looked up abruptly, in response to a metallic roar. The train had swung into reclaimed land again. Here a steel-mesh fence marked the right of way on either side—a barrier that paralleled the rails as far as the eye could reach. Behind it a great shipyard boiled with controlled frenzy. There was another crash as he watched: he saw the prewelded superstructure of a freighter nest home on a waiting hull and heard the whir of winches swinging the cranes free. The drills seemed to chatter even before the huskies in dungarees could swarm to deck and catwalks. From the train the workers resembled woodpeckers on Mars. The din they were raising shook the windows of the Limited as it roared past.

So this was the Borland yard. He didn't need the stencil on the work gate to tell him that. Newsprint and the movies had explained the phenomenon of Calvin Borland, even in England. The Proteus who had moved so easily from mining to Wall Street—and now to the bustle of shipbuilding. The confident operator who had come down to the Gulf with the first power cable out of Tennessee Valley.

Borland had spent millions to drain the marshes around Milton, to build roads for his trailer towns in the scrub, to

3

block out his ways and tool sheds and assembly lines. His first keel had been laid with all the ease of a fable in steel. Chris remembered the story of the eight Liberty ships launched here in a single morning. The corvettes that spawned in the West Island extension like mosquitos in June. The transport that Borland's engineers had put into the water in just eleven days . . .

The train rocketed on through Proteus' own world—a mirage to Chris Land's eyes, for all its precision. The monstrous maturity of the machine had always awed him a little—even when he could grasp its function. After all, his surgeon's fingers had always fumbled at carburetors; in the westering light the activity at the yard was a battle of Titans for a prize he could not see.

God knows he should have prepared himself for this explosion of a childhood memory. America had begun to win the war at plants like Borland's. A native son might even be proud that the man had chosen Milton as his new outlet— that he had bought the old King place on the Hill and spent another fortune to restore the landscaping. Tonight Chris Land thought, *To hell with miracles! I want to rest.* He hitched his way to the door and entered the observation car. Sinking into an armchair, he closed his eyes in earnest.

Things will look better tomorrow, he promised himself. When you've baked awhile in the sun at St. Lucie and gone over the rigging of the *Lady Jane.* What right have you to sulk in your weariness? You've paid your debt to posterity and put its problems behind you. Things will look different when you've learned to swim a mile before breakfast again.

He dozed frankly, ignoring the buzz of expensive conversation from the sleek-jowled men all around him. A cotton-wool sleep, too fitful to be called rest. When the whistle whined he sat bolt upright, mildly startled to find that it was only a train signaling for the Junction, and not an approaching shell with his number daubed on the nose.

Chris raised the shade and peered out at the land. The pine barren was peppered with trailers. Jalopy jobs, for the most part, scattered haphazard between the palmetto clumps, thick as fleas along the macadam that overpassed the right of way. The mushroom town managed to look both new and forlorn. A thing of plywood and tin roofs, it spread into the barrens from the focal point of a garish movie house and six full-blown saloons. A long loading platform marked the official site of the Junction. Even the freight sheds, he noted, were slick with new paint and out-at-elbow from constant use. Unlike the cheap-jack houses behind them, they had an air of solidity.

He flicked the buildings beyond with a quick, unhappy look. Here, then, was a mudsill town, on Milton's doorstep, more transitory than the movie set it resembled. Like a movie set, it already looked abandoned. The unkempt children playing in the dog fennel did not soften that impression. These were wartime waifs—conditioned to the tourist cabin and the dust of migration. The brood of new gypsies, born to wisdom before their time. He shook off the thought as the train slackened speed, and let his eyes rest on the limousine parked beside the loading platform like a visitor from another cosmos.

He saw the uniformed chauffeur dart forward to snatch a pair of pale leather hatboxes from a maid. He saw an adoring porter join the procession with more bags. The girl crossing the cinder platform on disdainful spike heels was alien to this background—and yet it seemed to suit her, too. She looked slender in the gray *trotteur* that had certainly come out of Paris ahead of the Wehrmacht; she looked sulky and vaguely unhappy, though Chris could not have said why.

He watched her trim retreating back as she nodded to the chauffeur. When she stepped into the car he had an all-too-brief glimpse of a pair of long, tanned legs, perfect beyond the dreams of advertising. A girl like that, Chris thought, could afford to let a dozen pairs of nylons rest in her dresser. He had had no time to resent her when the limousine purred toward the overpass. He saw her profile against the open window—cameo-fine and deeply tanned. Her face looked innocent of make-up, save for the heavily painted mouth. He watched her light a cigarette and inhale deeply; something about the gesture convinced him that she was both sulky and bored. But of course that was part of the tradition of rich men's daughters.

The train picked up speed again as it snored through the underpass. On the straightaway beyond he watched the limousine purr away for the turn. Here a private road crossed old cotton fields toward the King place—set on higher ground a good mile to the north, among the water oaks of Slave Hill.

Why had he known that she was Rosalie Borland, the shipbuilder's daughter? He had seen her in newsreels, of course—and had told himself that the camera lied. Really, she had no right to be lovely, with all those millions. She should have been vaguely square, like her father. . . . His mind dwelt on that heart-stopping curve from calf to thigh as she had stepped into the limousine. After all, it had been a long time since he had opened his eyes wide for a girl.

The last time came back to him now, complete with background. He had been lying deep in a seaward-facing meadow on Capri, with his head in Deirdre's lap. They had stolen ten days of Capri, to play out the oldest game that man has invented to soothe his progress to eternity—he from his unit, Deirdre from her office at the Naples AMG. . . . Chris had suggested Capri with *South Wind* in mind. But he knew that Deirdre would have joined him as readily in Amalfi or Sicily.

Now he could sit tranquilly and recapture the white curve of her throat—and how charmingly it had bronzed in that holiday of sun and badinage. The way her eyes had teased him that day in the meadow; and again that evening, on the terrace of their old inn set in its grove of olive trees. He had quite forgotten that this was once a Roman emperor's garden when she came into his arms. . . .

Was the French cynic right when he insisted that woman's virtue is man's greatest invention? It was pleasant to remind himself that Deirdre had played at love as easily as he—with no more regrets when their holiday ended. Women like that were rare in any language, he insisted. Especially in this great matriarchy of America. He wondered how long he could content himself with the solitude of St. Lucie Cay. How long before he must come out of that lonely haven and resume the ancient bachelor game of prowling.

The whistle called again, and his porter came through the car to ask about his bags. Chris paused once in the vestibule to breathe and looked out fearfully at the suburbs of Milton. But the train had already dropped into the long cut between the icehouse and the turpentine sheds. He saw only a blur of neons against the early dusk, the flowering of the overhead block signal that slotted the Limited into its berth.

Five minutes later he followed his bags down the platform. It hardly mattered that the terminal was brand new, like everything else he had seen. Or that his redcap was a bustling stranger herding him through a concourse that resembled a football week end minus the glamour. Halfway to the taxi stand he changed his mind abruptly and told the porter to check his valises. He had been through enough of those tussles for a taxi: this time he'd walk into the esplanade and explore on foot. Uncle Jeff wouldn't be expecting him, thank heaven; he'd been careful to keep the time of his arrival a secret. Perhaps he'd drop into the hospital later, to see if the old man was operating. Perhaps he'd sit for an hour over shrimps and beer in the Cuban café on Water Street. Absorb the town through his senses, before he thought about it too keenly.

He paused in the arch that gave to the outdoors, blinking a little as the first air-raid siren screamed. As always, the sound tore at his reflexes cruelly: he caught himself in time, before he could duck to cover—in this case, the magazine stand. Instead he leaned shakily against a pillar in the entrance and fumbled for his pipe. Each time it was a trifle easier to come out of that other life. This was one corner of a blazing world where bombs did not fall. The lazy, half-amused stir of the drill was proof enough of that. Porters still moved into the taxi rank with their luggage. A bus snored away into the night, packed to the doors: the driver, he guessed, was eager to have a start when the next blue alert came.

Chris was smiling now. There was something touching about the way his countrymen played this game of death-by-proxy. He had the right to smile at their boredom. After all, he had given a sizable portion of a tibia to allow them to go on playing games in peace.

Beyond the station the city was blanketed in darkness. On the esplanade he could make out the shapes of new buildings. Beacons cut the sky, silhouetting the contour of the Old Church on Duval Square, the bulk of the deSoto Hotel, where he had danced his junior prom. He let his eyes lift when the beacons crossed on a passenger plane throbbing west. The night mail (he checked it automatically) bound for Dallas with a stop at Shreveport if there were high-priority passengers aboard.

The red alert began its banshee warble. Behind him, in the station, travelers were stalled in knots; the fluorescent lighting above the benches dimmed and died. He felt his senses pulling him away from that cave, into the clean night of the esplanade. At the front he had fought that same impulse often. It was only natural to seek out the thing that menaced you, as if, by seeing it, you could resist it more effectively.

7

He smiled in earnest as the voice of a train announcer poured out overhead. The drawl told him that he was home again, even though the welcome was impersonal.

"This is a red alert, folks. Jes' keep your places."

Chris settled against the cool solidity of the column and wiped his forehead. It wasn't pleasant to admit that the sirens had jolted the delicate balance of his sympathetic nervous system. Wounded men had described the phenomenon, so he could diagnose his own case perfectly. Not that he wasn't well enough, he insisted. Nerve scars just took a long time to heal.

When the blue alert sounded again he let the rush of pent-up travel carry him into the esplanade: soldiers on leave, brief-cased businessmen, a hodge-podge of workers in overalls who managed to look prosperous despite their grimy hands. . . . He avoided the crush at the bus station and walked down the alley of date palms that led across the esplanade into deSoto Street. The hotel looked different as he approached. Even in the blackout he could see that it had acquired a marquee and a doorman in a zombie uniform.

He scarcely looked up when the all-clear sounded and the lights winked on in Duval Square. The beat of a juke box in the Sugar Bowl told him what had happened to the town's oldest pharmacy. He wasn't surprised to find the iron awning gone from the Surprise Store—to note that the store had changed from a small dry-goods shop to a bustling mart, jammed with yard workers.

Three years ago, when he had left Milton for good, the town had lived for its naval stores, the lumber mill, the small shipyard in the curve of the harbor. Its central square had held the classic pattern of the South: the contentment that waited for business, and yawned a bit while it waited. All of Milton had been like that: the faded white houses, the deep, sunbitten peace of their gardens, the public peace of the square itself. Old men had played checkers here by the hour, under the great live oaks. The clerks in the stores had lingered for five minutes of gossip before they had wrapped the most trivial purchase.

Now the war had needled mild enterprise to fever pitch. Borland had absorbed the shipyard and the lumber mill. It was a story that repeated itself endlessly, all over America; it was a routine essential to wartime. What right had he to resent this intrusion on his memories? Win, lose, or draw, you always lost your memories in a war.

He could find the old town easily enough by turning into Stuart Street. That corner would be unchanged, he knew. He pictured his uncle's house, in its frame of mossed boughs, tranquil as an old aristocrat who still keeps up his front. The house was like its owner in that. Geoffrey Land would never lose his poise, even if the small hospital he had founded bled him white.

Tomorrow would have to do for that reunion. Tonight he was in no mood to face the cold clarity of his uncle's mind. A taxi drifted up to the traffic light, miraculously empty. Chris got in on an impulse, told the driver to take him to St. Lucie, and waved away his objections with a bill. Maybe I'll be stranded on the Gulf tonight, he thought. I hardly think I'll mind.

The taxi fled down Main and swerved into Water Street: the driver was insolently eager to return for more fares. The Milton water front had always been tough, in Milton's way. Tonight a dozen cafés lured the crowds idling down the wide sidewalk. Girls smiled into the taxi at every light: painted, hard-as-nails girls who had never learned their profession in this once-mild tenderloin. Escobar's shrimp house, it seemed, was their special rendezvous. Chris grinned as he recalled his plan to dine there and talk fishing with the Cuban proprietor. So far Milton had stolen his appetite. If he fished tonight, it would be in the dark well of his mind.

Once again he closed his eyes and tried to doze through this last lap of his home-coming. But the bustle of the town still intruded: the blare of the juke boxes, the pound of heels on the pavements, the shouted invitation of a sailor to a girl. Even if I were blind, he thought, I'd know the town has changed. Its drawl is gone; the voice that has replaced it is brash and busy and insincere. A double-talk that jangles in the brain.

His taxi swerved, and he looked through the window, determined to reproach Milton no more tonight. They were on the causeway that led to Island Park. Across the bay a few lights winked in the modified blackout. Behind him the clatter of Water Street was already muffled in the looming docks. He watched a freighter move toward the harbor boom, and for the first time in that long, anxious day he felt a surge of relief. At least he was headed for open water now. Nothing could have touched his private hideaway at St. Lucie.

Thinking of the boathouse and the yawl at anchor there, he made up his mind to sleep at St. Lucie tonight, even if it meant missing dinner. He needed those hours alone to shake down his nerves. To say nothing of his plans for tomorrow.

Island Park, a five-mile beach facing the Gulf, was mercifully quiet tonight after they had passed the amusement center.

Like a hundred other coastal towns from Galveston to Tampa, Milton had channeled its harbor through a stone breakwater and built its summer cottages along the inevitable sand island that protected its bay from the Gulf and the winter storms. Island Park was treeless, sun-steeped, and pleasantly forlorn. A place of cottages deep in dunes and mullet nets drying on palmetto frames. On the bay side crazy fishermen's wharves walked into the shallows. On the beach palm-thatch huts made impromptu picnic spots in the glare of noon.

St. Lucie Cay (its name a relic of Spanish colonial days) was little more than an overgrown sandspit at the eastern end of the island. One hundred yards of dunes separated the last house from the tidal cut; a spider-legged bridge, just wide enough to admit a single car, straddled the tide rip. The cay itself had been bulkheaded solidly years ago, seeded with Bermuda grass, and planted with windbreaks. Three summer cottages stood in agreeable privacy among the oleanders and the tall Australian pines. One belonged to old Doc Embree, a retired medical man with a taste for Byron, bourbon, and argument. The others were the property of the Land brothers: Dr. Jeff and Dr. George, Chris's father. Dr. George had sold his to the Milton Bank a few months before his death, when Chris had moved on to Lakeview and a surgical career. He had reserved the boathouse, the dock, and the yawl for his son, in case Chris should return to Milton on holiday.

Chris had passed his youth on the cay. His young manhood was tied up in that boathouse and the memory of a hundred sunny mornings. Fishing for grouper with Roy, his father's Negro houseman. Reading for exams in the shade of the tiny porch that stepped down directly to dock and bay. Swimming by moonlight, to clear a brain fogged by too much anatomy. His books were still on the shelves, he knew; Roy

10

had stocked the little galley against his return. His yacht-rigged yawl (he could see her now, bobbing in the dock basin with sails furled) was ready to put to sea tomorrow.

He shouted to his driver to stop before they reached the bridge. Stepping out to the white sheen of the oyster road, he paid the man and waited impatiently until the taxi had roared away. Its presence was the only jarring note. When it had vanished among the dunes, he knew that he was home at last.

The bridge was fitted with a wicket and closed after dark to discourage joy riders. His key turned smoothly in the lock. Another minute, and the sand of the cay crunched under his feet. Coarse brown Gulf sand, still faintly warm from the sun.

He walked once around for the sheer joy of home-coming. The Gulf side first: he kicked off his shoes here and waded deep in the phosphorescent water. A shoal of mullet, feeding inshore, flashed by like a visible welcome—a reminder that he could sail south tomorrow, with no landfall this side of Cuba. Or southeast, to troll for bass among the coastal mangroves. He turned to the bay side of the cay almost with reluctance and dodged nimbly under Doc Embree's wharf. The old man's house was dark: Chris wondered if he was still at White Sulphur, nursing his liver. Uncle Jeff's cottage was shuttered: he wasn't likely to open it this summer, with a son dead in Buna and a hospital staggering under a Nemesis of debt. . . . Chris moved on, past the third cottage that had once been his father's, and frowned briefly at the lighted living room. Tonight he had wanted St. Lucie to himself.

Still frowning, he carried his shoes down to the stringpiece of his dock. The *Lady Jane* looked trim as ever in the starlight. The deck was holystoned, the woodwork painted: Roy had evidently worked hard against his return. He hoped that Roy would continue to serve him on week ends. His uncle had written that the former houseman was now making seventy a week at the Borland yards, but Roy's devotion to the Lands was little short of feudal. . . . Chris dropped to the deck of the yawl and laid one hand on the boom. He thanked Roy silently for making this part of his home-coming personal.

Standing with his legs braced, imagining himself already heeling in a following wind, he stripped off his tunic and

11

threw it into the cockpit. It was good to make that boyish gesture in the dark. He stepped out of his pinks and threw them after the tunic. After all, he had seldom spent a night in the boathouse, even in the dead of the short Southern winter, without a swim before bed.

Diving cleanly from the stern, he reveled in the familiar caress of the bay against his bare skin. Inshore the water was lukewarm as a bath; he swam boldly out, rejoicing again that Milton was only a vague shape across miles of bay. Far out the freighter blinked at the harbor boom before it slipped into the Gulf for its long haul to the Florida Straits. He watched it for a while, until the hull blended with the night, and then, floating lazily, counting the remembered stars, he forgot the freighter and all other symbols of the war.

I've earned my key to this private heaven, he told himself. Who'll reproach me if I insist that my life is no more important than a rainy morning in bed—or a sunny morning among the mangroves at South Island? Later, of course, I'll put my life in some kind of order. People are talking already about winning the peace: talking *ad nauseam* and brandishing blueprints from every editorial page, every best-seller counter. Eventually, I suppose, I'll join the chorus. Tonight I'm a boy again, swimming after a star I can see but never touch. Tonight I'm swimming a bit farther into the soothing dark and planning the voyage I'll take when I'm rested again.

His lips formed the words from Tennyson, without conscious thought:

> "There lies the port; the vessel puffs her sail:
> There gloom the dark, broad seas. . . . .
> . . . . the deep
> Moans round with many voices. Come, my friends,
> 'Tis not too late to seek a newer world. . . ."

In the dark a voice said clearly, "It's never too late for that, Dr. Land."

He rolled in the water like a panicky porpoise. When he put out his hand to make sure he wasn't dreaming, his fingers brushed the cool flesh of a woman's arm.

12

CHRIS SAID, "I beg your pardon." It seemed an absurd remark to make, three hundred feet offshore in a moonless bay. "Did I startle you?"

He heard laughter in the dark. Friendly laughter, with no siren overtone. "I'm afraid I startled *you*, Major."

"How did you know that I——"

"When you unlocked the bridge wicket just now, I guessed your name. There are three cottages and one boathouse on St. Lucie. You were too slim to be Dr. Embree and too tall for Dr. Jeff——"

"I gather that you're renting my father's old cottage?"

The voice said easily, "Shall we stop being detectives? I am Dr. Karen Agard."

He nodded solemnly in the dark, remembering his uncle's letters. Dr. Jeff had mentioned a refugee, recommended to him some months ago by the Public Health Service. Somehow he had not expected to meet Dr. Agard like this. There was a swirl in the water as a tanned arm thrust toward him. He could see her vaguely now: brown gleam of shoulders in the lake of phosphorus her motion had created; a wet aureole of hair that looked blonde even in the dark; the flash of a smile. Her handshake was firm and cool; he remembered to swim away just in time. When her shoulder lifted above the water line, he guessed that Dr. Agard was long and sleek—and as innocent of covering as he.

His voice was a bit huskier than he had wished. "Uncle Jeff is a poor correspondent. I wish he'd told me more about you."

"I have been his assistant since spring."

"Surgical?"

"X ray and anesthetist. Lab on the side. I'm really a biochemist." She swam a little closer as he retreated. The foreign flavor in her voice was slight but definite; where had he read that Scandinavians could see in the dark? His shoulder touched the side of the yawl, and he sounded deliberately. Swimming down the sandy bottom for a few long strokes, he hoped she would take the chance to swarm aboard unobserved. But she was still in the water when he broke surface—steadying herself in the swell with a hand on a gunwale.

"Perhaps you do not believe me, Dr. Land."

"Of course I do. Why on earth——"

"But you are avoiding me."

He managed a smile. "How d'you know? It's too dark."

"Also you are blushing. You see, I know a great deal about you. I suppose that is unfair."

"For example?"

"You are what is called a Southern gentleman. You do not approve of a girl who swims alone at night."

He found he was laughing. "Southern gentleman or not, I'm plain nervous. You see I—forgot my bathing suit."

"What of it? So did I. It is dark enough——"

"It isn't that dark."

Karen Agard tossed back her short mane of hair. "Then put on your uniform and join me for dinner." She smiled with eyes as well as lips. It was tantalizing to glimpse just enough of her face to guess that she was lovely, without being sure.

"Tomorrow," she said, "your uncle will introduce us properly. Tonight I will answer questions. If you are to work with us at the hospital——"

"Who said I was staying in Milton?"

"It is only that you are a doctor. There is so much work here for doctors. Your uncle thought—or should I say, he *hoped . . . ?*" The voice was edged with question.

"Can we skip Uncle Jeff for a while? And may I tell you about myself my own way?"

Once more she put out her hand and shook his gravely. "In five minutes, then—at my cottage."

He held his breath as she grasped the gunwale, but she did not swarm aboard. Instead she sounded with scarcely a ripple and vanished under the yawl's keel. A few seconds later he heard her voice from the far side.

"You are right, Major—about the dark. Don't look for a moment, please."

He dove deeply in turn, digging both fists in the bottom and staying under till his brain buzzed. He heard her call from the dock as he swam gingerly back to the yawl. She was standing on the stringpiece—a tall, unconcerned figure in a terry-cloth robe. The lighter flashed in her hand, and he saw that she held a cigarette between her lips. Her patrician, broad-browed face was all he had hoped for; her eyes were a deep blue, even in the lighter flame.

"Cocktails will be waiting when you're dressed," she said. "I know you can find the way."

He boarded the yawl when her back was turned and stood in the cockpit, watching her white shape ghost up the walk to the cottage. At the moment he didn't know if he was glad or sorry that his fumble for solitude had been spoiled.

Knotting his tie on the dock's end and lighting a cigarette of his own, he began to relax from swim as well as surprise. Evidently Uncle Jeff and his handsome assistant had discussed him rather thoroughly—right down to his plans for the future. Perhaps it would do him good to look at Milton, and himself, through foreign eyes. It might sharpen his own thinking to let her assume he was back to stay.

He took his time with the cigarette, giving her ten minutes instead of five before he walked up to the low screened porch that faced the Gulf. Remembering to knock just in time, he entered the white-walled living room. Dr. Agard, he noted, had added enough of her own to accent her personality without disturbing the slightly dog-eared charm. The old couch still sprawled beside the fieldstone hearth, and the open shelf still held books that looked thoroughly read. Even the tarnished bar tray still stood inviolate in its special corner, magnificent with a tall new shaker and Swedish goblets crusted with signs of the zodiac.

His eyes roamed for other signs of her. The pictures were mostly impressionists of the cooler sort, save for the Gauguin above the mantel. He was admiring the mad browns of Tahiti when his hostess backed in from the kitchen with a tray of canapés, flicking the door shut with a competent hip and letting in an aroma of boiling shrimp. She brought her own aura of relaxation: a tall, lithe figure in a white silk play suit, whose smile was welcome without coquetry. He found he had looked at her twice before he remembered she was beautiful.

"Who told you that shrimp is my favorite?"

"Your uncle, of course. Will you pour the martinis?"

15

"Don't tell me you prepared this for me?"

"Shrimp pilaff and creole salad," she said. "As it happens, it is my favorite too, when I give myself a holiday at St. Lucie. Later I will offer you a real Danish pastry and aquavit."

"Are you sure I'm not——"

"Please. I expected Captain Travers tonight, but he disappointed me." She answered his inquiry as he handed her a glass. "Paul Travers, the new health officer. I forgot that you have been away."

The martini was perfect right down to the dash of absinthe. Chris smiled his appreciation and sank into the comfort of a basket chair.

"One part of me is utterly content," he said. "Another part keeps firing questions. Shall I suppress it?"

"Ask me what you like," said Karen Agard. "It is only fair, when I have asked so much about you." She refilled his glass and smiled without archness. "It happens that there is nothing in the least strange about me. I came where I could work best, that is all."

"Here, in Milton?"

"I do not wish to sound dramatic, but I am a scientist. Your town needs all the science it can get. Your town has an American disease called a boom."

"We've recovered from booms before."

"This one is not even healthy. There are too many complications. A fever called war. Money in pockets that have been empty for over ten years. And buzzards everywhere. My metaphor is bad, perhaps, but you follow me. Also, you blame me for speaking, because I am a refugee."

"Are you really?"

"Technically, I suppose." Her chin went up. "I am a Norwegian, educated in London and America. I have no near relatives at home but cousins. Some of them may be heroes now; some, no doubt, are quislings. I cannot pretend to know. You see, I am not a member of the underground. I did not even escape down a fiord when the Nazis came. In the spring of 'forty I was already in a New York research laboratory, hard at work on the typhus virus. I worked there until last fall, when Captain Travers said I should come here."

"Do you take orders from him?"

"I take his advice," she said. "He is an epidemiologist with

16

the Public Health, on loan to the department here. When he said I could be useful, I came to Milton too."

So Milton is that sort of powder keg, Chris thought. He pictured the trailer city on the made land around the shipyard. A good epidemic could run through that sort of congestion like wildfire. Certainly the U.S.P.H.S., desperately short of doctors, would never loan an epidemiologist without a definite need.

"D'you give Travers part of your time, then?"

"I work for your uncle," she said. "Tomorrow you will find how much *he* needs assistance. Of course I help Paul when I can. I have my own laboratory at the hospital for culture work. In the evenings I manage a clinic for the workers' children." She put down her glass and got up. "Do not make me sound overworked. It is no more than any doctor should do here."

Chris considered. "Don't make me feel like a tourist in my own home town."

"Tomorrow," said Karen Agard, "you will be working just as hard." She led the way to the dining alcove without waiting for an answer.

Chris pulled out her chair and sat down across from her without disturbing the implication of her statement. He felt her eyes search him while she served the fragrant pilaff and tossed the salad in a huge wooden bowl. What would she say if he confessed that he'd hoped for a long rest at St. Lucie—and planned to return to Lakeview in the fall, to resume his teaching career?

She spoke without preamble. "May I be pompous for a moment?"

"Do, please. It's your party."

"All of us must fight where we can, Major. It is perhaps heartbreaking if that place is home. But it is fortunate, too. When such a battle is won, it counts in the heart." Karen Agard smiled, but her eyes were grave above the smile. "Now I am really solemn. I say tomorrow's battle must be won here, and not abroad."

Chris let her eyes hold him on that challenge. She was right, of course. Milton was only a corner of America—more confused than most by the backwash of war. The medical pattern was only a part of that dislocation, but it was an important part.

He spoke slowly. "Tomorrow's battle. Are you suggesting that we fight it here, today?"

"Isn't that why you came back?"

Dr. Agard crossed the living room to open the screen door on the night. For a moment she stood there, shaking her hair free of its bandanna. Her eyes were on the Gulf of Mexico; her fingers kneaded the wet, pale blonde curls of her short bob. She might have forgotten his presence after that abrupt question, but Chris knew that she was waiting for his answer.

"To tell the truth, Karen, I haven't decided."

"You will decide soon, Chris."

Apparently she had taken their use of first names in her stride. Her hand touched his shoulder lightly before she resumed her place.

"All of us must decide," she said. "How hard we mean to go on fighting—and how long. Truly, that is my last solemn remark tonight."

"Haven't I the right to catch my breath?"

"Have you ever done that, really?"

He grinned in earnest. "I see you've checked on me pretty thoroughly."

"You would not take your father's money in the depression. You worked your way through Lakeview; I know your surgical rating there—your uncle is much too proud of you to keep it a secret. He could use a good surgeon, Chris. So could my clinic. So could Paul."

"I thought the P.H. boys hoed their own row."

"People help each other here today," said Karen. "Everyone but the buzzards—and *they* help each other too."

"That's the second time you've mentioned buzzards. Be specific."

"Medical shysters, then. Must I name names? The town swarms with them."

"What town doesn't, in wartime?"

"Here they are organized." Karen controlled her voice with an effort. "Ask your uncle about them tomorrow. About the refugees Kornmann and Moreau. And the compensation clinic. Gilbert Dwight, the doctor who manages them all. Ask your uncle what would happen if typhus broke out in the flats."

She got up abruptly and led the way to the living room. "We will not discuss it now, will we? It is my night off, and

18

you are catching your breath." She turned to the bookshelf, returning instantly with a bottle and liqueur glasses.

Chris said, "I'm staying in Milton. Right here on the cay. I plan to sleep till noon and sail my yawl till sundown. After a month or so I'll decide between Uncle Jeff and Lakeview. Will that do for now?"

"Just how ill are you, Chris?"

"They must have told you I had a bone graft."

"You were swimming tonight."

"I may repent tomorrow."

Karen studied her glass. "Suppose I give you a week?"

Chris laughed aloud. "Has it occurred to you that you're rather rude?"

"On the contrary, I am only welcoming you. Where you belong." Again her chin came up. Her eyes were viking blue in the lamplight as she weighed him. "Of course you will join us on your own. Tomorrow, perhaps. We can wait till then——"

"We?"

"All of us. Your uncle, Paul and Roz Borland."

"Who let her in the picture?"

"I did. Months ago. You might call her our *liaison*. That is, she moves between two camps at will. When Dwight protests my clinic, she persuades her father to build it. When I need vaccine, she writes me a check. It is convenient, at least——"

"What will she do for me?"

"I can't say, Chris. If she likes you, perhaps she will ask her father to buy you."

They were laughing together now. "The ground bait is alluring," he said. "Now if you'll take a day off occasionally and sail with me——"

"If you do not play beyond my time limit, I will even bring Rosalie."

"Somehow I can't picture you knowing the Borlands," said Chris. "Is it my turn to be rude?"

"Not at all. Cal Borland and his daughter are both decent people. Wild, but decent . . ." Karen paused, considering the adjectives. "I think that is accurate. He has made his money fast, but he knows where he means to go. Roz is different: she has the money, but no destination. The money is a wall that shuts out reality."

"Isn't that a familiar American trap?"

"You will understand me when you have met her."

"I understand you now."

"With your head, perhaps. Rosalie Borland is a strange girl. In her you will find most of what makes your country great—most of what pulls it to pieces——" She reached for the phone as it rang a second time.

Settled in his chair as Karen Agard picked up the receiver, Chris wondered a little at his irritation. The mention of Rosalie Borland had interested him, of course, but he was in no mood to discuss the phenomenon of the poor-little-rich-girl now. The tabloids had told him quite enough about Roz Borland while he lay in a deck chair on Virginia Beach. Karen's right again, he thought. Catching up on the escapades of that brat is like refreshing your memory on all the paradoxes of America. . . . He came back to Karen at the phone. She was talking excitedly to Captain Paul Travers. Sketching the Public Health man in his mind's eye, he decided that Travers would have glasses, an Adam's apple, and the usual statistics. It was instructive to recognize this flash of resentment; at least he was thinking of Karen Agard as a woman as well as a dynamo.

When she turned from the phone at last, he sensed her urgency before she spoke. "Paul's on a case ten miles out. Diphtheria. He thinks it's laryngeal."

Chris sat bolt upright. "Don't tell me a Public Health man is treating——"

"He cannot stay, of course. That is why he asks me to come. Will you help?"

"If you think you can use me."

"Would I ask you otherwise? You can take that nap in the sun tomorrow." She had said it quite without reproach, but the challenge between them was tangible now.

Chris said easily, "Diphtheria is a bit more urgent than a soldier's rest cure. Lead on, Karen."

Dr. Agard was already moving toward her bedroom door, and unfastening the top buttons of her play suit en route. Now she paused and looked at him thoughtfully. "I am glad to meet you just like this. I was curious to learn the sort of man you are." She gave him a smile that began in her eyes. "Of course I knew already that you were a hero. With so many men that is beginning and ending."

He got to his feet belatedly and stared after her as the door closed. At that moment he didn't want her to change into a uniform—and another personality. He resented the command in that telephone—her acceptance even more. Suddenly he knew that he wanted her for himself, for hours more. To talk out the thoughts she had brought to the surface. . . . Somehow he must convince this intruder in his world that he could be relied on—for what? He took a turn of the room, forgetting that he was still supposed to limp a little, and glared again at the closed bedroom door.

"Bring the car 'round, Chris. It'll save time."

"Coming up," he said mechanically, and walked into the night without a backward glance.

Halfway to the garage he remembered that he hadn't asked about the keys. But Karen Agard was the sort of girl who slept with her door unlocked and her keys always in the ignition. He knew that instantly. Just as he knew that her car would be a trim roadster with the top down. That he would sit under the wheel at her door and wait for her—letting the night shape its pattern for him, quite outside his volition.

3

THE CAR LIGHTS picked out a whitewashed house in a grove of pines; Karen cut her motor and coasted into the yard under an umbrella of chinaberry trees. Chris took in the details automatically as he stepped out. They reminded him of a hundred small farmyards in the South, with one difference: the people who lived here now were not farmers. You guessed without looking that the barn held nothing but a jalopy. That the fields beyond were thick with trailers.

A man in a captain's uniform came out to the sagging porch. A slender, oldish man who looked tired but competent in the spill of lamplight. He shook hands with Chris as they met in the sand yard.

"So glad you could come, Major."

"Does it look bad?"

"Criminal's the word, sir." The man's voice dropped. "This is a yard worker, with five young ones. We inoculated four,

21

but the fifth was in the back country, visiting. A few days ago she developed a sore throat, but the parents are both at the yards, so no one reported it. Yesterday they took her in to Dwight——"

"The company doctor?"

"Dwight handles all Borland's compensation cases. He gave her sulfadiazine and sent her home."

"Without taking a smear?"

"Exactly. Dwight is a very busy man."

The word had come out more like a curse than a name. Chris looked hard at the speaker, noting the insignia of the Public Health Service on his lapels. Noting, too, that Paul Travers had glasses, an Adam's apple, and a saturnine manner, just as he had surmised. At the moment it suited him perfectly.

Travers said, "Dwight evidently hoped the diazine would take care of everything."

"Mention that in your report, Paul."

They both turned as Karen got out of the car with a tracheotomy set in her hands. In her crisp white uniform she was even more vital, her energy channeled to a definite end. Both men stepped aside wordlessly to let her go up the steps.

"Don't hold forth on Dwight," she said as she entered. "Let Chris find out for himself."

The health officer shook hands a second time. "Sorry we didn't meet under a better star."

"You're leaving us so soon?"

"Karen knows what to do, and I've a batch of serum waiting in Milton."

He left as casually as he had come. Chris stood for a moment watching the health officer's car disappear down the road to town. It was hard to define the man's quiet display of strength; certainly he had made no effort to impress. Public Health men were apt to be like that, he thought. Even when they weren't snubbed off by local doctors, they were generally too rushed to be polite.

He hesitated before he went back to Karen's roadster. A familiar black bag was waiting for him in the rumble: a surgeon's kit, complete with ampules of serum. Karen had snatched it from her hospital office in their dash to this back-country rendezvous with tragedy. Already Chris guessed that no other word would describe what was waiting for him inside those dirty-white walls.

22

Travers' whole manner had underlined the facts. The reference to the company doctor's neglect had added only a grim footnote. Chris struck fist to palm as he stood with a foot still on the running board. He felt a dull glow of anger at this doctor whom he had not yet seen. Certainly the man's handling of the case was all but incredible. A smear from the throat would have established the diagnosis instantly. Instead Dwight had merely followed the circus technique of so many doctors, who seemed to rely on the half-grasped miracle of the sulfa derivative as a cure all.

The devious ways of the compensation field had always belonged to the seamy side of medicine; Chris had collided before this with racketeers who grew fat on company contracts. In the Army it had been easy to forget such dodges, to pretend that medicine could go on at home as before. Here —as Karen's manner had implied—was concrete evidence to the contrary.

He forced his mind back to the job at hand. Once again he reminded himself that he was discharged from the Army and not yet licensed to practice as a civilian. His mind skipped that detail for the facts. Diphtheria was a rarity nowadays, even in the culture broth of a trailer camp. Chris brought the textbook picture clear. Globoid bacteria, insanely active. Predilection, the throat. Beginning with the tonsils, they could spread back to the larynx in a matter of hours, kill off superficial tissue, form a whitish membrane which gradually encroached on the airway. Sometimes it swelled to a point where air was shut off entirely. Even if it was merely jarred loose, it might fill the narrow space. In either event, suffocation was automatic. Incision of the windpipe was the only remedy at that stage—or the introduction of tubing into the larynx proper, which served to hold the airway open until the swelling could be abated by serum.

Karen called from the doorway, and he came out of his textbook picture. Walking up the steps, he knew that he was taking his first real step into the home front; he took it now, with all the eagerness of a war horse scenting battle.

The door gave directly to the farmhouse kitchen, a classic picture of America at war. Two small children slept on floor pallets; in an alcove he saw a jerry-built tier of bunks, sagging under another load of sleepers. The parents, both in overalls, sat stolidly at the kitchen table. For a moment the scene was no more real than a blurred photograph in a casebook. Then

23

the father raised his head, and the table lamp showed the badge on his overall strap. Chris read the name of the Borland Yards: the words completed the picture, gave it meaning. The child that was dying in the bedroom beyond was a casualty of war, though she had never seen a battlefield.

Chris forced assurance into his face, letting his hand rest on the father's shoulder before he followed Karen into the bedroom. The child, a slender girl of five or six, lay under a sheet in the cheap double bed. Chris examined her for a moment without speaking, as Karen brought the lamp closer. Suddenly he realized that it had been over three years since he had treated a child. Operating in station hospitals from New Jersey to Naples, in sandbagged dugouts, in the amphitheater of the Ospedale Maggiore in Rome, he had worked always against a background of khaki. His patients had been young men brimming with health until they stumbled in their first till with Mars. . . . Most of them—a grateful percentage, in fact—had fought back to health with amazing fortitude when surgery had tipped the scale in their favor.

The small form in this bed made another pattern of despair. He continued his examination, noting the swollen face, the blue lips, the cheeks already dark from oxygen lack. Here was no reserve of strength or confidence; life itself had already retreated in this squalid room—too far, perhaps, for any skill to lure it back.

Chris dropped his bag and picked up the child's wrist. Automatically he noted the waxy skin and the dark blue of the rich vascular bed beneath the fingernails. The pulse was fast, the beats tumbling over each other. When he increased the pressure on the artery at the wrist, the beat faded altogether—a sure sign that the heart was beginning to falter at its job. With each breath the child's body shook the bed beneath her. An eerie whistling sound tore through the larynx; the hollow space at ribs and collarbone deepened, showing how the muscles were laboring as the small lungs fought for air.

Karen handed him a flashlight and a wooden blade. The child made no resistance as he studied the throat. The entire area was covered with the expected whitish membrane; again Chris wondered how even the most haphazard doctor could have failed in this diagnosis. Other diseases of the throat might suggest diphtheria, particularly the streptococcic infections. But nothing else gave quite that ominous, dirty-white picture.

He moved to the child's chest. Here, too, evidence of a laboring heart was visible; the skin seemed to flutter as the twisting components of the heartbeat thrust the organ itself against the chest wall. There was only a faint, weak thud as he applied the stethoscope. He moved beyond, and frowned at the fine, moist crackling that came from the lungs. The picture was complete when he tapped across the chest itself, measuring the dullish area which conformed to the size of the heart.

"Has it begun to dilate?"

Chris nodded grimly. Karen was only a presence at his elbow now. "The toxin must have reached the myocardium. Did Travers give her any serum?"

Karen indicated an empty ampule on the night table. "Intravenous—just after he phoned me."

Chris could picture the job. With no competent hands to assist the puncture, it wasn't a simple matter to insert a needle in these small, depressed veins. "I'm afraid it's time for another."

Karen had already unwrapped one of the packages in the surgical kit. Inserting a needle in the ampule, she handed it across the bed and stepped forward to apply an alcohol swab to the pitifully slender arm. Chris searched for a point of puncture as Karen squeezed the flesh in an effort to fill the veins. Lowered pressure had also lowered the tension in the veins themselves; for a moment it was impossible to note even a sign of change. Then his stroking fingers outlined a small swelling. He thrust the needle in, feeling it go through tissue and vascular wall. When he pulled gently back on the syringe, blood spurted into the barrel—blood so dark from cyanosis that it was almost black in the lamplight.

Karen released the pressure, and he began to inject. Care was needed here as well, for there was always danger when serum was injected directly. Any sensitivity in the body, any abnormal reaction, would be multiplied a hundredfold by the direct contact of the serum with the vital centers; anaphylactic shock of this kind was always accompanied by rapid swelling of the mucous membrane of the nose and throat, and there was no room for such swelling. The slightest decrease in the laryngeal opening now would mean suffocation.

Karen spoke softly. "Can you keep the needle in?"

It was always a ticklish job to switch to a new ampule while the needle remained in the vein. But it was worth the risk. He had been fortunate indeed to find the vein he was using.

"Ready," he said. Karen bent beside him, pressing hard against his shoulder to co-ordinate her motion with his own. Her fingers were quick as she changed ampules. They did not speak as the fresh ampule began to inject. This time he held his breath for another reason—feeling the clean solidity of her body against his own.

"That's got it, I think," he said. "We'll repeat with glucose when we're sure the reaction is favorable."

Karen nodded, and moved away at last. "You're a good doctor, for a surgeon."

He shrugged and looked down again at the child. There was no apparent change as yet: if anything, the pulse was weaker. Still, there was no deep oxygen lack to justify an immediate tracheotomy. Most of the deadly symptoms pointed to poisoning of the heart itself; and there was now an ample supply of antitoxin in the child's blood stream, racing to combat that noxious influence. The battle was joined within. They could only wait, in readiness for an emergency. If the heart was too far damaged, nothing would save the small patient now.

"Better start on that glucose," he said. "If it's as bad as it looks, the heart will have something to work on."

The glucose was concentrated in an ampule, like the serum. Only the sugar itself was needed here: the addition of a large amount of fluid to the circulation, in the dilute solution ordinarily used, was contraindicated at a time like this. When the new injection was completed, Chris stepped back from the bed and smoothed his frown away. There had been no need to pretend with Karen, but he knew he must face the parents now.

"Want to steal time for a smoke?"

Karen shook her head. "It's your turn for that, Doctor. I've been in harness—you've just come back."

Chris nodded his thanks and opened the door to the kitchen. For a moment the scene before him was immobile as the waxworks in a dusty corner of a museum. Then he realized that the parents had dropped off where they sat—

26

wearied by hours of overtime, dulled by the comfort of having two doctors at work in their bedroom.

He went into the yard on tiptoe and sat for a while on Karen's running board. A breeze was stirring in the pines now: even here he could breathe the salt tang of the Gulf. Above him the branches of the chinaberry tree sighed a dry answer to that breath of the sea, a whisper of leaves and berries gone sere with summer heat. The sound did not blot out the pitiful fight for life going on just inside the bedroom window.

Chris got up abruptly and walked down the shoulder of the road. A lopsided touring car snored past, packed to the mudguards with men. Most of them were still in work clothes; all of them were singing drunk. He took a quick step into the palmettos as the car swerved toward him, righted, and weaved out of sight around the curb.

Suddenly he felt that he was wanted in the farmhouse and hurried back. There was no sign of Karen on the porch, but a vague shape rose up from the running board. He recognized the father's bulk and composed himself. Probably the man had only feigned sleep when he passed through the kitchen. Probably he had been steeling himself for the news.

"How is she, Doc?"

"We've injected serum and glucose. So far there's been no real change."

"Will you have to operate?"

"We're hoping the serum will bring her 'round."

"What about her heart?"

"Frankly, that's what is troubling me."

The father said, "She's going to die. I've known it since night."

It was a statement of fact that asked for no confirmation. Chris hesitated, then fumbled in his tunic for cigarettes. He offered one to the man before he lighted his own. Watching him expel smoke gustily, he wondered again at the layman's instinct that could cut through most clinical patter to the truth.

"Don't give up hope," he said. "I won't deny that things look bad, but we'll do all we can."

The father lifted his shoulders in a gesture of despair. "I'm sure of that, Doc. You and the lady are the right kind. Not like that company fellow we went to yesterday."

Chris did not answer. His opinion of Dr. Dwight, sight unseen, was already eloquent enough.

The father said, "He was too busy to give us more than a brush-off. He just wrote out a prescription."

"Did he say what the trouble was?"

"Only that she had a sore throat. That's all he had time for."

Chris spoke automatically. "There aren't many doctors left, you know. Most of them are overseas."

"Two of them had time to come here tonight. Three, counting that Public Health fellow."

"I'm not in practice here. I'm still getting over a bone graft."

"I know. I saw the ribbon." The man drew on his cigarette. "I got a bullet myself last time, at St. Mihiel. Nothing bad, you understand. But they gave me a medal too."

He considered that for a moment. "Funny, isn't it, how they could sell us the same story twice? Last time we were making the world safe for America. Now we're making it safe for *everyone*, including the Eskimos. We get miracles daily, and more on the way. Serum and sulfa and this penicillin. Unions with teeth, and old-age money. Company docs, when we go to work in a shipyard. But my kid's in there dying just the same."

Again Chris spoke automatically. "Sulfa's no help in diphtheria."

"Then why didn't Dwight guess it was diphtheria?"

Chris shrugged and turned away. Ethics or not, he could apologize no more for a profession that allowed that sort of doctor to stay alive.

The man said, with no trace of emotion, "Poor folks like me still get the short end where the doctors are concerned. Maybe we'll be better off when the government takes over. Kids don't die of diphtheria in the Army."

It was a familiar argument, and Chris accepted it mutely. The man was wrong, of course, but he could hardly convince him of that now. Perhaps he wasn't too wrong, where his own background was concerned. Families of that class got no medical care at all under the present setup—save the type offered by compensation racketeers like Dwight.

"We took the other children to the government clinic," the man stated in that same flat tone. "Dr. Agard gave 'em

28

the injections. I'd of been glad to pay for the shots, but they didn't charge us a thing."

"The Public Health Service tries to prevent disease," said Chris. "It's not their job to treat. Dr. Travers gave serum to-night only because the case was urgent."

"Suppose they could cure as well as prevent. Don't tell me the world wouldn't be a damn sight better off. If I'd taken the girl to Dr. Agard's clinic, even—the one she runs on the Flats—I'll bet you *she'd* have known what the trouble was."

"Dr. Agard is a very fine physician."

"I know that too. And she does her doctorin' free. Suppose my girl had had serum straight off. She wouldn't be dying now."

"No," Chris admitted. "If you could have taken her to a doctor earlier——"

"Earlier? I called a doctor night before last. Every doctor on that compensation board. Said they were too busy, the lot of 'em. Not only Dwight, but Kornmann and Moreau too. Then I tried the County Hospital; you know, all Borland's cases are taken there. But they wouldn't take my girl. Said they couldn't handle contagious diseases . . ."

His voice trailed off as Chris turned. Something had changed inside the house. Then he realized that the horrid, rhythmic crowing from the child's room had ceased. It was a silence that pulled him indoors more abruptly than any scream for help.

Back in the room again, he saw the picture in a glance. Something had choked off the girl's breathing completely— a swelling of the lining from serum reaction, a slipping of the membrane that filled the larynx. Already the blue shadow of oxygen lack had suffused the skin; the muscles between the ribs stood out in the agonized attempt to draw breath into a suffocating body.

Karen, at the night table, was working with the smooth haste of despair. He counted all the instruments for a trache-otomy, even as he reached for operating gloves. Karen, he saw, had already assumed that he would do the job. He could hardly pause now to explain that he would be operating without a license. His future as a surgeon in this state—or any state—was hardly important when measured against a child's fight for life. Even if he knew the fight had been lost in advance, in another doctor's consulting room.

29

He found that he had already powdered his hands and drawn on the gloves. Once again he counted the instruments from the emergency kit: scalpel, clamps, a tracheotomy tube, dressings. Karen was wrapping the child in a sheet now—mummy-wise, so that no spasmodic movement could disturb his work. His eyes questioned her as he picked up the scapel, and she answered him with a nod, drawing the child's head over the edge of the bed, extending the neck so that it was freely visible.

His motions were automatic now. He wiped the skin at the neck with a sponge saturated in antiseptic and felt for the larynx. His fingers located it with quick, sure pressure, then moved downward, testing the small swelling that was the isthmus of the thyroid, the narrow band of glandular tissue that straddled the windpipe at this point, like the strap of an old-fashioned saddlebag. Below this point there was a free space where the windpipe could be opened without damage.

He lifted the knife. It was almost three months since he had made an incision. As always, he felt that moment of unreasoned panic, when the scalpel seemed awkward in his fingers. Then he remembered Dr. Powers' lecture on tracheotomy, back in medical school. It had been short and to the point. "Make a hole in the trachea, gentlemen. Make it with anything you can find, a can opener if need be. But get the hole open."

The knife came down. There was no need for anesthesia here: the child was too deep in coma to feel pain. The tissues parted under the pressure of the blade, but there was little bleeding—the circulation, too, was almost gone. Wiping away the small stain, he cut again—severing the muscles smoothly, exposing the shining cartilage bands of the trachea itself.

It took more pressure to cut through this obstruction, but he forced the scalpel to bite its way until he had made a slit down the wall of the windpipe, just under an inch in length. A curved clamp came instantly into his hand. He inserted it into the opening, spreading the blades to let the air rush in.

The effect was instantaneous as air whistled into the child's straining lungs, to speed vitally needed oxygen through the body—to the heart, already toxic almost past going; to brain cells so sensitive that complete deprivation of oxygen for a matter only of seconds can turn man into a vegetating animal. Chris watched the bluish color fade from the girl's skin as he held the clamp wide to maintain the breathing space. Perhaps there was hope, after all—now that the serum had begun its work as well. He turned to Karen and tried to convince himself that the small patient between them had a fighting chance.

Karen said only, "Thanks, Chris. Are you sorry you came?"

He didn't answer as he took up the tracheotomy tube. It was in two parts: a large outer tube, curved for easy inserting, and a smaller section to fit into its sheath. Holding the opening wide, Chris slipped the apparatus into place and whisked the clamp aside. Karen bent to attach the tape on the outer sleeve, knotting it snugly about the child's neck to prevent dislocation if a fit of coughing set in.

Chris counted the pulse while she worked. She did not meet his eyes as she rose from the bedside.

"It's steadier, I suppose?"

"A little—but not enough, I'm afraid. I've already told the father. Or rather, I've let him tell me."

"Then you don't think she'll live?"

"Do you?"

It was Karen's turn to sit down at the bedside without answering. Chris looked at his watch before he took another chair. This was the wait that every doctor dreads: the long, hopeless pause when nothing more can slow the approach of death, when the doctor knows he is helpless yet does not dare to turn aside.

At intervals in the hours that followed he took the child's pulse and noted the increase grimly. At four in the morning Karen took the temperature. Chris stared at his watch again to verify the time. It seemed incredible that they had passed most of the night in that room.

Karen looked up and shook her head: the strain of their vigil had taken them beyond words long ago. He studied her notation on the chart—fever, 106. A temperature of that kind was nearly always terminal; he did not need the diminuendo of the child's breathing to warn him that the end was approaching.

At intervals in the next half hour Karen injected stimulants with weary competence. Both of them knew that the heart was past help now. When the sound of respiration died at last, Chris passed over the stethoscope. As the attending physician, Karen must, of course, give the verdict.

Once again she handed him the fever chart without speaking. He read the final notation: patient died, 4:36 A.M.

31

"You'll fill out the certificate?"

"Paul left it here. It's all in order."

So the Public Health officer had known that they were fighting a losing battle. He had even made up the records in advance, leaving it to Karen to add the ghastly postscript.

Chris sat quietly for a moment while she signed the form. Then he stirred himself to action and began gathering up their equipment. Karen folded the form into her notebook and rose to help.

"Thanks again, Chris."

He saw that she was crying. They were tears of anger, he knew; the kind of tears that did not ask for comfort. This was the baffled rage of the heart, when death is not inevitable, but needless. He put out a hand to her and pressed her shoulder warmly.

"Thanks to *you*," he said.

"For what?"

"For opening my eyes so soon. Shall we finish our talk tomorrow—about Milton's future and mine?"

"It's tomorrow now," said Karen.

He managed a wan smile. "Thanks for that reminder, too."

Then they went into the kitchen to face the parents—already stirring sleepily, to prepare for the morning shift at Borland's yards.

4

THE PHONE wakened Chris without startling him. He swung his feet from bed to boathouse floor and blinked at his surroundings, comforted to discover that six hours' sleep could rest him completely again. When his hand went out to the phone with no effort at orientation, he knew that he was home.

A woman's voice, unfamiliar and stirring, said, "Is that you, Major?"

He thought of Karen and shook his head. Already he'd

have known Karen's voice, even in this fuzzy moment. "Major Land here."

"This is Rosalie Borland. I've just talked to Karen and thought I'd call. Could I drive out to St. Lucie this afternoon and meet you informally?"

Chris sat up, wide-awake. He could picture her perfectly, in the expensive plantation setting on Slave Hill. Lolling over a late breakfast, perhaps, with a cigarette and an idle moment. Deciding, on the spur of that moment, to attach the latest hero to return from the wars. Yearning—like a million well-insulated females—to brush that war with her lazy hands.

But he kept his voice mild. "Could you tell me what this is all about?"

Her laugh was low and throaty. The sort of laugh that is provocative, regardless of motive. "I think that'll wait until we meet."

"Just what did Karen——" He swallowed the rest. This wasn't like Karen at all. She had said that he must not meet Rosalie Borland too soon. Already he was beginning to see why.

Rosalie said, "I want to go over our plans for you. Admit that's neighborly."

"Did you say *our* plans?"

"Karen's and mine. I haven't discussed all of mine with her yet. That's why I wanted to see you first."

He had an impulse to bang up the phone and knew it was unreasonable. The voice at the other end had managed to be both friendly and faintly mocking; he wondered if he was playing Ulysses to an invisible Circe when he turned back to it.

"As it happens, Miss Borland, I've several calls to make in town. Perhaps I could drive to Slave Hill around one."

"I'm lunching with Dr. Moreau in a half hour. Jean Moreau. Have you had time to meet him?"

Chris remembered the name. Dr. Moreau was one of the refugee surgeons in Dwight's clinic. Part of the incubus that Karen had asked him to challenge. Karen had also called Rosalie the liaison between the two camps. Perhaps he should translate that cryptic remark on his own.

"Dr. Moreau? I've not had the pleasure."

"I'm bringing you together soon, of course. Jean was at Dunkirk, so you'll have lots in common."

"Why?"

33

The voice ignored the question. "Shall we say St. Lucie? Around four?"

"Are you bringing the Frenchman?"

"Just us," said Rosalie Borland.

"Why?"

"You sound human now, Major. Let's meet on Karen's veranda. We'll have an hour to argue before she gets back from her clinic."

He was wide-awake when he hung up, and furious enough. When Roy came in from the galley kitchen with his breakfast, he needed an effort to get out a greeting the houseboy deserved. Roy—he was a lean fifty now—had been his father's servant, and his own, since Chris could remember. This morning his wide grin welcomed a favorite son back where he belonged. So did the breakfast that had been ritual at St. Lucie: grits in cream, ham and eggs, and the sort of beaten biscuits only Roy could make.

"Who told you I was home?"

The houseboy's grin widened. "Dr. Agard. But I been comin' out 'most every day, jes' on the chance."

"You sure did the yawl proud, Roy."

"When we goin' out for snapper, Mist' Chris?"

"Give me time to get my strength." Chris looked at Roy narrowly. "How come you're here at all? I thought you were getting rich at Borland's."

"Not too rich t'come here mawnins, Mist' Chris." Roy flexed his powerful hands. "Never thought I'd take to rivetin' at my age, but I declare, it does agree with me."

They laughed together at a joke of their own. Roy's laziness had been a standing reproach in the Land family—probably because it was so little deserved. The Negro owned a neat truck farm in Blue Hollow; his two tall sons had gone on from Tech to see action with the Air Force in Sicily. It was touching to find Roy back at his old job, quite as a matter of course. . . . Chris wondered how to explain that Roy's free time belonged to his farm now. Not to an evacuee who had outdozed his convalescence.

After a second coffee he felt ready to face the phone again. Karen answered almost as soon as he was put through to the hospital.

"I thought Roz would call you."

"Just what did you tell her, and why? And now we're on the subject, how well do you know this young duchess?"

34

"We were at Vassar together. Roommates for a whole year, until she was sent down for commuting to the Stork Club."

Chris took a deep breath. This wasn't the Karen he remembered from that blurred horror they'd lived through in the dark. At the moment she seemed to have Rosalie Borland's manner, as well as her vocabulary. He forced himself to relax. After all, man has but one course when women conspire in his behalf—to yield, and keep his back to wall.

"Just how busy are you, Karen?"

"I can talk, if that's what you mean. Your uncle Jeff is out on a call. I'm in the office, checking bills."

"Then answer one question. Last night you wanted to keep me out of Rosalie's way. Why knock our heads together now?"

"That was last night. You're stronger than I thought."

"Be frank. What does she want with a busted crock like me?"

"I think she wants to introduce you to her father." Karen's voice twinkled. "Cal Borland has made more than one young man's fortune. Why shouldn't he make yours too?"

"Suppose I don't want to meet her father? What could I say to a colossus like Cal Borland?"

"Right now I wouldn't know. But it might surprise you both." There was a pause on the wire, a small chuckle. "Don't you *want* to make your fortune? Most Americans do."

"I'm planning to make it my own way, with your permission. Suppose I start by coming in as a surgeon for Uncle Jeff?"

Her chuckle changed abruptly to a gasp of delight. "I thought you'd decided last night, Chris. But I didn't dare ask."

He was a bit surprised himself, now the words were out. Just when had his mind taken the hard shape of decision—to stay in Milton, come what may? To fight to restore the Milton he had known? He shook his head solemnly on that one: the Milton he had known would never return. His job—like that of every citizen—was to help his particular Milton to its niche in the future.

Karen said, "Are you there, Chris?"

He took the plunge in earnest. "You're Uncle Jeff's assistant. What'll he want for half interest?"

"Chris! You wouldn't——"

"And don't read over those unpaid bills to me," he warned.

"I know that story by heart, too. Furthermore, if you tell him I called, I'll fire you in person. This is one scheme I'm breaking my own way."

He did not permit himself to think while he paced the strip of beach before the boathouse in the hot late morning, waiting for the garage to send over his car. Nor did he let himself notice Milton too closely when he had parked in Duval Square again and mounted the sedate steps of the Seaboard Bank. . . . Only when he had slid under the wheel again did he give his mind the luxury of a complete turnover. He found that it was ticking as smoothly as the engine of his father's battered coupé. He let it tick on merrily as he drove down the side street to Uncle Jeff's hospital.

Chris stopped just outside of the short curve of driveway and stared up at the well-remembered façade. After three years of war the grounds were more than a little unkempt; the cheerful stucco of the entrance was frankly down at heel. What did that matter, when he could remember that the wards occupied that low wing to the left? The operating room beyond, masked, as always, in an arbor of bougainvillaea. Then the private rooms—all twenty of them. Beyond that was the lab and the office where Karen was working now. He played with the temptation to take Karen to lunch, and banished it—knowing that he must be alone until he had seen Uncle Jeff and burned his bridges firmly.

He let his thoughts tick on, with Uncle Jeff for a starter. Geoffrey Land had poured his life into that building, from the day he had formed his first partnership with his brother George. Together they had built up their hospital from a four-bed surgery to the modest miracle that had continued to pay its way (despite its free clinic) until the depression. Even then the brothers had kept their doors open, by dipping into capital. When Chris had gone off to Lakeview, the town had just begun to get on its feet again; the hospital had been sound as a nut when his father died.

Since then he had needed no reports from Seward Harper, his father's executor at the bank, to know that things had gone steadily downhill behind that cheerful front. It wasn't Uncle Jeff's fault that he was better at materia medica than surgery, and a better surgeon than a businessman. No one could blame his brother for turning his stock into cash just before his death. George Land's son was already a promising surgeon

36

on the staff at Lakeview—and George Land had felt that Chris deserved the means to plan his own life in his own way.

Chris sat on under the wheel of the coupé, staring at the sun-faded façade; the hospital stared back at him with its dog-eared dignity intact. Crusades, he thought, had been planned in stranger fortresses than this. . . . Abruptly he turned on his ignition and drove back toward the square. He had just remembered that Uncle Jeff always dined at home, sharp on the stroke of noon—usually with Dr. Embree, if the old crab was really back from White Sulphur. That gave him ten more minutes to check on the deSoto Building—perhaps to brush elbows with the thing he had come home to fight. A medical poseur like Gilbert Dwight would be sure to locate in Milton's solitary skyscraper.

The deSoto Building stood at a corner of the square, beside the hotel: sixteen proud stories of white limestone, with facings of Georgia marble. Parking at another meter in the bustling esplanade, Chris studied the line of men waiting at the side entrance. From their clothes, he knew that most of them were yard workers. From the slips clutched in their fists, he assumed that they were waiting for Dwight's medical discharge.

Most of the faces looked healthy enough. Of course this was the showcase of the compensation racket: the period of log-rolling and kickbacks, however profitable, must be written off eventually. Tragedy could hardly stalk down this line of once-broken men whom Gilbert Dwight and his staff had mended so skillfully—and with such exquisite delay. . . . Chris pounded his steering wheel softly with one taut fist. Was he unfair to complete his picture of Dwight on Karen's savage remarks and the evidence offered by a single piece of murderous neglect? Should he join the line now and have it out with the man, face to face?

It seemed evident that Dwight had invaded Milton like a buzzard. Still he deserved a warning that a buzzard hunt was now in the making. It would be a revelation to walk into the man's office—even if he could picture it perfectly, from the too-pretty receptionist to the potpourri on the glass-topped modern desk:

"The name is Land, Doctor. I've come to set up practice here."

"Glad to welcome you, Dr. Land. Will you lunch with me?"

"Certainly not. I don't break bread with enemies. Must I

explain that I shan't sleep too soundly until I've put you on the next train north?"

"Now just a moment, young man——"

The church bell boomed noon, as it had done on Duval Square for over a century. Chris grinned at his own melodrama, dropped another coin in the taximeter, and backed into the noontide traffic swirling around the date palms. The impulse had been pure heroics, of course. Now that he had made up his mind, he could afford to turn his back on Gilbert Dwight for a while.

Uncle Jeff's house was an easy drive from the square, and he enjoyed every moment of it. Stuart Street was a pattern of tranquil green light, where the water oaks made their arch above the macadam. Nothing stirred there, save the sprinklers on a dozen old lawns. The houses, he noted, brooded as gently as ever on their secrets: white, sun-faded houses with doorways drowned in summer bloom. All the overtones of the Old South were here in force, but this was in no sense a show street in Milton. These houses had been built to live in, to preserve a heritage that had never really submitted to change.

Chris wondered how many years remained to Stuart Street in the whirling pattern of tomorrow. How long before its owners moved to boardinghouses or hung out tourist signs of their own. . . . Geoffrey Land would be the last to go, he added grimly as he turned up the flagged walk that led across his uncle's lawn.

The two men seated in the deep shade of the veranda were a part of the unchanging picture. Even before he had quit practice Dr. Cato Embree had lunched almost daily with his friend Dr. Geoffrey Land. Residents could set their watches by his progress from his own trim porch to the veranda of the Land house—where a preprandial bourbon, argument, and a bristling gesture of friendliness had enlivened a thousand noons. Chris could hear Embree now, pounding his chair arm and damning the Administration as only a Southern Democrat can damn.

Chris felt his pulse quicken. Here, at last, was the true dynamic of the South: a frail ghost in white linen, with blue fire for eyes and a white tragedian's lock. Here was Uncle Jeff, benign as time in his rumpled gabardine: a leonine man with an unexpected, twisted smile and gentle hands. Both of those hands were held out now as Chris ran up the walk.

"Karen said you were back. I couldn't believe it."

He's aged in the last three years, Chris thought. The sort of aging that means resignation. He doesn't look as though he had a first-rate bellow left. Not even a bellow for the status quo that makes old Embree so exasperating. . . . He put out his hand to the retired firebrand—surprised, as always, that a man as slight as the doc could have such an iron grip.

Embree said judiciously, "Young hellion, it's about time you turned up. And don't stare at us; your uncle Jeff won't blow away. He won't even curse you for sneaking into town without a wire."

They beamed at him together out of their common past. Chris said slowly, "I know I should have wired——"

But Uncle Jeff was already steering them into the white-paneled parlor—and charging to the dining room to order bourbon and an extra plate. The room received Chris with its friendliness unchanged. He knew it by heart, of course; he and Bill Land had always been like brothers. Bill was buried in a New Guinea grave today, but his photo still laughed down at Chris from the tall highboy. The whole room was like that: lived in, but a little forlorn. An old man's retreat, it admitted that its owner had seen better days—but insisted that he was none the less a gentleman for a bookcase with a cracked pane, and a sagging sofa.

Embree echoed the thought as he settled into a wing-back chair that would have brought a gleam to an antique dealer's eye. "Hadn't you heard, Chris? We're poor, and we don't give a tinker's damn. Not if the hospital keeps its doors open——"

"We, Doc?"

"You know I own ten shares of stock. D'you see me running out?"

Chris grinned and took the well-remembered love seat with a broken spring. Cato Embree, despite his sharp tongue, had always made a good thing of medicine. And yet, when he had retired at sixty, he had no tangible assets but his Stuart Street home and a rickety mortgage or two. Seward Harper, who knew as much as most bankers, said that Embree lived by dining out. Of course Seward knew as well as anyone that the old doctor had salted away a cool hundred thousand in government bonds, despite a vague suspicion of any institution as far north as Washington. . . .

"Are things really that bad in Milton?"

"Things are wonderful in Milton, if you play ball with the right club." Doc Embree tossed back his tragedian's lock.

39

"Don't get me started on the medical muddle here, boy. Not till I've had my bourbon." He leaned forward and tapped Chris's leg. "Let's have a look at that tibia."

Uncle Jeff had come back with the bottle; he dropped to one knee as Chris hitched up his trouser cuff. He felt no hesitation in showing the scar to these inquiring eyes. He had shown Uncle Jeff all his hurts as far back as he could remember.

"Two and a quarter inches of bone graft. It'll take me into a football game today."

The old doctors nodded in unison. Embree snorted. "Why not? They've got all the good surgeons in the Army."

"Where else would you have them, Cato?"

"We could use a few in Milton."

Chris said, "You've got one now, if he's welcome—and good enough."

Uncle Jeff looked up slowly. For a moment he seemed about to speak: then he went over to the side table that had always served him as a bar. The mixing of bourbon, mint, and soda was a rite that permitted no interruptions.

Embree had no such reticence. "Don't tell me you mean to practice here?"

"I'm coming into the hospital, if Uncle Jeff will have me."

Again his uncle turned and seemed about to speak. Chris was grateful for the dimness in the room; he had a shrewd notion that Uncle Jeff's eyes had misted a little.

"Of course he'll have you," said Embree. "He's been fighting the sheriff for months, with only Karen to help." The little doctor took the frosted glass that Uncle Jeff proffered. "Course I can't guarantee you'll keep your mind on your job, with that lady viking under the same roof. If I was twenty again— or even forty——"

"Shut up, Cato," said Uncle Jeff. He came over to Chris almost diffidently. "Karen said you'd dined with her and gone out on a call. I gather she's told you something of our troubles."

"Seward Harper finished the story at the bank," said Chris. "That's why I'm coming in."

"What about Lakeview? Didn't you plan to go back and teach?"

"Perhaps I will, when the war's over. Unfortunately, it's still to be won."

"You've done your stretch at that, son."

40

"I'm talking of the home front. The war is right here in Milton, and the doctors seem to be losing."

"Jeff's planning to give up," barked Embree. "Dwight and his crowd are willing to buy him out tomorrow. God knows their offer is generous enough——"

Uncle Jeff's eyes flashed. "You know damned well I refused it."

"Seward mentioned the figure this morning," said Chris. "Gilbert Dwight offered you twenty-five thousand dollars outright. Would you give me a half interest for that amount?"

Embree said, "Don't be a fool, boy."

And Uncle Jeff added in the same breath, "That's your dad's money, Chris. Your security——"

"Don't pull out the organ stops," said Chris. "I expect dividends."

He put a hard fist against his uncle's shoulder, forcing the older man to meet his eyes. "Seward said you'd *have* to listen to me. He said it's either Dad's money or foreclosure. Dwight's offer would barely cover the mortgage. With cash of our own, we can catch up on back payments. Put the hospital on its feet——"

He let the rest go, feeling the mute acceptance in his uncle's eyes. The heart-warming glow had come back; the confidence of a man who has fumbled too long in a strange world.

Uncle Jeff said, "If it's what you really want . . ."

There was no need for more. They had known each other too long for that. Uncle Jeff let his hand rest on his nephew's arm for a moment before he got up—briskly, now, with his massive shoulders squared.

"Dinner is waiting, gentlemen. Shall we go in?"

Cato Embree pushed back his soup plate. Chris did not flinch when he leveled a forensic finger in his direction.

By his standards, Chris thought, I *am* a damned fool. All his life the doc has clung to security and fought change. To him the war is a spell of bad weather for Milton to live down. . . . He plans to outlast it, just as he outlasted the depression: by sitting tight, cashing his bond coupons, and doing nothing.

He frowned at his plate as the fiery little doctor began talking. He, too, had been planning to outlast the storm. To settle with his own dividends and think things over. Until

Karen Agard had reminded him that the time for planning was short.

Embree said, "I repeat, Chris. You are a damned fool. Furthermore, you know it. Let old Jeff sell out and retire. Damn his old hide, he's too senile to be running anything bigger'n an outboard motor."

Dr. Jeff said tranquilly, "I'll retire the day of my funeral, Cato." He smiled at Chris across the table. "At that, son, you'd better hear him out. If you decide to withdraw that offer——"

"Not a chance of that," said Chris. "Naturally I know what an honest doctor is up against when heavy industry moves in on a town like Milton."

"Everyone works for Borland nowadays," said Embree. "You can't be against him. If you're a doctor, that means you work for Dwight."

"Why can't we handle shipyard cases on our own?"

"Because Dwight has the yards sewed up."

Chris listened patiently while Embree sketched the familiar pattern. Expansion in a restricted area, and industrial health —the twin problems of any war boom—had been met by the Borland interests in the usual way. The medical unit which Gilbert Dwight headed had entered Milton fully organized: Dwight had built his clinic beside the County Hospital, which had been filled with company cases from the day it opened. As practice multiplied, Dwight had taken in other doctors: Moreau, the French surgeon from New York; a Viennese specialist named Kornmann; a medical man and a laboratory technician, also on the refugee list. He had even gone to the Milton Medical Society to sign up a diagnostician—one of the few physicians in Milton who had managed to ignore the war.

"Old Baskin, the horse doctor," said Embree. "You surely remember *him,* Chris. Got himself a disability rating and jumped into Dwight's pen like a rabbit."

"So far it sounds legal," said Chris. "How well has it worked?"

Embree snorted in earnest. "Both Moreau and Dwight are first-class surgeons, if you take their word for it. I must say Dwight's is ironclad: I looked it up myself, last time I was in Washington. Moreau's another breed of cat, of course, with a temporary license: Hitler's sitting on *his* credentials now, to hear him tell it. . . . Most of Milton has taken 'em on faith, needless to add. Dwight has just got himself elected president of the County Society. Course he's thick as thieves with the gang at the Capitol."

Uncle Jeff put in a mild word. "We've had no epidemics so far. Naturally the accident rate has been high. Always is when unskilled hands move in on a new job."

Cato Embree slapped the table with a thin but furious hand. "Never mind if they're shysters or geniuses. I'll come to that in a minute. Right now I'm telling Chris that their racket has milked this town dry, as far as the old doctors are concerned. For all the boom, they can't make a living in Milton. Not unless they move in with Dwight and think his thoughts."

He half rose from his chair: the forensic finger was imitating a semaphore now, under Chris's nose. "Seven doctors in all, working day and night in that bandits' clinic—and charging what they like for outside practice. Seven political logrollers—five of 'em refugees. D'you think *they'll* fade into the European fog when other Milton doctors start coming back from the war? D'you think that you can outsmart 'em now?"

"Dwight isn't a refugee."

"No, worse luck. He's just a bad American. A slick New Yorker with a bedside manner. Been on Borland's pay roll for years, and expects to stay on."

Chris considered the portrait of Gilbert Dwight as Embree shaped it with bold strokes. In such hands a compensation clinic could turn over a fortune. Chris reviewed the standard methods of the dishonest doctor: keep the patient coming back, load him with twice the dressings he needs, keep him sick even if he wants to be well. Build on the fact that many workmen prefer to loaf on half pay rather than earn overtime. . . . How many in that long line outside Dwight's office were goldbrickers? How many honest craftsmen really yearned to get in harness again—and wondered why a simple industrial accident should take so long to heal?

The compensation racket, Chris pursued, was hard to expose, and harder to combat from the outside. An industrial clinic, working within the factory, did not solve the problem: in such a setup the patient usually received undertreatment rather than coddling. Even when it was provable that doctors lost no business because of them, free clinics usually died a-borning when men like Dwight ruled the local medical society. Sometimes it seemed that a certain type of doctor was opposed to any measure that lowered the sickness rate. Remembering last night's tragedy at the farmhouse, Chris was ready to put Gilbert Dwight's name on that list. His fist curled. Already he regretted the impulse that had turned him aside from Dwight's office.

Doc Embree's voice went on above his musings. "Have I got to draw blueprints at your age, Chris? You know exactly how Dwight operates his gold mine. According to our state law, Borland's must pay any doctor that treats a worker. Said worker, of course, being free to choose his physician. The Medical Society even makes rules about rates, to keep physicians from undercutting one another."

"Bring me up-to-date," urged Chris. "Remember I've been out of this for three years." Embree's remarks were as familiar to him as original sin; but it was a standing convention at Uncle Jeff's to supply a guest with an audience.

"One way to get around the Medical Society—if it's too honest—is to make a deal with an insurance agent. God knows they're not all crooks; most of 'em find it pays to follow the law literally—give the workers a list of ethical doctors in case of accident. But others aren't above talking turkey with a shyster who'll shade his rates a little. In Dwight's position it's simple. He comes here as Borland's man before the word gets 'round; he makes a deal with the company agent to get Borland's compensation work; he puts Borland's foremen on his pay roll, just to be sure his lists are posted, and no others."

"In other words, sold to the highest bidder?"

"Exactly. Who's on Dwight's list? The refugee crew I just named—and old Baskin, for local color. Before the yards were half open they had the men in their pockets. So help me, it wasn't three months before they *all* had private offices in town, grabbing our own boys' practice with both hands. Who could stop 'em, with every Milton doctor under forty in a uniform?"

Uncle Jeff smiled wanly. "Don't ask Southern boys to keep out of a fight, Cato."

"It's the same up North," said Embree. "Heaven forgive me for saying it, but the Yanks like a scrap as much as we. In the meantime it's a field day for refugees and riffraff."

Uncle Jeff said, "Don't run down all the refugees. Remember Karen."

"Could I forget her? I'm not saying the Nazis didn't drive a few good men out of Europe. I'm saying a lot of bloodsuckers pulled out from under, even before the storm broke. I'm saying a lot of that stripe like it here and plan to stay.

And that includes Dwight's janizaries. Most of 'em are working for him now on a straight salary basis and licking his hand in gratitude. If you ask me, I doubt if the great man bothers to look at a dozen patients a week."

Chris met the blue blaze of Embree's eyes. "A smart bookkeeper, eh?"

"A fat cat in a cream pitcher."

"Of course it works to everyone's advantage."

"Everyone's. Dwight is a rich man now. Moreau's his go-between, and getting rich too: making friends all over the state, doing Caesareans like a movie star. As I say, the others are cashing in big, in a local way. . . . As for the compensation clinic—well, the insurance boys are taking it and liking it. At least, they pay Dwight a flat fee—and know he won't parlay his cases beyond reason."

Embree thumped the table and glared at his audience. "Nobody loses but the war effort and Borland. Am I right, Jeff?"

Uncle Jeff smiled wryly. "What's the solution? State medicine?"

"Hell and Maria, no! But it's coming, as sure as taxes, if good men don't gang up on the sharks."

"I reckon that's why Chris has come back. I reckon we all know that no matter how bad the spirit of competition is, the quality of medicine goes down when you remove it."

"Who's denying that?"

"Dwight, for one. The politicos in Washington deny it too —when they try to jam through their bills for government control."

"So what? Do we bury Hippocrates and take it?"

Chris heard his own voice cut through the wrangle. "There *is* one answer, gentlemen. Group medicine, on a prepayment plan. I'm shooting for that here, with Uncle Jeff's permission."

"Clinic against clinic, eh?"

"Why not? Uncle Jeff has *always* run that hospital as a big free clinic—that's the main reason he's broke. All I want to do is put the hospital in running order—and get our money in advance. From Borland himself, if he'll take us on—and why shouldn't he? The prepayment system has already proved itself at the Kaiser yards. We can try it here, as an antidote to Dwight."

"What'll you use for doctors?"

"We've a nucleus now. Karen in lab, Uncle Jeff on the

45

medical end, myself in the O.R." Chris chuckled as he saw his uncle's face light up. "We might even take in Doc Embree as consultant—if he'd give up making speeches and come back to harness."

"Don't tempt me, boy," snapped Embree. "Just tell me again who you'll use for patients."

"Everyone in Milton who is dissatisfied, or believes in progress with a home-grown label, or is loyal to Uncle Jeff. Everyone we can grab at the yards."

"Dwight will fight you for every sore finger."

"Good. I'll start by fighting him for the business at West Island. That's still wide open."

The shipyard Chris had mentioned stood at the far end of Milton. In the past it had manufactured sailing craft and small fishing boats. Now, of course, it had garnered its share of the wartime boom and the wartime headaches. The bank had controlled its finances since the depression. Seward Harper had told Chris an interesting story of that financing, and he hastened to elaborate it now.

"Borland has been using West Island as a subassembly for some time. Last month he took over the receivership *in toto*. Seward has been doubling in brass as manager: Borland didn't want people to know that he's the actual owner today. . . . Of course the bank's been handling its own accident insurance and has refused to do business with a group. But that method simply hasn't panned out. Right now Seward is willing to experiment, if he can find an honest outlet. Why can't we elect ourselves?"

Uncle Jeff let out his breath in a long whistle. "Why didn't Seward come to me with this?"

"Because he's a realist," said Chris. "He thought you'd have to give in to Dwight. Now, of course, he's all for us—if we're for *him*."

"Sold," said Uncle Jeff. "You can name the figure."

But Cato Embree could keep out of no conversation for long. "Why hasn't Borland turned this over to his white-headed boy? Doesn't he think Dwight is efficient?"

"Apparently he feels Dwight has all the work he can handle."

"And why should he consider you?"

"I'm not sure he will," said Chris. "But I know Seward is on our side. And I'm meeting Borland himself, through his daughter."

He was mildly appalled by his words, but it was too late to call them back. He saw his uncle's brows go up; he watched Embree lean across the table with real excitement in his eyes.

"Since when have you known that barelegged hellion?"

"I'm meeting her this afternoon," said Chris. "Through Karen," he added for his uncle's benefit. "You see, Uncle Jeff, we're all working on your side."

The older doctor said, "Karen Agard is a remarkable scientist and a remarkable woman. I still think it was pure luck that she should choose to come to me on Paul Travers' word. I won't say what I think of *your* return, Chris. I haven't words to thank you."

"Do you approve of my methods?"

"More power to you if you can convince Borland. I never thought of you as a politician before, but——"

"Nor did I, until eleven this morning," said Chris. "Naturally I can't guarantee results until I meet Miss Borland"—he grinned at Embree—"and test the power of my charm."

Embree shook with laughter. "I'll back you in that sweepstake, boy. You're the kind who doesn't know his strength where women are concerned. That kind always runs up the records."

Chris grinned at his uncle now. "Maybe this conversation has gone far enough. In another minute the doc will be telling us of his conquests at twenty."

"Don't sneer, you rascal," said Embree. "It was a good youth while it lasted."

They pushed back their chairs and moved out to the veranda. Uncle Jeff said, "Would you like to drop in at the hospital before your—shall I say your rendezvous?"

"Why d'you think my car's at the curb?"

They waved good-by to Embree as the coupé took the curve for the hill and coughed its way easily up the slope. Chris looked back at the little doctor. With his after-dinner cigar at a brave angle, his Panama riding high on his blizzard of white hair, Cato Embree could have passed for a small but indignant bantam. In a way he represented all that was best in medicine: iron integrity, an instinctive hatred of sham—and a flair for the dramatic that has cured more patients than doctors dare admit. But the worst of medicine elbowed for room within that same tight skull: impatience

47

with change, a firm belief in the lone-wolf path to success that hobbles specialist and plodding G.P. alike.

Dr. Jeff put the thought into words. "Maybe we're old fogies here in Milton, Chris. We haven't given up our right to criticize. And we know how to appreciate a friend in need." He cleared his throat in one of his rare moments of embarrassment. "I hope I can prove that to you now."

It was more than enough to seal the bond between them. Uncle Jeff was not the demonstrative sort: emotions had a way of choking somewhere inside. When they swung into the hospital driveway he was already talking of Paul Travers and his ominous notes on trailer town.

"Brill's disease is a plain name for murine typhus in the South. Paul says he can smell an epidemic in the making, down there in that filled-in marsh." He flicked a finger in the direction of the lab. "Karen's been working on some choice specimens he picked up in jalopy city. Of course you'll remember how that marsh was overrun with rats in the old days. Some of 'em migrated; most of 'em have moved in with the new settlers and fought over their garbage pails. I won't discuss the migrations of their fleas."

Chris felt his mind make a familiar hiatus. Karen had already spoken of these storm signals. If rats still flourished under the wheels of trailer town, it would be a simple matter for their vermin to spread typhus to the ends of Borland's empire.

"Have you any patients now?"

"No cases yet, thank heaven. Dwight's got a couple in his back room, according to reports: Travers is doing his best to make sure of it. . . . In fact, my patient today is a rebound from a family that Dwight has hospitalized. Pyloric stenosis. Karen brought it in from her children's clinic outside the yards."

"Charity again, eh?"

"I'm afraid that's the name, son."

They walked into the antechamber that gave to the familiar tiled curve of the operating room. Uncle Jeff said quite casually, "Will you take this case, or shall I?"

"I'm afraid I'll have to wait for my license." Chris bit his lip on that recollection. Once again he remembered he was in for trouble if the news of last night's work reached the wrong ears. He explained the matter briefly to his uncle,

48

while the older doctor scrubbed. But Uncle Jeff merely looked up at him with approving eyes.

"Don't call me an idealist, son. In your way, you're just as incurable."

"What will happen to me if the fact gets out?"

"Anything from suspension to loss of your license. Depending on who found out—and how strong his pull was with the State Medical." Dr. Jeff looked up as the operating-room door opened on a muted stir beyond. A sterile nurse came up with his mask and gown. Chris stepped back a pace, to receive a similar gown from a probationer.

"Don't let your fingers itch, son," said his uncle. "We'll have your license down from the Capitol in a day or so. Karen can pull the wires for that."

They looked at the tall figure in the doorway, with a small bundle in her arms. Karen Agard said, "If you're talking about Dr. Land's license, it's on its way now. I filed for it by telephone this morning."

Her eyes were quite as blue as Chris remembered above the gauze mask. For an instant they rested on him with warm and untroubled friendliness. A viking's eyes to go with a viking manner, thought Chris. Eyes that accepted you completely or not at all.

Dr. Jeff said, "This is my new partner, Karen. Or did you two fix that all up between you?"

Karen said, "I tried, at least."

"You'll take his orders for your trouble, then." Uncle Jeff chuckled. "Don't give him an argument on a diagnosis, even when you're right. And never look at him like that when he's operating."

"I'll remember," said Karen. Her eyes still held Chris: they snapped away abruptly now as she turned back to the operating room and laid her bundle on the table.

The baby was sleeping quietly, thanks to a preoperative barbiturate. Chris watched Karen stretch their small patient on the table and secure his arms and legs with bandages and cotton pads. The child was emaciated from loss of food; in this strange condition, when the pylorus grew too fast for the body's need, it tended to shut the outlet of the stomach and block that vital section of the alimentary tract. As growth increased, vomiting became more frequent and the obstruction more ominous. Finally, when the closure was complete, nothing could pass from stomach to intestine, and the child

49

slowly starved from lack of foods and fluids. Glucose could still be given by vein, of course; fluids, injected beneath the skin, relieved dehydration for a time; in the end such measures could not maintain the body needs. Only by surgery could these tiny victims of their own muscle growth be saved.

Watching his uncle prepare the patient, Chris asked, "What anesthetic will you use?"

"Local," said Dr. Jeff. "Karen will give the baby ether if he needs it."

Chris nodded. "I've almost always been able to handle them with local."

Dr. Jeff bent down to inject novocain into the baby's abdominal wall, in a vertical area just above and to the right of the navel. The tissues were delicate; as he made the small incision he closed the bleeding vessels with delicate mosquito clamps. The scalpel severed the tough sheath that covered the abdominal muscles and separated them deftly to expose the peritoneum.

Chris found himself leaning over his uncle's shoulder to follow the operative pattern. He remembered his own first incision of this sort, at the baby clinic in Lakeview. It had been his first year as a surgical intern; he could still see his patient, incredibly small on the huge operating table. He remembered how utterly helpless the baby had seemed—how huge his fingers had felt as they began their work of exploration.

Dr. Jeff made a clean, bold slit in the peritoneum, exposing the dark surface of the liver beneath. An incision of this sort, correctly placed, always exposed the liver first—which could then be lifted above the operating field to show the stomach, and the whitish, sausage-shaped muscle tumor at the end of it.

Gently the old doctor lifted the dark, sharp edge of the liver; with a piece of saline-moistened gauze he pinched up the stomach wall and brought his objective into view. The obstructing muscle tumor came up easily into the wound, without pulling. So far the child had not stirred; the novocain had taken care of pain for a time, and he still slept on under the barbiturate.

Dr. Jeff slit the top of his circular muscle layer which had grown completely around the stomach in this area. Then, with a small clamp, he began separating the fibers themselves, breaking through tissue gently by separating the points of the instrument.

50

"Rammstedt's method," he said.

Chris nodded his approval. Time had proved that this was the best technique to break muscle fibers. There was no need here for a scalpel; the surgeon's job was done, once that circular band of gristle was separated and the membrane lining of the stomach was visible.

Like so many of the surgeon's routine jobs, this one was tedious as well as delicate. It took Dr. Jeff perhaps a half hour of slow dissection with the clamp before the obstruction was completely relieved and the tumor lay in the operating field like a watermelon with a slice removed.

Chris stepped back from the table while his uncle dropped the patient's stomach into place and let the liver return to its normal position beneath the wound. The older doctor's hands had been smoothly fluent throughout. There was no difficulty now with the operative closure, no pushing of delicate organs through the incision, no stimulation of the baby to break his dreamless repose.

"Nice work, Doctor," said Chris.

Dr. Jeff shook his head. "You could have done it in half the time, son. Old hands have to move more slowly." He made an inclusive gesture of welcome. This is your domain as of now, the gesture said. Beginning tomorrow, I move back to my consulting room, where I belong. The gesture took in Karen, of course: Chris gathered that when Uncle Jeff pushed up his mask and gave them both his slow, easy grin.

"I hope this plan of yours turns out well," said Uncle Jeff. "Even if it doesn't, I'll enjoy it."

The probational wheeled the patient back to the baby's ward, and they walked into the scrub room in a compact group. When Karen, too, pushed up her mask, Chris saw the happiness in her face. A serene kind of happiness, with no hint of passion. Yet when she put her hand on his arm he was mildly astonished at the burning pressure of her fingers.

"I'm so glad, Chris."

"Let's hope you don't change your mind. I'm a slave driver, you know."

She let her hand drop, feeling Uncle Jeff's eyes. "So am I," she remarked. "It's nearly three. Don't forget you've a date with Roz Borland in an hour. It might be important."

"It might, at that. Now I'm in this fight, I'm leaving no stone unturned."

51

"Don't forget Dr. Dwight."

"Must you spoil my crusader's glow so soon?"

Karen said evenly, "Dwight telephoned here an hour ago and asked for you. He likes to know all the new doctors in Milton; could you drop in at his office now, on your way to Rosalie?"

5

HIS OFFICE is just what I expected, thought Chris. The same muted elegance. Same thick mahogany. Same receptionist, tired but pretty, giving honest workmen the brush-off in the reception room. It reminds you of a banker's sanctum, not a doctor's. And yet the man himself looks every inch a doctor. A nice young dynamo, complete with horn-rims and a Ph.D. brow. Bouncing and thoroughly self-assured. How could a fellow that young keep out of the Army? Did he classify himself 4-F?

Never mind that now, Chris warned himself. Of course Gilbert Dwight would be clean-cut, urbane, charming. This isn't the first time that evil has invented a plausible mask. . . . *Your* job right now is to sit tight and remember that he's too smooth to be honest. Those gray eyes are hard as marbles, for all their friendly sparkle.

Dwight had been talking of the war—and his regret that he could not take an active part. Now he leaned forward to balance a paper cutter on his palm. For a moment he stared down at his reflection in the glass desk top. The lattice behind him was golden with the Southern afternoon; it served to accent the alert tanned profile, the well-modeled jaw with its deceptive boyish dimple.

Dwight said, against Chris's silence, "Perhaps I shouldn't reproach myself too much, Major. In a way, Milton is a war front too."

"An important front," said Chris.

"You plan to locate here at once, I believe."

"I'm considering it."

"Forgive me if I hear too much—but I know that you've already made your decision."

The man's smile was as bland as ever; his voice had not varied in timbre, but the eyes behind those horn-rims focused and held. This, it seemed, was his first challenge. Something to be met head on or not at all.

Chris said, "You might explain that."

"How I know of your plans? My dear doctor, I have friends at the Seaboard Bank. You are about to go in with your uncle —with the West Island yards as a probable nest egg. Is that specific enough?"

"Do I have your blessing?"

"Why not?" Dwight leaned across the table earnestly. "Every new doctor in Milton is an asset. God knows *I've* all the cases I can handle." He made a lightning pause; when he went on his tone was silky, confidential. "Of course we should co-operate. That's why I asked you to drop in."

Chris considered the bait warily. He knew that Seward Harper had been using all his influence to get him the West Island contract—even before he was sure that Chris would consider such an opportunity. Did this attitude of Dwight's mean that Seward had succeeded? Or was Dwight building to a more devious end?

"Understand me, Major," said Dwight. "I've been Borland's medical specialist for some time now. Had I wished, I could have undertaken this new work merely by extending my staff. No matter what your figure is, I could go below it if I wished. Surely these are sound reasons for agreement between us."

Chris said, "I'm not sure I understand."

"I think you follow me perfectly."

"Are you suggesting I come in with you?"

"Co-operation is the word, Major."

"Are you sure it isn't logrolling?"

Dwight had a rich, full-bodied laugh. He used it to advantage now. "I was warned of your candor. May I say I— appreciate the sample?"

"Why use big words, Dwight? From your point of view, wouldn't it be simpler if I just joined the party?"

"Much. As you know, I've already offered your uncle liberal terms. I think it's only a question of time before you see the light. Medical care for Borland's is a big job; it should be handled as a unit."

"How do you know I'm a good doctor?"

"Your Lakeview record speaks for you, of course. To say nothing of your energy."

He's fishing now, thought Chris. West Island may not be mine, but it isn't his either. Not at this moment. . . . He came back with a start to Dwight's smooth drone:

"Not many doctors would leap into harness again before they were out of uniform. I'm sorry if that's a scrambled word-picture: you know what I mean."

Chris suppressed a frown. So far the heavy artillery was clearly on Dwight's side. A blueprint of his plans was on the desk between them. Dwight had accepted the challenge and predicted the outcome. Now, it seemed, he knew that Chris had operated the previous night without a license.

Dwight said, "There's work here for all of us, Major. Can't we share it sensibly?"

"One town, one melon?"

"You put things admirably. One organized group of doctors, working as a team, is the only answer to our health problem in wartime. Of course the fact that such an arrangement can be most profitable is only a by-product."

Chris felt the blood knock at his temples. "Do you feel that your organization can offer health protection here today?"

"Would I be here otherwise?"

"You might."

Dwight's expression was unchanged. He said mildly, "It's your turn to explain yourself now."

"You seem to know a great deal about me," said Chris. "Let's see how well I know you. You've two surgical assistants —both refugees. Three medical men, same status. A local doctor who'd have lost his license years ago if he didn't have relatives at the Capitol. To my mind, that's not a team in any language. I don't see how your group can handle Borland's work adequately—let alone branch into private practice."

Dwight said affably, "May I file a denial? The record speaks at Borland's. As for our private practice—and I'll admit it's extensive—what would you have? People simply prefer us to the old plugs war has left behind. No offense to your uncle, of course: to my mind, Uncle Jeff's eternal." He spread his hands and offered Chris his best smile. "Apparently you've had time to hear stories about us, Major. Surely you've no right to belittle our refugee physicians. Your own uncle employs one—and an attractive one at that."

Chris spaced his words—and controlled his temper. "Let me offer one example of trouble in the making. The rats in trailer town——"

"Human or otherwise, Major?"

"There's a Public Health man on the spot, lining up a report on an incipient typhus epidemic."

"Don't mention Travers, please. That pious meddler has been a thorn in everyone's side."

"Suppose he's right? Are you prepared for trouble when it comes?"

"Isn't that my affair?"

"The public health is everyone's affair."

"Of course, if we can't talk the same language——"

Chris found he was no calmer. "You might order me from your office. I didn't come here to fight, but I'm doing a first-rate job."

Dwight was still affable, on the surface at least. "Why should we fight at all? There's enough business for us both, even if we can't join forces."

Damn his manners, thought Chris. He's getting cooler by the minute, and I'm almost shouting. "I'll tell you why we're fighting," he said. "There's a certain shipyard family on your list. The name is Dawkins. Five children in a back-country farmhouse. One of them died last night, of diphtheria. Shall I tell you why?"

"Don't bother, Major. I have the case on record." Dwight looked at his nails. "Dr. Agard filed the certificate of death this morning. The child was my patient, of course; it isn't the first time she took over without consulting me. You, I believe, injected serum and performed a tracheotomy, without a license——"

"The father could reach no other doctor," said Chris. "Dr. Agard was summoned by Travers. I went along as consultant. The child would have suffocated without surgery."

"The child died," said Dwight.

"She might have lived, with the proper diagnosis. You might at least have turned her over to a medical man."

"The child died," said Dwight. "You operated without a license. That could interest the State Medical."

Chris got to his feet, feeling relief surge through his limbs as he brought Gilbert Dwight up too, without quite touching him. He's half a head taller than I, thought Chris. But I've a hunch I can outreach him. How would that dimpled jaw stand up under a haymaker? He dismissed the boyish hope. Dwight was much too clever to show his feelings now. Perhaps he was one of those completely evil persons who manage to exist without visible emotions.

Dwight said, "I was only joking, of course. At least we can suspend our little quarrel until you've seen Borland. Until I learn just how unreasonable you intend to be."

Chris said, "We aren't quarreling, Dwight. We're at war. To be honest, that's all I had to say."

He was rather proud of his departure. Of the self-control that made him close the consulting-room door gently. Walking through the reception room, he still felt the boredom in those hard gray eyes. The man had looked at him incuriously —with no hint of fear, or even of contempt. For the first time Chris realized that he was a familiar phenomenon in the life of Gilbert Dwight. That a doctor of Dwight's stamp might well spend a lifetime staring down integrity.

At least the meeting had gone as he'd expected. It was something to know that the battle was already joined. From this point on he'd be fighting with most of Dwight's own weapons. He'd even make love to Rosalie Borland, if he could walk down that tightrope to her father's favor.

His mind checked off that decision quite painlessly as he walked into the corridor of the deSoto Building just in time to see Rosalie Borland herself step into the elevator. Perhaps it's an omen, he thought, watching her escort click his heels and assist her over the imaginary obstacle of the car door. Odd that he should study Roz Borland's companion and not the girl herself. The man was tall and a bit too sleek. The sort of sleekness that advertised the foreigner—even without the too-wide Panama, the extra pinch at the waist of the beautifully cut tweeds. The snap of his shoulders had all the arrogance of a distinguished visitor who finds slumming a not unpleasant novelty.

Of course this was Jean Moreau, the French refugee surgeon with whom Rosalie had lunched. He guessed, too, that Moreau had come back to Dwight for orders before he delivered Rosalie to St. Lucie. The conviction was strong enough to take him into the next elevator on the jump.

They were getting into Moreau's convertible when Chris

stepped out to the glare of afternoon. It was a car like its owner—long, off-white, and aggressively expensive. . . . Moreau had parked it squarely at the curb, in defiance of the space-saving taximeters. Rosalie Borland was just settling beside the wheel as Chris pulled up short in the shadow of the lobby.

Chris took his first long look at her—and found himself savoring it completely. It was pleasant to find that she was quite as disturbing as her photographs. Disturbing, and appealing too, he added, with a sharp stir of nostalgia. Looking at Roz Borland was like looking back at the yesterdays that had tortured you on a foreign beachhead—when America was only a cracked snapshot to be cherished—when home was a pin-up on the wall of a Quonset hut, a snatch of melody that brought back a country club deep in elms and kisses stolen in the shadow of a moonlit bunker.

Rosalie, he reflected, was all that and more to homesick eyes. She was the spirit he had lost and found again—lithe and laughing, and a little wistful under its American patina of assurance. The fact that her figure could transform slacks and a polo shirt into a style all her own was only a part of the picture. Chris didn't even mind if her laughter was for Moreau alone. He stood quietly in the shadow of the lobby while she scolded the refugee in bright, inaccurate French. Then Moreau slammed the car door and whisked into traffic, with an international scowl for the policeman at the corner.

What if she had forgotten their date at St. Lucie? Chris ran down to his own battered coupé and kicked at the starter. Backing into the stream of cars with a carelessness that matched Moreau's, he risked his life to catch Rosalie Borland at the first traffic light.

Like most games, the tag with Moreau's convertible had lost its novelty before he was half across the causeway. The Frenchman, he observed, could drive like an inspired dervish; he did not worry too much about Rosalie's safety, even when the white fender of the convertible seemed to graze a passing bus. Moreau obeyed the speed limit, at least; it was a simple matter to keep his rear bumper in view in the stream of jeeps and workers' jalopies. To study the toss of Rosalie's head and the way her coppery page-boy bob went mad in the whip of wind from the Gulf.

Chris cut his motor and coasted to a stop in the lee of a

dune just before the macadam ended. Now that he had passed the last traffic trap, Moreau had taken the oyster road with his foot on the floor; the white convertible seemed to merge with its dust as it took the last turn to St. Lucie Cay. Chris sat on under his wheel and watched the dust settle. He felt calm enough now, as his mind framed the things he must say. How long he would let her wait for him on Karen's porch. How he would alter his argument, if Moreau insisted on waiting with her.

The second question canceled out when the puff of dust reappeared among the dunes. Moreau drove by with his eyes hard on the road: Chris noted, with no surprise, that the Frenchman was one of the handsomest men he had ever seen. A sullen blond Norman, he hazarded, spoiled by flattery and easy living. At the moment Dr. Moreau might have passed for a child who has just been deprived of his favorite sweet. She's sent him packing, thought Chris with an unreasonable lift of his heart. For the next hour she's all mine. He kicked the starter and remembered to drive slowly down the oyster road.

A plume of smoke curled at the boathouse chimney, to show that Roy had made good use of his day off. Beyond, Karen's bungalow offered a trim face to the glare from the Gulf. The mats were down on the western railings, making a cave of coolness; when he crossed the lawn Chris saw that Rosalie Borland had stretched out here in a basket chair, quite as though she had owned it forever.

He walked toward her steadily, noting for the first time that her face was almost gaunt in repose. The long fingers holding a cigarette were stained with nicotine. In the half-light her eyes were neither green nor hazel. They followed him lazily as he came up the step. Chris stared back into them boldly, still determined that she must break their silence.

When she spoke, her directness jarred him a little. He had expected a junior-league parroting—or perhaps a husky contralto born of too many cocktails at lunch. But Rosalie Borland's voice was as natural as the lazy surf behind them.

"You're early," she said. "Does that mean you're anxious?"

"Speak for yourself, Miss Borland," said Chris. "You *are* Miss Borland?"

"Don't I resemble my photographs? You're the image of yours—except that your uniform is cleaner."

She had a provocative handshake. The sort of handshake that started lightly and grew on you. Chris reached for his cigarette and a professional manner.

"Was I photographed recently?"

"In the ruins of a church outside Civitavecchia. The caption said you'd been operating in the apse under shellfire."

Chris stared back briefly at the memory. It had been one of those firemen's days after the fall of Rome. A backwash of war, without heroics or violent headaches. He remembered the clamp on that boy's femoral artery, the emergency dressing, the shout for stretcher-bearers. Then up into the sun for a cigarette and a breath of clean air—free, for a moment, from the endless round of scalpel and hemostat, from the hopeless begging of a hundred eyes. . . . He hadn't noticed the grubby little man with the Leica and the correspondent's arm band. Obviously it was the sort of picture an afternoon paper would blow into a story on a dull day. A fat paragraph of caption, expertly angled to transform routine into romance on the home front. The fact that he had received his own wound a scant hour afterward—too late for that same press deadline—was only an ironic footnote.

He came back to Rosalie and said grimly, "I'm afraid I didn't look my best that day. It was an informal pose."

"I liked you well enough." Her eyes narrowed in frank appraisal. "In fact, I made up my mind to use you—if you ever came close enough to grab."

"Thanks. I'm on my guard now."

The girl sat down on the veranda rail and flexed her long legs. "Isn't it my privilege, if you profit from it?"

"Keep right on," said Chris. "I'm good at games, even when I don't know the rules."

"Only this isn't a game. I enjoy them too, sometimes. Today I'm a very serious person. Didn't Karen tell you that?"

It was a dare, and Chris accepted it promptly. "Karen summed you up in a rather catty phrase last night. She said that your father's money had insulated you from reality. Was she right?"

Rosalie Borland opened her green eyes wide at him. He accepted the stare—and leaned forward to light his cigarette from her own. "Surely you've been told that before?"

"I won't say that Karen's wrong. I can't say I feel insulated, but—naturally Dad's money has spoiled me. Take you, for instance."

"Why me?"

"I'm fitting you into a plan I have. If you just won't fit, I'll be heartbroken. Tell me that's wrong. Or even pigheaded. I'm trying, just the same. And you're listening."

Chris kept his poker face intact. It was interesting to learn so soon that she was vulnerable under that bright mask. Vulnerable as only a rich man's daughter can be, when she finds that some things cannot be reserved by telephone or paid for by check. He said quietly, "I'm a surgeon, not a psychoanalyst. I still enjoy listening."

Rosalie Borland flipped her cigarette at the Gulf of Mexico. "If you're planning to go into practice here, you'll need a lot of business fast. What say I introduce you to Dad and give you a head start?"

"As painlessly as that?"

"Please don't scowl. Karen and I *did* go to Vassar together, you know. She *did* tell me you'd planned to stand up to Dwight. Can't I contribute?"

"I wasn't scowling. I was gaping."

"Can't I be unselfish without someone's jaw dropping?"

"Not in my dictionary, Miss Borland."

"Call me Roz," she said. "It's nicer than calling me names in your mind."

"Stop me if I'm wrong, Roz, but—*I'm* just a name to you, as of now. This offer has a string attached. Tell me how badly it chokes before I thank you."

Rosalie Borland studied him through lowered lids. "You won't choke, Major—may I call you Chris, now we've let down our hair?"

"Call me anything you like. I know I'm rude——"

"The fact is, I've a protégé. Name of Jean Moreau. A surgeon. I wouldn't know, of course, but I'd guess he's a good one."

"Would you mind starting over?"

"Tell me first how tolerant you really are. About Jean, for example."

"I'm afraid we haven't met."

"You haven't met me, formally. But I imagine you've a few opinions. You were studying Jean carefully when you trailed us out of town."

Chris grinned over his cigarette. "I guess that's your round."

"We aren't fighting, are we? We're just saying what we think."

"About Moreau."

"You think he's hand in glove with Dwight. That isn't true. You think he's a chiseler in the American boardinghouse, too."

"Check," said Chris. "Correct me if I'm wrong."

Rosalie said solemnly, "Jean escaped to Algiers just before Hitler took over. He's earned his living in London and in New York——"

"Why isn't he with de Gaulle?"

"He was," said Rosalie, triumphant. "Until he was wounded at Sfax. Maybe he isn't a bit different from you—or is that too hard to grasp?"

Chris said, "He's with Dwight."

"That's my doing, too. We met six months ago, at a Long Island house party. I liked him and decided to help him. So I told Father to get him a job." She spoke precisely, with the lazy emphasis of a princess. "Father put him in Dwight's medical unit. Don't blame him if he's tried to make a living since."

"Judging by the exterior, he's done quite well."

"All right, Chris. You think that Dwight's dishonest. So do I, now I've talked this out with Karen. Can't you see that this is another reason for rescuing Jean?"

"Why not let him stay—and get rich?"

Rosalie said, "You needn't tar him with that brush. You see, I mean to marry him, the next time he asks me."

Her hand shook as she drew on a fresh cigarette. Chris saw her completely in that gesture. Why, she's only a mixed-up kid, he thought. A bored kid who's run after one uniform too many—and wonders why she's still bored. Abruptly he was sorry that he hadn't stopped Dr. Jean Moreau on the oyster road. At this moment a blueprint on Moreau seemed even more essential than a declaration of war on Dwight. Even if he hadn't thrown Rosalie off-center, he added grimly. Even if the battle of Sfax wasn't an American-British show, with practically no Fighting French involved . . .

Rosalie said, "I'm in love with Jean, and I don't care who knows it. Do you think I'm a little crazy—telling you?"

"A little."

"But you won't be down on Jean until you've given him a chance?"

"What sort of chance?"

61

"I want you to take him in with you when you go to work for Dad."

Chris let out his breath in a sigh of relief. At least this topsy-turvy meeting had assumed a pattern.

"You mean—admit him to Uncle Jeff's hospital?"

"That's the string. Don't pretend it's hurting you, either."

"Have you discussed this with Moreau?"

"Certainly not. Jean is much too proud to accept favors. He thinks I'm meeting you here for social reasons." She gave a strained laugh. "Of course I don't mind if he's a little jealous."

Chris hesitated. Obviously this was no time to express his real opinion of Moreau. Or to inform Rosalie that the Frenchman had already found his groove and would certainly refuse to budge for any inducement Uncle Jeff might offer. Somehow you didn't explain things like that to the Rosalie Borlands. It was simpler, in the long run, to let them bump their own noses.

He said only, "I'm not quite clear about your offer. Frankly, I don't think you've worked it out yourself."

"But I have. Right now Dad's only *thinking* about giving you the West Island contract. If I took you to him to-night——"

"Just where is your father now?"

"At home," said Rosalie. "If you can call that white mausoleum home. He's been fighting lawyers since morning; that always puts him in a good humor. So if I just took you by the hand and introduced you——"

"Why can't I make a date on my own?"

"He won't see you that easily, Chris. He never does."

"Any bets?"

He was disconcerted to find that she stood eye to eye with him: the dare in her eyes was something he could hardly ignore if he meant to keep his ego intact. She looks like a frozen tantrum, he thought. For the life of me, I don't know if she's going to scream or bite.

He said quietly, "Come off it, Roz. I don't bribe, and I don't take orders, unless they make sense. If I land this contract, I'll talk to Moreau. If he sounds honest—which I frankly doubt—I'll make him an offer I'm sure he'll never accept. Right now I'm talking business with your dad, on my own. Want to listen in?"

When she did not speak he knew that he had made his

point. But he didn't quite risk turning his back on her. Instead he leaned hard on the bungalow door and felt his tension unreel as he remembered that Karen never locked it. He had the absurd conviction that Rosalie's bright copper hair was rising from her temples, like the coiffure of a modern Medusa. At the same time he knew that he could turn his back on her with safety now as he picked up Karen's phone.

The operator connected him instantly with Slave Hill. Any call to Borland's, it seemed, had priority on the Milton switchboard. Chris braced his shoulders as he heard the bored voice of a butler. With Borland's daughter generating electricity on the veranda, he could hardly muff this attack.

"Major Land calling Mr. Borland."

"Does he expect your call, Major?"

"Naturally."

"One moment, please."

For once he could glory in the fact that he had spent the last three years giving orders to enlisted technicians. Without even barking, he had sensed a break-through. When the next voice came on the wire, he was sure of it.

"Yes, Major Land?"

It was a jowly voice, crackling with authority. The sort of voice that could dictate clearly through cigar smoke and frighten a secretary with a whisper. Chris braced his shoulders in earnest.

"Do you know why I'm calling, Mr. Borland?"

"Of course."

"I'd like to talk contract on West Island. When can we get together?"

"What's wrong with now?"

"You mean this afternoon?"

"Why not?" said Borland. "Do you have a car, or shall I send for you?"

Chris swallowed hard. "I can drive over in about twenty minutes. Shall I bring Seward Harper?"

"Harper is with me now," said Borland. "He's been trying to reach you for an hour."

Chris stared at the phone as he hung up. Somehow the instrument had never seemed quite so magical before. He turned back to Roz Borland, keeping his voice steady.

"Glad we didn't bet?"

But the veranda was empty. He saw her a moment later, when he had crossed the lawn and climbed into his car. She was standing on the beach with folded arms, staring hard at the horizon. Even as he watched, a lazy wave curled about her ankles, wetting her slacks halfway to the knee. She did not turn when he called.

"I'm driving to Slave Hill now. Can I take you home?"

He let two of his wheels bite into beach sand and swung close to see that she was crying. It didn't surprise him greatly. Professional experience had told him long ago that girls in love cry with ease. Almost as easily, in fact, as girls who have never loved or been loved. . . . In Roz Borland's case his behavior was only an added cause for tears.

"Sorry I couldn't make promises," he said. "And I hope you don't marry him until you've checked a little further. If I remember Balzac and Proust, Frenchmen make poor husbands."

She whirled on him in earnest then, but he had already wrenched the car back to the road. When the wheels rattled the boards of the bridge again, he turned for a final wave and saw that she was standing in the road with pure murder in her eyes.

6

AT THE EDGE OF TOWN Main Street blossomed abruptly into four-lane macadam, a teaming dark artery that swept across the vast fill to the main gate of the Borland yards. Chris edged his coupé into the stream of trucks and jalopies, pleased that his progress should be retarded for a while. He had driven across the island at top speed. After all, he needed time to marshal his thoughts for the ordeal ahead. A battle was in the offing: he sensed that instinctively, regardless of what enemies might be present at the conference.

Just how much had Cal Borland been swayed in his favor? Watching the torches in the yards sputter like giant candles on the edge of the dusk, he knew that he must discount that question in advance. It was only sound strategy to assume that he must sell his plan for prepaid medical care from the beginning. He wasn't quite ready to do that, he told himself candidly; yet he must create that impression. Borland would hardly put his trust in a doctor who wasn't sure of himself and his facts, who was unready to assume full responsibility for his plans.

Perhaps he should have waited to meet the shipbuilder through his daughter. He let his mind linger on that strategy for a moment, glad that he had chosen the bolder course. Obviously he should have insisted that Rosalie Borland drive home with him, now that he had secured an appointment on his own merits. . . . Remembering her as she had stood there in the shallows of the Gulf with tears and fury in her eyes, he could take solid pleasure in the fact that he had bested her in their first encounter. A brat of that kind deserved to be slapped hard on occasion, as part of her upbringing. By the same token she would have to discover, quite on her own, that Dr. Jean Moreau was a heel with international trimming.

He was skirting the steel-mesh fence of the yards now: behind that efficient barrier the skeletons of a dozen half-finished ships teemed with activity in the glare of the floodlights. For once he could ignore that challenge as he kept his thoughts in focus on the meeting he had sought so eagerly. . . . The cool night breeze from the Gulf kept his spirits buoyant, even as it mingled with the tar-and-paint stench of the yards; as the coupé took the overpass at the railroad right of way, another element was added to the stench—the acerb odor of garbage, filling the skirts of trailer town with an almost visible miasma. Chris frowned as he located the refuse dump that trailer town had chosen, on the edge of the shipyards themselves. Here on the rise steam shovels had scooped a great hollow to accommodate a railroad spur and a sooty row of coal tipples; evidently the cinder road that curved around this hollow, on the way to trailer town itself, had offered the squatters a too-easy solution to the problem of waste. The slopes of the hollow, Chris noted, were streaked with the livid odors of decay: at the bottom, where a generation of tin cans fraternized with waste from a thousand wartime dinner pails, the dump was a hummocky, evil monument to man's carelessness. Chris drew a deep breath and forced himself to follow the circle of cinder road toward trailer town. Studying the dump from every angle, he weighed the aftermath that this squalid city on wheels was courting. . . .

The gray shadow that skittered under his wheels and vanished down the malodorous slope put a dramatic period on his thoughts. At first he was sure that he had just escaped running down a cat; when the animal turned he saw that it would have given most cats pause. Long-tailed, pointed of ear and snout, the creature fixed him with a yellow and contemptuous eye. It was a huge marsh rat, already gorged, on its way to search out other tidbits; apparently it had already foraged at will among the open waste cans of trailer town. Chris frowned in earnest as he pictured that foray. How many squalid dwellings had the animal penetrated? How many parasites had it left behind—fleas as adventurous as their host, bearing an almost pure culture of the *rickettsia mooseri*, the endemic murine typhus that Southern doctors call Brill's disease?

He drove cautiously through the streets of trailer town, avoiding the children who seemed to swarm under both mudguards. On the next rise he left the dank odor of humanity's waste behind him; he was driving through a fine stand of yellow pine now, breathing the clean tang of the needles, the acrid medicinal odor of the rosin dripping from a hundred white slashes in the boles. He remembered the road well. As a boy he had tramped through these same pine barrens to fish in the tidal river that bisected the bottom land of the old King plantation. The tidal river was still there, he saw—widened to accommodate the bustle of the yards. Here it had kept much of its sleepy calm, despite a brand-new boathouse nested in a grove of water oaks.

The cotton fields swept away to the west and north, to end at the slope of Slave Hill itself. Chris took the road that skirted the boathouse landing. It was odd to see a trim launch riding at its moorings, where he remembered only marsh grass and desolation. The fields that had waved snow-white with cotton in August offered him a desolation of another sort. In the old days black hands had picked down these long rows, dragging the huge bags bulging with staple; in boom years he had worked in the King fields himself for pin money. Now the land had gone back to dog fennel, palmetto, and scrub pine, a living sacrifice to carelessness, greed, and the boll weevil. The shipyards had bridged the gap for poverty awhile; once again he wondered why he felt no gratitude to Borland for this largess.

The road was rising now, to the man-made slope of Slave

Hill; Chris could just make out the fieldstone wall that surrounded the grounds. Fieldstones from England, he remembered, brought in ballast to gratify a rich planter's whim—sweated up this slope on black men's backs to shut out the master's domain from the eyes of field hands. . . . The coquina gateposts were unchanged, a relic from the days when a Spanish alcalde had made this his summer home. Borland's architects had added only a steel gate and a caretaker's cranny. The caretaker himself stepped out as Chris coasted to a stop—a uniformed guard with a holstered pistol at his hip, a logical extension of the force that barred all corners of the Borland empire to unwanted outsiders.

The uniform brought its automatic response: Chris flicked out his wallet, with his Army A.G.O. card.

"Dr. Land—by appointment."

The man read the card through and nodded briefly. "They're expecting you, Major." He took in the empty rumble with a brief but competent glance. "Follow that avenue of oaks; you can't go wrong." The steel gate slid back without sound as the man returned to his cubbyhole. Chris smiled wryly as he eased the coupé through. Here were two facets of Cal Borland's efficiency: a guard that checked you with impersonal competence, a gate that opened on oiled runners, without a whisper. . . .

The car followed the curving driveway famous in a hundred albums: a wide white oyster road, arched by great live oaks that Spanish hands had planted, the boughs heavy with their weight of moss. Beyond, the lawns were green, handtailored miracles in the starlight, building in proud terraces to the swan lake in its frame of magnolia and blue gum, a minor Versailles complete to the last white Venus masked in leaves, the last marble balustrade and boxwood hedge.

Slave Hill, Chris reflected, was only the fitting climax to that half hour's drive from the Island. It was quite proper that trailer town, the wasted cotton fields, and the empty tidal river should lie at its foot; proper, too, that a cold-eyed Cerberus should open its gate to him with reluctant hands. . . . As liege lord, Borland had every right to sit in this proud white house and look down on his vassals, including Dr. Christopher Land.

He shook off the fancy and forced his mind back to the proper century. This was Borland's world, and it was his privilege to tailor it as he pleased; he would form no more judgments of the man until they had met face to face.

Ghost-white in the evening, the great manor house seemed to float between earth and heaven—a place of vast wings and tall slate roofs, anchored to its apron of lawn and terrace by the soaring Greek portico. Even the Borland architects had paused here, leaving the tall Corinthian columns untouched. Only the fanlighted doorway had been restored from photographs. Indirect lighting framed the tall mahogany door and the knocker shaped like a mailed fist. Chris had remembered that knocker when it was green with rust. Tonight it shone with a hundred yellow highlights. . . . He smoothed his frown as he got out of his car. The old King place was as authentic as time; in that soft floodlighting it looked precisely like a three-toned whisky ad.

"Good evenin', suh."

The soft Southern accent was a part of that three-toned aura. Chris looked up at the dark, white-haired figure standing in the portico. A black major-domo, he thought, as synthetic as that indirect lighting. In another moment he'll reach into the tails of that bottle-green coat and offer me a mint julep.

"Why, it's Mist' Chris!"

Chris ran up the steps and held out his hands. "Robert! It's good to see you!" Robert had been butler when the Kings had fought off the sheriff on this same portico. Robert had watched young Francis King drink himself to death in the best Southern tradition. . . . For all that, Chris heard his voice frame the inevitable question:

"What are *you* doing here, Robert?"

The old Negro chuckled. "Reckon you'd call me the official welcomer, suh." Already his voice had faded to the correct impersonal note; he seemed to recede within himself as he turned to the great brass knocker and struck a resonant blow.

"Allow me to show you inside, Mist' Chris."

He was gone when Chris turned again. The great hall in which he stood was empty as a museum and quite as distinguished. A gleaming place of endless parquet, great rosewood stair newel, and high white walls thick with ancestors. Four stories up to the fourth-floor skylight, Chris told himself. Twenty-eight bedrooms, haunted by daubers and mud swallows when Francis King died. He wondered what miracles Borland's money had wrought in those upper stories.

Certainly he had spent a fortune refurbishing the King ancestors, right down to the last dapper brigadier who had died not too far from here in a futile effort to deflect Sherman from Atlanta.

He tried to picture Roz Borland on that great stairway and gave up painlessly. Roz was capable of sliding down the banister in broad daylight, and thumbing her nose at every portrait she passed.

"May I take your hat, sir?"

This major-domo was English, and flawless to the last broken vein in his claret-colored face. Chris glanced over his shoulder and saw an impassive footman step out of a white-columned doorway to the left. When the man nodded slightly the Englishman stepped aside with a small, grave bow. Chris knew that he had been given the stamp of approval by a private detective disguised as a servant.

The butler said, "This way, Major Land."

"How did you know my name?"

"Telephoned up from the gatehouse, sir. You'll find Mr. Borland in the library. The other gentlemen will be here shortly."

Chris nodded grimly as he turned toward the columned doorway; the bodyguard in mufti stepped back with his stare intact. So this is to be a free-for-all, he thought. Borland's asking Dwight and his crowd to the party, just to bring out the best in me.

He was still digesting that thought when the library door swung open. A booming voice within assailed his eardrums. He knew without asking that the man at the desk was Calvin Borland. Even in the white linen suit he was small, with massive, almost simian arms and shoulders. The face above the loose-knotted cravat was weathered rather than tanned, the face of a man who tried to cover every detail of an outdoor empire in these long workdays of war. Chris got a flash of white teeth around a cigar, of eyes like sparks of blue fire. Then Borland was back on the telephone—shouting again at Washington.

Chris turned gratefully to Seward Harper as he heaved up from an armchair. The banker was tall and rather baggy in his unpressed seersucker: bankers in Milton, in Seward's apprentice years, had found it profitable to look a little like back-country farmers, and Seward was too old to change. A shrewd eye and a mouth like a well-tailored purse belied the softness of his drawl. Chris sensed the undertone of excitement as they walked together into a recess of a tall leaded window.

"Keep your chin up, boy," said Seward. "I think it's in the bag."

"You mean you've sold me, sight unseen?"

"Not you, Chris. He's made up his mind, with no needling from us. West Island needs a medical unit, that's all. You're it, if you talk fast enough and know all the answers."

"What'll Dwight say to that?"

"He'll throw the book at you, of course. But Dwight's got all the work he can handle, with that left-handed crew—and Dwight knows it. I think he'll knuckle down if you leave him in peace."

Chris chuckled. "Come again, Seward. I declared war on that hand-curried monkey a few hours ago. In his office, to his face. All-out war, with no secret weapons barred."

They turned back to the room as Borland's bark rose to a crescendo. Chris took in the great, high-ceiled library for the first time: when you entered Cal Borland's lair, it seemed, you noticed the man first and details later. Borland had touched nothing in the library, from the deep leather chairs to the busts of the philosophers atop each glass-fronted case. The Kings' hand-tooled leather sets looked as unread as ever, but the room was lived-in now. This was a corner of the Borland beehive, for all its vastness. Its occupant could afford to ignore the echoes.

Borland addressed the telephone competently. "See Don, then. If he won't make sense, see Jimmy. I've got to have those castings on schedule, and they know it. This time I won't fly to Washington to beat it into their brains." He banged up the receiver and turned to Chris. "Glad to see you, Major. That's the last interruption."

The palm that touched Chris's hand was hard with calluses. Once again Chris remembered that the man had risen from his own workbench. Apparently he was not too proud to keep his skill burnished today.

Borland said easily, "Harper's been selling me your clinic for the past hour. Are you ready to finish the job?"

The man's blue eyes held a hard challenge that did not match the easy geniality of his words. Chris knew that he was being appraised even now, before he could speak.

"If you're ready to listen——"

70

Borland said, "Don't waste time telling me who you are. I had Lakeview on the phone this afternoon and talked to Powers. You couldn't improve on his report."

Chris relaxed a little. Trust Powsie to go to bat where a former pupil was concerned.

"What'll you have, then? Facts and figures?"

"Harper's told me how much it'll cost. I'm willing to gamble that much for results. The facts are simple: you've a working hospital, the beginning of a staff, and a few new wrinkles. Maybe I can use all of that—including the wrinkles. Maybe not. It depends on how I react to you."

Borland's voice had the same easy purr, but the gleam in his eye was sharp as ever. "That's why I called this meeting."

"You mean why you invited Dwight too?"

"Exactly. When I take on a new man I like to study all the angles. See how he handles himself with the opposition— if there *is* opposition to a new man, and there generally is. Watch his footwork and how he throws his punches——"

Chris held up a detaining palm. "Save it, Mr. Borland. I'm ready."

"Then wet your whistle. When you start talking you'll have to talk fast."

Chris turned as the catfoot butler came up with a tray. He accepted a bourbon and soda with a small inward sigh. He'd hoped for a tranquil discussion of his scheme, but there was no point in asking for that now. If he judged Borland correctly, the shipbuilder would see that he got fair treatment in the rough-and-tumble ahead. But there'd be no favors. He had something to sell, and it was up to him to sell it. On the barrelhead, and despite Dwight's heckling.

Borland took his own drink and downed it in three long swallows. "All right, Percy. Let the other team in."

No one spoke while the butler crossed the room. Borland chuckled and threw his dead cigar at the fireplace. Seen without the smoke screen, he was a bulldog in granite. A wary bulldog about to referee a dogfight of his own.

"Believe it or not, his name *is* Percy," he remarked in a heavy whisper. "Bought him from a fellow in London ten years ago, and I still can't get used to him."

But Chris was watching the butler as he opened the double doors at the end of the room and stood aside with perfect punctilio. Four men marched in from the study beyond, for all the world like jurors in a melodrama. Gilbert Dwight, with his best smile turned toward his employer; Jean Moreau, disdainful as ever in his dapper tweeds, flicking Chris with a quick, insolent stare; a roly-poly with a Junker haircut and hard, near-sighted eyes behind thick horn-rims; a man in work clothes, with the slouch of a bear and fists to match Borland's.

The shipbuilder named them easily, with his eyes on Chris. "The bull-of-the-woods is Scanlon, my yard foreman. The fat one is Kornmann, as you may have gathered. Dwight tells me that you introduced yourself this afternoon. . . . The handsome one with the manners is Moreau. Don't waste time shaking hands. You'll be calling each other names soon enough."

Moreau came forward regardless and struck palms with Chris. The Frenchman had surgeon's steel in his fingers and a hot brown stare. Once again Chris admitted that Roz Borland could hardly be blamed for yielding to that brand of charm.

Moreau said, "Don't mind our host, Major. He has been called a tycoon too often; it goes to his head."

"Sit down, Jean," said Borland. "You know you're here to listen, not talk."

"As you will, *mon capitaine.*"

The Frenchman gave Borland a quick heel click; for all his offhand manner, there was obedience in the gesture. Dwight had already taken a comfortable armchair and made a prayer book of his hands. Kornmann took up most of a love seat with a heavy sigh and kneaded his pudgy fingers. . . . Thank God he's one refugee that looks the part, thought Chris. Those paws are probably itching for my throat right now, even if he won't lower himself by looking at me.

Scanlon ignored Borland's nod and leaned against a bookcase with folded arms. The foreman's stare was forthright: at the moment he seemed to be sizing Chris up, with all the frankness of a yard boss who believes that all men are shirkers.

Every head turned as Paul Travers walked in from the hall. The Public Health man looked just as rushed as ever as he shook hands with Borland; the quick grin he threw over the shipbuilder's shoulder was for Chris alone. Watching Dwight's face go sour, Chris permitted himself to relax a little more. This meeting was beginning to take focus, now that Travers was invited too. . . . If Borland is interested in Travers' work, he thought, Borland's my man. He was still

72

certain that the U.S.P.H.S. would never send one of its crack epidemiologists for a vacation on the Gulf of Mexico.

"You'll notice that Travers isn't shaking hands either," said Borland. "He and Dwight have called each other names before. Notice also, Major, that you're about to be tossed to the wolves. Shall I open the meeting, Travers, or d'you want the honor?"

The Public Health man cleared his throat and looked hard at Dwight. "Our purpose, as I understand it, is to do something about health conditions at the yards."

Borland chuckled. "Seward Harper wouldn't put it just that way. *He* came here to sell me a medical crew for my West Island unit. Maybe there's a connection at that; we'll let Major Land sell us that angle in just a moment. Right now I'm telling you why I called you doctors together. Scanlon informs me—or should I say he admits?—that our loss of time rate from sickness is mounting. I'm the biggest boss in Milton, so that burns my pocketbook. I'm willing to pay within reason to have it stopped. You doctors should be interested in helping me to keep up my production."

Travers said quietly, "The United States Public Health Service is interested in the welfare of the people."

Borland reached for another cigar with a gesture of irritation. "It's the same thing, and you know it. If they'e sick they can't work, and everything stops. Where would this country be without peak production? Where would the war be?" He shot a quick glance at Chris. "Are you with me in that, Major?"

When Chris spoke he found that he had taken Travers' tone. "The best health measure is early and thorough treatment of disease."

Kornmann snorted audibly, and Borland looked up with a frown. "Speak up, Doctor. This is no time for sulks."

The Austrian's accent was ponderous and butter-thick. "But it iss so childish, *nein?* To say vot one already knows."

Chris said crisply, "Unfortunately, Doctor, we don't always practice what we know." He had not missed the gleam of hatred in the man's eyes; in a way he welcomed it. Open, glaring hatred of that kind could be met, and countered. Dwight's bland silence was an enemy of another stripe.

Borland went back to Travers. "What's the health situation in Milton now?"

73

"Bad," said the epidemiologist. "In your trailer town it's worse."

"Be specific, man. Just what's the danger?"

"We've managed to stave off a real epidemic so far——"

"Just who is 'we'?"

Travers let his eye roam round the circle of doctors. "I refer to Dr. Karen Agard and myself—and to the full cooperation of Dr. Geoffrey Land, the major's uncle."

"Does that imply that Dwight and his assistants have refused to cooperate?"

"I'm not implying, Mr. Borland—I'm stating a fact."

No one stirred in the room. Borland bit into his cigar with his face unchanged. "Go on, Travers. This is your inning, I guess."

"Through Dr. Agard's child clinic we've pretty well immunized the workers' families against typhoid, smallpox—and, except in a few backward cases, diphtheria." Travers shot a quick look at Dwight, who ignored the thrust with perfect composure. "Living conditions continue to be appalling, however. Crowding—the disposal of garbage and waste——"

"Are you telling me that that's my concern as an employer?"

"You could have done something about the crowding when you laid out your yards."

Borland said without bitterness, "I tried to arrange for prefabricated housing through the Milton Chamber of Commerce. The local building and loan boys turned thumbs down; seems they wanted to cash in on that racket themselves. So I filled in around my work gates and let trailer town grow as it would."

Travers flushed. "I guess that was before my time. At least you can give financial aid to a clinic for those who can't pay for their treatment."

"I'm in business, not politics. What d'you think of that idea, Scanlon?"

The foreman's voice boomed across the room: the foghorn accent of a man accustomed to talk above the chatter of pneumatic drills. "Meat balls will always live like pigs, boss; and it's meat balls who built trailer town. They'll always get drunk—and sick—when it suits 'em." He cast a half-contemptuous, half-amused glance at Travers. "You should boss a few Monday shifts, Doc—you'd learn things."

Travers ignored the sneer. "At least that garbage dump could be destroyed."

"I've looked into that," said Scanlon. "We've got fifty thousand dollars' worth of coal piled within range of that dump. It'd be too risky."

"What's more important, coal or lives?"

Scanlon spat calmly into the tall colonial fireplace. "Ask the cashier, Doc. I wouldn't know. Why don't you stop the workers from dumping garbage there? Make the city extend its pickup."

"That's impossible in wartime. The pickup in Milton is inadequate enough."

"Are you asking the boss to use *his* trucks at the dump?"

"I think it would pay dividends in the end."

Kornmann said heavily, "The garbage—it does nothing but smell."

"What about the rats that live around the dump?"

"Rats? Always there iss rats."

"You've got me there, Doctor," said Travers, and walked to the window frame. He's working hard to keep down his temper, thought Chris, and half rose from his chair. Borland flicked him with a glance, and he sat down again. Travers has been banging his head against this wall for a long time now, he thought. A Public Health man should be used to this kind of beating.

Gilbert Dwight spoke for the first time: a cool tone that poured like spring water over Kornmann's porcine mutter.

"Surely it's time you stopped waving that typhus flag at us, Travers."

Travers spoke without turning. "It happens to be my job. Sorry if it—annoys you."

"But we proved at the last meeting of the Medical Society that there's no danger of murine typhus spreading into Milton."

Borland put up his hand. "I don't follow this battle, Doctors. Just what is murine typhus?"

Travers spoke ahead of Dwight. "Murine typhus is the endemic form of the disease. That is, it is always present in many communities—particularly Southern seaports. In wartime it shows a tendency to increase."

Chris squirmed in his chair as he listened. Travers was on the line with his facts. Why was it that facts, in themselves, carried so little conviction? The Public Health man was a bang-up specialist in his line—and yet, perhaps because of his government badge, perhaps because of a doctrinaire manner, he was not holding his audience. Not even Borland, whose nod must decide their fortunes.

Borland said heavily, "They had that trouble in Europe in the last war. I remember the disease well now."

"Actually it is caused by a different organism. And the symptoms are less severe. Besides, it is transmitted by the fleas from infected rats."

"Like the bubonic plague?"

"Almost precisely. Ordinary typhus is transmitted by lice, direct."

"You see?" murmured Dwight. "A real epidemic of typhus is impossible."

"Work in Dr. Agard's clinic awhile, and you'll eat those words," said Travers hotly.

"Really, Doctor——"

"Shall I show you what we spend for insecticides in a month?" Travers turned on Borland. "And you say you won't help us to——"

"I haven't said that yet," Borland snapped. "Just complete your picture."

"It's simple enough. Given enough people with murine typhus—which means a large enough reservoir of infected rats—put them into unsanitary environments where lice might accumulate, and the pattern changes. Endemic changes to epidemic. In this case, real epidemic typhus. You saw what that did in the trenches in World War I."

"No one has proved that the pattern changes," said Dwight patiently. "Yours is an epidemiological theory, nothing more."

Travers turned to Chris. "What's the Army's opinion on that point, Major?"

Chris fixed Dwight with his eye. "It's more than an opinion now, I'm afraid. There have been too many cases of typhus changing its vector, becoming louse-borne." Again he spoke straight at Dwight. "Surely you remember the report on Mexican laborers imported from louse-ridden areas to work in the States?"

Dwight said, "I remember the case perfectly, Dr. Land. And I remain unconvinced."

"How many cases have been reported at the County Hospital?" asked Borland.

"I know of just two." Dwight's voice was silky now and a

76

trifle bored. "About the normal number for a community in this latitude."

Travers cut in sharply. "What about the cases your own staff has treated as fever of undetermined origin?"

"I know of only a few such cases, Doctor. We regard none of them as contagious." Dwight turned to Borland. "Dr. Kornmann will be happy to send you a detailed report if——"

Borland's granite stare was intact as he shook his head. "You'll need better proof of those fears, Travers; for the present we'll carry on as we were."

The Public Health man shrugged gloomily. "May I say I expected just that from you?"

"You may indeed—if you'll take a back seat for a moment. It's Major Land's turn to sell his product now."

Once more Chris looked around the circle. The enemy doctors' faces were contained masks: only Moreau flicked an elegant eyebrow as their eyes met. The Frenchman had not spoken since the argument began, but he had made his presence felt. For no definite reason, Chris guessed that he was playing Dwight's game for reasons of his own. Certainly he could never count on Moreau as an ally, but . . . He put the thought aside and turned to Seward Harper.

"Just how much does Mr. Borland already know of my plan?"

"Only that you're prepared to handle West Island on a prepayment basis," said the banker crisply. He smiled as he turned to Dwight. "Of course he knows how much his end will cost if he approves."

Chris said generally, "I'm turning my uncle's hospital into a group clinic for that purpose."

"What about compensation cases?" Scanlon interjected.

"Dr. Land's clinic would take those also."

"West Island cases, you mean?"

"West Island will do for a starter," said Chris. "After we've proved ourselves, we'll take all comers."

A heavy silence filled the room. Now that the challenge was in the open, even Dwight seemed unwilling to speak. Chris watched him lay a restraining hand on his henchman's arm as Kornmann gave another deep-throated rumble.

Chris said quickly, "Compensation work is always essential to a clinic of this kind. Especially at the beginning, when care of the workers' families doesn't quite pay its own way."

Scanlon cleared his throat. "I get you, Doc. No matter how you slice it, Mr. Borland pays for your charity project."

"On the contrary. His contribution is a direct payment to guarantee the health of his workers—with the worker matching dollar for dollar as the project builds. We all know the futility of charity in the industrial setup. It's the ideal ground-breaker for state medicine."

Borland said, "Is your group formed now?"

"It will be, within the next two weeks." Chris hoped that his voice carried conviction. Mentally he reminded himself to telegraph Jim Reynolds tonight, to see if he was willing to try a year of free-lancing. Jim had come over in his convoy; he should be out of Walter Reed by now. Young Terry Stone would be looking for a practice too, the moment he was released from his Balkan frame. Then there was Captain Sam Bernstein, who had already written to Chris to inquire about openings in the South. Six doctors for a start, counting Uncle Jeff, Karen, and himself. . . . He heard his voice go on:

"I'll begin with a staff of five specialists and standard equipment. I'm sure we can handle your West Island personnel adequately."

Borland said, "I'll take your word on that. What about the money angle? You and Harper know what I'm risking. What'll the workers pay?"

Chris said quite steadily, "Collections would be made direct, on a one-per-cent basis. If you like, we might call this the One-Per-Cent Plan, where personnel is concerned. That's what would come out of your West Island pay roll every month, with a two-dollar minimum on each check. Management would make up the difference in the few cases where an employee's salary was inadequate. With wartime minimums, that's no headache."

"And just who is selling a one-per-cent deduction to the union?"

"You are," said Chris tranquilly. "I hardly think I'd be here tonight if you weren't confident of union support."

Borland rumbled with laughter, though his face was still expressionless. "I guess that's your round, Land. Pudge Carrol is the CIO delegate, in case you didn't know. He's on his way here now to call me a few names. To be honest, he's been trying to sell me this insurance plan for a year. Tonight I'll be selling *him*."

78

"Does that mean I'm in?"

"Not unless you keep talking fast. What about your own union—the A.M.A.?"

Dwight cut in with a perfect show of manners. "What Dr. Land proposes is contract practice. It is forbidden by the American Medical Association."

"Does that mean you'll protest if he tries it here?"

The compensation doctor shrugged. "I have no personal objection to the experiment. All forward-looking doctors will risk a great deal to forestall the coming of state medicine. Unfortunately, it's been proved that schemes of this kind are impractical."

Seward Harper leaned forward. "I question that, Doctor. What about the Ross-Loos group in Los Angeles? What about the Kaiser Plan?"

"They haven't established their worth as yet."

For the first time Chris let his temper rip through the polite exchange. "For God's sake, man, what do you need to convince you?"

Dwight smiled at him, unruffled. "Ten years would do, I think."

"In ten years the future of medicine will be decided. If obstructionists are still in the saddle, it will all be operated by the government."

"Come, Dr. Land. Is that label meant for me?"

But Borland had already slapped the desk top. "Skip the dogfight, Doctors. Right now I'm building ships, and I want my men on the job. Can you promise me that much at West Island, Land?"

"Definitely," said Chris.

"Very well. Let's say I take your word on that too. How do I collect this one per cent from my personnel?"

"The procedure would be similar to the Kaiser Plan. Your office would collect the insurance from every worker every month and turn it over to the business manager of my clinic. In addition, patients would be urged to come in with their compensation injuries. For that, of course, we'd set up a dispensary at the yard, to provide immediate medical care. Cases needing hospitalization would be transferred to town at once."

"What about dependents?"

"The hospital would handle them on the same basis. One per cent for a wife. One half per cent for children."

"How about the additional bookkeeping?"

"I've considered that too," said Seward Harper. "One additional full-time bookkeeper should be able to handle the Health Fund——"

"So already it has a name?" This was Kornmann, porcine as ever, and damp of forehead under his long silence.

Chris said quietly, "Can you suggest a better one, Doctor?" His own fists were curling as they exchanged glares. This time the Austrian dropped his eyes without replying. Dwight took up the needling.

"Assuming you can make both ends meet, Dr. Land— which I doubt—what's the exact clinical picture? How can you guarantee health on the assembly-line method?"

"It depends on teamwork, of course," said Chris. "I've promised Mr. Borland that. Teamwork of the sort that takes pride in keeping the patient well—not the reverse."

Kornmann was already on his feet, with an animal bellow. "Do you insinuate——"

"I'm stating a fact, Doctor. My cases will be treated from every possible angle—and returned to duty in the shortest time. Can you say the same for straight compensation practice?"

Dwight flicked a white hand for silence. "Just what do you mean by that, Doctor?"

Chris felt his heart pump in his throat, but he went on steadily. "I'll say it to your face, Dwight, gladly. We both know that the worst element of the medical profession always drifts toward compensation practice——"

"Meaning my colleagues and me?"

"Meaning, Doctor, that your type of practice must follow an inevitable pattern: chiseling, kickbacks, prolonged treatment, padded fees. The group clinic I'm sponsoring could never assume that pattern, even if the temptation existed. We are paid for our results in advance; only we can suffer if we don't deliver. Not the employer's work schedule or his premium payments."

But Dwight kept his temper, with no show of effort. "My books are open to Mr. Borland's accountants at any time," he said. "Mr. Scanlon will vouch for them, I'm sure. You've said a great deal about ethics tonight, Doctor. Do you mind if I point out a few practical flaws in your plan?"

"Do, please. I hope I've anticipated them."

"To begin with, how can you be sure of your staff?"

Chris crossed his fingers and prayed. "Isn't that my affair?"

80

"Certainly, Doctor. I referred to the small number, not to individual competence. I also refer to the fact that you are bound to be challenged by the State Medical Society. Practically all doctors who have ventured into contract practice have lost their licenses."

Travers cut in grimly. "Most of those licenses were given back by the Supreme Court, Dwight."

"If you please, Captain——"

"Go ahead. But keep your facts straight. Dr. Land has been overseas. I'm up-to-date."

For the first time, Chris noted, Dwight was almost angry. Pale color stained his cheeks as his eyes narrowed behind those impressive horn-rims. For a moment he paused, removing the glasses and polishing the shining lenses, as though he could polish away his spleen in the same gesture.

"My next point is really serious. Clinics of this type can never stand an epidemic. Especially the kind that Dr. Travers produces from his sleeve on every possible occasion."

"And which you blandly assure us will never come."

"Perhaps not typhus. I refer to influenza, polio, dysentery——"

For once Travers was silent; Chris tried to keep his own face impassive as he turned to judge the effect of this thrust on Borland. Dwight had not hesitated to fight the Public Health man with his own weapons; the strategy was sound. Every medical man in the room knew the answer in advance. With poor sanitary provisions, an epidemic of dysentery could work its own blitzkrieg in trailer town. No privately financed clinic could hope to control that menace.

Unexpectedly, it was Borland himself who came to Chris's aid. The shipbuilder's tone was almost cordial now; with his first words, Chris cut the reins on his hope.

Borland said steadily, "Epidemics are another story, Dwight. That'd make you wrong, Travers right, and me responsible. Naturally I'd throw my weight on Land's side if he had that to cope with."

Chris settled in his chair with a long sigh. Facing the drawbacks that Dwight had itemized, he could welcome the coming battle now. Organized medicine in Milton would be against him—that went without saying; doctors, en bloc, could always be counted on to support the status quo, to resist blindly anything labeled with the stigma of social medicine. He could beat down that sort of perverted thinking if

81

Borland could be counted on in the pinches—and Borland had just given his word.

Dwight was talking on regardless, a wily campaigner who fought a skillful rear-guard action even as he left the field:

"What about the choice of physician? The A.M.A. has always insisted that——"

"May I remind you that we have a hospital already in operation? As need arises, I'll add to my staff of residents. Every doctor in the group may have his private practice on the side."

"Would it be bad manners to inquire about finances? You'll need a sizable backlog to indulge in any real expansion."

Chris ignored Dwight and addressed Borland directly. "My father left me in excellent financial condition. I needn't add that I'm putting all I have into this project." From the corner of his eye he watched slow smiles spread over the faces of Dwight and Kornmann. Only Moreau sat on, smoking placidly with his handsome Gallic stare unchanged. I guess that completes our plan of battle, Chris told himself. Nothing would please them more than to put me in my place and leave me penniless in the process.

Aloud he said, "I think I'm a good risk, Mr. Borland. Am I in?"

"Of course you're in," said Borland. "I told Harper that an hour ago, but he doesn't know English."

The banker let out his breath in a long, low chuckle—the restrained laugh that had closed a thousand deals at the Seaboard. "You said he'd have to jump through the hoops first."

"Maybe he should jump through one more. This is the money question, Land. Why are you betting on yourself like this when you know you'll never get rich in this sort of practice?" The shipbuilder was on his feet now, sweeping the faces before him. "Speak up, man. A little simon-pure idealism might put these crapehangers where they belong. God knows *I* had my share once—until I hired my first bookkeeper."

Chris found himself hesitating for the first time that evening. "Maybe it's just that I want medicine to keep moving," he said, feeling for the words. "I certainly can't stand by and watch it rot in the strait jacket of another Washington bureau. God knows I'm not a pioneer: the plan I'm following isn't novel. It just needs proving. If teamwork in our profession comes to mean more than logrolling—if we, among

82

ourselves, can plan group treatment, encourage the mass of the people to pay as they go, and buy themselves better medical care than they've ever had——"

Chris abandoned the sentence, knowing that it was one of those pious hopes he could never enclose in a phrase. "The cost of illness is a very real thing, Mr. Borland. Let's say we're a young and healthy country. So young that we've never bothered to insure ourselves adequately against a hundred rainy days." The glum silence and Borland's attention were his reward. He plunged on regardless: "Some of the answers have been beaten out on the political anvil in the past decade. Others have been drowned in alphabet soup. The next generation will decide on the choice medicine should have made. I'm voting for the middle road."

Once again Chris looked around the circle of faces. He found no echo there, save in Borland's eye. In that flash he realized that this was no conference of a feudal lord and his vassals. Borland might sit on Slave Hill, surrounded by the jalopies of trailer town. For all that, Borland was just. He had to be just, to keep his empire in gear. He had to move fast, to keep in line with a chaotic present. On occasion it was even necessary for him to make snap judgments: for example, in the minor matter of health—minor, indeed, where an employer like Borland was concerned. . . . For the first time he grasped the relation of Borland to Dwight, the clever charlatan who had been lucky enough to deliver the goods so far.

Chris said, "I think doctors can work for the common good and keep their outside patients. I think my clinic is the answer to government control; I think it'll prove, so far as Milton is concerned, that doctors can rise above the profit motive long enough in each working day to keep the Borland shipyards well. Of course I may be wrong. In that case I'll go back to teaching—which is probably where I'll belong."

Once again he let his voice trail: speechmaking was not his forte, and he realized that he had been talking a great deal this evening.

Borland said only, "Some ideals pay off in the long pull, Land. Maybe you'll be lucky; at least you'll get a fair trial from me." He glanced at Dwight. "Any more sneers, gentlemen?"

Chris recognized the note of dismissal. He rose in the heavy silence and shook hands with the shipbuilder. No one stirred as he turned toward the door; only Travers raised two crossed fingers in a gesture of benediction. He could not quite resist pausing on the threshold for a parting shot.

"Don't think I'm in business for my health, Mr. Borland, any more than you. When I've proved how much more efficient our method is than Dr. Dwight's, I expect to take over all medical practice at the yards."

It had been a schoolboy exit: Chris faced the fact with no regrets as he walked out to the portico. Robert, he saw, had vanished. A grimy anachronism had replaced him—a chunky man in overalls and steel helmet, seated comfortably with his back against an immaculate white pillar, smoking a corncob. The anachronism waved a friendly greeting as he approached.

"Evening, Major. It *is* Major Land, I know. A fellow in my position knows everything before it happens. How does it feel to win a battle on the home front?"

Chris blinked as he shook the workman's hard hand—and recovered as he accepted a light for his cigarette. "Are you Mr. Carrol?"

"Pudge to you, Major. Or should I just say 'Doc,' now you're getting out of uniform?" The union leader's voice was raucous as well as friendly, the kind of voice that seemed always on the point of breaking into a laugh. "You see, I *do* know all about you. Had a complete report on you—and your clinic scheme—from Harper this noon. . . . Must I add that I'm on your side, or was Borland cute enough to tell you that himself?"

Chris laughed. "He even admitted that you'd been trying to sell him my idea for some time."

"Some time is right, Doc. Don't think I won't enjoy rubbing that in tonight. And don't think I'm waiting out here like a poor relation, either. Cal will see me the minute I bang that knocker. . . . Just gives me a kick, smoking a pipe in all this phony splendor." Carrol knocked out his ashes against the pillar and stood up for a luxurious stretch. "Besides, it gives that house dick of Cal's the screaming meemies to have me sitting here. Still thinks I carry bombs—God knows why."

He put an arm through Chris's and led him down the colonnade, dropping his voice to a whisper. "Are the chiselers still trying to include you out?"

"They tried hard," Chris admitted. "It seems the boss had

his mind made up in advance." His own words chilled him a little. They reminded him how easy this triumph had been. By blind luck he had walked into Borland's world at the precise moment when Borland needed him. His job was to widen that need: so far he had hardly begun.

The union leader brought him back. "I know the Kaiser system backwards, Doc. Course they run that on a big-time scale. Still think you can swing West Island at four bits and up from my side?"

"Plus compensation—just."

"I thought you were shaving it thin."

"We've got to shave it thin for a while, to prove that low-cost insurance really works. Providing the clinic is efficient and honest."

"You'll include physical checkups?"

"That's a cardinal point in the scheme, Pudge. Low-cost insurance has to nip illness in the bud, if it's going to earn its keep. And that isn't all. We'll include every family that's willing to take group insurance. Even when he's well, sickness in the family can keep a man from work. If he knows that his kids are getting adequate care——" He shot a quick glance at the union leader. "Naturally family care is optional in the scheme. The more groups we get, the better chance we'll have to——"

"They'll come in or else," said Carrol. "That's another way I earn my keep, Doc. Got any other arguments?"

"Of course we'll provide health education and do what we can to cut down accidents."

"Don't let Dwight catch you out after dark."

"D'you mean that Dwight would dare to——"

"Don't pin me down," said Pudge. "I have hunches sometimes. . . . Take this health education, now. Is it in line with what Dr. Agard's doing for the kids in jalopy city?"

"We'll work through that free clinic directly."

The grip on Chris's arm tightened. Pudge said, "I've a little emergency fund in the war chest, Doc. It's yours, if you and Karen Agard can use it. I know what she's done down there on her own."

Again it was Chris's turn to blink. This was hardly the picture of a union boss that had come out to the foxholes.

"You could help us over a hump right now."

"Name it, Doc."

"Dr. Travers feels that there's definite danger of a typhus

epidemic from the rats. He asked permission from Borland to burn out the dump——"

"And Scanlon knifed him?"

"Exactly. Both Travers and I would like nothing better than the chance to vaccinate a group of the workers against typhus—if only to bring home the danger."

"Why not vaccinate everybody?"

"I don't think we're strong enough to buck Dwight at the main yard. Besides, murine typhus isn't usually considered dangerous enough to justify a widespread inoculation. But we both think that cases of typhus are being reported as other diseases. If we could safeguard West Island crews, for example—and an epidemic came——"

"I get you. Dwight would be out on a limb at the main yard. It could even cost him his contract with Borland."

"You understand I have no proof."

"You don't need proof to sell me vaccine. How much would a hundred-per-cent vaccination at West Island cost?"

"About a thousand dollars."

"I'll send you a check tomorrow."

"But we haven't actually signed the contract."

Pudge laughed aloud. "I'm seeing Borland, ain't I?"

He walked into the house on that, just as Seward Harper came out—his tin hat at a cocky angle, his dungarees slapping as he marched down the shining parquet of the great hallway. Chris let out his breath in a low whistle and grinned as Harper came down the colonnade to meet him.

"Making friends with all sides, Chris?"

"Does he always take your breath away?"

"Pudge is an all-out guy, even when he likes you. Want to take a turn of the gardens before you go?"

The two men walked down a graveled path that led to an alley of giant magnolias. Chris saw without surprise that Borland's architects had restored the old slave quarters, there in a hollow behind the kitchen wing. He remembered the small, windowless cabins when they had been rotten with age and memories. Tonight, as always, the Gulf breeze sang long-ago in the leaves overhead. But the old coquina walls were whitewashed now: the freshly thatched roofs gleamed in the starlight like neat hats in a row. Chris paused to glance over the first threshold. He had killed a blacksnake on that same doorstep years ago, its body big with a swallowed field mouse. Somehow that memory was much more real than the quaintly furnished interior, complete beyond any abolitionist's dream.

Seward Harper said, "I liked it better when you could flush rabbits here. We can still do business with the new tenant."

"Thanks for the vote of confidence, Seward. You don't think I'm biting off more than I can chew?"

The banker shook his head. "It's a big cud, boy, but I'm counting on you to handle it. Naturally, as your financial adviser, I should warn you to hold out a nest egg. Only I don't think you'd listen."

"Not after I've talked to Carrol. He's cheered me. Don't ask me why."

"Pudge is a slice of earth; he cheers up everyone but his enemies. Even Borland enjoys fighting him. It was one hell of a fight at first, I can tell you; Pudge stood up to the old man like a stone wall, and I think he respected him for it. Anyhow, the WLB okayed the raise."

Chris laughed. "He promised to bring in as many whole families as he could. We've got to move in the next few weeks, Seward, or——"

"Carrol will give you all the head start he can. He wants a healthy force as badly as Borland—if only for overtime." Harper shook his head. "No, that isn't fair to Pudge. He sees it in terms of war bonds too; he believes that busy men keep out of mischief—that some of them will even open bank accounts. I tell you, he's brought in a lot of small accounts to us. Ordinarily we wouldn't expect transients of that kind to use a bank at all."

"He sounds as though he could charm them into buying health insurance too."

"Isn't that the next step in the pattern? Pudge has his eye on tomorrow. He knows that the unions are going to have to toe the line when the war's over. If he can keep a jump ahead on plans like this——"

They walked back to the apron of grass before the house. Chris kicked at the mudguard of his coupé. It looked no less shabby in this magnificence. For all that, an obscure impulse urged him to linger, much as he hated the sleek new lines that Borland's architect had imposed on the past.

"If there's nothing else, Seward——"

"Nothing but the papers," said the banker. "You can stop in my office and sign them tomorrow." He looked back at the great white blur of the house and flexed his arms like a boxer preparing for the ring. "This is one contract I'm going to enjoy drawing. It's always fun to haggle with a big shot and watch 'em pinch the pennies."

"Maybe that's why they're big shots," said Chris, and got into the car.

"Maybe," said Seward Harper as they shook hands. "God knows the Kings never pinched, did they, boy?"

Chris drove slowly across the Flats to trailer town. Nerves, and an instinctive hatred of Gilbert Dwight, had kept his chin up at Borland's; now that the skirmish was over, he could admit that he was a little afraid.

Seward had said, *You can handle it, boy.* But could he, really? It wasn't the medical aspect of group practice that worried him: after all, he had worked as a member of a team —in uniform—for nearly three years. Karen and Uncle Jeff were definite: if his three Army friends came in, he knew that he could see through any emergency. All of them would work a twenty-four-hour shift to make the One-Per-Cent Plan a success.

No, the trouble would come from outside his clinic walls. It went deeper than the menace of Dwight, down to the ancient roots of greed, down to the hatred of change. The whole weight of the profession might well be turned against him in this venture. Did he have the right to expose old friends to that chance?

Jim Reynolds was a dour crusader; he guessed that Jim could take it. Terry was an unknown quantity so far as the plan itself was concerned, but Terry was young and resilient and able to bounce up for more. What of Sam Bernstein? Sam had just been discharged from the Army for an ulcer, after more than two years at cantonments—a busy obstetrician, whose job was to make sure that soldiers' wives had their babies in hospitals, if hospitals were available. Sam had given up a profitable practice to younger doctors with deferments. It would be a long road back at best—a heartbreaking road. Was it fair to ask Sam to risk the loss of his license, risk association with a possible failure, risk being tarred with the brush of "socialized medicine"?

Or Karen Agard. The war was exploding into its climax; it might well end before they could bring their clinic over the hump. Returning doctors were bound to resent her presence in America; she, too, had everything to lose and little to gain. How could he embarrass straightforward, honest

Karen—already a lifetime friend of twenty-four hours' standing? Or was she more than a friend, after what they'd risked together in that squalid farmhouse? Watching his headlights slash the dark road ahead, he let his pulses race with the memory of her—her low, throaty laugh out there in the starlit bay, the satin sheen of her arms and throat as she swam forward to take his hand.

He cut his motor abruptly and jammed down on the brake as a figure loomed up in the double-track macadam ahead. Cursed when the figure plodded on into his headlights, forcing him to wrench two wheels into the grass to avoid a collision.

"Can't you walk on the shoulder?"

"Can't you give a lady a lift?"

He saw that it was Rosalie Borland, still in slacks and still glaring. Her hair was whipped up into a bright-colored kerchief, the only concession to her sex. Otherwise he might well have passed her in the dark, taking her for a yard worker who had missed a car pool.

Roz said, "Sorry, Doctor. I saw you coming and knew you wouldn't stop unless I scared you first."

"At least I'm glad we're friends enough for that."

Roz said, "Let's not call any names until we're sure. I'll tell you this much: I'd like to see what makes you tick."

"No luck this afternoon?" he asked, and wondered why his voice was shaking. "I thought we understood each other quite well."

"Come off it, Major," the girl said. Her voice was still colorless; only her eyes betrayed her anger. "You gave me a brush, and you know it. If you ask me, I'm a fool to come back for more."

Chris found that he had won back both his balance and his temper. "Never mind that now. Jump in, and I'll take you home."

"I'll settle for a drink instead. You're a home-town boy. D'you know a good roadhouse?"

He sat under the wheel and stared at her, wondering if he had heard her correctly. Then, as her glare dissolved into laughter, he realized that she was baiting him.

"Surely you went to roadhouses as a boy. Or were you too busy?"

He found that he had opened the door and meshed the gears. "Get in," he said. "The Miramar is just a mile down Bayshore Road. I hope it won't shock you."

Rosalie Borland said, "Good. I love the Miramar."

He backed the car and took the first side road with his throttle wide as he dared. Without turning, he knew that she was relaxed beside him, with her kerchiefed head resting on the worn upholstery. When he stole a glance at her as they whisked under an arc light he saw that her face, in repose, was tranquil as a child's and just as disarming.

7

THE MIRAMAR, Chris observed, was one Milton institution that had taken the boom in its stride. The Miramar had begun its existence as a bootleggers' dump, in an old boat shed where the oyster road met the curve of the Gulf. Later it had acquired a kitchen wing, white paint, and a sagging veranda that overlooked the sea. Still later it had added a dance floor, conveniently private wall booths, and a juke box like a neon sunburst. Tonight, though the juke box beat eight to the bar, the rambling white façade was a relic of another time—a slightly bawdy façade that had outlived prohibition and depression and now offered trailer town the same frowzy welcome.

Chris found the low-ceiled gloom unchanged as he followed Rosalie into a wall booth. Tables and bar were nearly empty. The dozen guests—most of them still in overalls—stared at him rather than at the girl. After all, he thought, she's dressed for a trailer-town roadhouse. Girls in slacks were a dime a dozen on the Flats; uniforms were something else again. Well, he'd be out of O.D. this time tomorrow—and girding for a battle of another sort.

"Bourbon and water, Joe," said Rosalie to the waiter. "The major will take bourbon too. He's a native."

Chris watched the waiter amble away with their order. He remembered the man vaguely—a shrimper who had practiced rumrunning on the side. The barman mixing their drinks had been a henchman of Dutch Charlie's, the bootleg king who had owned every still in the piny woods. Chris wondered if their highballs had come from Charlie today and decided in the affirmative. The collective thirst of trailer town could hardly be solved legitimately in this ration-tight year.

Rosalie said, "D'you mind the quiet?"

"On the contrary."

"The Miramar is always quiet at this time. The swing shift is in and the day shift is still washing up."

"What about the night shift?"

"You *have* been away, Dr. Land. The night shift quits at dawn. That means they're tight by 8 A.M. and fighting till noon. Give the boys time to sleep it off."

He guessed that she spoke from firsthand knowledge and wondered why he wasn't shocked. Evidently she had visited this roadhouse often, dressed as she was tonight. He could see her clearly as the place filled up, dancing with huskies fresh from the yards—perhaps even pretending to be one of them. . . . A rich man's daughter, slumming for the fun of it? He hoped that her interest went deeper than that. He hoped that Roz Borland was trying to rub off her insulation in these off-the-record wanderings.

He put part of the thought into words. "Why did you come here with me? What have I got that you want?"

The girl smiled at him over her glass. Her malaise, it seemed, had vanished with the first sip of Charlie's corn. "Don't crowd me, Doctor. I'll use you in time, I promise you."

"You tried this afternoon, I believe."

"I gather you got to first base with Dad, all by your lonesome."

"A bit farther than that, I think."

She listened quietly while he told her of the meeting on Slave Hill.

"So he's playing you against Dwight. Are you frightened?"

"If I am, I'm trying not to show it. At least I'm getting my contract without strings."

"Don't rub that in, please," said Rosalie.

"Be honest. Can you picture your friend Moreau deserting Dwight—and joining my team?"

"Now that I know you better—no."

Chris lifted his glass in a silent toast. "The beginning of wisdom," he said.

91

Her brows knitted again; he watched the spark smolder in her hazel eyes. "I'm not that young."

"You gave a good imitation this afternoon. Princess Pat intriguing behind the Sun King's throne. It's too bad the Sun King had already made up his mind."

"I asked you once not to rub it in."

Chris leaned across the darkened wall booth to touch her hand. A sullenly hot hand, beaded with moisture from the highball glass. "Consider the subject closed, Roz. Just let me add that I think your heart's in the right place. I even think you were trying to help *me* as well as France." He leaned back slowly to study her over his glass. "For that excellent reason I'll offer Dr. Jean Moreau a job—after he has shown me his credentials."

"Jean's papers were left behind in Paris. I told you how he got out in 'forty."

"Then I'll offer him a job on trial—and bet you ten to one he refuses."

"Why ask him at all, then?"

Chris thought his answer out loud. "Because I can use a good surgeon—and I've a hunch he's good. Another hunch tells me that he's using Dwight. Not vice versa. Of course he's using you too, but you seem to enjoy it. So we won't mention that."

"No," said Rosalie, "we won't mention that." Her voice was steady now and not in the least unhappy. "If you'll let me, I might even say I was a fool this afternoon. Playing Lady Bountiful——"

"And Machiavelli."

"Shall I apologize for both?"

Her eyes were opened wide to him now, inviting him to look as deeply as he liked. But he drew back into his corner, puzzled once again by the thud of his heart.

Aloud he said, "Don't try to be charming in this background, Roz. I'd have used you myself if I'd needed you. Fortunately your father had already decided to use *me*. Can't we cry quits on that?"

Rosalie wasn't listening, he noted with a faint sense of pique. She said easily, "It's quite an experience, being turned down flat. Most people jump fences when I make my offers. I was ready to crown you at the time. Now that I've cooled off, I rather think I like it."

She had only to crook a finger, he noted, to attract the

barman's eye. He shook his head as the waiter ambled over with refills for them both.

"Leave it, Joe," said Rosalie. "I'll get to it in time." She leveled a finger at Chris and sighted down it with light, teasing eyes. "You're easy to talk to, Chris, now I've got you placed."

"Just where do I belong?"

"On the wrong side of thirty. Not too far. You remember what it's like to be young—and remembering makes you lonely." Again the finger wiggled—under his nose this time. "Know what that makes you? A pushover in any language, including the Scandinavian. A do-gooder, because you haven't a girl of your own to keep you up-to-date."

Her eyes dared him, but he looked down at his glass. "Stop me if I'm wrong, Chris. If you and Karen——"

He took up the second highball and drank deep. "Skip Karen, please. Tell me your troubles instead. I'll be a real do-gooder and listen—if you'll stay away from Moreau."

"But Jean is my headache. Right now I've no medicine for it—and it's all your fault. A fine doctor you turned out to be."

"You mean I'm right about him?"

"You and Karen both. I know just what he wants, and I don't care."

"Didn't you say that once today?"

"Check. If the war was over, I'd go to France with him tomorrow and buy him a château. Or, if he really owns one, I'd rebuild what the Nazis left behind." She leaned across the table and slapped Chris's cheek lightly. "Listen, can't you? Doctors always listen. Doctors and bartenders."

So this is why she brought me here, thought Chris. Hearing her with half his mind, he began to work out the enigma of Rosalie Borland. She thinks she is free and strong, he reflected, but she is caged and stubborn. She pretends to herself that she can sway her father, when she knows in her heart that she can never deflect that hard integrity. Knowing she is useless, she has adventures to compensate—like that long tramp through trailer town. An evening, strictly incognito, at the Miramar. Or she accumulates protégés like Moreau.

Rosalie said, "You think I'm unhappy because of Jean. That I'm getting tight so I can let down my hair. Maybe you're right."

But I don't think that, Chris told himself with an inward

smile. I think you're much too healthy, under that needled boredom, to take an obvious escape. Right now I think you're acting to the hilt and rather enjoying yourself. . . .

Aloud he said, "Doesn't it upset you to discuss your latest love affair in public?"

"You aren't my public. You're my doctor."

"I'm your public too. Believe me, I followed all your love affairs with interest. Even from a foxhole in Italy. . . . We got the tabloids there, you know."

Rosalie said, "You might have shown more taste in your reading."

"Perhaps. But, you see, my interest was clinical and quite proper. You've always been a problem to me—even in that foxhole."

In his mind's eye he pictured her with those other men who had made the headlines. Roz sunning in a *maillot* on Eden Roc, with the left-wing son of a noble lord, the summer after Munich. Roz on a toboggan at Sun Valley, with a much-married movie producer. Roz at the New York Horse Show with an Italian cavalry captain. According to Winchell, she had actually been engaged to that one for all of three months. . . .

Moreau, he assured himself, was only the current face in the gallery. It was ridiculous that she should go on playing this collector's game. What had she gained, hugging this elegant flotsam to her heart, pretending that hand-kissing was love? The others had gone on: to a job gained through Borland, if they were worth Borland's notice; to the next rung of the social ladder. Moreau was obviously ready to start that climb now. Or did Roz understand all that clearly—and cling to the same game because she was too weak to make her own rules?

"What do you want?" he demanded.

"Now or tomorrow?" She let her fingers curl and uncurl around the glass. "That's easy, Chris. I want an end of war and double-talk. I want Jean to get back his land in France —and his job. I want to go to Paris and marry him there."

"Sure it isn't just Paris again you want—and not the Frenchman?"

Her eyes met his without wavering. "You think I'm a butterfly as well as a fool, don't you?"

"Answer three questions on the nail, Roz. When did your mother die?"

"When I was three. Dad was tracking down his first million then."

"Who raised you—your father?"

"He was much too busy." Rosalie Borland considered. "I had a governess I was rather fond of. Several of them, in fact. . . . Dad didn't believe in governesses, though. He decided to buy me an education outside the family mansion the day I was fourteen. Don't ask me how many finishing schools I attended; I generally left before I was acclimatized."

"Question number three is just as simple. When did you get your first real allowance?"

"The day I was ready for Vassar. I was eighteen then; the trust fund was in my name. Dad couldn't have stopped it if he wanted to."

"The sort of trust fund that you could never quite spend?"

"Right again, Chris—and you've a hell of a nerve."

"Don't pretend you aren't enjoying it. And don't say you could be anything but a butterfly, with that background."

Rosalie Borland considered him for a long moment. "Won't you believe I enjoy helping people—even when they disappoint me? I know that Jean wants to go home—before the war ends, if he can. Perhaps there isn't one chance in ten that he'll"—she paused, and her eyes dropped—"that he'll ask me to follow him, legally or otherwise. Does that mean I can't make plans for him?"

"Not at all. Especially if you enjoy it. Perhaps it's a fair enough substitute for living. But if that's the best you can do, I wish you wouldn't confide in me."

"I'll confide in you all I like," she said. "You're a doctor, and you're soothing. Especially when you get mad. If it hurts too much, you can send me a bill later."

"It's quite painless, and I'll give you some good advice free. You want Paris again. Well and good. But you must do your part to bring it back, if you want to enjoy it truly. Until you do—well, I'd say that Jean Moreau was a luxury you can't afford. Even you, Roz. And you can afford plenty."

"But I *have* done my part." She half rose in her corner of the booth, with her knuckles white on the table edge. For the first time he noticed how she resembled her father. "Damn you, anyhow! What right have you to——"

He ignored the outburst. "I know. You've sold war bonds, given blood, and worked at the USO—all with photographs. I read the captions while I was convalescing at Walter Reed."

He drew a deep breath to steady his voice and wondered why he should be so angry. "Don't you see you were only coasting—having fun in uniform? Doesn't your conscience trip you now, when you wake up and wonder how you'll survive another day?"

He guessed that she was angry too—angrier, in fact, than she had been in a long while. It hurt him a little that she hadn't shown it more, after that brief barrage of cursing. Rosalie said only, "Thanks for pulling me apart. Am I hopeless, or do you have a remedy?"

"You might try the WAC and find out what boredom really means—to say nothing of the kind of patriotism that can stand up under monotony. If you prefer home life, I imagine the yards could use another rookie."

He knew that he sounded grim and avuncular. He knew that this was no way to charm Roz Borland from her groove. Her generation had been caught between the home front and the grimmest war in history. Deprived of the safety valve of gaiety, it was sure to rebel at blueprints, personal as well as cosmic. For all that, he forced himself to go on:

"I know it isn't too pleasant, being young today. Your youth is spread so thin—over the seven seas, in fact. So much of it is growing old before its time."

Her eyes mocked him. "You should know, Major."

"Leave me out of this. I've got a reason for ticking. Why haven't you? How can I give you a prescription until you've stopped chasing fun for its own sake?" He found that he had banged the table top with his fist, without regretting it. "Or, if you must have fun, why go to Jean Moreau? And why tell your troubles to pickups like me?"

"I wouldn't call any more names," said Roz. "Not out loud. Jean is about to join the party."

Moreau came across the sleazy dance floor with all the ease of a prowling cat. His smile was fixed, intent. Chris found that he had just time to rise before the Frenchman sat down in their booth—with perfect manners, though he had not been asked. Once again he wondered why the man should infuriate him without a tangible reason. Perhaps it was that offhand blend of good manners and contempt. The insouciance of the well-bred foreigner, who lets the American know, wordlessly, that he considers him a red Indian—and dares him to resent it.

96

Moreau spoke, to Rosalie alone. *"Si je suis de trop, chérie——"*

"Speak English, Jean," said Rosalie. "There's a gentleman present. You know I'm always thrilled when you shadow me. Who told you I was here?"

"Usually you are at the Miramar when you are late to dinner."

"Has Dad missed me?"

"That I cannot say. When I left he was on the long-distance."

Chris sat back and let them enter their private world. In a moment he would protest at being so beautifully ignored. For the present the man's manner fascinated him. Though he was speaking of ordinary things, Moreau gave every word an air. Even the picture of Cal Borland on long-distance conveyed a hint of intrigue, or retribution to come, where Rosalie was concerned. . . .

Moreau said, "Why must you pretend to be what you are not? Why must you forget our dinner date?"

But Rosalie only crooked a finger at the waiter. From his corner of the booth Chris saw that the questions had fascinated her too—touched her, even, in a way his sober analysis had missed completely. In that flash she was a bewildered child no longer; she had taken on the spurious sheen of a woman of the world, fencing gaily with the man she loved—and sometimes kept waiting.

Rosalie said, "I've a whole hour to dress for our dinner date. Can't I go slumming, in the meantime, with my psychoanalyst?"

"I like to know where you are," said Moreau. "Besides, I understood that Dr. Land was a surgeon."

"Call him what you like," said Roz. "He's been carving up my ego. You came just in time, Jean. . . . Incidentally, do you two know each other?"

She turned to Chris triumphantly. *You* have taken me apart, the gesture said. *He*, with a few teasing words, has made me whole again. Now do you see why I prefer his company to yours—or any man's?

Chris said, "I met Dr. Moreau this evening, in a business way. It's pleasant to meet him socially."

Moreau, he noted, could bow even when seated. Moreau said, "I may join you, then?"

"Why not, since you're already here?"

"That is one reason I like America," said the Frenchman. "First, the old-fashioned politeness of the South—then the wisecrack. It leaves one bewildered, but it is vital too."

The waiter came up on the run with two highballs on a tray. Chris said, "One of those is yours, Doctor, if you drink bourbon. As Miss Borland's psychoanalyst, I think she's had enough. Especially if she's dining out with you."

Roz Borland had already reached for her drink, but Moreau flipped her hand aside with a quick, delicate pressure of his fingers. "Dr. Land is quite right, *mignonne*. Two is your limit when we dine at East Point with the commanding general."

Chris smiled inwardly at the exchange. East Point was the Army cantonment across the wide mouth of the bay: it featured a sedate club and a permanent Officers' Row. He wondered if the commanding general was a friend of the Borlands—if the general's wife was ailing. Moreau's handsome nostrils had assumed a professional flare as he mentioned the name.

Rosalie said, "Never mind the general tonight, Jean. You know he's bringing you his gallstones on Monday."

"If you please, my dear——"

"Why can't we dine here?"

"Is it so great an effort to make yourself beautiful and your escort proud?"

Rosalie's hands made sudden fists on the table. "I wanted you two to know each other. At least you might fight over me instead of stealing my drinks."

Moreau snapped to his feet and bowed from the waist. "Dance with me just once, Rosalie. That always soothes you. Then I'll take you home."

Roz got to her feet sulkily enough, but she was smiling when she went into Moreau's arms. The floor was beginning to fill now with a motley crew in overalls and windbreakers. Some of the men danced with their helmets still on their heads; nearly all the women were in slacks, though a sprinkling of girls from Water Street had begun to drift into the bar. One of these ladies of the evening came up promptly to the booth when she saw that Chris was alone. He waved her aside impatiently and turned to watch the progress of Moreau and Rosalie on the dance floor.

The Frenchman moved through that stomping crowd with his feline grace unruffled. Oddly enough, his immaculate tweeds did not look out of place against the tawdry background. After all, Chris reflected, he's probably spent a life-time dancing for his dinner, in all the bistros of the world. . . . He corrected the estimate sharply. Jean Moreau was neither a gigolo nor a professional charlatan like Dwight; with no positive proof, he was sure of that. What right had he to assume that the fellow was bad for Rosalie? The girl was obviously enjoying herself now to the hilt; watching the Frenchman whirl her expertly in boogie rhythm, watching her long lashes flutter down as she rested her cheek against his, Chris knew that she was in another world.

He told hims f resolutely that it was a pleasure-hungry world, that Rosalie's energy should be directed elsewhere if she meant to find her niche in the changing American dream. Like all generalities, the reflection brought him little com-fort. At the moment it was more important to stare at the crowd that had swallowed Moreau and Rosalie in its grimy heart. To wish that *he* could dance with that same easy assur-ance to the throb of a roadhouse juke box. . . .

Chris looked up with a start—and saw that Moreau was standing above him, quite alone.

"You were right, Doctor. Two drinks of this raw alcohol is enough for her. My gesture toward the dance floor was only a subterfuge." Moreau took up one of the untasted highballs and drank deeply. "At the moment she is both happy and comatose."

Chris found that he had bounced to his feet, to the immi-nent peril of the drinks. "What have you done to her?"

"Do not be alarmed, my friend. At this moment our Rosalie is in a taxi, bound for Slave Hill. The night air will revive her. In an hour she will be dressed for dinner and waiting for me."

Moreau spread thin brown hands on the table. Chris watched the fingers curl like prehensile snakes in the half-light. "I said *our* Rosalie by design, Doctor: I'm sure we've a common interest. Shall we explore it together?"

The Frenchman raised his glass to Chris, but Chris did not return the gesture. He felt his face freeze under the other man's regard. As always, it was disconcerting to find that a stranger understood you perfectly. Chris hated to ad-mit that he was interested in Roz because she was vitally and disturbingly herself.

Moreau said, "Of course, if you insist on playing the Southern gentleman, we can always drink. I've a curettage at noon tomorrow, but tonight is my own."

"What about your date with Rosalie?"

"So we return to Rosalie, without delay. It will do her no harm to wait. Or even to dine with her father for a change."

"What about the general's gallstones?"

"As Rosalie said, they will keep nicely till Monday. Then, my friend, I shall take them out at a hospital in New Orleans. As expensively as possible, of course." Moreau lifted a tensile finger and spanged an empty glass to attract the waiter. "You see, Doctor, I lay my cards on the table. I am a refugee in America for one reason—to make money, as rapidly as possible. So far I do not find that difficult. I am an excellent surgeon, with an aura of romance about me; I have many friends to bring me contacts. The Borlands, among others——"

Chris felt the rasp in his voice as he broke in. "Do you think it wise—telling me all this?"

"Precisely. You already think ill of me, since I work through Dwight. Permit me to correct your estimate. I am black, yes; but not quite so black as you paint me."

"I assure you I've formed no estimate——"

"Must we pretend, now we are alone? You hate me on sight, because you see that Rosalie is—how shall I put it delicately?—attracted to me."

"Can't we leave Rosalie out of this?"

"Not possibly, since she is the agent who brings us together. I am still wondering why."

Chris said bluntly, "Rosalie thinks you're the one honest man in a nest of shysters. She'd like to lift you out by the neck and present you to me." He permitted himself a rueful grin as the waiter brought fresh drinks. "I promised to offer you a place on my staff—just to give you the privilege of refusing."

Moreau studied him out of half-mournful, half-mocking eyes. "Rosalie, as always, is a romantic. Almost as romantic as you, Doctor. And why not? You Americans are a young nation still. Romance is a luxury you can afford. It is different with continentals. Our poetry is packaged for export only."

"Aren't you straying from the subject?"

"Not at all. I only ask you to believe this: so far I have cost Rosalie Borland nothing. I would not spoil my record by coming to you. Even if you'd take me."

100

"Not until I'd checked on you thoroughly."

"Then we are even from the start. Shall I explore your mind a little deeper? You think I am not honest—and you are wrong. My price is high, but I give the values the rich demand. . . . You think I use my friends—including Rosalie. In this you are completely right. Tell me, Doctor, what else are friends for?"

Chris found that he was listening almost tranquilly now. The fellow isn't a bad Frenchman after all, he told himself. No bad Frenchman would talk this frankly, even when it's off the record. He's just a careful, out-for-himself Frenchman who knows how to exploit a gold mine. And then he thought of the other careful ones, the men who had sent their money to Wall Street years before Munich, the cautious patriots who had jumped on the Vichy band wagon and turned this same bland face to the world. He had rubbed elbows with them often in New York: the too-fat, loud-spoken Frenchman who infests Park Avenue and first nights and the last available seats in parlor cars.

Moreau said, "Shall I sum you up in a phrase? You are an American idealist, of the type that only a war for survival can produce. Today you would make your profession over. Tomorrow, I hope, you will see the light and go back to making money, as all good Americans should."

Chris let him go on, in stolid silence. Not all refugees were cynical, he told himself. Or crapulous, or querulous about rationing, or reluctant to rise in restaurants when the national anthem was played. Thousands of them have eaten their hearts out on starvation wages; thousands more are dying in foreign legions. And then he reminded himself that every war had produced that same patient breed: born to starve and die, while the cynics (with their fortunes intact) bought the political front for the new peace.

"With your record," said Moreau, "you could make twenty thousand as a surgeon, even in this corner of America. I am making three times that now, in spite of your insane income taxes. . . . Give me a few more months, and I shall have what I want of you. I shall go back to France and restore what was mine before the vandals came."

Chris kept his voice level. "You mean with the Fighting French?"

Moreau shrugged a negative. "I was a liaison officer for a while. With your own shock troops in Tunisia—at Sfax and

101

Bizerte. But the French Committee and I do not see eye to eye. There are, as you know, many opinions on the future of France. More opinions, perhaps, than there are Frenchmen."

The man's voice had the harsh ring of truth; once again Chris revised his estimate. Jean Moreau was not essentially bad: he was merely selfish. The sort of enlightened egoist who has stood foursquare against change since governments began. The feudal lord at his own tight crossroad, exacting his toll till doomsday. The rich specialist who would go on robbing the rich and ignoring the poor, come war or peace. . . .

"Do not confuse me with the men of Vichy," said the Frenchman. "I am neither a fascist nor a ghoul; I am only a good doctor who believes in success. It pains me that we cannot be friends—that you will not give up this mad scheme for a clinic and go back to money-making for its own sake." Once again he gave that queer, negative shrug. "I am uncomfortable with Americans who talk of international police and the brave new world. To my ear they are babbling a language they can speak without understanding. . . . Perhaps your millionaire is obsolete. At least he knew what he wanted."

With no sense of personal control, Chris saw his hand bang the table top for silence. He knew then that he was angry, and cold in his anger. "Where would my world be— and your France—if America had nursed its nest egg first and played with patriotism later?"

Moreau shrugged. "Perhaps we deserved to die. Why did you trouble to rescue us?"

"I don't know, damn you. Or rather, I know perfectly. You've been the guardian at the East since the days of Clovis. Whether we thought it out or not, we decided it was worth while giving you another chance. Along with the British, of course." Chris thought briefly of what he had said. Even at the moment he knew that he had simplified history to the point of absurdity. "Are you worth the risk?" he asked. "Can you put yourself in Class A again and pitch in?"

Moreau studied his drink for a while without answering. "I wonder," he said at last. "Just as I wonder about the great, soft heart of America. How long will it go on beating for all the world?"

"I wonder too," said Chris as he signaled to the waiter. He waved aside Moreau's gesture with a billfold and hated himself for enjoying it. "No, Doctor, this is all on me. After all, you joined the party late." He got up carefully, watching for *non sequiturs,* and committing one instantly, for all his care. "Will you continue this discussion in the fresh air, or would fresh air embarrass you?"

They walked together to the parking lot. Chris saw that Moreau had parked his sleek white convertible beside his own battered coupé. The Frenchman lit a cigarette with an appropriate, and no less irritating, pause. "Answer this frankly, please. Do you dislike me because Rosalie Borland enjoys my company? . . . Come, Major. Are you afraid I will steal her too?"

Chris said, "I asked you once to leave her out of this."

"But Rosalie is the symbol of your dislike, Doctor. If we discuss Rosalie, with one mind, we understand each other completely."

Chris said levelly, "If I thought she was unhappy because of you——" Then he made his voice calm, with an effort. "But she isn't, really. You're just something she'll outgrow. . . . Is that frank enough, Doctor, or shall I go on?"

"Go on, please," said Moreau. "You are charming—now you're in the open." He watched Chris owlishly as the other finished his cigarette and flipped it into the Gulf. "Why not come out a little more? Why not admit that this is not American chivalry—that you want her for yourself?"

Chris said, "If you think I want a bundle of nerves——" and cursed his frankness immediately.

"American males are always marrying bundles of nerves. That is one of the things I do not understand about Americans."

"Do you mind if we skip our marriage habits?"

"And Rosalie too? But she *is* a bundle of nerves, Major. Perhaps you regret the phrase; it is none the less exact. She will require expert treatment before she can call herself mature. Do you feel qualified to supply it?"

Chris turned to his car, fighting for control. So help me, he thought, if he goes on purring another moment I'll swing at him. Yet he paused with a foot on the running board, letting Moreau's voice follow him, with all its implications:

"She is unhappy now, Major. Believe me, the fault is not mine. American women are so often unhappy. Is it because they have everything they desire—except men who really amuse them? Are they bored by their security? Or is it simply that they still feel useless, for all their Army Corps and ship welding—and know there is no cure?"

Chris said, "If you don't mind, I'll say good night."

"Not before we settle the Rosalie question, Major. Give me time to get rich again, and I'll amuse her as she deserves to be amused. I'll marry her, too, if her father meets my price."

It happened, Chris found, quite simply. His left arm swept round with him as he turned; his left hand, palm out, struck Moreau's cheek a stinging blow. The Frenchman staggered, then came up with his grin unchanged.

"So we must fight for her this way?"

Chris said evenly, "Never mind why we're fighting. Put up your hands."

It was sophomoric, he knew; it was more than a trifle ridiculous. It was also a pure and glorious release to wade into Jean Moreau with both fists flailing. To send his man spinning with an old-fashioned one-two and watch him reel under the double blow. To stalk him carefully as he staggered back—and then rush him for the knockout. . . .

A sledge hammer from nowhere connected with his left temple, dropping him in his tracks. He groped his way up to a knee and an elbow just in time to see Moreau pivot on one toe with all the grace of a ballet dancer. Too late he remembered that the French box with feet as well as hands.

"*La savate*, Doctor," said Moreau. "Will you have another sample?"

But Chris had already rushed him a second time, breaking the next crafty kick with a hunched shoulder. It was absurdly simple to handle the Frenchman once he was inside his guard. A smash above the heart, to line him up; a haymaker, straight up from the gravel of the parking lot. Moreau would have fallen face forward this time. Chris deflected him neatly, so that he collapsed on his knees, with his chin resting on one of his own white-walled tires.

No one had come out of the roadhouse to witness the brief fracas. The bouncer at the Miramar washed his hands of the parking lot. Fights in the bar, which cut down on customers' drinking time, were his only real concern.

Chris waited with both fists cocked as Moreau came out of the punch and pulled himself up to his running board. Watching the man shake the stars out of his head, he saw with satisfaction that the cynic's grin was gone from his face. For

all that, the Frenchman was smiling again as he looked up—
a smile that held no hint of malice.

Moreau said amiably, "Pardon the oversight. I'd quite forgotten you were a Southern gentleman." Chris took a step
closer, and he held up a detaining palm. "Don't resent me
again, please. I'll cry uncle—or whatever it is one cries in
America."

Chris heard him chuckle quietly in the darkness behind
him as he got into his own battered coupé and kicked at the
starter. He roared out of the parking lot without looking
back. On the road to Milton he threw back his head and
laughed too. He wasn't quite sure, then, if he was laughing
at himself or at Moreau. He knew that he had been sophomoric, even childish. He knew that it would be some time
before he brought the real reason for those fisticuffs into the
open and faced it calmly. But he felt more alive than he had
felt since he stepped off the train. . . .

Still in a pleasant daze, he parked in the curve of the hospital driveway and slipped in at the well-remembered emergency entrance. A sleepy orderly snapped to attention in the
receiving room, but Chris waved him aside with a cheery
greeting. His mind informed him that he had a half interest
in this little world now; he had to touch it again with his
hands to make the thought come true. . . . On the practical
side, he had to wash the grime from face and knuckles before he faced Uncle Jeff—or Karen.

When he was presentable again he walked contentedly
toward the buzz of voices in the scrub room. Uncle Jeff,
draped to the chin in an operating gown, pushed up his mask
to give him his familiar soothing smile.

"Evening, partner. Mind if I call you that so soon?"

"So Seward told you what happened. I wanted to surprise
you."

Uncle Jeff said slowly, "You couldn't do that, son. I knew
you'd bring it off."

Once again there was no need for more between them.
Detecting a slight huskiness in his uncle's voice, Chris shucked
off his coat and held out his arms for an observer's gown.

"Mind if I watch the job?"

"It isn't at all dramatic. Just an ordinary case of posterior
presentation."

"Just what I've been waiting for. Obstetrics is the one thing
I didn't get a lot of in the Army."

They walked into the operating room ahead of the student nurses with that same comfortable camaraderie between them. Chris saw without surprise that Karen Agard was already bent over the anesthetic machine. It was a comfort to see her there—and something else besides. He let his mind explore the reason behind that extra pulse in his throat as he hoisted himself to the observer's stool and smiled down at her.

"Mind if the new partner sits in?"

Even an operating gown could not hide the contours of her figure, and no cap could hope to conceal the pale gold sheen of her hair. The eyes that met his were quiet with happiness. Already we're a team, he thought. I know we'll work together perfectly, even if that extra pulse keeps jumping when I remember the shoulders under that white gown, the way she laughed at me out in the Gulf last night. . . .

Now Karen said only, "This is our last case, Chris. You've got to tell me everything afterward."

Her long, facile fingers tested the dials before her. He felt the pulse die painlessly, felt himself move into the clinical pattern of his job-to-be. Dr. Jeff, who had already draped the patient between them, nodded to Karen as he stepped into the hard bath of light above the table. The anesthetic mask went down. Chris checked the operative setup and saw with satisfaction that Uncle Jeff had omitted nothing, regardless of his financial status at the moment. There had been no stinting of the things which counted: the drapes which prevented the transmission of infection to its most fertile soil—the womb freshly bereft of its small occupant.

Uncle Jeff spoke generally, quite as though he were addressing an amphitheater instead of an audience of two:

"This is a simple occiput posterior. We'll take the little gentleman's head and turn him 'round—so he can come down the way he should."

Chris watched the smooth, unhurried hands as they picked up the instruments and began to insert the blades in the birth canal—a fluid technique that encompassed the baby's head without undue pressure. Now, with the blades locked in place, he began to exert gentle traction. A downward traction and rotation that balanced nicely until he felt the child's body begin its response to his urging, to adjust itself normally to the contours of the birth canal.

Karen, Chris saw, was doing her part to perfection. In

cases of this sort the anesthetist had a nice problem of adjustment. Too little anesthesia failed to relax the muscles, and thus interfered with the normal climax of the operation. Too much might be even more serious, causing a sudden cessation of breathing when the stimulus of the operation was removed.

Uncle Jeff said easily, "There. That should do it. Our young friend completed his somersault this very instant. Give her the oxygen, will you, Karen?"

Karen tripped a valve on the machine and forced oxygen into the breathing bag. By increasing the oxygen flowing into the mother's body, she was pouring the vital gas through a still-pulsating umbilical cord, into the blood stream of the child as well. This, too, was a vital element in this type of delivery. In a few moments the child would be adjusting itself to a completely new environment. Thanks to Karen's skilled fingers, he would have a head start when he began the function of respiration.

Chris watched breathlessly as, the delivery accomplished, Dr. Jeff clamped and cut the cord—watched him squeeze the child in his hands, jackknifing the tiny body to compress the lungs and stimulate breathing. He knew that the others around the table were waiting just as tensely. Here, as always, was the dramatic climax of a delivery. If the baby did not breathe, every other precaution was wasted. There was always the chance that mucus might plug the bronchial passage, or the abnormal development of the thymus gland. Lungs might fail to expand. Occasionally the delicate respiratory center of the brain would refuse to respond to the mounting accumulation of carbon dioxide in the blood stream, for all the signaling of the still-beating heart.

All of them waited now for the tiny wailing cry that is such a welcome sound in the delivery room. Dr. Jeff had already inserted a suction syringe deep into the respiratory passage, to remove any obstructing mucus, but this did not set up the automatic movements of breathing. Chris saw his forehead furrow above the mask as he glanced back at the patient. She needed him too, at this critical moment, needed skilled hands to massage the uterus, to set up the contractions that would snub off any hemorrhage from the spongy network of blood vessels that had supplied the child with food and oxygen.

Chris heard a voice he recognized as his own. "Lay the baby on the table, Uncle. I'll bring it 'round."

Dr. Jeff's brow cleared as he stretched the baby on a side table and turned back to the mother. Chris had already taken up a piece of sterile gauze to cover the baby's mouth. Quite without conscious planning, he began the time-honored method of inducing respiration in the newly born—mouth-to-mouth breathing, filling the child's unexpanded lungs with air from his own body.

Again and again he exhaled gently, with a hand on the child's chest. Already he could feel the ribs lift upward and outward as the tiny chest expanded. Removing his lips, he gently compressed the chest cavity until all the air was exhaled—and waited hopefully before inflating the child's lungs once again with his own. Already he noted a definite lessening of the bluish color of oxygen lack that had developed so rapidly in the baby's lips and ears. Exhaling once again through the gauze, he drew back and saw that the child's lips were almost pink. There was a commotion under his hand as the tiny chest contracted of its own accord, a quavering wail like no other sound in the world to a doctor's ears.

He heard one of the nurses laugh, a little hysterically; another came forward to assist with the infant. Karen's eyes were warm across the table, and he sensed that Uncle Jeff was smiling behind his mask. Abruptly he felt a little foolish and reminded himself that any of the student nurses could have done the job as well. And yet, for the first time, he felt identified with the world he had chosen.

Karen was waiting in the front office when he came back from the women's ward and a final check on the baby wailing in his nursery bassinet.

"Your uncle has jumped across town on a call," she said. "I expect to hear everything just the same. It'll bear retelling tomorrow."

Chris saw that she was still wearing her uniform under a short polo coat. "Don't tell me this is your clinic night?"

"I can give you just an hour. Then you can drive me to the Flats, if you're not too tired. Paul Travers will pick me up there when I'm finished. He's using my car to make his rounds tonight."

Chris laughed. "Don't you take time out for food?"

"That's just what we're doing," said Karen calmly. "Believe it or not, there's a sirloin waiting for you at your favorite dive on Water Street. I arranged for it by phone, on the chance you'd come back and report to us."

She dropped her impersonal manner on that and gave him both her hands. "Must I tell you again how *glad* I am?"

"Don't waste my time," he ordered. "Lead me to that steak."

He marveled at the soothing quality of their silence as they drove across town together. Roz Borland—snuggled in that same corner of his coupé like a sulky but relaxed kitten —had stabbed at his nerves by her mere presence. Karen, he reflected, was normal stimulation, no more. He caught himself just in time, before he could move closer and let his knee touch hers, if only to put the comparison to the test.

Instead he began to tell her of his crowded day from the beginning. She listened calmly throughout, encouraging him with just the right questions. Karen Agard—he decided it quite suddenly—would be an ideal confidante in any language. Last night she had helped him to clarify his own reasons for returning to Milton. Tonight, when those same reasons had exploded him into a full-fledged and rather alarming crusade, her acceptance justified everything.

On Water Street he slid into a vacant spot at the curb and sat on under the wheel, reluctant to break his narrative by entering the garish café across the sidewalk. The Cuban's place was no less tawdry than he had remembered from last night's glimpse. A background like this might suit Roz Borland's hectic charms; Karen Agard was another story.

He said tentatively, "I wish we'd picked a quieter spot——" and broke off in confusion when he saw how her eyes were shining.

Karen said, "The things you're telling me will stand up against any background. Don't stop, please. Not even when they bring the steak."

Chris grinned. "I was thinking of the clientele."

But she only took his arm gaily as they crossed the sidewalk. "If you mean the little harlots, don't worry. Why should *I* mind them if you don't?"

A swarthy waiter led them through the miasma of smoke and garlic with a flourish imported from Cuba via New Orleans. Once again that night Chris found himself walking behind a lovely woman to a wall booth, in a restaurant that could be classified only as a dive. This time the background reached him but dimly. Karen's interest was more important than the stares of the harpies they passed—or the limericks a drunken yard worker was shouting to a chorus at the piano. Karen's interest—and the dynamic future they might share with Uncle Jeff—was a refuge that would sustain him for a long time. The exact number of beds they'd add to the wards (and whether Jim Reynolds would be more useful in lab or dispensary) were questions more engrossing than the memory of Roz Borland's mocking hazel eyes. Or the equally mocking quirk of Jean Moreau's smile.

Despite that, he found himself telling her of his bout with the Frenchman, after the soothing therapy of a two-inch sirloin smothered in the restaurant's special sauce of onions and pepper.

Karen said unexpectedly, "Jean has used those same arguments on me, so I understand perfectly. I, too, have felt a desire to murder him on occasion."

"Don't ask me to explain it, but—for a moment nothing was more important than knocking him cold. If only to shut off those sneers about America."

"Are you sure it was America you were defending—and not Roz?"

"I'm not at all sure." Chris hesitated, then opened his mind wide to the possibility for the first time. "Maybe he's partly right, at that. Maybe Roz Borland does sum up what's wrong with us."

"Jean Moreau will never understand America," said Karen. "His mind is too narrow for that. So, I suppose, are the minds of many Americans."

"Dwight, for instance?"

"No, not Dwight. He, I'm afraid, is pure evil. Men like Dwight are always a race apart; there is no cure for them but death. But Moreau is a good Frenchman, as you said. The Americans I speak of are patriots too. Like him, they have their own definition of democracy: the right to get rich in their own way; the old pioneer privilege of stepping on their enemies' faces as they go up. Not even America can permit such men to flourish forever. Such men are fascists, even when they hate fascism with their hearts."

It was Karen's first long speech; she looked down at her plate and flushed a little. Then her chin went up, and she continued resolutely:

"Perhaps they are right about you. Perhaps you are a do-gooder who bites off more than he chews." She laughed as her American broke down. "Perhaps it does not matter in the long run. You are like Paul Travers in that: you'll fight until you die. Such men leave their mark."

Chris chuckled. "Don't embarrass me, please. I'm just a doctor who wants to treat his patients in his own way, with no help from the government. For God's sake, don't call me a crusader."

"Moreau would call you that, wouldn't he? He's said as much to Paul, to his face."

Chris's chuckle deepened. "Women aren't supposed to admire the type. I'm surprised that you——"

Her eyes were suddenly languid as they met his. "Of course I admire you both—for other reasons."

"Thanks for lumping me with Travers. He's a swell guy, but he chills me a little." Abruptly he wondered he if he had affected Roz Borland tonight in the same fashion that Travers affected *him*—and cursed Roz Borland again for intruding.

Karen said quickly, "It's Paul's misfortune that he speaks truth too bluntly. He should have been a bacteriologist, and nothing more. . . . You, I think, are different. You stir people's emotions, even when you're making them better themselves. It's a rare talent, Chris. I know you won't waste it."

He laughed aloud, marveling at the easy way she reassured him. "If you're referring to the lecture I gave Roz Borland—I assure you it didn't ruffle her self-esteem."

"Don't be too sure of that. I wouldn't even say that that fight with Jean was wasted."

"Will he challenge me to a duel tomorrow?"

"I think he'll respect you for your anger. I even think he'll go out of his way to help you against Dwight." Karen Agard rested two elbows on the scarred table top. "Never mind all these people, Chris—and their little motives for hating us. Or even for loving us. . . . People are unmanageable; microbes are consistent when you know their habits."

"And much more fun to destroy."

Karen said, with all the lilt of a poet planning a new epic, "Tell me more about your plan to make Pudge Carrol pay for our vaccine."

"And kill a few rats for us—when we're better friends."

"And the dispensary—could you really afford to open a branch at my shack on the Flats?"

They were off again—two scientists, lost in a private heaven all their own. . . .

It was Chris who reminded her that it was time to drive to that same shack on the Flats—the one-woman clinic that Karen had established with her own elbow grease and guile.

He said, "Personally, I'd much rather take you for a sail in my yawl. There are several hundred things we haven't argued out."

"We can argue tomorrow, can't we?"

"Tomorrow I expect to be too busy to argue."

Now, coasting his coupé to a stop in the cinder patch before the shack, he wished he'd been firmer about that sail. After all, there was nothing essential about tonight's chore: a lecture to the mothers of trailer town on first aid, with emphasis on child care. He'd fit that sort of thing into his larger program tomorrow, just as he'd absorb Karen's jerry-built clinic in the larger plans he was making for compensation work at West Island. . . . Tonight, he thought resentfully, we've a right to talk each other out.

Thinking this, he did not blame his hand for closing on hers as she reached for the car door.

"When do I see you again?"

"Tomorrow at the hospital—when I report for orders."

"Can't I come back and pick you up?"

"I've told you Paul is coming. We've a few back-country calls to make."

"Doesn't your day ever end, Doctor?"

Her mouth was close to his as she smiled at him in the dark. "Speak for yourself, Doctor."

He had a definite desire to move closer, and resisted it heroically. "Don't you ever have the impulse to cut loose from it all?"

"Frequently," said Karen. "So will you, when you've been back awhile."

"How will we fight it off?"

"Picnics will help," said Karen. "Especially if you're generous with that yawl of yours. Your houseman tells me the groupers will be running off South Island in another month." She smiled, and her mouth was still very close to his. "Your nerves will last till then, I'm sure."

"Don't be too sure," he said.

"Please do," she said, "if it helps."

Her lips were sweet and yielding under his, but it was a kiss of acceptance rather than a kiss of passion. She did not resist when he put his arm around her.

112

"It helps, all right," he said. "It helps tremendously. I've been away a long time, you know."

Her soft laughter teased him in the dark. "Away from parked cars, you mean?"

"Away from you," he said, and meant it.

"That's a real compliment, Chris."

He drew her even closer in the dark. This time it was she who put her lips on his. A long, hard kiss that sent his senses reeling; a kiss that dissolved self-doubt in a sudden burst of flame. For a moment he was too startled to respond. . . . When he released her at last, he saw that her eyes were shining.

"Remember, I've a class in first aid," she said, and ran across the cinders to the down-at-heel building that housed her clinic.

He sat for a long while under the wheel, staring at the light that fell through the grimy windowpanes, waiting for the thud of his heart to taper off. It had been a long time since a girl had kissed him like that. Since Deirdre, in fact —and the sea-girt Capri meadow. With Deirdre it had been the satisfaction of a mutual need: Capri had taken care of the romance. With Karen——

In that flash he knew that Karen had kissed him to give his taut nerves release; that the passionate embrace was only an overtone to their comradeship-to-come. He had no right to misinterpret her gesture. And yet he sat on, staring at the run-down house where she had set up her small citadel of science, wishing he could lure her out again. Wondering what would happen if Travers was late—if he waited until that droning first-aid class was over.

Eventually, as his mind simmered down to realities again, he kicked his starter and drove back to St. Lucie. An early moon had begun to silver the bay as he parked his car beside the boathouse. The *Lady Jane*, bobbing at her moorings, was a tangible invitation, but he did not go aboard.

Looked at from any angle, it had been quite a day. Two women had entered his life boldly—to challenge him as a man, not as a doctor. Professionally, he had assisted at the dramas of birth, healing, and death. Standing in the clear white light of the operating theater, he had promised himself a finish fight for the kind of medicine he loved. He had been kissed soundly by one refugee—and had knocked out another. . . . Dr. Christopher Land grinned at his own thoughts in the dark. The offshore breeze was perfect for a long, sweet tack across the bay. He knew it was the last temptation he would resist tonight. This time the wind's song in the rigging of the *Lady Jane* was a call to battle.

8

HE WAS BATTLING MOREAU once again, and losing, thanks to the Frenchman's flying heels. Roz Borland was acting as an obviously one-sided referee; Karen was a composite audience of one, screaming at him to rise from the canvas and hit back. . . . Chris rose on one elbow as Roy's voice bored through the cotton wool.

He heard the Negro houseman clearly through his drowsiness: "This my early day at the yard, Mist' Chris. Got your breakfuss all laid out."

Chris stayed on one elbow with an effort. "On your way, Roy. I'll manage." As he settled into his pillow again he wondered—for the thirtieth time that month—why he hadn't been sleeping enough lately.

At the same time his mind whisked over the memory of Jim Reynolds, who was doing such a wonderful job with Karen in lab and doubling in brass at the West Island dispensary. Jim would be giving full time at the hospital in another week, when Terry put his Balkan frame aside and joined them. Young Terry Stone, a born clinic manager, and an ideal man to handle the many-sided problems at their West Island branch. . . . At the same moment he remembered that Sam Bernstein was in town—his credentials in order and roaring for work. He had a date to meet Sam, and Paul Travers, in just an hour. In just forty minutes, he told himself ruefully, swinging his feet to the floor as his eye caught the inexorable message of the alarm clock at his elbow.

He forced himself to walk over to the window and stare out at the pale blue sheen of the bay. At this hour the water was a milky mirror for the summer morning; the fisherman, trolling his crabline in the miragelike distance, was the only break in the endless panorama of water merged with sky. For all that deceptive calm, he could smell a breeze in the making, where the last sandspit of St. Lucie Cay curved south to meet the Gulf. Another wonderful day for a sail. He saw himself at the tiller as the *Lady Jane* plunged seaward with a bone in her teeth—away from the patients that streamed through the Bayshore Clinic. Away from the headaches that plagued him daily. . . .

That fever case, admitted last night to the contagious ward. No way of proving yet that it was murine typhus, though both he and Uncle Jeff were sure of it.

The child he had operated on in the small hours of this morning—too late to reach the ruptured appendix. No amount of education, it seemed, could prevent people from waiting to call the doctor; even with medical care prepaid, they still dosed themselves until it was too late. Or almost too late. . . . He had every hope of saving the child, even if the clinic staff must work overtime now with plasma units, with the intricate but effective Miller-Abbott tubes which now prevented the lethal distention so fatal in peritonitis.

Then there was that puzzling bone case from the plant. Another snapped humerus, the third in two weeks on that shift. He made a mental note to drive to West Island and check on safety appliances once again. His first survey had shown several places where accidents might occur; only constant vigilance would insure that his advice was carried out.

After he had shaved he pulled on a pair of trunks and walked out to the pier. The yawl bobbed gently in the wake of a passing shrimp boat. Chris waved an answer to the helmsman's greeting and plunged cleanly into the bay, to follow the boat's wake awhile with a brisk racing crawl. Then, as the water quieted to a sleepy mirror again, he floated on his back to study the sky. Already the soft blue was changing to the blaze of full daylight. It was still restful to swim alone, to watch a single gull wheel high above him, a mere white fleck against the morning.

Regretfully he turned over and swam briskly back to his stringpiece. He was a working man now, an executive heavy with responsibility; no longer could he afford to waste even a minute in a day that barely sufficed to cover the tasks he had allotted himself.

Slipping his feet into wooden-soled espadrilles, he stalked gauntly up the path to the boathouse, for all the world like his own conscience on parade. Through the silent screen of Australian pines he glanced up at Karen's cottage and blessed its nearness once again. Knowing her had been the one tranquil spot in the month that had just raced by. Their long quiet talks in the evening, when they'd been spared the bustle of an emergency call. Sunday-morning picnics on her veranda, when he and Paul Travers had wolfed crab meat and beer and lazed for a delicious hour afterward, too comfortable to think of swimming. . . . Karen, it seemed, was made of sterner stuff: he remembered her now through half-closed lids, every inch a viking as she raced inshore with the lazy surf. Remembered the breath-taking lines of her body, revealed so casually by the brief white halter top she wore. . . .

Since the time he had taken her in his arms, there in the thick dark of trailer town, it had seemed only natural that they should kiss good night when they parted at her doorstep. He had forced himself to keep their short embraces as platonic as a kiss can be, to ignore the hint of passion he had sensed more than once in those full and eager lips. Stronger men than he would have probably yielded long ago, he told himself testily, and opened his eyes wide at Karen's cottage. The place looked empty in that moist morning light. He reminded himself that Karen had gone on to the hospital an hour ago to help Jim and the resident intern set up the clinic for the morning rush, that Uncle Jeff was not due to return until afternoon from White Sulphur—where he had gone to visit an ailing but unregenerate Embree. Another reason to hurry across the causeway to Milton. Thanks to this brief relaxation, he was already late.

Even now the white shirt and seersucker felt strange after the uniform he had folded, with no regrets, into his father's clothespress. He roared across the causeway with his foot on the floor, relying once again on the protection of the bright new "MD" on his license plate. Travers and Sam Bernstein were already at breakfast when he walked into the small hospital dining room. Sam would begin his duties at the clinic today; Paul, as usual, had dropped in to beat his drum for sanitation in trailer town.

Three years in the Medical Corps had done little to reduce Sam Bernstein's girth. In hospital white he looked even more the contented rolypoly that Chris remembered from

Lakeview. Before the war this façade had helped the little obstetrician to a successful practice in Baltimore: expectant mothers, sensing a vague affinity with their own *embonpoint,* had put their troubles in Sam's hands without a qualm.

Now Sam said, "Don't ask me for compliments, Chris. I've looked the shebang over, and it's perfect. In fact, I've only one complaint."

"Your speciality, I suppose."

"Check," said the obstetrician. "I'll give you my ideas on that after you've eaten. You may need strength."

Chris grinned as he went to the diet kitchen to shout his order. He knew what Sam had in mind, and knew it would not be pleasant to refuse.

"Get off your hobbyhorse a minute, Sam," said Paul. "Tell Chris what you really think of the clinic. Not that he needs a build-up. That's *his* specialty."

Chris laughed. "Don't fish for me, Paul. Sam has already bestowed the accolade. As he says, all the place needs is one more good doctor. I've got him, as of now."

Bernstein's round face beamed. "I guess that makes us even. Now tell me when I get busy, so I can brace myself."

"The real rush starts around ten."

"And you'll need all your hands for the first week," put in Paul Travers.

Karen Agard came in from the diet kitchen and sat down with the others. "I'll take my coffee here, if this isn't an all-male huddle."

"You're in," Chris assured her. "How's our appendix?"

"Doing nicely, now we've established drainage. I'm transfusing her again in an hour."

He nodded his approval. "Last night, Sam, I introduced this young lady as our right arm. Begin to see why?"

Sam said, "From where I sit, I'd say she's more than that."

Karen blushed at the compliment as she turned to Paul Travers. "Jim and I autopsied those guinea pigs an hour ago. It's there, all right." She looked slyly at Chris. "Surely you don't mind if I do that much for the public health?"

Paul explained to Sam Bernstein. "The other day I did a little rat-catching down on the Flats. Took some from the garbage dump and some from workers' trailers. Thick with fleas, the lot of 'em."

"Wasn't that rather risky? I hear you've a lot of typhus around here."

"Karen and I are both immune. We took the vaccine as soon as we set up shop here. My hunch said that the fleas were definitely infected, so we put them under the pestle, and Karen inoculated the guinea pigs."

"How many autopsied positive?"

"Every one," said Karen.

Sam whistled. "That's a pretty high incidence."

"I guess you win your bet, Paul," said Chris. "Are you telling Borland?"

"Not now. I'm afraid he's too busy for it to register. What I'm really praying for is that vaccine."

Chris turned again to Sam Bernstein. "The local union kicked in for typhus vaccine, but it's been slow in coming. We're planning to inoculate our whole bailiwick as an experiment."

"Are you that worried?"

Paul Travers nodded solemnly. "Yes, now we've put the experiment on the line." He took out his watch with a sigh. "It's always later than I think. Can you steal a half hour to check on that dump with me, Chris? I want you behind me when I make my next report."

Chris nodded and pushed back his chair. "Want to come along, Sam?"

Bernstein said, "Can't you let your new broom sweep clean? I'm going through the wards with Dr. Agard. . . . And don't gulp that coffee like a commuter, Chris. You've still got time to hear my beef."

Chris said, "I know it now, Sam. You're a specialist with no place to practice your specialty. You want me to readmit maternity cases."

Bernstein squared off from the table and addressed them generally. "You all know I was in charge of obstetrics at every camp G.H.Q. sent me to."

"Don't tell me you handled patients at the local hospitals?"

"Good Lord, no. If the Army delivered every soldier's offspring, we'd have no room for the wounded. My job was to find doctors who'd take maternity cases for the amount Uncle Sam pays. Even that was simpler than lining up hospitals to take the gals at Army rates. . . . Come off it, Chris. You know what I want."

"You're asking me to let in soldiers' wives at fifty dollars a case, is that it?"

"God knows the soldier can't sweeten the Army allotment,"

said Sam. "God also knows most of 'em have to, before the average private baby-snatcher will deliver their wives. . . . And that isn't all. I think I know my trade; it still beats me how many patients I'd swear were ideal for normal delivery develop complications that mean operative deliveries, even sections."

Chris looked up quickly. "Legitimate ones?"

The pudgy obstetrician shrugged. "You know the Caesarean racket as well as I do. I'll bet my brand-new license that outside of the big clinics less than half the Caesareans done today are really necessary. I'll go further. Most of the needless ones are done by men least qualified to hold a scalpel."

"Like our friend Kornmann," said Paul.

"Don't mention Kornmann to me," said Sam. "I heard all about that racketeer when I was two counties away. He's done twice as many sections as any other surgeon in Milton, hasn't he?"

Chris said, "I see you've come to me with statistics."

"Chapter and verse. A few years back there was a report analyzing about five hundred deaths from sections, all over America. Do you know that in many of those cases the disproportion between the baby's head and the birth canal had not even been measured?"

"Think it over, Chris," said Paul. "If you let in these Army cases, you'll be muscling in on a pretty lucrative racket."

Karen said quietly, "Dr. Jeff and I went into the problem of Army admissions some time ago. East Point is the only big camp near Milton, but it's big enough. It would probably run close to fifty deliveries a month."

Sam said, "I could handle fifty, with the new wing you're putting in, and pull my weight besides. It'd be worth doing the job on clinic time to show up Kornmann. Have I got to tell you how much Army pay that Austrian is drawing down?"

Chris got up firmly this time. "I can't give you a definite answer now, Sam. I'm up to my eyes in organization. But I'll try to work it out, I promise you."

Sam Bernstein's face fell—but not too far. He knew the quality of Chris Land's promises. "Suppose I agree not to brace you for another month. Will that do?"

"That'll do nicely," laughed Chris. "Now suppose you stay with Karen for an hour and prove what sort of new broom you are. *I've* got to double up with the Public Health Service."

Driving across the Flats with Travers, Chris let his mind dabble with the melancholy deceptions of arithmetic. Fifty maternity cases per month, at Army rates, would bring in twenty-five hundred dollars to the new clinic. With the additional beds he had ordered, they could probably swing it at cost—or slightly less. Taking an added flyer at this time, of course, would narrow the margin of safety he had allowed himself. Already he had written off most of Borland's fifteen thousand for new equipment; in another week he'd be writing checks against his own nest egg as well. . . . All this before a dollar had come in from the West Island pay rolls. And yet he had no right to employ a specialist like Sam without permitting that specialist to use his skill.

He filed the whole matter, regretfully, for future reference—and turned to the Public Health man:

"You must be really worried to drag me out of my groove like this."

Paul nodded solemnly. "Believe it or not, I'm beginning to get Milton worried too. Most of the merchants are pretty well sold on ratproofing their buildings. So it won't hit the town too hard when and if it really comes. We'll have a bang-up object lesson for Borland right here at his work gate. Of course, if I could prove that Dwight and his crowd were taking cases without reporting them———"

"I still can't believe he'd risk that."

"He's got to take those risks to get rich, Chris. Remember, Borland also pays him a salary as medical director of the main yard. That means he's supposed to dream up measures to prevent accidents as well as disease."

Chris smiled grimly. "Just as I've made a survey at West Island and recommended safety devices?"

"Precisely. Only it doesn't work that way with Dwight." Travers honked viciously at a draggletail rat that had just scurried across the road ahead. "He can't lose sight of the fact that every extra patient is extra income for him and his little army of chiselers."

Chris said slowly, "Much as I distrust the man, I can't believe that he'd deliberately———"

"Wait till you've been at this awhile longer. Wait until the same crack-up occurs on a job time after time. I'm not hinting that Dwight encourages accidents by sins of omission. I'm stating that he prepares them, with the help of Scanlon."

Chris started to protest, remembered the broken humerus on his list for today's checkups, and held his peace. The aura of the dump had already assailed their nostrils before they could coast down the next gentle slope. Paul stopped the car.

"I've talked the city into building an incinerator out here. Of course it'll be months before they can get the materials."

"Borland could throw one together in a few weeks if——"

"If Scanlon would okay it. That sourpuss never will."

"Don't tell me that's Dwight's doing too."

"This time it's the coal tipples," said Paul. "Not that Dwight isn't interested in leaving things just as they are on the Flats."

They walked along the edge of the coal tipples and looked down at the great smoking heap of refuse. In the past week, at Paul Travers' urging, the city had thrown up a jerry-built fence around the area. Already there were paths from fence to trailer town, and evidence—equally well marked—that still more refuse had been tossed over the fence itself.

"Look well," said Paul. "That's the only reason I brought you out. Incidentally, have I thanked you for coming? The U.S.P.H.S. sends us out to handle things like this: most of the time doctors stare us down as though we were enemy spies."

Chris said, "You must know me better by now."

Travers opened his case and passed over a cigarette. They smoked in unison, in a vain effort to forget the aura of decay. "All right, Chris. I know you're on my side, but—are you worrying about this typhus threat the way *I* worry?"

"Maybe I would if I had time."

"Sorry. You know as well as I what's going to happen if we give the virus an even break. Let's say it doesn't get that break, that Dwight's gamble wins and my science loses. We'll get several hundred cases. A half dozen may die—unless the virus gets stronger. Unless it really rampages through those cases and begins to resemble the real thing."

Paul tossed his cigarette over the fence and watched it turn gently as it descended into the steaming miasma below. "A good fire would take care of that particular threat. Without the dump, the rats would have to spread out for a living —the ones that weren't killed by the heat. We could spread the disease out that way."

"Unless it becomes louse-borne in the meantime?"

"Does that worry you, Chris? Or must I do my worrying alone?"

"Give me time to get my business in fighting trim," said Chris. "I'll join you in that worry." He swept trailer town with an inclusive glance. "When people must live in soap-boxes and bathe when they can, what else can you expect?"

Travers nodded solemnly. "As a bacteriologist on a lark, I ought to be glad of this proving ground. We've never been able to study the change from flea to louse-borne typhus adequately. Let's say it happens, just as we fear. I could write it up for some medical journal and get myself a promotion." He steered Chris firmly toward the car. "I'm never at my best when I descend to sophistry. Besides, it's time you got back to that treadmill."

They drove to town in silence. Chris stole a quick glance at his companion and asked himself once again why the man inspired loyalty rather than friendship, respect rather than admiration. He ignored the question as he broke the silence:

"What's on your calendar for today, Paul?"

"I'm catching the plane for the Capitol in just an hour. Did you know we were already drafting plans to control malaria when our boys come back from the South Pacific? Have you thought what's in store for us—with all those healthy young spleens packed full of parasites waiting to break out a chill and form a dinner for the first anopheles that comes along?"

Chris whistled softly. Suddenly he realized how puny his troubles were alongside Paul's. After all, the Public Health man had a right to be doctrinaire at times.

"I don't envy you your job," he said slowly. "Maybe I'm lucky to do my fighting with a scalpel."

Back at the hospital again—and conscious, as always, that he was a trifle late—Chris hurried to his office and changed to a white work gown. Sam Bernstein was already at his elbow as he turned toward the door.

"Want some fun, Chris?"

"Hospital fun?"

"Not this time, brother. Downstairs, in the clinic. Just want you to check on your new broom."

They went down the whitewashed corridor to the basement. As always, Chris could not help pausing at the end of the long room to survey his medical mill in action. The waiting room was jammed with workers and their families. In their fenced-off corner was a group of mothers and their babies, come early to take advantage of Karen's clinic, with free examination and pediatric advice. By putting the babies on record when they were well, she could follow them more intelligently in the critical months ahead. There would be no inoculations missed among the families who worked at West Island; no repetition of the tragedy that had snuffed out a life in the Dawkins farmhouse.

His eye moved to the far side of the room, to check an older man, florid of face, patient of mien, who waited his turn on the bench. A cardiac case, if his internship at Lakeview counted for anything. He would go eventually to one of the busy cubicles beyond the examining office, where the metabolism tests and the electrocardiographic examinations were made. As his eye roved down the bench he could almost guess who would need a further checkup—with or without X rays and hospitalization.

That room, he told himself, represented medical care that would mount into the thousands on individual doctors' ledgers. The babies alone would ordinarily cost their families one hundred dollars apiece in their first year, if only for normal checkups, inoculations, and the inevitable small illnesses of early childhood. A Borland worker paid roughly nine dollars to achieve protection for the same period—and his was admittedly only a small experiment in prepayment. Organized on a national scale, medical care of this type could certainly be offered to the low-salaried worker at a far lower scale.

Chris squared his shoulders to that challenge. Perhaps he was only a cosmic dreamer, like Travers; perhaps the Dwights of this world would nip his schemes in the bud. He would still try to prove that a thing like this could last over the long pull, that America need not be nursed to health by government doctors. He would prove that people did not have to abandon the traditional relationship of doctor and patient. The contact would be maintained on a larger base, that was all.

He swung back to the present as Bernstein called him into a small examining room beside the main office. Sam was already bent over the chest of a patient who lay on the examining table. He looked up owlishly as Chris entered, and took the tips of his stethoscope from his ears.

123

"This is Dr. Land, Mr. Pryzinsky," he said. "The chief of the clinic."

Chris smiled down reassuringly at the dark little Slav on the table between them, but the man only turned away and mumbled into his beard. He was a type of patient all too familiar to the clinical worker; Chris had treated a hundred such at Lakeview. Automatically he took in the overbright eyes, the increased respiration, the dark brown reek of poverty. . . . As Bernstein detailed the case history he tested the pulse, noting its hurried rhythm.

"The patient became ill two days ago. Felt bad all over." The layman's phrase for what doctors call general malaise. "Last night he felt much worse. Had a chill——"

"Any malaria before?"

"None. And there's none in this neck of the woods."

It was true enough. The threat of malaria was something a Southern city understood perfectly. Milton's founding fathers had needed little prodding from Paul to clean the anopheles mosquito from the area.

Sam said, "That's about all he can tell us. Fever one hundred and two——"

"What about the blood work?"

"It's being done now."

Chris nodded and turned to the patient. "We'll have to put you in the hospital for a few days, Mr. Pryzinsky. Until we decide just what's wrong."

The man's great, liquid eyes were wide with disbelief. Eyes that stared humidly out of a whiskered visage that could have gone into a revolutionary cartoon without retouching.

"But, Doctaire—I cannot pay."

Chris smiled. "You've already paid for the whole thing. You're covered by the insurance scheme at the plant, aren't you?"

Sam shook his head in the background. "He's at the big yard, Chris. Not in the plan. English not too good, you understand. Came here by mistake when he should have gone to Dwight."

Chris frowned. Here, at last, was a perfect example of what he was fighting. The patient was probably developing typhus; they'd know for certain when they had the final blood report. That meant he would be sick for weeks. Since the mortality rate for murine typhus increased rapidly after fifty, he might even die. Could he correct Sam's error and send this unwashed bundle of infection on to Dwight? In that compensation mill he'd receive only nominal care at best; if he died, the Bayshore Clinic would be indirectly responsible. The head of Bayshore Clinic made his decision quickly.

"We'll take you into the hospital anyway," he said, and turned quickly as Sam plucked his sleeve. Both of them stared at a tiny moving spot on the white surface of the examining table. Sam snatched a magnifying glass from the instrument shelf. Under it the perambulating spot developed legs and a horny carapace.

"So help me, an arthropod."

"Surprised?"

"On the contrary. But——"

Chris kept down the excitement in his tone as the clinical picture came clear. Here was a patient with typhus—it *had* to be typhus now. A patient who was, literally, lousy. If murine typhus could really also become louse-borne (and all epidemiologists felt sure it was), here was a golden chance to prove it.

The plan exploded into words. "Get this man into isolation at once, Sam. Spread sheets on floor and bed and strip him. Get all the parasites you can, and have Jim make an emulsion. We're going to inject another guinea pig and pray."

Bernstein had already telephoned the wards when a nurse tapped on the door. "Could you see Dr. Agard a moment, Dr. Land?"

He went into the examining room where Karen was working, forcing his face to reassume its professional mask. Karen would hear of this in detail later on: there was simply no time to break the routine with such news, now that the job was out of his hands. As always, the children's sanctum was bedlam on a minor scale. Nurses weighed babies and took temperatures all down a long table. Nurses gave inoculations, took blood counts and busy notes. . . . In nearly every case the patients registered their protests in no uncertain terms. The baby Karen was examining merely blew bubbles and waved four pudgy limbs like a grounded acrobat.

Karen said crisply, "You'll have to decide this case, Dr. Lan "

He bent closer, fighting down a momentary wave of nausea. Deformities in children sometimes affected him that way. In this case the baby's harelip was an almost classic V, a split which evidently extended back through the jaw itself.

"What about the palate?" he asked.

"Complete cleft," said Karen. They exchanged a glance. Both of them knew that that made correction of the deformity doubly complex. To repair the lip itself was a minor plastic operation nowadays. Reconstruction of the palate was something else again, a job that could require several staged operations.

"Is the family in the plan?"

Karen nodded. "Your banker wanted you to insist on a complete checkup before you'd take anyone," she reminded him. "It would have saved you things like this."

"I couldn't begin by hedging."

Her eyes were warm with approval; he watched her sway a fraction toward him before she became briskly professional again. "Of course you couldn't, Doctor," she murmured, and he knew once again that she was merely matching his reactions with her own. He went over to the baby's mother, who was waiting stolidly in a corner of the room. Another Slav, he noted absently. A Slav considerably cleaner than his prize incubator, Pryzinsky.

"We can repair the lip. But it may take several operations to do the rest."

The woman's face fell. "It is too much to ask, Doctor. How do we pay?"

Each day he had answered that inevitable question by rote: "You've paid already. The insurance takes care of everything," and asked himself, once again, how long that answer would have meaning. The smile that spread over the mother's troubled face was enough answer for his doubts—a partial reward, at least, for weary muscles and lost sleep.

"You can arrange about admission, Dr. Agard. We'll operate as soon as the child is ready. Now may I go on to my own surgery?"

Back in his own examining room, he felt that he was beginning work at last; his own cases gave balance to his day, after the still-unfamiliar routine of serving as consultant to the other sections. Jim Reynolds and Sam would spell each other as admitting officers this morning; he knew he could trust them on that end. The best any admitting officer could do was ask a few pointed questions, coupled, in some cases, with a brief examination. That was about what the average G.P. or compensation physician did for a patient, before sending him on his way with a placebo. Here the rough sorting was only a beginning of treatment. When patients had been shuttled into the proper corner of the clinic, a thorough examination would determine the .real trouble—the sort of checkup that only the specialist could make. If a diagnosis was still impossible, further appointments were made for lab work or X ray. The patient ill enough for hospitalization was admitted after the first interview.

Now, in his own consulting room, Chris found his own selection of patients waiting. Most of them had reported for minor surgery. An inevitable rookie, with a broken wrist to be set; another rookie, with an equally inevitable broken finger. Abscesses to be opened and drained. A case of recurrent abdominal pain, which he sent up to the hospital proper for an X ray study of stomach and alimentary canal—a case that might be an early ulcer or one of those kidney dilations which go under the long name of hydronephrosis.

The last man was the fracture case he'd handled early that morning. The arm was doing well, thanks to the novocain and the plaster splint which the patient carried nonchalantly in a sling. The check X ray now showed good position.

"Feels funny to be up and walking," said the patient. "Friend of mine got clipped this way last month, and they put him in the hospital."

"Do you feel enough pain to want hospitalization?"

"Not me, Doc. Don't get me wrong. The way you got me fixed, it don't hurt at all. I just don't see why Dr. Dwight had to put Gus in bed for a month and bury him in splints."

Chris applied the new bandage snugly. "Is your friend back at work yet?"

"Not Gus. *He's* ridin' compensation."

Chris took out his own compensation-report blank. Last night he'd been too tired to fill in all the details.

"Where did this accident occur?"

"An overhead crane came loose and clipped me. Just like I said about Gus. Ratchet didn't hold."

Chris looked up. "I inspected those West Island ratchets last week—and ordered them filed deeper."

"Looks like your order didn't go through, Doc. Maybe you ought to check on it."

"I'm checking right now," said Chris. "Feel well enough to come along?"

The man said, "Why not? I was going to hitch a ride and gab awhile at lunch."

It was a fairish drive to West Island, and he cursed the necessity adequately as he pushed the coupé through the Milton traffic. Things like this, he reflected, should not be part of a doctor's routine; but there was no help for it now. Especially if he uncovered what he expected to find.

At the plant gate Chris and his injured partner showed their passes. They walked down the plank-floored midway together, through an obbligato of rivets. Every drill on the shift seemed to be chattering like a horde of metallic monkeys. The injured worker shouted cheerily above the din.

"This clinic of yours is sure a fine thing, Doc. Over at the main yards there's talk about your not havin' good doctors, but over here we're more'n satisfied."

Chris moved a bit closer as they walked. The trip, it seemed, was paying dividends already. "What kind of talk?"

"Well, you know how yard workers shoot the breeze . . ." The man hesitated, then started over. "One of the boys was visiting a pal from Borland's main assembly. At the County Hospital, it was. Pal's got some kind of fever. Said he'd heard that your staff was all broken-down medics who couldn't make a livin' in a livery stable."

Chris's lips tightened. He had been expecting this sort of rumor. A smear campaign, handled by an expert of Gilbert Dwight's caliber, could be an effective thing.

"Did you remember anything about me in particular?" If he knew his smear campaign, the answer was already in his brain.

Again the man hesitated. "Mind you, *I* don't swallow a word of it. You did a swell job on this arm. But they're sayin' at the County Hospital that you were kicked out of the Army —that you weren't wounded at all."

Chris found that he had paused on the boardwalk, in the full glare of noon, to pull up his trouser leg and show the great, livid scar that would always mark the bone graft.

"Does *that* look as though I barked my shin in the dark?"

"Mind you, Doc, I didn't say that!"

Chris laughed aloud, slapped the man's shoulder, and walked on without another word. This was more than he had expected; it was hard to believe that even Dwight could go so low. He surmised that it was Kornmann who had started the actual tongue-wagging. A doctor who would do a Caesarean section on a soldier's wife—and attach a soldier's pay —was capable of anything.

They turned down a side path and entered one of the great work stages. A donkey engine shrieked its warning as it went by. Chris and his companion stepped into the shadow of a half-finished hull that had apparently been assembled like a giant jigsaw of steel. Even before the man pointed, Chris recognized the crane that swung idly over their heads; the number daubed on the cab was an additional reminder that this was the mechanism he had condemned a week ago.

Chris turned to a foreman salting a gargantuan sandwich in the shadow of the ship's hull.

"Weren't you here when I tested that crane last week?"

"That's right, Doctor."

"You heard me say it was unsafe—that the ratchet was worn?"

The foreman bit deep into his sandwich. "Hell, Doctor, I coulda told you that without a check—and more'n a week ago."

"Was anything done about it?"

"Not a thing."

Chris controlled his tone and smiled at the injured man beside him. "Thanks for giving me an idea."

"Thanks for the lift, Doc."

He knew that the two workmen were staring at him; at the moment he was too angry to care much. There were coin-box phones just inside the gate, and he stepped into one to call Seward Harper. Six days ago he had sent the banker an urgent report on the crane; it was unlike Seward not to have acted on it immediately. Still, he had to be sure before he made his next move.

The banker sounded busy but really concerned. "Of course I sent your letter through, Chris."

"Through to where?"

"Borland is handling all his maintenance at West Island through the main plant. It saves duplicating repair crews."

"Does that mean Scanlon got my letter?"

"I suppose. Naturally I assumed the defect had been corrected long ago. Is anything wrong?"

Chris remembered Paul Travers' barefaced accusation; at the time it had seemed incredible to him. "There's been another accident," he said. "Fortunately not serious. I'm seeing Scanlon about it at once."

He could sense Seward's hesitation, even on the phone. But the banker's voice was firm when he spoke. "Yes, Chris— I think you should do just that."

Once again he edged the coupé into the bustling ship-yard traffic for a long cross-town drive. Once again he cursed fluently at the obstructionists who had spoiled his morning. Evil, he reflected, is not always a positive quality, and seldom visible; evil can be compounded of wasted time and uselessly taut nerves, rather than an open threat. . . .

At Borland's main gate he wasted another two minutes arguing with the keeper as to the validity of his pass. Scanlon's office, he was told at length, was just behind the main repair shop. A beehive enclosed in beaverboard, trembling on its joists at the crash-bang world outside.

A secretary (it seemed odd for Scanlon to have a secretary, but she was both pretty and competent) looked at Chris doubtfully across the glass partition inside.

"I'm afraid he's busy. If you haven't an appointment——"

"It's about an accident to a worker. I must see him at once." Chris stared at the ground-glass cubicle beyond and saw only the foreman's bull-like silhouette against the pane. "If you'll pardon me, I'm going in now."

He walked past the girl's protests and pushed open the door. The silhouette changed into the bulky, sunburned torso of Scanlon himself—stripped down to an undershirt, and elbow-deep in blueprints. Evidently he had heard part of Chris's colloquy; at any rate, he had prepared his best scowl for the intruder.

"This is my busy day, Doc."

Chris braced himself as the jet of tobacco juice rang a bull's-eye in the battered cuspidor six inches from his foot. There was a chair in the cluttered office, but the foreman did not offer it. Instead he held Chris's eyes for a long, insolent moment before he picked up a T square and returned, even more insolently, to his work.

Chris said, "Do you think I'd break in on you like this if it wasn't important?"

"I wouldn't know, Doc. Speak your piece."

"Early this morning there was an accident at West Island."

"Sure. I got the report myself, now Mr. Borland's out of town. What about it?"

"It was only a broken arm. But it might have been a death."

Scanlon worked on busily. "So a man dies. That's what we carry insurance for. You aren't a good businessman, Doc. Accidents should mean more income for you."

"You're forgetting how I do business, Scanlon. My clinic is paid to *save* working time, not to waste it. So, I take it, are you."

"Just what d'you mean by that?"

"Only this. The broken arm at West Island was caused by a defective crane—a machine I ordered overhauled a week ago."

"Did you say 'ordered,' Doc?"

"You heard me."

Their voices were quiet enough, but Chris could feel the stale air in the office vibrate between them. "You also have my letter," he said. "Seward Harper sent it to you."

"Sure. I remember your letter too. Are you an engineer, maybe?"

"Of course I'm not."

The foreman heaved to his feet, with both fists on his blueprints. "Then why don't you ride your own racket and let me manage mine?"

"Does that mean you refuse to replace the ratchet?"

"It means I don't answer questions from amateurs, Doc. It means Cal Borland trusts me to keep his yards moving my way—not yours. Have I got to remind you again I'm busy?"

For once Chris found he could keep his temper. "Not at all, Mr. Scanlon. I've found out all I want to know."

Walking back to his car, he felt his spirits rising. The foreman's place in the enemy ranks was certain now; his attitude was only one more proof of how deeply the battle was joined, even though it was strictly subsurface as yet. Dwight's camp had undoubtedly started the whispering campaign; Dwight had paid Scanlon to thwart him at every turn.

He knew that he should lay the facts before Borland, but he put that obvious temptation aside. Scanlon's reputation as a production wizard was well established at both yards— and Scanlon was certainly prepared to combat him with the sort of chapter and verse he could never supply. At this stage of the clinic's progress the shipbuilder would take his foreman's word on an engineering problem, not his.

He beat an energetic tattoo on his horn before he whisked by a truck tottering under its load of boiler plate. Beyond, a side road opened out from the coastal highway to the suburbs of Milton. He was going back in earnest now: to his own home town, to the hospital he was building there with heart and brain and hands. The clinic would be on its feet in a few weeks more—a living proof to Borland that he had chosen wisely. In the meantime he'd fight Dwight and Scanlon in his own way. It would be a fight he could enjoy, now that he was beginning to gauge their methods.

But his exhilaration died instantly when he drove under the portico of the Bayshore Clinic and found Karen waiting. The message in her face was plain, even without the blood-stains on her white work gown.

Karen said, "We've phoned everywhere for you."

He was out of the car with no sense of transition, hurrying with her through the emergency entrance.

"Accident case?"

"Roy," she said evenly. "Your houseman. It looks like internal hemorrhage. Sam's preparing him for the table now."

9

SAM BERNSTEIN was waiting at the door of the emergency room. The pudgy obstetrician looked calm as ever on the surface. Chris forced calm into his own voice as he shucked off his street coat. Roy would hear them through the half-open door, if he was still conscious.

"How did it happen?"

"Truck skidded, not two blocks from here. This colored boy was the driver's helper." Sam hesitated a moment. "Karen tells me that he works for you."

"Roy's been with the family for thirty years."

"No wonder he asked to be brought here."

They went into the room in a group. Roy lay on the table —a grotesque, gray-faced Roy in his denim work clothes, his face contorted with pain, his knees hunched against it. Chris took in the picture at a glance; the blood on the floor, the empty plasma unit on its frame beside the patient, the houseman's labored breathing. His eyes moved on to the Negro's head and the dark mat of blood in his wool.

Sam said, "Scalp wound's superficial. I stitched that while we waited for you. Want another plasma unit?"

Chris nodded as his fingers left Roy's pulse. The beat had been hard to find at first. Everything in the houseman's position pointed to the profound shock that went with hemorrhage. Roy's eyelids fluttered as Chris straightened his legs gently and devoted his attention to the taut muscles of the abdomen.

"What's the meaning of this, Roy?"

The Negro's voice was vague; even in that short span he had relaxed. " 'Lo, Mist' Chris. Sure glad I'm here, suh."

"Where does it hurt most?"

The Negro moved his hand toward the upper abdomen and vaguely toward the left flank. "Door jammed into me right hard when we turned over." His eyes opened wide now, to scan Chris's impassive face anxiously. "Is it bad, Mist' Chris?"

Chris said cheerfully, "Not if you can still talk after coming this far." There was no time to change his angle of observation, to see if the deep sigh from Roy was a sign of trust or approaching coma. The situation, even at this phase, was obviously too desperate.

Karen said, "The plasma's ready."

"Will you start it, Sam?"

He continued his check as Bernstein went after a vein with a new unit. Muscular tension was an infallible index of trouble in a case of this kind, and he explored carefully across the upper abdomen. On the right side there was the ordinary springy response; he could feel the tension growing as he moved across to the other flank. Beneath the ribs on that side the muscles were boardlike; he could feel Roy wince as he bore down to test the deeper tissue. He let his fingers move gently to the back, but there was no change.

"What's the blood pressure?"

Karen said levelly, "Seventy over forty."

Chris frowned. "That calls for cortin."

"Waiting," said Sam Bernstein.

Watching them adjust the clear ampule to the tubing of the plasma unit, Chris wondered if it was too late even for cortin. That magically potent extract of the cortex of the

133

suprarenal gland had always worked wonders for him before —along with its synthetic brother that went under the chemical name of desoxycorticosterone. Would it help now in controlling the widespread constriction of the tiny blood vessels all over the body? What if the deadlock that shut down the flow of blood through vital tissues was still unbroken?

Chris moved back from the table for a few anxious moments while the cortin mingled with the plasma flowing into the sick man's veins. At the moment he could not even consider removing Roy to the operating table where he so obviously belonged. The situation was still too critical to risk the slightest strain on a flagging circulation.

He spoke guardedly to Sam. "Looks like a ruptured spleen."

"That was my diagnosis too. Of course you're the boy to go after it."

"Are they setting up for an emergency now?"

Karen said, "The O.R. is ready when you are, Doctor."

Chris turned back to Roy and tested the pulse again. Situated as it was, high on the left side of the abdominal cavity, the spleen was no easy surgical goal; a spleen ruptured by a blow was doubly hard to deliver. He remembered the intern's vulgar but accurate picture: a ruptured spleen was like a smashed bag of raspberries spilling pulp and juice everywhere. For its weight, the spleen was easily the greatest blood container in the body; when smashed, blood still poured through in a steady stream, until the encasing action of the tissues around it brought about a stop in the flow.

This was the optimal moment for operative attack, when the bleeding stopped—perhaps for an hour, perhaps for a week. No one could even estimate the timing beforehand; at best it was a trap for the surgically unsure—a trap that sometimes lured the doctor into believing that the condition was under control, only to have bleeding break out afresh. In that event, death was the reward of mistaken judgment.

In Roy's case, of course, the problem was complicated by shock. Maximum relief was imperative, before the patient could be subjected to the even graver shock of the operation, when life itself would be constantly in the balance until the blood supply of the damaged organ was completely controlled. And yet Chris dared not hesitate too long before he went in. His mind closed and steadied on the hard choice. It did not occur to him that, at the very outset of his career in Milton, he was tackling one of the most dangerous problems on the surgeon's list; he did not remind himself that a surgeon is known, not for the number of his successful operations, but for the paucity of his deaths.

Karen and Sam, he realized, had slipped out of the room while he stood beside the table. They, too, had known what his decision would be; like model acolytes, they had gone upstairs for a moment to give the operating theater a final check. He bent over the pressure dial at Roy's arm and saw that it was rising. It was almost at ninety now; that second plasma unit had made it feasible to put Roy on the table at last. There was a tap on the door, and he turned to give his orders to Karen. To his amazement, two white-coated strangers stood in the hall outside, with a wheeled ambulance stretcher between them.

"Got a man named Benson here, Doc—Roy Benson?"

Chris eyed the stretcher. "Who are you?"

The first white-coat took a step into the room. "We got an order to take him to the County Hospital."

The other spoke from the hall. "That must be him on the table, Bill. Scanlon said it was the nigger helper on the truck."

Chris started to speak and felt the words choke in his throat. He pushed the first white-coat into the hall and shut the door behind him.

"Who gave you this order?"

White-coat said, unruffled, "You heard us, Doc. Scanlon, the super at the main yard. . . . Why didn't you look at the nigger's badge before you admitted him?"

"This man was injured only a few blocks from here," said Chris. His voice, he noted with satisfaction, was wonderfully calm now. "He happens to be a family servant of mine. Naturally he asked to be brought here."

"Listen, Doc"—White-coat had begun to sputter a little now—"I got orders to bring this man back. Doesn't he know he's on Dr. Dwight's compensation roll?"

"The patient is in a dangerous condition. I refuse to have him moved."

"Then let me talk to the head man here."

"*I'm* the head man here. I'm Dr. Land. Will you go to that phone and tell Dr. Dwight I refuse to have my patient moved?"

White-coat dropped his eyes before Chris's level stare and turned toward the phone in the emergency office. His companion merely shrugged and trailed him with the stretcher. Chris completed the grotesque procession, keeping his rage intact. He knew that it was risky to leave Roy alone in the examining room behind them; at the moment, however, it seemed more important to rid his hospital of these leeches.

Chris stood in the office doorway while the call went through. If Dwight was making any objections, the man at this end of the wire gave no sign of it. Halfway through the call he turned to Chris again.

"What's your boy in for, Dr. Land?"

"Tell Dwight that I'm about to perform a splenectomy." Chris kept the sarcasm out of his voice with an effort. "Don't tell him that it's both difficult and dangerous. I'm sure he'll know."

He knew that he was in possession as he spoke. Dwight would be unwilling to lose a patient and a fee. On the other hand, Dwight would be only too happy to let him risk his reputation on a job like this, and hope that he would fail.

The man spoke again from the phone. "He says it's okay if he can send over Dr. Moreau as an observer."

Chris swallowed hard. Somehow he had not expected this. But he kept his voice steady. "Dr. Moreau may watch if he wishes. Now will you get that ambulance out of my driveway?"

In the elevator he stood beside Roy's trolley stretcher, massaging a light dose of morphia into the blood stream. General anesthesia would come later, of course; a little morphia now would smooth the induction of ether in a patient still tense with diminishing shock. Once again his fingers moved over the abdomen, seeking for a change in rigidity between wall and flank. The boardlike tension, he noted, was fixed and somewhat extended. The picture was clear now: blood had spread from the localized area around the spleen into the general peritoneal cavity. Now, if at all, was the time to operate; a fresh hemorrhage and deepening shock would spell the end.

He was not surprised to see Jean Moreau waiting at the door of the anesthetic room when the stretcher rolled into the upper corridor. A sleek and contained figure against the white bulk of Sam Bernstein, who barred the doorway. Behind the two men Karen worked serenely at her dials. Chris found himself returning the Frenchman's bow. If there was resentment in Moreau's manner, it was not apparent to an outsider.

Sam jerked a thumb at Moreau. "Is he on the visiting list?"

Moreau said, "With your permission, Doctor."

Chris nodded. "Dr. Moreau is here with my permission. Will someone help him into a gown?"

He ignored the Frenchman successfully while he scrubbed for the ordeal ahead. But Moreau was already at his elbow as he turned for a final check on Roy. A sleek but dramatic figure now, complete to the tips of pale rubber gloves.

Chris stared at the gloves. "I told Dr. Dwight that you might come in as an observer, Doctor. Not as an assistant."

Moreau said, "I would not dream of assisting, Dr. Land. But may I evaluate the case?"

Sam came forward again, but Chris restrained him. The Frenchman made a careful check of Roy's abdomen. Watching those facile hands, Chris admitted regretfully that the Frenchman knew his business. He was a trifle rough in his pressure: that seemed to be a characteristic of the continental surgeon, Chris knew. Only rarely did they develop the sure lightness that characterized the English and American technique. For all that, it was obvious that Moreau was thorough in his field as he stepped back from the table.

"What is the blood pressure?"

Karen spoke without looking up from her preparations. "One hundred and ten."

"He could be safely moved, then. You still refuse, Dr. Land?"

Sam said, not too patiently, "Listen, Doctor, if you came here to argue——"

But Moreau continued to address Chris directly. "It is more a warning than an argument, Dr. Land. Your operative build-up, I see, is excellent. The risks are still great. Especially since you are working with our patient." Even in an operating gown he managed to bow with his familiar catlike grace. "If I could spare you that risk, I would be only too happy."

Chris looked up in amazement. The Frenchman sounded utterly sincere. "Is this your own idea or Dwight's?"

"My own, I assure you."

"So you'd assume the risk in my place?"

"If you will permit me."

The mocking eyes above the mask continued their challenge. He knows just what Dwight will do if I slip, thought

137

Chris. He knows it'll be a trump in their hand, and yet he wants to spare me. . . . He shook his head. Moreau was a psychic puzzle he could not pause to solve at this moment. He spoke crisply:

"I must decline the offer. You were admitted to this operation as an observer only. If you'll take your place . . ."

He watched the other's eyes widen above the mask and thought he saw a gleam of respect as the Frenchman turned toward the operating room. No one could have moved with more agility to the observer's stool. Even Sam Bernstein's charade of a bow had not spoiled the man's aplomb.

Chris looked down at Roy to make sure that he was comatose under the morphia. "Am I right, Karen?"

"Right as you'll ever be," she whispered softly. "Even if we haven't a donor that matches. Shall we wait?"

Chris hesitated. He had counted on a transfusion before he began; it was even more dangerous to go into the operation without a reservoir of blood waiting to head off trouble. A further drop in pressure could be controlled to a certain extent by plasma, but it could never entirely replace blood lost by hemorrhage; eventually the time would come when only red bloods cells, the oxygen bearers, would serve the purpose. But could he risk waiting for more donors to match against Roy? At any moment now the change he was waiting to forestall might be upon them: once the bleeding spleen reopened, the fight was over.

He heard his voice frame his decision quietly enough. "We're going ahead. Prepare for autotransfusion."

Karen stiffened at the word, then nodded in solemn agreement. Autotransfusion was a heroic measure in operations of this type—entailing, as it did, the use of the reservoir of the patient's own blood as it accumulated in the body cavity. Removed from the peritoneum, mixed with a citrate solution, it was then injected directly into the circulation, where it could take up its vital work immediately. Here was a technique that involved no matching or delay; but it was a tricky procedure at best, and used only in great emergencies.

He knew that he could leave the anesthesia in Karen's hands now, knew that the background preparation would go on without him. A nurse held a sterile gown as he stepped to the door of the scrub room; another nurse whipped out the powdered, sterile gloves and drew them taut. With a small section of gauze he completed the fitting of rubber to fingers, massaging carefully along the joints until there were no wrinkles, until the gloves lay snug against his flesh, offering no obstacle to the messages that tactile flesh must soon relay to brain.

While he completed this final detail he surveyed the operating room itself, as a soldier might con a battlefield. Two nurses were scrubbed and waiting, one for the dressings and packs, one to handle the instruments and suture needles on the adjustable Mayo table. He inspected both setups automatically: the warm packs and sponges, the razored scalpels in a row, the silk and cotton sutures. The instrument nurse was already completing the adjustment of the transfusion machine on a side table—a tall glass cylinder marked off by centimeters.

The anesthetist—he knew it was Karen in cap and mask, but he thought of her as a unit in the team now—wheeled the softly breathing patient under the floodlight. His assistant —it was Sam Bernstein, of course—stepped into that hard white glow from the outer rim of darkness. He examined the patient one last time—he was Roy no longer, but a problem to be solved.

"What's the pressure now?"

"One hundred. It's dropped a little."

He nodded. A slight drop was only to be expected. "Better continue the plasma. We can keep the needle in——"

"What incision, Doctor?"

He looked at Sam across the table as Sam solemnly held up two crossed fingers. He needed no other vote of confidence.

"A left subcostal." This was the best approach to that confined area, between the ribs and the curve of the diaphragm, where the spleen lay—a diagonal incision through skin and muscle to parallel the ribs on the left side. To use it a surgeon had to be confident of his diagnosis, for it sharply limited the area in which he could work. For this reason many surgeons preferred the vertical incision which widened the actual operative field but made exposure of the spleen itself sometimes more difficult.

Sam was painting the area with crimson antiseptic, using pledgets of gauze at the end of a long forceps. Karen had already arranged a small, flat sandbag beneath the patient's left side, turning him slightly and elevating the area where the surgeon must work. Chris stood aside for a moment while

139

the body was draped: towel squares, a windowed sheet exposing the stained rectangle of skin through which he would enter. He glanced at Karen, bracing himself for her nod.

"The patient is ready, Doctor."

"Scalpel!"

The steel slapped hard against his gloved right hand. He weighed the knife for a second between his fingers before he drew it across the body just below the ribs, laying the skin open cleanly down to the glistening fibrous covering of the muscles. He clamped off the instant small spurt of blood. Sam was already draping the incision with wet towels, covering all the skin so that no infection might be introduced from that almost-impossible-to-sterilize area. The scalpel moved on, cutting through the fascial sheath, continuing across the pulpy red fibers of the muscles themselves, severing tissue that retracted to expose the layer beneath. Already the peritoneum was visible—the thin lining membrane of the abdominal cavity. He glanced quickly at Karen.

"I'm ready to go in. How's the pressure?"

"Still dropping. Plasma running full."

He completed his incision, exposing the peritoneum fully, noting again that instead of its normal, glistening white it was a dark blue color, infallible indicator that the cavity beneath was filled with blood. He had seen that warning many times—less frequently in splenectomy, much more often in the dramatic and dangerous complications of childbearing.

"We've plenty of hemorrhage," he told Karen. "I'll work fast for that autotransfusion."

"He certainly needs it."

As Sam paralleled his move, Chris took up a clamp and tented the thin layer of the peritoneum. This was no time for inconsidered hurry. In opening this delicate structure it was possible for an inexpert operator to push the blade of the knife too deeply, damaging the organs which lay beneath. Glancing at the instrument nurse, he received an affirmative nod. The glass cylinder of the transfusion machine was ready to receive the blood, the citrate waiting to mix with the vital fluid to prevent clotting.

He nicked the peritoneum with the blade. Into the opening he inserted the points of surgical scissors, enlarging it to practical dimensions. Blood poured into the incision as he held up the abdominal wall with a narrow-bladed retractor; he scooped it from the wound, poured it into the cylinder;

the nurse agitated it slowly, mixing it with the citrate solution.

He did not wait to check the start of the actual transfusion. When the dark red mixture in the cylinder had reached the level of a quart or more, he took up a large instrument with a ratchet and inserted the jaws into the wound. Spreading the jaws, he opened it wide, letting the ratchet catch and hold as he released the pressure. A self-retaining retractor such as this would hold the wound firmly open, giving him free room to work.

He inserted his gloved hand carefully, to explore deep in the abdomen. Under his fingers he could feel the rhythm of the great artery, the aorta, which coursed through the body here, carrying blood to the organs of the trunk and limbs. Neither the volume nor the rate was to his liking.

Karen echoed his thought, behind the white-tented sheet at the table's head. "The pressure's going down."

Chris reached high now in the left upper abdomen. His fingers encountered soft clotted blood, and he pushed this aside, seeking for the feel of solid tissue, the contour of the damaged spleen. Here was his goal at last: a smooth, rounded structure with a clot-filled rent in its side. His hand was deep out of sight, but his fingers were eyes now, telling him that this was the organ he was seeking, that this was but one of many tears that had extended deep into its substance.

Karen said, "Pulse poor, Doctor. Respiration shallow."

"I've almost got it," he said. "Kidney pedicle clamp, please."

The long, curved clamp came into his hand. Designed for working deep in a wound, it was an ideal instrument to control the blood vessels going to the spleen. He met Sam's worried eyes across the table and knew what he was thinking. The pedicle would have to be clamped blind: there was no time now to work for good exposure. Working by feel rather than vision, surgeons often caught a small portion of intestine or stomach in the clamp without realizing its presence. But there was simply no other choice at the moment. Blood was flowing fresh against his hand as it groped deep inside the patient's body. The wound must be controlled quickly, or control would no longer be necessary.

Carefully he slid the clamp along the inside of his hand until the open jaws engulfed the stalk on which the spleen hung—the pedicle that contained the arteries pumping blood into what was now little better than a damaged sieve. His fingers, taut on the outer end of the clamp, felt the jaws engage something solid. With an unspoken prayer that it was the stalk—and nothing else—he squeezed the handle, heard the satisfying click as the ratchet went home, and held like a vise.

"I've got it," he said softly to Sam. "I've got the pedicle." As he spoke he heard Karen's voice above the sheet:

"The pulse is gone, Doctor."

"Watch the clamp, will you, Sam?"

He checked the transfusion and saw that the patient's own blood was already feeding back into his veins. With circulation re-established, they might succeed even now; more than a quart had been salvaged, and he was satisfied that no more blood was leaving the damaged spleen. But if the pulse was really gone, there was little hope—unless the heart could be shocked awake again—or teased awake. . . .

"Can you feel the heart, Sam?" He was already stripping off gown and gloves, contaminated by that move around the table to check the transfusion.

Sam's hand went into the wound and out again. "It's faint, but it's moving."

Karen said, "The patient isn't breathing, Doctor. I'll use the bag." It was an effective form of artificial respiration. Simply by squeezing the breathing bag at intervals, the operator could force air into the lungs via the anesthetic machine. In simple cases of respiratory failure during anesthesia, breathing could be maintained for hours.

Chris was pulling on fresh gloves now. "I can massage the heart, if necessary," he said, and bent over the operative area once again. There was no evidence of fresh bleeding, and he did not examine the clamp further. Instead he reached high in the center of the wound and felt for the base of the heart, as it lay against the muscular sheaf of the diaphragm. As Sam had said, there was little real movement; the organ was almost gone, thanks to loss of blood and shock.

"Adrenalin hypo, please. And a long needle."

Karen said, "I can reach the precordial——"

Chris shook his head. She was needed badly where she was; any change in the rhythm of that artificial respiration might spell their doom.

"I'll inject directly through the diaphragm." With the heart in his hand, he knew he could shove the needle upward. Of course it was usual for the anesthetist to go in directly through the ribs, over the heart itself. He had never seen an injection performed from this angle, but it was perfectly feasible.

He slipped syringe and needle into his palm, which was supporting the heart through the diaphragm, inching the needle forward until its point touched the base of the great pump itself. He held his breath and pushed upward. There was resistance of the muscle as the needle passed through, and then a sudden release of tension as it penetrated the heart chamber itself. Blood shot into the syringe as he pulled back on the plunger, a sure sign that he was inside the heart. Quickly he injected the dose of adrenalin, whisked out the needle, and, via the diaphragm, began active massage.

Manipulating the organ in a steady rhythm, simulating as well as mere fingers could the routine of a normal beat, he waited anxiously for a change. Somewhere, somehow, one of the tiny centers of nervous control must take over that job, exploding an impulse that would take up the natural function again, the contraction of muscles that went by the name of heartbeat.

There was no response. When he looked at Karen she shook her head faintly. But he would not accept the dictum that a patient who no longer breathed of his own accord, whose heart no longer showed a perceptible beat, was no longer alive. He knew that he was right, in this case at least; knew it for a certainty when he felt the first faint pulsation under his fingers.

Chris skipped a beat in the rhythm of his massage, and the heart under his fingers made up the lack. Faintly, as yet, but definitely. He resumed the rhythm, knowing that the battle was not yet won, that the organ was still too quiescent to resume entirely of its own accord. But he could not quite keep the triumph from his voice.

"It's coming back. I can feel it now."

He saw Karen's eyes glow at the news. The instrument nurse staggered slightly and grasped at the table for support. We're a team, he told himself exultantly. We brought it off. It was an odd feeling, to come out of the concentration that surgery demanded, to realize that others' tension had been on a par with his own.

Karen said, "I can feel it in the wrist now."

The breathing bag filled suddenly as the patient expelled

143

a deep breath. Karen stopped her pressure as the bag filled and emptied with Roy's normal respiration.

Across the table Sam said, "I guess that does it, Chris."

"We can close now. I'll put a ligature around this pedicle." He scooped more blood from the peritoneal cavity, until he could expose the jaws of the clamp holding the pedicle of the spleen firmly closed. Above him he heard Sam Bernstein breathe deep as they both saw that he had placed the clamp correctly, if blindly, without so much as grazing another organ. Carefully he stitched the tissues of the splenic stalk with strands of dark, heavy silk and knotted them securely. Only then did he incise the damaged spleen itself—a smashed bag of raspberries that was harmless now. His eye followed it briefly as he tossed it wetly aside. Then he turned back to the pedicle, making the ligature certain by stitching in a second heavy suture. Sure that there was no more bleeding, he cut the ends of the ties and straightened to look at Karen.

"What's the pressure now?" He knew in advance that it was coming up, for he had felt the pulsation of the aorta as he worked—if anything, stronger than it had been when he entered.

"Eighty," she said, "and getting stronger. Pulse one ten."

"Closing sutures, please."

He thrust the needles rapidly as they came into his hand, tying the strong white cotton threads, bringing the edges of the wound together as neatly as the mouth of a Scotchman's purse. When he had strapped the last pad of gauze into place, Roy was breathing evenly. He stripped off his mask and allowed himself to smile for the first time.

"Blood pressure one hundred," said Karen. "May I have him now, Doctor?"

"He's all yours, Doctor. I needn't add that that was a fine anesthetic."

"May I offer *my* congratulations?"

Chris turned with a slight start as Moreau got down from the observer's stool. He had expected to feel that presence above him as he worked, like a white vulture hovering in the penumbra. Actually he had forgotten the Frenchman completely, long before the first incision.

They walked into the scrub room together as Karen wheeled Roy toward the wards. Sam hovered in the background with an anxious eye cocked in their direction. Chris knew that the little obstetrician was a scrapper when aroused; now that the long pull of the operation was over, he'd like nothing better than the job of ejecting Moreau from Bayshore—by force, if need be.

But the Frenchman was obviously on his way even now. As he scrubbed powder from his hands Chris watched the other shuck his observer's gown in one batlike flurry of his arms and slip on a street coat—a perfectly cut white flannel, with a cornflower in the lapel.

Moreau said, "It is a pleasure to watch your work, Doctor. The patient could not have been safer—even in my own hands. Must I say more than that?"

Chris said, "Thanks for the compliment. It isn't necessary to be polite, you know. You were here to make a report."

"Precisely. For your sake, I am sorry it will be so . . . favorable."

"Would you mind saying that again?"

"Surely my meaning is clear. If you had failed today, our mutual friend would hold a card against you. I do not think he would have played that card. Not immediately, at least. He would have waited—hoping that you were a poor doctor —hoping you would defeat yourself on your own."

They exchanged cold glances across the antiseptic reek of the small, tiled room. Then Moreau turned to the door with a final shrug. *"Now,* Dr. Land, I must tell Dwight that you are as good a surgeon as I. Such praise will make him unhappy, I can assure you. So unhappy that he will probably play other cards—which you cannot trump. . . . Wait, please. Let us not hate each other too soon. I can tell you no more; you must believe me when I say that I work with Dwight but do not share his thoughts." The Frenchman spread eloquent hands. "I can say only that it is dangerous, here in Milton, to be so good a doctor—and so stubborn an idealist. What can I add but *au revoir—et bonne chance?"*

He went out on that—jauntily, humming a little, and twirling the cornflower in his lapel until it presented its brightest face to the world.

ALONE IN HIS OFFICE, Chris sank down at his desk with Jean Moreau's exit line ringing in his ears. As usual, of course, the Frenchman was right: Chris admitted that much to himself without too protracted a struggle. His success with Roy just now would cause Dwight to hate him all the more—assuming that Dwight was capable of such emotion as hate. . . . The compensation doctor was a rather unsatisfactory devil in that respect; a shadow of evil who pulled wires in the background and remained ice cold through most crises.

Now, it seemed, the minor crisis of Roy would broaden soon into open warfare with the rival group. Moreau's warning had certainly been solemn enough. Had Roy died on the table—had the clinic's prestige gone down—Dwight might have hesitated before striking with heavier artillery. With Roy alive, and the clinic flourishing, his enemy could not stay his hand forever.

Chris sat up straight in his armchair, knowing that he could yield no longer to its comforts. He looked thoughtfully at the luncheon tray on his desk and asked himself how long it had been since breakfast. There was seldom time for lunch, in the formal sense, since the clinic had started rolling in earnest. This same tray had chased him all over the hospital: he was lucky to have ten minutes to devote to it in privacy.

A student nurse was at the office door before he could quite finish. Even before she spoke he could guess how quickly the work had piled up. Most of his personnel had been concentrated in the operating room for the past two hours.

"How many are waiting?"

"You've two dozen patients alone, Doctor. Some of them have been here since noon."

He got up briskly, shaking off weariness like a visible threat. "I'll see the first one now, in the treatment room."

The afternoon took its pattern from that moment: the sense of hurry without bustle that would mark a thousand afternoons in the world he had chosen as his own. If the battle for Roy's life had been a peak in his day, this was the valley; only his weariness made it seem a slough of despond, and he shook off that melancholy comparison as he fitted his energies to the groove again. Medical practice, he reminded himself, is not an adventure for the light of heart: much of it is mere dull routine, the minor patching of troubles that should never be, of malingering that masqueraded as illness, of genuine psychic blocks that were not illness at all.

His first case was real enough—a Colles's fracture, with the characteristic upward deformity of the wrist. It went quickly to X ray, and from there to the operating room, where he injected novocain into the broken bone ends while he waited for the plate. There was no doubt about the fracture, but this was compensation work, and it required a full report. For all he knew, the sallow little man nursing his pain on the table was another spy of Dwight's—or a chiseler working on his own, ready to turn even an accident to his profit. Doctors as cautious as he had been sued before this for their failure to X ray.

It was midafternoon before he could steal a moment for the lab and Karen. He saw at a glance that she, too, was working against a letdown. Jim Reynolds was assisting her with his usual dour competence. As Chris entered he held up a small portion of reddish fluid in a sterile test tube.

"Eau de vie d'arthropod," said Jim. "Or should we say *eau de la mort?"* Jim had picked up his ticket home in the suburbs of Havre; he was still proud of his smattering of French. Now he put down the emulsion and added soberly, "As you see, Chris, your host was generous. Shall we try it and pray?"

"Still doubt we've a vector here, Jim?"

"A scientist never doubts," said Jim Reynolds, and handed the lethal test tube to Karen. Chris watched her dip into the chicken-wire enclosure across the room and extract a remarkably bored guinea pig. He wondered if the result would be as important as any of them hoped for. Even if it were positive, even if Paul Travers put on the heat, they had no assurance that the health authorities would act. And yet Chris knew that a positive reaction would point the way for every doctor in his clinic. They'd be sure, at long last, that the time was ripe for rat killing—and more than one species of rat was down on their list.

Karen shook out a syringe and drew the crimson fluid into the barrel. The guinea pig still looked bored as she swabbed his shaved midriff with iodine. So skillfully did she thrust in the needle that the little animal did not even flinch.

"We'll know in a week," she said.

"Come off it, Karen," said Jim. "This isn't enough for the Journal of the A.M.A. You know that as well as I. So does Chris."

"We'll know," she said.

There was no time for more. The same student nurse who was Chris's own private Cerberus had already put her head in at the laboratory door.

"One more patient, Doctor. From West Island. If you'd like to clear your office——"

"Coming, Miss Deane." Chris glanced at Karen. "I came here to ask you to dinner. How are your chances?"

Karen smiled tranquilly. "Bad. How are yours?"

"Worse," he said. "Shall we check in another half hour?"

"I'll stop by, Doctor," she said, professional as ever in front of Jim Reynolds. Jim, Chris reminded himself, was a bang-up doctor; he was apt to be a bit ribald at times, where office friendships were concerned.

In the treatment room he saw only a woman in slacks, seated with her back to him, her hand lying on a towel on the table. He spoke by rote as the nurse handed him the clinic record.

"How did this happen?"

"Sorry, Doctor. I tried to catch a rivet in a bucket—and missed."

He stalked around the table and found himself staring down at Roz Borland—an impish Roz, complete to grease-stained work clothes, her smile unspoiled by a smudge or two.

Roz said, "Don't gape. Remember, you were back of this."

"Since when?"

"Since a month ago. Now I'm a grease monkey on the day shift. If you must know, I started just three days after our talk at the Miramar."

He remembered the nurse at his elbow, and made himself bend over the injured hand. "This is a simple burn. Why wasn't it treated at the yard?"

148

"The dispensary was closed between shifts," said Rosalie. "I was told to come here."

He reminded himself that Jim had been held at the hospital, thanks to the emergency. Next week, with Terry Stone on the job at West Island, he would not be plagued with things like this, at the fag end of a busy day. . . . Now he could only shrug and pick up a needle from the instrument case. She did not flinch as he drained fluid from a blister that had already formed, applied ointment, and dressed the finger with weary competence.

Roz said, "I started a note to you—thanking you for the advice. Then I decided to thank you in person."

"You like it, then?"

"If I told you how much, you wouldn't believe me."

"I might." Again he was conscious of the attentive nurse at his elbow. "Come into my office, while I make out your card," he added, and stared down at the unfamiliar name under her photograph in the clinic files. Then he led the way to his sanctum, ignoring the question in his assistant's eye. Both of them knew that the cards for most patients were made out in the examining room.

For once he felt no sense of relaxation as he closed his office door. He made out her card on the desk leaf, forcing himself to pass over the way she took his swivel chair, the way she curled up in its comfort, like a spent kitten.

"Helen Ogilvie," he said. "Who gave you that alias?"

"Pudge christened me," she said. "Pudge Carrol, the union boss. Dad made him my guardian at West Island when he saw there was no holding me."

"Why not work under your own name?"

"Come, Doctor. You yourself accused me of toiling to the light of flashlight bulbs. Think of the splash it'd make if my fellow workers knew who I really was."

Her smile, he saw, was as disturbing as ever under its patina of shipyard grime. The eyes were something else again. Something had vanished from those hazel depths; in that flash he realized that it was the hectic muddle that had stood between them at their last meeting.

He pulled himself back to realities on that and said sincerely: "Just what do you do at West Island?"

"I've told you. Grease monkey and general nuisance. Right now I'm helping the foreman in the tool shed—and training to be a riveter someday, if I'm that good." The light in her clear hazel eyes had not changed. "You've no idea what those four weeks have done for me, Chris—or have you?"

He controlled his interest with an effort and said flatly: "I may, when the returns are in. Just how did your dad react to the idea?"

"Raised the roof, of course—until he understood that I meant it." There was a dimple in her smile now; her off-center cynicism, he gathered, was coming back fast. "It's just as well he doesn't know you inspired me. He'd probably have fired you on the spot."

"Is he still boiling?"

"Right now he's being rather sweet about it all. I think he's secretly pleased that I'm useful at last. Why aren't you?"

"Remember, I'm your doctor. I must suspend judgment until the prescription takes." But he couldn't quite keep from staring. Part of his mind assured him that this was only another game, of which she must soon tire. Another part—and he admitted freely that it was involved with his emotions—repeated the conviction that she was quite genuine this time. That she would stay on this job for the duration, without flashlights.

"It's taken now," said Roz. "Your prescription, I mean. Come out of that psychoanalyst's whiskers and admire me a little. I don't just look like a shipyard rookie—I am one. And I'm sticking."

"Even if they make you a welder?"

"A riveter," she corrected him solemnly. "That's my life's wish right now. To hold a drill in both fists and stitch up a Liberty Ship for the sea. . . . It's nice to have a life wish that you can touch with both hands. It makes living so much simpler."

He breathed deep and kept his voice calm. "Does it really?"

Roz spoke with the air of thinking aloud. "What amazes me is the fact that it took *you* to show me the way. Why didn't I think of this on my own?"

"Don't you remember? You were too busy enjoying life. With Moreau," he added, and hated himself instantly for the remark.

"But I still go dancing with Jean."

"At the Miramar?"

"At East Point too. Now that I've got the cramps out of

my legs, I enjoy it more than ever. . . . Don't look so sour. Surely a girl can discuss cramps with her doctor."

"What about the general's gallstones?"

"Jean handled those, of course. With his customary éclat." Her impish grin deepened. "Speaking of major operations, I hear you did a lulu yourself this morning."

"Who told you?"

"Jean. You see, he's generous with his praise. Why can't you return the compliment?"

"Maybe you were right about Moreau in some ways," Chris conceded. "I still think I'm right about him in others. Sorry to sound like a bad sport, but—we just happen to stand for different things. Even if we do agree on an operation."

"I heard about the fight," said Roz.

He looked up, startled. "How?"

"From an authority, no less—Dutch Charlie. He saw it all from the steps of the Miramar." Her eyes challenged him now, but they were oddly tender too. "Charlie said you waded in like his own bouncer."

"If you don't mind, I'd——"

"But I do mind. It was high time someone beat Jean's ears back. Believe me, he's been better for it since." She put out a quick brown hand and touched his. Even now he could not help noting the faint white streaks where her rings had been. "Thanks for the K.O. too, Chris. It's something to know that you fought over me for myself—and not for what you hoped to get out of me."

Chris said stonily, "I'll accept Dutch Charlie's compliment on my footwork. Why assume we were fighting over you?"

"What else could you fight over, on such short notice?"

"If you must know, I socked our mutual friend for just one reason. I didn't like the way he saluted the flag." Chris got up, still holding her eyes. "If that's old-fashioned symbolism, you may make the most of it."

"In other words, you two will never get together?"

"Sorry if I've been ungallant, but—you've said it."

"What about us, Chris?"

There was an odd appeal in her voice, a wistful note he had never heard there before. At that precise moment he admitted, once and for all, the existence of a real person under her sleek front—a person who could be completely honest about herself. He could even believe that Roz Borland

151

was trying to work out her own salvation, with her own formula.

Believing her, he let his hand cover hers on the desk. A slender hand, tanned by four real weeks of toil: a vital hand for all its fragile loveliness. A strange excitement coursed through his veins as he felt her fingers respond to his pressure. It took a real effort this time, but he managed to put his professional manner between them once again—a facile mask that shut out emotion for the moment. She would never know how near he had come to taking her in his arms to comfort her. No, he told himself in a savage burst of honesty. He wanted her in his arms for her own sake—because she was slender and vital and desirable. Because he had lived too long on the abstractions that Jean Moreau dissected with such fluent ease.

Roz said, "Of course, if I'm wasting your time with a first-degree burn——"

He released her hand on that and picked up the compensation card.

"That's what I'm here for—Miss Ogilvie. If this injury hadn't been treated properly, it might have kept you from work tomorrow."

"So you think I'll be fit for work tomorrow?"

Chris handed back her card—and stayed carefully behind his mask. "That's how I've certified you. This clinic isn't a feather bed, you know. Nor, I'm glad to say, is the union your Mr. Carrol manages so well. Punch that card on time tomorrow, Miss Ogilvie, or you'll be docked."

She met the challenge head on. "Thanks for reminding me of my place, Doctor. Believe me, I'm quite content to stay there." She went over to the door; he sat immobile at the desk, trying hard to ignore the fact that her long legs were exciting, even in dungaree slacks.

From the doorway she said, "From eight to four I'm a machine that gets better every day. It does well enough, right now, for *raison d'être*. From four o'clock on I'm still Roz Borland. I'll have your scalp yet, Chris—after working hours."

She went out on that, without looking back. He found that he was on his feet now, smoking a cigarette in short, nervous puffs as he paced the narrow strip of carpet behind his desk. In the past months he had fought out more than one problem on that strip of worn matting; somehow the solution to this one eluded him completely.

It was a relief when Karen came in and he could give up his one-sided debate. In fact, the whole debate seemed slightly ridiculous as their eyes met.

"You've seen her too," he said.

"Naturally. Isn't it marvelous?"

"D'you think she'll last?"

"Oddly enough, yes. She's enough like her father for that. Women machinists are born and not made, you know."

Chris sank into his swivel chair again and smiled wanly. "Tell me more about your sex."

Karen smiled. "I was only wondering how the men will react when they come back from war and discover how many women machinists *have* been born, all these centuries. Think of it—all those dishpan hands that might have managed a lathe instead. Isn't it a little frightening, now that dishes can be washed by machinery too?"

"Just how does this social evolution apply to Roz?"

"Don't pretend to be stupid. In my opinion she's had a talent at her finger tips all these years without even knowing it. Quite by accident you've helped her to discover it—and given her the only solid happiness she's ever known. I think you can take a bow, Chris."

"Did Roz tell you that?"

"Surely you must know she came here to thank you?"

Chris kept his eyes on the desk blotter. He said gruffly, "I happen to be a surgeon, not a psychiatrist. If she makes a go of this, it'll be something she's worked out on her own. Besides, I know you backwards. You've come in here to butter me up for another job."

"See? You *are* a psychiatrist too."

Chris groaned. "About this time each evening I begin to wish I were twins. Let's have it, you Simon Legree."

Karen shook her head. "I'm going to let Sergeant Sanders tell it."

"Since when is the Army coming to Bayshore Clinic?"

"Maybe it would be better if they did."

"If this is a plug for Sam's maternity ward——"

Karen's face was grave. "Call it that if you like. I want you to hear the sergeant's story from the beginning and make up your own mind." Abruptly, with a quick glance at the closed office door, she bent over his chair and kissed him. It was the first kiss she had given him in business hours, and he re-

153

ceived it in astonished silence. . . . He did not even stir as she turned to go.

Karen said, "You're a little dense about Roz Borland. I think I can trust you with the sergeant."

It was a full minute before he recovered himself and pressed the buzzer under his desk—a signal that told his admitting office that Dr. Land was ready for business again.

Technical Sergeant Sanders was a slim boy in a sun-faded uniform—as far removed from the noncom of legend as an automatic rifle from a bludgeon. Chris watched him pityingly now as he sat forward on the armchair and twisted his cap in his hands.

"It isn't me, Doctor. It's my wife."

"I gathered that from Dr. Agard. Is your wife with you?"

"No sir. She's in the County Hospital. You see, Captain Bernstein took care of her. Up to a month ago, when I was transferred from Blanding."

Chris frowned inwardly. He might have guessed that Sam was behind this visit. "You mean she's going to have a baby?"

"She had it last week. They operated on her and took it."

"A Caesarean section?"

"That's what they called it, Doctor."

"Who performed the operation?"

"Dr. Kornmann."

The boy's voice was shaking. Chris leaned over the desk to hand him a cigarette. "You might tell this from the beginning, Sergeant."

"As long as my wife was under Captain Bernstein's care she got along fine." The sergeant hesitated. "He'd even arranged with a doctor over in St. Augustine to handle the delivery, at the regular Army rate. Then, as I say, I was transferred to the Ground Force at East Point. Being outside of Captain Bernstein's territory, I figured I'd bothered him enough. So I went to the County Hospital on my own——"

"Is that when Dr. Kornmann took over?"

Sanders nodded gloomily. "He said he was too busy to take us at first. Finally he agreed to handle the case if I'd pay him a hundred over what the government allows. Said his regular fee was twice that. . . . Course I could handle the money end, with my stripes . . ." The boy paused again; the fingers that held the cigarette were shaking.

Chris did not rush him, now that the pattern was taking shape. In the past few years doctors remaining in civil practice had been worked off their feet. Yet most of them still delivered soldiers' wives with the fifty-dollar government allotment. It hardly paid them for their trouble, he knew; it was the contribution most of them made for their inability to enter the Army. A few—or were they so few?—had moved in on this situation like vultures. Like Kornmann, he added grimly, who certainly resembled an overstuffed carrion bird. . . . Doctors of this stripe would use even this need as an excuse to up their fees. Even a buck private could dig up a few extra dollars in an emergency; a technical sergeant, of course, was a prize package for that type of racketeer.

The sergeant said, "When her time came, I took my wife to the hospital. She was having hard pains even then; we'd already phoned Dr. Kornmann. He was busy on another case, he said. But he came in about an hour——"

"I hope everything was all right after that."

"First he said she'd be okay. But after about twelve hours he said——" The sergeant swallowed hard, searching for the phrase.

Chris prompted gently. "Was the birth canal too small?"

"That's it, Doctor. He said he'd strongly advise that operation you mentioned—that Caesarean. And that it'd cost me another hundred, if I wanted our baby born alive."

The pattern, Chris reflected, was still classic. No competent obstetrician would make so sudden a decision; correct measurements were always taken beforehand, to make sure there was no obstruction. If dystocia existed, Kornmann should have known of it in advance. This dramatic gesture had obviously been made to impress the father, and for no other reason.

The sergeant said, "He told me she was getting a high fever too. He couldn't let her go any longer."

"When did he make the section?"

"Five days ago. She seemed to come out of it okay until that night. Then she got a chill."

"Was that the first bad sign?"

"The very first. Next morning she was delirious. But Dr. Kornmann still wasn't worried. Said he'd bring her out of it with sulfa drugs."

Another pat assumption, Chris thought grimly. He remembered his first night in Milton—and the tracheotomy he had performed in that back-country farmhouse. He remembered

Gilbert Dwight's prescription: like Kornmann, he had relied on sulfa to cover a criminal diagnosis.

"Did the sulfa help?"

"No sir. Not a bit."

Again Chris nodded grimly. Puerperal infection, the dangerous and often fatal inflammation that sometimes followed childbirth, was also a persistent camp follower in the case of a hasty Caesarean. Infections of this type, when sections were performed after the trouble had already begun (indicated clearly in this case by the rising fever before delivery), were nearly always caused by anerobic germs—an oxygen-hating streptococcus which was not even stunned by any type of sulfa drug.

"Did she have penicillin too?"

"Yes sir. We got a special allowance and started it two days ago. But it didn't help either." The boy's voice broke in earnest now. "Today they said at the hospital they'd done all they could—that my wife would just have to die."

"And the baby?"

"The baby's fine." The young sergeant looked up haggardly. "Maybe I'm wasting your time with this, Doctor. But if there's an outside chance, I thought——"

"From what you said, everything that could be done has been."

"I know, sir. That's what Dr. Bernstein told me."

"You don't mean he's back on the case."

"We had a talk, that's all. Wanted me to see you. Said if anybody could do anything——"

Chris nodded agreement. He did not even damn his friend for putting him into a very awkward corner. Anyone would be reluctant to close an avenue of escape for this young father. Except Kornmann, perhaps—and Chris guessed that even Kornmann would step aside, now he had banked his fee, if he could keep his own skirts clean.

"Would you like me to see your wife?" Though it was almost certain that he could do nothing, Chris knew that it would help the boy to feel that he had exhausted every hope.

"You mustn't expect a miracle," he added gently. Failure of penicillin and the sulfas had only underlined the picture of anerobic streptococcus. Nothing short of hysterectomy— the removal of a hopelessly infected womb—could alter that picture now. Of course that job should have been done five days ago, at the time of the original Caesarean section. No one but a charlatan would have operated in an ordinary manner on a case deep in labor and showing clear signs of infection.

The sergeant said quietly, "I'm not expecting miracles, sir. But Dr. Bernstein said that if anyone could pass a miracle, it was Dr. Land."

Chris got to his feet and said formally, "Dr. Bernstein is too good a friend, I'm afraid. You understand that you must first speak to Dr. Kornmann and ask for a consultation. If he calls me in, I'll be glad to see your wife this evening."

"I'll talk to him right now, sir. Where can they get you?"

"Here, until six. Our switchboard will trail me after that." Technical Sergeant Sanders whipped into a model salute in the doorframe and went out with a smart about-face. For a moment Chris stood looking after him. Army punctilio seemed to belong to another world now, but it was good to be reminded of it at times. To say nothing of the boy's blind faith in a miracle that would surely never come.

He pulled himself back to the present and went into the emergency room. A number of late-comers were still waiting on the benches. Karen, who had just finished her own clinic, was working over a finger laceration.

"What'd you make of it, Doctor?"

"Puerperal infection. Probably with an anerobic strep."

"That was Sam's thought too. Nothing to be done, I suppose?"

"Probably not. Still, I said I'd see her in consultation."

Karen looked at him levelly over their patient's bowed head—a hirsute cracker from the deep back country, who had obviously deserted the plow handle for better wages. A patient who sat with hunched shoulders as this jargon flowed above his head and waited for the horrors that had not yet come.

Karen said, "They won't like that." She had no need to explain who *they* were.

"I suppose not. There's an even chance they won't even consider it. What have you here?"

"Lacerated extensor tendon. You'll want to repair it. I've sent for the instruments."

He glanced toward the side table and saw that a nurse had already come in with a tray from the operating room. As he scrubbed at the wall basin he wondered again at the cool efficiency that let Karen anticipate every detail of their routine. Her competent fingers brushed his cheek as they tied on mask and operating cap: that gesture, too, was part of the pattern they had made.

Scrubbing finished, he pulled on his gloves and injected novocain, with a reassuring smile for their scared but stolid patient. With the novocain block complete at the base of the finger, he studied the wound itself. The clean cut across the back of the little finger had not severed the tendon, for the tendon had not retracted completely into its sheath, as it normally would in the case of a complete incision. He cleansed the wound gently and examined its depths. Again he was struck by the surgical precision of the gash.

"How did this happen?"

"Been ridin' a stamper all day, Doc—then I go home and nick mahself with mah own razor, damn' if I don't."

"Sure it wasn't someone else's razor in that crap game?"

Their patient grinned for the first time. "Don't ask me t'swear on the Bible, Doc. But I kep' the winnin's, damn' if I didn't."

Chris chuckled as he went to work; here, at least, was a traumatic picture that seemed completely honest. Lifting a gossamer strand of black silk, he pushed the attached needle through the fibrous tissue of the tendon. Working as close to the cut as eye and touch would permit, he looped his thread to prevent slipping, repeated the stitch at the other side of the wound, drawing the severed ends of the tendon together, joining them as snugly as any housewife would have dared. A couple of extra sutures were needed to close the skin before he applied the small splint that Karen held out to him. The aftermath of another crap game was history now, the sort of history that no Southern doctor would write into a compensation report.

Karen watched their patient lumber out, with his great shoulders squared at last.

"A neat job, Doctor."

"Thank the Army, not me. Remember there's nothing more important to an officer than snug buttons."

"If you're not careful, you'll make someone a good wife."

"Any suggestions?"

She wrinkled her nose at him, in the brief breathing spell they allowed themselves. It was impossible, he thought, that this poised viking could wrinkle her nose at anyone. Impossible that she should have kissed him a half hour ago, as he

158

sat in his office chair. Yet she had managed both gestures perfectly.

"Perhaps I should call your next case, Doctor. I think we're both forgetting where we are."

They worked smoothly together to clear the clinic. It was after five when the last patient had departed. Jim Reynolds, en route to one of his private cases, came through the empty room to say good night.

"No cracks, boss-lady," he told Karen. "Dr. Jeff is spelling me till I get back."

"I thought Dr. Jeff was still at White Sulphur."

"So did I, until I looked in just now. He got off the train an hour ago."

Chris was already on his way to his uncle's office. It was totally unlike Uncle Jeff to return to Bayshore without making his presence known. But there was no change in the neat consulting room: his uncle was as much a part of it as ever—a neat, white-coated figure who smiled faintly as Chris entered.

"Don't scold me, Chris. I wanted to be by myself for a little while." He pointed to the folded newspaper on the desk between them, and a circled item.

"The *Gazette* might have run his picture. He deserved that, the old shellback."

But Chris was reading of the death of Cato Embree— ". . . for many years before his retirement, one of Milton's most prominent physicians"—at White Sulphur two days ago. Dr. Embree, it seemed, had visited White Sulphur frequently, to treat an obscure liver complaint, which had caught up with him at last. Interment would be private, at his sister's home in Louisiana. . . . There was a half column in all, in the best style of the small-city paper that has not quite outgrown the flourish of village rhetoric.

Uncle Jeff said, "Cato died just before I arrived. And it wasn't an obscure liver complaint. It was cirrhosis, pure and simple. If you ask me, the rascal went out with a glass of bourbon in his hand." The old doctor polished his spectacles and looked owlishly at his nephew. "As you see, I'm over the shock by now. I'm even trying to take it the way he'd have liked. Remember how he was always promising to leave a bequest in his will—so his friends could have a party after the funeral?"

Chris put the paper down gently, with his eyes on his uncle. But the older man seemed calm enough.

"I'm glad he went like this, aren't you?"

Uncle Jeff nodded. His smile deepened. "I'm not even going to the funeral. My place is here, Chris—that's another thing Cato would have understood perfectly. In fact, I've just one regret: that he didn't live long enough to see us put this clinic over. It would have given me such pleasure to say 'I told you so.' "

Chris found that he was smiling too; it seemed odd to smile, with this news between them, and yet it seemed right too. "What's this—a back-hand accolade?"

"Call it what you like, son—*I'm* happy here. For thirty years I've wanted to limit my work to internal medicine—but I had too many friends. . . . Cato would have shown 'em the door: I wasn't so smart. I was born a medical man, Chris—until you came along I was a G.P. in spite of myself. Can't say I haven't enjoyed it, but this is pure pleasure now." The old doctor's eyes twinkled. "If you knew what it means—to be able to order an ECG on anybody—even if he can't afford it——"

Even if we can't afford it, Chris added silently. For the tenth time that day he let his mind grapple with the unfamiliar demon of arithmetic.

"A lot of doctors feel that way, Uncle Jeff. If enough of them come our way——"

Sam Bernstein put his head around the door. "Here's one now," he said. "Should my ears be burning? And may I speak with you at your leisure, Chris?"

Back in his own office, Chris faced his friend with the deepest scowl he could assume.

"I thought you'd left for the day."

"Me?" Sam's round face was as innocent as a two-year-old's. "Sorry, but I brought in a case. Looks like pneumonia. I'll have to get some sulfa going before I can think of dinner." He made an artful pause. "By the way, did a Sergeant Sanders drop in?"

"He did indeed."

"What did you do with him?"

"I offered to see his wife in consultation. Just as you thought I would, you old conniver."

160

"Okay, Chris. I'll unmask. The kid happens to be a friend of mine. I wanted to help him if I could."

"Kornmann told him the girl was too small to have a child normally."

"Kornmann's a ruddy liar. I examined that young lady myself, while we were all at Blanding. With a good anesthetist, I'd deliver her of triplets."

"She had fever when he operated."

"Is that news to you? I had quite a talk with our refugee shark this afternoon. He'd have murdered that child for an extra hundred bucks."

"Isn't that exactly what he's done?"

The phone rang at Chris's elbow. Switchboard said, "Will you talk to the County Hospital, Dr. Land?"

He smiled grimly at Sam. "Speaking of devils——"

But it was a bored intern's voice, not Kornmann's. The Austrian specialist, it seemed, would like Dr. Land to see Mrs. Sanders in consultation. Mrs. Sanders was the wife of an Army sergeant—a rather special case. Did Dr. Land remember?

Chris snapped, "I remember perfectly. Put Kornmann on now."

"Dr. Kornmann is out on an emergency. He asked me to give you the message."

Chris considered. In the face of rank discourtesy such as this, he was more than justified in refusing to make the consultation. But that would hardly help Sanders or his wife.

"All right. I'll be over in twenty minutes."

Sam was watching him narrowly as he hung up the phone. "Do I gather that Kornmann is afraid to show his face?"

"It begins to look that way. Want to come along?"

"Do I not. Give me time to order for this pneumonia patient. Maybe we can pin down that butcher between us."

The County Hospital was only a short drive from the Bayshore Clinic, on a small hilltop across the railroad tracks. Chris remembered that hilltop well as they drove up the high-banked road in the dusk: a certain real-estate company had bought new offices when the city had decided to purchase the site; a certain mayor had left office under a cloud. . . . Some of that gloom had hung over the County Hospital since it had opened its doors; only with the arrival of the shipyards had the place come into its own. Tonight every window blazed with light along the rambling ground floor as Chris parked

161

his coupé; even the student nurse who looked up from the chart desk had the polish that comes with prosperity.

"Mrs. Sanders' chart? Certainly, Dr. Land."

He heard Sam breathe hard with unholy wrath as they checked the graph together. The chart told the story of the case in jagged silhouette: an irregular series of peaks, each coming in the late afternoon, each tagged with the cryptic word "chill." There was no trending downward in that spiking; in fact, the afternoon reading had reached a higher level than that of the previous day.

"What about penicillin?"

The sleek young nurse flicked her record book. "Six hundred thousand units intramuscularly, Doctor."

It was not a heavy dose, Chris thought. Still, it was enough to have its effect on the temperature curve, if penicillin was indicated in this case. He flipped on through the chart, to read the description of the operation itself: the typed name indicated that it had been written up by the assistant, a Dr. Brenner.

"Kornmann's stooge," said Bernstein in a not-too-inaudible whisper. "If you can imagine Kornmann with a stooge. Fellow classmate of the Vienna diploma mill. Descriptive, isn't it? 'Uterus opened. Pus encountered between uterine wall and membranes.' Shall I call that by its right name?"

Chris read the last word of stiff English. It had been a classical type of Caesarean section: he could not doubt that now. A murderous technique that had spilled purulent material into the peritoneal cavity as it cut through the great blood spaces of the uterine wall; a lethal technique that had injected teeming millions of bacteria into the blood stream of the patient as surely as if they had been introduced with syringe and needle.

Sam Bernstein spoke through tight lips. "Why didn't he cut her throat? It'd have been quicker."

Chris nodded slightly toward the nurse. Apparently absorbed with her temperature graphs, she was undoubtedly drinking in every word. He put down the chart and moved toward the ward in which the patient was lying.

The picture he saw there would have been familiar enough to the obstetrician of a century ago, when infection ran rampant through every lying-in hospital and many women entered their doors to pass through again on their way to the deadhouse. Modern obstetric technique had all but done away

162

with puerperal infection. There was no way to keep the occasional operator from performing a Caesarean section when labor was prolonged, even when the only excuse was the man's own ineptitude. A time like this cried out for the trained obstetric operator, the specialist dextrous at the difficult delivery—or, failing that, the surgeon capable of performing a section which did not involve the spread of infection through the body. Neglect of these precautions was a crime, though it could not be punished by ordinary means. Kornmann and his assistant were proof of that: already they had covered their tracks in a barrage of generalities.

The girl in the hospital cot—she was hardly more—turned her head as Chris and Sam came round the screen. Her eyes, Chris noted, were brilliant with fever and delirium, her breathing rapid; he knew that the fingers plucking absently at the sheet would be burning hot, for all their surface pallor. Her husband sat hopelessly beside her; he leaped to his feet in a quick robot salute.

Sam said, "Forget it, Mike. How often must I explain we've both been beached?"

The boy flushed as he shook Chris's extended hand. "It was good of you to come, sir. I hope you don't think that I——"

Chris let his free hand fall on a tense khaki shoulder. "Forget that too. All you've got to do now is wait outside till we've made an examination." He took the bedside chair the sergeant had vacated and touched the patient's burning wrist. "How do you feel, Mrs. Sanders?"

The girl focused her attention with an effort; her lips framed a fever-bright smile. "Fine," she said. "I feel fine . . . fine." Her eyes moved on to the white surface of the wall beside her, and she flicked at an imaginary insect on the sheet.

Chris examined her gently. He noted the distended abdomen, in this case the fatal evidence of a beginning ileus, the paralysis of the intestines that accompanied peritonitis. The skin was bone-dry, despite the fact that the chart had shown an intake of well over the usual minimum of three quarts. The entire picture fitted the diagnosis he had made before he had seen the patient. He had seen the aftermath of this before, on the autopsy table; had seen the great blood spaces of the recently gravid uterus filled with the products of infection, the reservoirs from which bacteria and their by-products flooded the patient's blood stream, sending the temperature rocketing, roweling the body with the chills of septicemia.

There was no cure for Mrs. Michael Sanders, he told himself—nothing, that is, but the removal, in toto, of that infected uterus. Perhaps it was even too late for a hysterectomy. Most of the surgeons he knew would have been definite enough on that score. He drew Sam Bernstein into the hall to check on that conclusion.

"What d'you think, Sam?"

"She's a goner."

Chris nodded slowly. "All the blood spaces of the uterus thrombosed and infected to the hilt."

"I saw a case like that last year, on the P.M. table. They'd treated her with everything in the book."

"Penicillin?"

"That too. Got a special order. We thought for a while we had it."

"Did you control the septicemia?" Chris was interested now. He watched Bernstein like a cat, letting his fingers clasp and unclasp about the fountain pen in his hand.

Sam looked at him curiously. "Sure. We sterilized the blood for a while—until the bugs kept on coming."

"From the infected uterus."

"Undoubtedly. Why?"

"What if that uterus had come out in time? Would your patient have lived?"

Bernstein's eyes widened. "Could be. I wouldn't dare guess, even."

"Would you dare to guess on this case?"

"Now hold on, Chris."

"You said the blood was sterile. Prompt removal of the uterus *could* have brought infection under control. That's the answer, Sam—I'm sure of it." His voice rose in his excitement. A passing nurse looked at him in astonishment, remembered her training, and moved on.

Sam had read his thoughts by now. He said hoarsely, "You couldn't take a chance like that. No one has taken it before."

"Maybe no one had just this setup before. She'll die without a hysterectomy, you know that."

"Even Kornmann knows that much. That's why he's lying doggo."

"Then it's worth the chance. If Sanders gives me a green light, I'm going in."

164

The little obstetrician gripped his arm. "Whoa there, son! You can't take flyers like this, with the clinic on your shoulders. Not with Dr. Jeff and Karen to think of. Suppose you do go in—and this girl dies. There's less than a fifty-fifty chance of her living, you know that."

"I'd say it was less than one in ten."

"Then think what Dwight will make of this if you fail. You pulled through with your houseboy this noon; this girl is another story. Do you know how fast they'll hustle you out of Bayshore—out of this town?"

"Suppose I'm willing to risk that?"

"To cover Kornmann's stupidity?"

"To hell with Kornmann. I'm saving a life, if I can."

They had dropped their voices to a whisper as a figure approached them down the corridor. Sam shrugged. "It's your throat, Chris. Cut it if you like. . . . Here's the sergeant now."

Sanders' face was white as he came once again to attention. Looking at the boy with wide-open eyes—now that he had made up his own mind—Chris saw for the first time that punctilio was the façade he was holding against the world; that discipline, in this terrible hour, was his antidote for despair.

Seeing the boy clear, he made up his mind. At his nod Sanders followed him into a vacant office that opened into the corridor, sat down with him on a wide leather sofa, accepted a cigarette. Sam, Chris noticed, was much too agitated to smoke. He puffed for a moment in silence, while he waited for the boy's agonized eyes to meet his own.

Sanders said, "Do you think, sir——"

Chris said, "I think there's an outside chance. If you'll consent to a hysterectomy."

He looked hard at Sam, who said flatly, "That's removal of the uterus, Mike. It's acting as a reservoir of infection. We haven't a chance otherwise."

"It's—pretty dangerous, isn't it?"

Chris said, "So dangerous that Dr. Bernstein doesn't think I should undertake it."

"Only because Dr. Land will be criticized for operating at all," said Sam. "At this late date," he added—for no one's benefit but his own. Sanders, they both saw, was too bewildered to react to details now.

When he spoke at last, his voice was strangled but firm

enough. He's been well trained, thought Chris admiringly. He knows that sergeants don't weep. Even when they're in a private room, with people they can trust.

"What are her chances, Dr. Land?"

"With an immediate operation, perhaps one in ten. That's only an estimate, of course."

The sergeant spoke firmly now, without the impediment of tears in his throat. "I haven't much money any more. Dr. Kornmann took——"

"Don't worry about that. I wouldn't operate without moving her to my own hospital."

"Is it safe to move her?"

"We think so. We'd want her where Dr. Bernstein and I could see her constantly."

The boy in uniform said, "I'll take a chance then, sir. If she can't live the way she is, I want you to operate."

Chris held out his hand. "I'll do my best then, Sergeant. We'll order the ambulance at once. What about donors?"

The boy smiled for the first time. "I've got enough friends at East Point to handle that. Six of 'em are matched now, and waiting to be called."

Chris looked at his watch. "In that case we'll have her on the table in an hour. Suppose you hop to a phone and get those donors on their way to Bayshore."

They hurried out of the office in a group, just in time to see a figure hover at the entrance to the women's ward, shrug beefy shoulders, and move on.

"Kornmann, as I live and breathe," said Sam in another of those furious stage whispers. "I didn't think he'd have the nerve."

The Austrian turned as he heard his name. Chris watched with pleasure while a hectic flush mounted from his collar, to lose itself in the bristles of his military haircut.

"Good afternoon, gentlemen. You have examined her, *hein?*"

"Thoroughly," said Sam.

"And you agree with me that it iss a hopeless case?" Kornmann stared coldly at the young sergeant as he spoke. It was a brutal pronouncement, a typical *herrenvolk* approach. Chris clenched his fist to keep from slamming it into the puffy complacency before him.

"I don't agree with you at all," he said quietly. "I think there's an outside chance of saving her."

166

"She hass a septicemia."

"What did you expect?" snapped Bernstein. "When a doctor does a needless section with infection already developing?"

Kornmann's neck swelled like a pouter pigeon; for a moment Chris waited confidently for the man's collar to burst. Would Sam have the privilege of smashing him to a pulp after all?

Sam said quietly, "Hit me if you don't like my language, Kornmann. For my money, you're a butcher with a bad haircut. Or was the Kaiser in your mother's woodpile?"

They faced each other in the wide hospital corridor, the grotesque caricature of a so-called Master Race and the pudgy New York Jew, with hate like a living thing between them. But it was the Austrian whose eyes dropped first.

"There are such things as libel laws, Doctor," he said softly.

Chris accepted the change in tone without comment; he had guessed from the outset that Kornmann was hog fat to his soul. "I agree that there is septicemia," he said. "In my opinion an emergency hysterectomy may remove the focus." He pushed a gaping young sergeant toward the phone booth and faced the Austrian squarely. "Sergeant Sanders has given me full authority to proceed. Will you withdraw from the case in my favor?"

"A hysterectomy?" Kornmann's jaw had dropped at the idea; his small, close-set eyes began to sparkle now. Chris could almost see the wheels turning behind the man's knitted brows. "An interesting idea, Dr. Land. A daring idea. Has it ever been tried?"

"Not to my knowledge."

"In that case, I envy you your courage." The Austrian had been careful to star the noun with a cynical inflection. "What can I do but step aside?"

"You mean you don't object?" barked Sam.

"How can I object? Sanders has called Dr. Land in for consultation. He has accepted his verdict over mine." The beefy doctor shrugged again. "Will you operate here?"

Chris said, "I prefer to work in my own clinic."

"Shall I, then, order an ambulance?"

Sam said, "It's already ordered."

They exchanged bows with the hate of centuries still between them. Sam let out a low whistle as Kornmann stalked out of sight down the corridor.

"I didn't think he'd cave in so quickly. Don't tell me I scared him into it?"

Chris laughed. "No, you Brooklyn fire-eater. Can't you see he was burning to get rid of the case? It saves him a mortality, and he's sure I'll get one myself."

"And give him a bludgeon for your professional brains. Use your brain, Chris. Back out of a blind alley before it's too late."

Chris shook his head. "I'm operating the moment we can get her ready. You don't have to assist, Sam."

"Shut up," Bernstein growled. "Who got you into this, anyhow?"

Back at Bayshore they found Karen writing up a night emergency. As Chris had expected, she took the news quietly.

"Have you talked to Dr. Jeff?"

"I thought I'd keep him out of it."

Karen said, "He'd never forgive you if you did that. We're a group, aren't we?" She had already picked up the phone to dial Dr. Jeff's consulting room.

The warmth of that reaction still lingered when Chris took up the phone and heard his uncle answer. It was all the incentive he needed to lay the case on the line, without mincing words.

Uncle Jeff said crisply, "I'll be in the O.R. the moment I've cleared my office."

"Does that mean you approve?"

"Surgery is your job, son. Whatever you say goes."

Chris sat down and lit a cigarette. As usual, he was perfectly calm, now the die was cast. "It's okay," he told Karen. "We'll get a transfusion into her while you're setting up. Sam can handle that."

He looked up, a bit startled to see that Bernstein had already anticipated his order. Karen smiled.

"I told you we're a team, Chris. What anesthetic?"

"What about a continuous caudal?"

"That's my department," she said. "I'll set up for it at once."

So his team had assembled, as simply as that, without even waiting for orders. Alone in his office, Chris sank deep into his armchair, disciplining his nerves into the absolute quiet that was essential to the job ahead, if this brief respite was to mean anything. His father had sat in this office before him —hundreds of times, perhaps, while he awaited his summons to the operating room. Had that other doctor ever faced the decision his son had made tonight?

Again he reminded himself that most surgeons would consider the operation he was waiting to perform a foolhardy procedure. Perhaps it was. A case like this was almost surely doomed in advance, in spite of the sulfas, penicillin, transfusion. In daring to remove an infection-ridden uterus, he might be using his skill in vain. Sam had not magnified the risk by an iota: loss of reputation would be the reward of failure, perhaps even a criminal action against him—for a doctor is always vulnerable to legal chicanery, especially when the risk he takes is justified.

Even if he succeeded . . . He remembered his success with Roy this morning, and the ominous warning from Moreau. Success with Mrs. Sanders would be another red flag. . . . Kornmann was probably making his report to Dwight at this very moment. The rival group would wait like patient spiders for the news: good or bad, they would be sure to move against him.

He stretched out deeply in the armchair and refused to let his mind stray from the main purpose. Personal gain would be a small thing beside the knowledge that he had saved a life. He heard his ambulance roar up to the emergency entrance: he could have watched his interns unload the patient, simply by turning his head, but he knew the pattern too well. He could picture the white-faced boy walking down the hall beside the wheeled stretcher—down to the door that barred further progress. He pictured him pacing the waiting room, lifting his head to follow the progress of each passing nurse, not quite sure to be glad or sorry that the footsteps had passed him by. . . . In another hour or so, if all went as he hoped, he could walk into that waiting room with good news. He could tell Sergeant Sanders that a butcher's blunder had been overcome, that a girl who might have died would live.

That, he repeated solemnly, would be reward enough for now.

11

He checked the transfusion setup while he awaited Karen's call and saw that preparations were complete. As Sanders had promised, several donors were in the anteroom; as an added precaution, ampules of plasma were ready at Sam's elbow. In a case of this type it was impossible to be too careful: a transfusion, or multiple transfusions, would control blood loss during the operation itself. He did not consider too lightly the prospect of an uncontrollable hemorrhage: tissues infected as these undoubtedly were might be difficult to hold with either suture or clamp.

A nurse signaled through the white swinging door, and he went to the dressing room to complete his scrubbing. Through the glass window to the operating theater he saw that Karen was setting up for caudal anesthesia, arranging the slender, malleable needles that could be knotted without breaking, connecting the tubing with the reservoir from which the drug itself would run.

Tonight he could thank his lucky stars that he had ordered this equipment when he took over the clinic. This new anesthetic method—injecting into the hollow space at the end of the spine, and forcing the solution outside the lining of the cord itself—had already accomplished wonders in obstetrics. More recently it had been adapted to regular abdominal majors. Little of the fluid absorbed into the body itself; in the case of a poor-risk patient there were none of the disturbing effects upon heart action that so often accompanied ordinary spinal anesthesia.

Watching Karen as he snapped on sterile gloves, he saw her turn to the sick woman at her side. Even in delirium there'd be no trouble in handling Mrs. Sanders now: morphia had soothed away reality for her long ago. He came into the room as Karen beckoned, and took up a small syringe filled with novocain. At the lower end of the spine he located the opening in the bony sacrum that gave access to the space he was seeking. Injecting a small wheal of novocain into the skin, he infiltrated the deeper tissue with a longer needle. Now he could be sure that there would be no reaction to pain, no flinching to interfere with the passage of the next needle—through which the anesthetic solution itself would be injected.

Here, ready in his hand, was the first minor crisis in the job ahead. He pushed the long, flexible needle through the skin, continuing the steady pressure until he felt it break through into the space inside the sacrum, between the meninges around the lower spinal cord. Whisking out the metal stylet, he stood for a moment watching the open end of the needle. If the meninges themselves had been penetrated, the anesthetic he was using would be contraindicated; drip from the spinal fluid would advise him of that at any moment now.

He took up a second syringe, half filled with novocain.

"We'll inject a little, to make certain it's not in the spinal canal."

Sam watched him inject ten cubic centimeters into the space he was testing. "How long do you wait?"

"Ten minutes will do. If the solution penetrates to the spinal fluid, we'll have spinal anesthesia, with loss of function of the legs."

"You mean that caudal anesthesia in this amount would have no effect on the motor function of the legs?"

Chris nodded, and compared his watch with the clock on the wall: it was one of those moments when extra words are superfluous. He watched Karen as she dissolved an ampule of the brown penicillin solution in a small amount of water. When it was finished she injected it into a regular bottle of salt solution already connected to a needle in the patient's veins. . . . His whole thoughts were concentrated on the hands of the clock above them; he hardly looked up when Dr. Jeff's masked face appeared like an anxious moon in the half-light beyond the table.

"Continuous penicillin, Chris?"

"We'll keep it working for days, if need be." He did not add that the next hour or so would tell them if therapy of any kind was needed. . . . The hand of the operating clock jumped with a barely audible click. Chris snatched up a needle and jabbed deeply into the patient's skin. A thorough-

171

going jab that would penetrate to the semiunconsciousness of the preanesthetic injections.

He all but shouted aloud as she groaned and flexed her leg. Sam was grinning too, across the table.

"There's no spinal block there, Chris."

He spoke tersely to Karen. "Start the injection at once, will you?" Back at the side table, he stripped away his gloves and held out his hands for a change. Karen had already begun to force the prescribed load of anesthetic solution into the space inside the sacrum. Traveling between meninges and bone, it would block off each nerve root as it left the spinal cord, raising the level of the anesthesia to the point needed for the operation. In this case the operative level need not be high: if necessary, operations could be performed in the upper abdomen under the same type of blocks.

Chris held out his hand for the scalpel. "How is her condition?"

Karen spoke as she worked. "Bad. Temperature one hundred and five."

One hundred and five was the highest point so far. At any moment a body-shaking chill might occur, jeopardizing the already slim margin they were working under. Across the table Sam's unspoken thoughts were in his eyes. It was not too late to stop, even now—to decide that the rising temperature meant a breakdown of some last barrier. True, the abdomen was already draped, the skin painted a crimson only a trifle less brilliant than the flush of the patient's fever. He could still wash his hands of the whole affair. Once he accepted the scalpel, there could be no drawing back.

He stretched a taut arm toward the Mayo table and felt the steel slap into his hand. His brain stood coldly aside for a moment, watching the knife move smoothly down the tensed skin for the full length of the proposed incision.

"Hemostats, please."

For a moment there was no sound but the click of the instruments as their jaws clamped down on blood vessels opened by the swift-moving knife.

"Coagulation."

In this type of operation it was quicker to coagulate each bleeder with the high-frequency current, avoiding the time lost in making individual ties. Sam's hands moved after his down the length of the wound, touching each clamp in turn with the electrode as Chris lifted it. Half heeding as he

172

worked, he heard the faint buzz from the machine, the hiss-and-popping sound as each tiny bit of tissue in the clamp cooked in the current . . . and lastly, the clatter of the clamp as his dancing fingers dropped it in the basin.

He took a fresh scalpel now, to attack the tense fascial layer throughout the length of the incision. The muscle appeared, its rich red tissue bulging through the opening. Carefully he separated the fibers to expose the infection-dulled sheen of the peritoneum. So far the operation had moved in record time.

"Condition unchanged?"

Karen answered, without raising her eyes, "Shall I start another transfusion?"

He nodded as he tended the peritoneum with Sam's aid and went in. Instantly cloudy fluid spilled through the edges of the wound.

"Suction, please."

The tubing dropped smoothly into the depths of the pelvic cavity. As the machine whirred, the receptacle below it gleamed with its yellow intake of pus.

"Peritonitis," said Sam Bernstein. "Peritonitis—and how."

Chris nodded, with his eyes on the incision. The whole picture was both ghastly and typical: the furry exudate on the bowel, the distended, quiet loops. Doctors called this adynamic ileus, a strange paralysis that had been a prelude to death in more cases than he cared to remember now.

He said only, "We can handle the peritonitis, Sam. Let's have that infected uterus."

The obstetrician bent with him over the wound. Already they could see the organ clearly. Kornmann's sutures, closing the incision through which the child had come five days ago, shone against its surface, like a cross-stitch in a nightmare.

"Balfour retractors."

Chris spread the metal frame, extending the arms until they had distended the incision, permitting easy access to the pelvis. Sam stood ready with a large pad moistened in saline; when Chris lifted the uterus, he whisked the pad under it, separating the bowel to expose the lower portion for the waiting clamps. Both of them knew that no partial surgery would suffice here, that the infection had spread through muscle and blood spaces. Nothing else could account for the boggy, unhealthy feel of a normally muscular organ.

"Large clamps."

With the uterus in his left hand, Chris placed a clamp across the broad ligaments on either side of the organ. Sam had already paralleled the move with a second clamp. The knife went down through the tissue between. A quick suture tied off the blood supply passing through the ligament; a minute's work completed the process on the other side. The uterus was now freed, held only by the tissues beside the lower portion, the cervix, through which coursed the main blood supply to the organ itself.

Here, he knew only too well, they would almost surely run into trouble.

"Large clamps, please."

This time he tested the instrument in his hand. It was of heavy metal, heavier even than the clamps he had been using. Here, of all places, he could not risk a slip that might release a stream of blood from an open vessel. He let the jaws bite gingerly around artery and vein, feeling the tissue of the pelvis fever-hot against his fingers. Then he held his breath and let the ratchet click home.

The clamp held. Wordlessly he passed a second clamp to Sam, who applied it on the other side. The scalpel severed the uterus from the stump of the cervix. He saw that there was little bleeding, though the blood vessels under his hand were filled with friable clot. Each of them, he knew, was teeming with bacteria. A slip of the knife, at this point, could mean an injection of death direct into the blood stream of himself or his assistant. It was the kind of accident that had nipped more than one promising surgical career in the bud.

The uterus came away into his hands at last. He dropped it into the ready basin and took the suture from the instrument nurse. The sharp needle bit through the tissues at the end of the clamp. He tied it tightly, noting as he did so how the suture material cut into the inflamed tissues. Grasping the other clamp gently, he made ready to control that too by a suture. A few moments more, and the worst would be over. Closing the abdominal wound would be only a matter of minutes.

He had turned his eyes toward the needle holder which the nurse was handing him when a sharp intake of breath from Sam made him glance back at the wound. What he saw made him drop the needle and reach for a pad of gauze. In the instant that he stuffed the gauze as a dam against

174

the dark flood welling beside the stump of the cervix, he knew what had happened.

It was a common accident in this kind of emergency, one of those imponderables that no operator could avoid when dealing with tissue in this stage of infection. While he worked against time, the clamp had bitten through the invaded tissue, cutting the uterine artery and perhaps the vein as well. The artery, surely—for the pressure of the gauze alone did not control the ooze of blood, only slowed it somewhat.

"Can you clamp?" asked Sam.

Chris shook his head. "We'll control by pressure until I can put in a stitch." He let his fingers move along the cervix, feeling for the tubular section of the artery that lay there. Thanks to the inflammation of the tissue, it was difficult to distinguish structures; yet the artery must be located promptly, or they were lost. He let out his breath as he found its pulse at last—a hurried pulse, faint but definite. His fingers closed. Immediately there was a slowing of the sweeping flow of crimson from the depths of the cavity.

"Sponge away, please."

Sam's gloved hand was already busy above his own. When the area was clear, he saw that there was no further flow. He spoke to Karen without daring to look up.

"How is she?"

"Blood pressure has dropped twenty points. I've stepped up the transfusion."

"Suture, please."

The dark thread streamed away from his hand as he began the all-important stitching. With the needle deep in the tissues beside his fingers, he made sure that the blood vessel he now controlled was within the loop of the ligature.

"Will you tie, Sam?"

Bernstein took up the ends of the ligature, set the knot, and pulled it tight. Only then did Chris release the pressure of his fingers. They waited, motionless above the wound, knowing that it was useless to proceed unless the tie had held. Nothing happened. The ligature, firmly anchored, had closed the damaged blood vessels.

Chris said only, "That was close."

"Too close." Sam's forehead was beaded with sweat.

"Drain, please."

Chris placed the soft rubber drain deep in the pelvis; an outlet was essential here, since he knew that infection still remained in the area of the cervix, for all that sweeping incision. They had done what they could for the patient; they must depend now on her natural resistance to turn the tide. Once again he thanked heaven that he had not stinted the clinic on equipment. Everything was at hand to help the body's fight back to health: penicillin, transfusions, plasma, glucose, the double-lumened suction tube . . .

"Closing sutures."

This was no time for the fancy surgery that devoted a half hour to insuring a hairline scar. Heavy sutures—thrust deep and tied across to rejoin the sundered abdominal wall—were the weapons of choice. Time saved by a quick closure could be devoted to helping the sick woman in other ways.

He tied the last stitch and turned back from the table to Karen. "Will you get her to her room at once? We'll give her an ice sponge."

Back in the scrub room there was no time to think of fatigue as he dressed. When he reached the sick woman's side again, Karen was already wrapping the patient in sheets wrung out in ice water.

"The old typhoid treatment."

"It should work here as well."

"I hope so."

There was no need to say more as they worked together. Experience had taught them both that a surgeon's battle has sometimes only started when it seems won.

Sam came into the room as they finished, carrying a Miller-Abbott tube. This lifesaver in many a case of peritonitis was really two tubes in one: a large sheath, connected to a metal tip by which continuous suction of a distended alimentary canal could be carried out, and a smaller tube with a balloon at the end, capable of inflating as it entered the intestine, relieving distention as it went.

Sam said, "I never had much luck getting these things through the stomach."

Chris turned aside from the bed. "I picked up a new twist on that in Rome. We'll put the tube down as far as the stomach and then inject mercury into the balloon. The weight will push it right along after that."

The three of them worked together for more than an hour, connecting the suction apparatus, replacing a penicillin needle vital to the continuous flow of the drug that would save Mrs. Sanders now, if anything could. The strange chemical process, by which a mold extract dealt death to germ invaders, was in charge of the case now.

It was well toward midnight when Sam gave up his place at the bedside to answer an emergency call; another half hour before Chris and Karen could turn the job over to a watchful nurse and repair to the diet kitchen for a snack. Karen took fruit juice from the refrigerator while Chris slumped into a chair. It was good to acknowledge that he was bone-tired now—good to sit quietly while Karen's deft hands prepared their meal.

Her voice was quiet, too. "You're working much too hard, you know."

"So are you."

"Perhaps we both need a day off, Chris."

"Make it a month, can't you?"

Karen said, not too severely, "We'll be lucky to get a Sunday. Suppose I took you up on that sailing date?"

He had a sudden, vivid picture of the *Lady Jane*, sails bellied in a following wind, and this tall viking babying the wheel. He let it build in his mind, feeling his nerves relax.

Karen said, "This girl should be out of danger by tomorrow, if she's coming out. And your houseman is resting like a two-year-old. Couldn't Sam handle the rest?"

"Yes, barring blitzkrieg by Dwight."

"Then why not take up my invitation?"

He covered her hand with his—not at all casually. "My yawl has been waiting for a month now. Suppose you take *me* up?"

"The snapper are running off South Island," she said. "We can take our tackle."

"Or we can just loaf, and learn each other's middle names."

She did not withdraw her hand. "Of course it all depends on Mrs. Sanders. What do you really think?"

"It's too soon to tell, of course." Her easy reminder brought him back. "Having that vessel break loose didn't help her any. I should have known better than to use clamps."

"Everyone does, Chris."

"That's no excuse, with the inflammation we found. I should have seen what was coming."

"Did you ever have it happen before?"

He grinned. "No, thank you. I suppose I was lucky this time. She didn't lose too much blood."

"That's better," said Karen. "Speaking of stubborn doctors, did Uncle Jeff give you the news on Cato?"

Chris's face sobered. "It's hard to believe he's gone. Maybe he was a troglodyte, but I loved him."

"Did you know he was half thinking of joining us? If he'd been younger——"

"Cato? Why, he'd never approve of a get-together like ours."

"Perhaps it was the fight ahead that attracted him, then. He told me he'd give ten years of his life to be with us."

"Then he wasn't as old as I thought. Or maybe I'm not the only one you affect that way."

She blushed but rarely; he thought it a pity, for the rich red that stained her throat was more than becoming. Yielding to a sudden impulse, he pulled her down to his knees and kissed her.

"Did I ever tell you that you're a lovely girl?"

Karen, unperturbed, brought another of those absurd wrinkles into her nose. "Often, Chris. Usually when you're tired, and happy. I suppose I should be flattered, drawing compliments from your best moments."

The kiss she gave him back was friendly but not ardent. For all that, it was a kiss with a promise; he accepted it for the present, without asking more. It was good to turn to life again like this, after cheating death for an hour; good to hold the promise of all their tomorrows in his hands.

Karen cupped his face in her own hands for one more kiss. Then she got up slowly from his knees. There was no provocation in the action, but he knew without asking that she had enjoyed being there.

"Suppose we check on that girl, Chris. Then you need some sleep."

When they looked into Mrs. Sanders' room they found her sleeping quietly under the drugs. Thanks to the ice sponge, the reading on her temperature chart was more than gratifying. The night special smiled up at them.

"You can go to bed with a clear conscience, Dr. Land."

And Karen added, "There's an empty room across the hall. I had the cot made up."

They said good night under the benign but watchful eyes of the night special. "Sure you aren't afraid to go home alone?" he asked.

"Why should I be?"

He watched her tall figure swing down the hall. After all, it was a question he could hardly answer, with one of his best nurses within earshot. And then, with the door of the empty room closed behind him, he realized how tired he really was. Too tired to do more than kick off his shoes before he was on the narrow hospital bed, asleep.

It was staring daylight when he wakened; his feet fumbled automatically for his shoes and found them instantly, thanks to the training of his intern days. Dousing his face in cold water, he looked at his rumpled hospital clothes and decided to ignore appearances for once. At the moment it was more important to know how Mrs. Sanders had passed the night.

The day special at the sick woman's bedside stood up and smiled. That was his answer, of course; but he took the chart just the same. The lowered pulse rate, the sharply dropping temperature curve, told him that the infection was losing ground. He moved the covers gently to study the operative wound; there was some drainage, of course, but the abdominal swelling had definitely subsided. The nurse smiled in earnest as she handed him the X ray he had ordered the night before. There was no mistaking the dark metallic blob of the mercury they'd put into the Miller-Abbott balloon. It was well on its way to relieve the small intestinal distention which was one of the greatest immediate threats to recovery.

The day special said, "She's taking fluids, Doctor. And the penicillin's going in splendidly."

He felt like shouting. It looked very much as though they had won the battle.

Outside, in the clean-washed air from the Gulf, he got into his car for the drive to St. Lucie. At the first turn to the Bayshore Road he did permit himself a small, exultant whistle. He found that he was still whistling as he rattled over the bridge to his boathouse landing. This was a medical victory for the Journal; balanced by the splenectomy he'd done on Roy, it went far to make up for the child he'd lost that first night in Milton.

At the boathouse steps he paused and glanced at the windbreak of Australian pines that separated his house from Karen's. Karen would be glad to know of their success, he told himself—and found that he had already sprinted across her lawn to hammer on the screen door of her veranda.

179

When there was no response he added his voice to the din he was making. "Karen! Are you up?"

Her voice came out to him, drowsy with sleep—just as he reminded himself to glance at his wrist watch and saw that it was barely seven.

"Chris?"

"Who else would have the nerve?"

"Come in," said Karen. "You know I don't lock doors."

The invitation sent his pulse hammering; he could not have said why. Yet he paused on the threshold of the living room, remembering once again that her bedroom was just beyond. The casual way she had unfastened the back of her play suit as she went through that same door a month ago . . . Now she came out yawning, her hair a pale aureole on her shoulders, her eyes foggy with sleep. She had thrown a filmy robe over what must have been an even more filmy nightdress; he forced his eyes away, not sure that the faintly visible pink glow through the fabric was not her flesh.

He knew that the pause had saved them both; he was comparatively sure of himself when he dared to raise his eyes and smile at her.

"I knew you would be."

"Would be what, Chris?"

"Lovely in the morning. As lovely as you are at night." He came forward and took her hands, forcing himself to make the gesture light. "You see, I don't just pay compliments when I'm exhausted."

"Surely you didn't rout me out to tell me that."

He crossed the room and took a cigarette, nursing his news a little. The letdown—now he had assured himself that it would not be cricket to take her into his arms—was more than compensated by the news he had brought her.

"I'll take even money that the Sanders girl gets well. Sorry —I couldn't wait to let you know."

Karen sat down on a chair arm and let out her breath in a delighted sigh. "You can wake me up any time for news like that. Now that it's over, I don't mind admitting I was worried."

"So was I. Did I show it?"

She shook her head loyally. "Not even when you went after that bleeder. Wait till Kornmann hears *this* news, Chris. Wait till Sam spreads it 'round at the next doctors' meeting."

"I'm not thinking of that," he said. "I suppose it's unprofessional, but I'm glad for the kids' sake. Both of them, I mean."

"Just for that, you earn breakfast," said Karen. "Do you want to go to the boathouse and shave while I make coffee and toast?"

"And kippers, the Norwegian way."

Her eyes laughed at him as she shooed him toward the door at last. "Do you like the Norwegian way?"

"If I told you how much, you'd give up nursing and open a restaurant."

His phone was ringing when he ran across the lawn to the boathouse. To his surprise, it was Seward Harper.

"Could you stop on your way to the hospital?"

"Don't tell me you're at your desk that early."

"Nowadays a banker must get up early to make anything. Or should I say *especially* a banker? You seem to be doing first-rate."

"What's in the wind?"

"It'll keep, boy. If I told you over the phone, you probably wouldn't believe it."

Chris dropped Karen off at the hospital and swung his coupé back toward Duval Square and the bank building. He wondered what new complication had come up to plague his existence. Offhand he could think of nothing. For once everything seemed eminently right.

Seward was already deep in work when he walked into the glass-walled sanctum. "From this distance you look happy enough," he said. "How's the clinic going?"

"At the moment it's ticking like a clock."

"What about the money end?"

"I haven't put in an adding machine yet, but I'd guess we're breaking even."

"You should." Seward took off his glasses and polished them slowly. Chris knew it was a trick he had when he was about to break a bit of news. At the moment he couldn't even guess if it was good or bad.

He said tentatively, "Any rumbles from Borland so far?"

"We had a general talk just before he went North. Barring an epidemic or another Act of God, I'd guess that he'll go on being pleased."

Chris nodded soberly. He knew that his success in this whole experiment of group practice depended on keeping Borland satisfied. The shipbuilder must be convinced that his

181

workers were getting at least as good medical care as they would have received in Gilbert Dwight's camp.

Seward said, "I didn't bring you here for a session of back-scratching, Chris. It's about Cato."

"Cato Embree?"

"Did you know he left something to the clinic before he died?"

Chris looked up in surprise. He vaguely remembered the conversation he had had last night with Karen, in the diet kitchen.

Seward said, "It was you he approved of, Chris. I reckon he thought there couldn't be much wrong with a project you'd underwritten."

"I thought we weren't back-scratching, Seward."

"Easy does it, boy. I'm only preparing you." The banker burrowed into his desk and came up with the papers he was seeking. "Cato was pretty cagey, you see. He even knew that you're incorporated so that inheritance taxes can't touch you. That means you get the whole hundred thousand, clear and clean."

Chris found his voice with an effort. "Stop me if I'm wrong. Did you say a hundred thousand?"

"On the line. No strings." Seward flipped through the papers under his hand. "I can put it in your account today, if you like. Cato left his estate in apple-pie order, and I'm his executor."

It was the sort of news you blinked at a moment before you digested it completely. As Chris sat blinking now he thought first of Sam Bernstein. His plump friend could go back to obstetrics now, instead of assisting at surgery. Terry or Jim could double at that chore when Uncle Jeff was engaged; he'd go into the open market, corral the best dispensary manager available. And of course he'd pick up the deed tonight for the old Slade mansion across the way. He'd been resisting the temptation to make it an annex to the wards for two weeks now. . . .

Seward said, "You can sign the papers later, if it hasn't percolated. I just wanted to break the news as gently as I could."

"Could I keep this as a separate fund, outside the account?"

"Of course. You and your uncle are the sole directors of the clinic's finances. But why?"

Chris spoke slowly. "I don't quite know. I suppose I'd

like to prove that this thing can carry itself. . . . With a hundred thousand in reserve, I can really experiment. Know I can back up my beliefs. Later—if my beliefs are sound—we could use it to found a memorial. A research lab, with 'Cato Embree' on the name plate."

Seward nodded. "The old man would have liked that." He passed over a sealed envelope. "Incidentally, here's a personal letter to you, explaining the bequest. Suppose I get Luke Fraser in to draw up the transfer papers? You can sign them at your leisure, if you want to keep the cash on ice."

Chris put the letter in his pocket. "Sounds like a good idea," he said vaguely. "Do you mind if I work this off my own way? I'm still a little dazed."

At the entrance of the large waiting room at Bayshore he paused for a moment, as he always did. The room was packed, as usual: a day's work waiting for each of them. In a clinic room he could see Sam Bernstein's bald head gleam pinkly as he bent over a patient. The little obstetrician looked up with a grin when Chris called good morning through the door.

"That girl's going to get well," he said. "I still can't believe it."

"Would you believe me if I said you'll have your own obstetrical clinic in about another month?"

Sam's eyes sparkled at the news, but he kept his voice sober. "Sure you can swing it, Chris?"

"No doubt about it. We're in the velvet."

He left Sam fairly dancing for joy at the news and moved down the hall to his uncle's office—remembered that Uncle Jeff was out on calls this morning and moved on to the lab. He had saved her for last; his mind still hesitated over the best way to tell her that the clinic was over the top.

This morning Dr. Agard looked every inch the scientist as she removed a smear from the microscope. Even her voice was professional.

"Would you care to examine this, Doctor?"

Chris focused the eyepiece as she returned the glass to the operating field. A cluster of brilliant red lines occupied the center of the smear, with the fainter shadows of cells in the background.

"Looks like acid-fast, doesn't it?" This staining feature

183

distinguished the tubercle bacillus from all others. Even when it was treated with acid, the brilliance remained.

Karen nodded and smiled. He wondered why the discovery should please her. "It's a sister of a pilebuck foreman. There are several children in the house. This one came in because of a cold, but she had a history of losing weight——"

"Did you X ray at once?"

She picked up the film from the table. There was no mistaking the fluffy shadow under the collarbone.

Karen said, "It could have been atypical pneumonia. But I checked the sputum, and there it is."

Chris chuckled in approval. "Now I see why you're so happy. This is one case we've caught in time."

"I'm starting a pneumothorax now. They're already arranging to send her to a sanatorium to continue the treatments."

It was another affirmation of his faith in this type of practice. Thanks to the low cost, the parents had sent the child for an early checkup, while the disease was still easy to treat. The average doctor, working on an average fee, might well have skipped the X ray to save the family's pocketbook.

Karen echoed the thought. "In private practice she'd have been treated for a cold and sent home."

"And spread her T.B. among the other kids. We'll show them yet, won't we? Thanks to Cato, we can't fail now."

He watched her lovely eyes widen as he told her of the legacy. He was hardly prepared for the sudden kiss she gave him.

Holding her at arm's length, he said, "I should inherit money more often. Won't you let me finish? I'm buying the Slade place now, for a maternity annex."

"I should kiss you again for that."

"Sam almost did, when I told him."

Her eyes held him as she drew away at last. "You're a modern miracle, Dr. Land—in case you didn't know."

"Right now I'm more interested in our holiday tomorrow. What about Paul Travers? Think he'd like to come along?"

He watched her narrowly, but her expression didn't change. "I already asked him. And you'd better get to your clinic now—legacy or no legacy."

Chris looked at his watch and whistled. "Without even time out to turn a cart wheel," he agreed. "Anything special waiting?"

"Jim Reynolds has a report he wants you to check. He's very secretive about it."

Jim's report was lying open on his desk when Chris walked into his cubicle; Jim himself came in as Chris was reading it, looking as harried as usual, but much happier.

"What d'you think of my blood count?" He took the paper from Chris's hands. "Did you notice the small number of platelets?"

"What's the history?"

"Frequent hemorrhages. General debility. Some fool of a doctor told this woman she had leukemia and would die. God knows why she came to us—except that her husband had already bought her the insurance, and they're both Scotch-Irish."

"She'll feel better when you tell her it's not leukemia, but a thrombocytopenic purpura."

"I told her that just now. She'll feel better still when you've taken out her spleen and made her well."

Chris threw an arm around Jim's stooped shoulder. "Who says they can beat this team in a fair fight?"

His mood carried through a morning packed with routine cases. He did not even realize how tired he was until late afternoon, when he found that he could steal a half hour for the barber's chair. It was something of a shock to open his eyes under the sting of a cold towel and realize that he had dozed through a haircut. . . .

Looking back on it later, he knew that he should have been more startled when a familiar voice rose out of a steam of towels in the next chair. An affable voice with ice in its heart, even when its owner assumed the tone of friendship.

"Good afternoon, Dr. Dwight."

At the moment he could see nothing but the man's immaculate sports oxfords under the apron of sprigged muslin. A manicure girl worked busily on a long white hand; the head barber, Chris noted automatically, was giving the compensation doctor the best facial that the Manucy Tonsorial Parlors boasted. Dwight smiled easily as the towel whisked aside, to expose his bland stare—the disdainful look of a sultan who could afford to take his ease and distribute good will to a rival.

"How's the Sanders girl?" he asked.

Chris spoke with his eyes still on the mirror. "Very well, thank you. She's going to live."

In the mirror Dwight's face was still smooth as a stone idol's. "I understand you went out on a limb with her."

"You might put it that way."

Dwight said, "It takes a real surgeon to do a hysterectomy on a case that's moribund. I'm afraid I must congratulate you."

Chris reached for his hat. It was incredible that this was the thing he must fight and crush. This cold, calm visage that smiled at all the right moments and uttered compliments that must sound sincere to any ears but his. He made his own voice as bland as Dwight's, and hated himself for the effect.

"It was the only chance of saving her."

"I agree with you entirely, of course. When the news gets around, it should help your clinic greatly. Not that it needs help, if my own reports are accurate."

Chris said, not at all affably, "They're accurate enough, Dwight. And thanks for your interest."

The bland mask replied, "Not at all, Land. Always glad to see someone make a success of a new thing."

Once again Chris congratulated himself on not slamming a door as he left the barbershop. Driving back to the hospital, a great deal more slowly than he had a right to drive, he asked himself what pleasure Dwight could get from this waiting game. Or had the compensation doctor already moved to take his enemy unawares?

Back in the clinic, there was no time to ponder the problem. It was well after six when he put aside his white office coat at last and reached for the gabardine he had donned that morning at the boathouse. The crackle of an envelope in the breast pocket reminded him of Cato Embree's last letter. He had been saving it until now, as a solace to end a busy day.

One look at the familiar scrawl told him that Cato had gone out in his stride:

DEAR CHRIS:

By the time you get this, I'll be wherever I'm going. Whichever place it is, I'll find some friends there, so it don't make a lot of difference. God knows I'm not paying it any mind.

Seward has already told you about the bequest. Have you gotten over being surprised? In a way, I'm surprised

186

myself: the things you're doing at the clinic now would never suit me or my ways. Don't even ask me if I approve of what you're doing to the medical picture as I knew it—when I rode circuit with my whole hospital in my saddlebags. You're going to meet trouble, and that's God's truth; but you'll come out on top, I'm sure of that. If you need cash in between, here it is—and God bless you, Chris.

Yr. Obdt. Servant
CATO EMBREE, M.D.

Chris put down the letter. He remembered Doc Embree twenty years ago—dosing him with sulphur and molasses in the spring, laughing as he grimaced at the quinine he was always prescribing for the ever-present malaria from the swamps. And the time he'd slashed his leg on the thorn tree, where he'd been rocking a hornet's nest. Cato had sewed him up then—and his burning blue eyes had dared him to let out a whimper. . . . Today, when he was rocking a hornet's nest of quite another sort, he could feel the old man's hand on his shoulder once again.

He looked up sharply, saw that Karen was standing in the doorway in her street clothes, and beckoned her into the office. She read the letter over his shoulder.

"Speaking of troglodytes——"

"There are good and bad breeds, you know," he said. "What I can't get over is his trust—not in me, but in my ideas. It's a great responsibility, having people trust you."

"You can shoulder it, Chris."

"I can try," he said. "In fact, I wouldn't talk like this if it hadn't been a long day."

Her tone lightened. "That's why I stopped in. To tell you I'm handling the commissary for the picnic tomorrow. All but the drinks: you and Paul can bring those."

"I need that holiday," he admitted. "I'm fagged out." He found that he had leaned against her as she stood beside him; that she had moved closer, with no hesitation, to cradle his head against her breast. For a moment his head swam with the faint, sharp perfume of her nearness; then, he knew not how or why, a deep sense of peace stole through his being. That was Karen's own magic, he told himself: abiding peace, and the promise of fulfillment to come. He knew that she had offered herself completely in that gesture, knew that

187

he could claim her when he would; even that knowledge was a part of the contentment that enveloped him.

How could he accept the gift of herself so quietly? It was an odd emotion, with none of the strangling heartbeat and dull, unreasoning rage that Roz Borland's visit had stirred in him. This emotion was quiet, desirable. He found himself wondering what it would be like to have Karen always beside him thus—at work and at home: part of his life, as essential to his happiness as she was to the success of the clinic. He raised his eyes to hers to put the thought into words and saw that she had read it in advance.

"We'll sail at seven, to get the tide," she said quietly. "See you don't oversleep."

She walked out on that, without another word. Watching her go, he knew that she had done right to break the spell. The question he had been about to ask her would keep indefinitely.

For all that, he sat on into the dusk, looking hard at the future. The boom of the clock on Duval Square reminded him that his day was ending on schedule, for once. He locked Cato's letter in his desk and walked down the hall to the wards, to look once again at Mrs. Sanders' chart. The sergeant was visiting her now, the nurse told him: Chris could guess that the boy's face was beaming, even without a glance around the screen that masked her bed.

He had intended to stop by for a word, but he did not disturb the tableau. Instead he found himself walking through the lower corridor, checking out automatically at the admissions desk, pausing in the entrance-way to breathe deep of the inevitable evening breeze from the Gulf.

The whiff of fresh air, joined to the tableau he had just glimpsed upstairs, restored his spirits completely. He was whistling again as he walked down the driveway; he did not even start as he approached his coupé and saw a tall weed of a man rise up from the running board.

"Dr. Christopher Land?"

He braced himself in earnest as the man's hand whipped toward him: but it was a paper he held, not a gun. A long, blue-bound paper that slapped into his half-extended palm a quarter second before the weedy individual vanished into darkness.

For a moment he stared down dully at the paper in his

hand. Then he went over to the instrument board of his car to read the typewritten words in a ruled square at the top:

> *Dawkins, Samuel L.*
> *Dawkins, Mary, et al.*
> *vs.*
> *Christopher Land, M.D.*

So he'd been slapped with a summons—the first he had ever seen in his years of practice. He skimmed through the legal bombast with a sinking heart. Someone named Dawkins was bringing a criminal action against him for malpractice: that much stood out clearly from the jungle of jaw-breaking phrases. So far the attack was familiar enough: he had testified as a witness before, when doctors he knew had been sued by patients. He knew that many of them were self-seekers who saw, in the embarrassment they could cause a doctor, a chance to force a lucrative settlement out of court.

But who was this Dawkins? Suddenly he remembered, in a blind flash of anger. That had been the name on the R.F.D. box at that back-country farm—the camp for migrant workers where he had gone with Karen on his first night in Milton. The rat's nest where he had worked in vain to save a child from diphtheria. His eyes skimmed down the summons:

"Did, without permission of the plaintiff, perform an operation upon the body of their daughter, Mary Ann, resulting in her death. . . ."

Dwight had known, then—even when he murmured those compliments from the barber's chair. Dwight was back of it all, of course: the fact that it was Dwight, not Chris, who was directly responsible for the death of Mary Ann would count for little with Mary Ann's father, after the right amount of money had changed hands.

Of course he could fight that brand of jackal. The imponderables back of the fight were something else again. He knew that organized medicine, with the die-hards at the helm, would welcome the chance to wield the blackjack of license removal upon him and his group. For a quarter century, now, the blackjack had been standard practice, thoroughly approved by the brass hats of the A.M.A. Stymied by a California reversal in the case of the Kaiser Plan, rebuked on the national stage by the Supreme Court decisions that had gone against them, brass hats of that type were never really beaten. They would support Dwight now, with all their power. If he fought this case, and lost, his chance to practice medicine at all would vanish into limbo.

He squared his shoulders against the threat that had pounced upon him out of the subtropic dark. By heaven, Cato had not trusted a man who'd take this sort of attack without striking back. Luke Fraser, he told himself automatically, was the lawyer to handle the details. He'd see Luke and Seward on Monday, and lay the facts on the line. Tell them that he and Karen had fought to save a life that night—a life that had been needlessly sacrificed to Dwight's medical bungling. Tell them that they were working side by side today, to make that sort of bungling impossible. . . . Monday was time enough for imponderables. Meanwhile there was Sunday and Karen and the open sea to look forward to. He thrust the paper into his pocket on that note and kicked the starter of his car.

12

WATCHING HIS BOWSPRIT dip in the first long swell from the Gulf, leaning on his tiller to pick up the port tack across the harbor's mouth to East Point, Chris felt the contentment of the morning seep into every pore. True, he could still turn his head and see Bayshore Clinic awaiting his return on the low rise behind him. At the moment Bayshore and Milton and the fears that Dwight's latest threat had raised were excluded firmly from his mind.

At the moment it was enough to feel the yawl come about as the boom swung—to laugh aloud as Paul Travers remembered once again to duck—just in time. To shout a needless command to Karen—an astonishing sailor in the briefest of white bra suits, who was handling the sheets for him with all the aplomb of a veteran.

At the moment he was utterly content, absorbed in the sweet-sailing yawl. He felt hardly a pang when Paul moved forward to sit beside Karen on the high starboard gunwale. Paul and Karen were old friends: they had a perfect right to dodge spindrift together. Beside, they were probably discussing nothing more intimate than that last inoculation. It was much too fine a morning for jealousy—especially as Paul wasn't coming on the picnic after all. In just seven minutes, now, he'd be dropping the Public Health man at East Point wharf, for his Army meeting. . . .

"Do either of you want to handle her awhile?"

Paul laughed aloud. "Right now I'm using my willpower to fight *mal de mer*."

And Karen said, "Why don't you come and join us for a moment? She'll sail herself."

"Join *me*," said Chris. "Skipper's orders."

Crew and passenger moved obediently down the gunwale —Karen nimble and barelegged in the whip of the wind, Paul Travers crabwise and awkward in his faded uniform.

Paul said, "I envy you, Chris. When did you find time to learn this?"

"After all, I had a boyhood. Some of it stuck to me."

The Public Health man sighed. "I wish I could say the same. All I can remember is Kansas corn—and how I hated to get up at four in the morning. And going to work in Topeka when I was fourteen, to save up for medical school."

Watching Karen's face, Chris wondered why he could summon up no stronger feeling than admiration. He and Paul had worked together closely this past month; besides giving him a head start with Borland, the Public Health man had helped him at every turn. There was still something dry and indoors about him, something that seemed oddly wan in the sea-bright day. Something that should have inspired pity—and just missed the mark. . . . Obviously this feeling was not shared by Karen. Her eyes were warm now as she turned to Paul.

"Give us time, Doctor. We'll teach you how to play."

But Paul only looked up with a smile as the wind lessened a little. Already they were coming into the protection of East Point: the jetty curved out to meet them, framing the bustling thoroughfare of the Army dock.

Paul said, "Make it your veranda next time, Karen—and another of those alfresco picnics. I play best on dry land, I'm afraid." He lifted his face in tentative homage to the sun. "Maybe I'll take up tennis at fifty. Or the rumba. Maybe I look fifty now. I feel it, with the hours I keep."

Five minutes later he was marching up the dock in a sergeant's wake, to mount a waiting jeep. Chris stared after him thoughtfully—and came back to his job as Karen called out for instructions.

"Cast off bowline. We're going places now."

It was ticklish sailing between the jetty and the western sand bars, but he had taken the *Lady Jane* through this pass a hundred times. The rollers were coming in steadily from the open Gulf, but he knew that the yawl would handle in the offshore wind. If that breeze held, they would reach South Island by noon, though it was still only a pencil smudge half lost in the heat haze on the horizon.

When their seaway had flattened out at last, he looked contritely at Karen—a relaxed goddess now, as she stretched full length on the cockpit cushions, intent on a sunburn.

"Maybe I should have asked before I took you outside——"

Karen gave a glorious yawn: he fought to keep his eyes on their course as her high, firm breasts swelled under the wisp of fabric that covered them. "The *Lady Jane* and I have been to South Island before, Chris. Quite on our own. Don't insult my seafaring ancestors."

Her long lashes fluttered; he guessed that she was watching him covertly as she dozed—or pretended to doze. There was no hint of artifice in her manner; yet she was utterly feminine today, from the shining mass of her loosened hair to the last warm brown curve of calf and ankle. . . . He let his glance stray back to her guardedly. All of her that he could see was that same rich sun-brown. He caught himself wondering just where her tan ended.

Karen said easily, "I'm sorry about Paul. Aren't you?"

The transition startled him. Without knowing why, he was sure that she had been thinking of him. Perhaps he and Paul were only two facets of a common interest in Karen Agard's mind. Perhaps she was working to teach them both to play, with varying success. . . . He banished the thought firmly, and spoke with the proper gallant flourish.

"Of course I'm not sorry. I wanted you to myself today."

She smiled, opening her eyes wide at him as she lay there at his feet. "Did you really, Chris? It's nice to be wanted—just for yourself."

Unaccountably, he found himself shying away from more

gallantry—and its obvious conclusion. "Besides, Paul would have been seasick by now. He was building up to it nicely when we docked him."

Karen's eyes twinkled as she studied him narrowly. Had she understood his reason for withdrawal? "Perhaps I wanted Paul along for an object lesson. Do you know just how old he is?"

"Hard on forty, I'd say."

"Paul Travers is just thirty-three. It shows what can happen to a man who won't take holidays, doesn't it?"

"Is that shot aimed at me?"

"Directly. Don't forget how to relax, Chris; it's the one thing Americans forget so easily. Paul can't help himself, I'm afraid; he's always worked so hard for everything he's had. Now that he's earned the right to a holiday, I suppose he'd be unhappy if it lasted too long. . . . I still haven't given up hope for him."

"What about present company? Do you think I'll learn?"

"Why else would I lure you here?"

So we're back where we started, he thought. Back to the you and I—with the possibility of exploration unlimited. Karen got up and stretched lazily in the sunlight before she came to sit beside him at the tiller. He was sure now that she knew what was troubling him; the knowledge steadied him a little. At least she wouldn't be too surprised when he asked her a question that had tormented him for some time now. When he told her—as untheatrically as possible—that he needed her as a partner at Bayshore Clinic—as a woman— as a wife.

Perhaps it wouldn't be quite fair to propose to her today; perhaps he should wait until he could foresee the outcome of the Dawkins suit that Dwight had built up against him. Once again he pushed that nightmare firmly into his subconscious; Karen's holiday would not be spoiled by business, least of all by that. . . . He eased away from the wind a bit and stared across his port bow, realizing that he had mistaken the chug of a launch for the pounding of his heart. Karen swayed with him as he leaned on the tiller; when he settled back on his course he found that she had moved wordlessly into the curve of his arm.

The launch came on fast, framed in an aureole of spray; with no seaway to spare, he saw that they meant to cut across his bows. He luffed sharply in time to avoid a collision, handed the tiller to Karen as the *Lady Jane* bounced crazily in the passing swell, and ran forward to handle his stay sheets. Once again the launch cut in toward him. He shook a fist in its direction, noting that it was a luxury cabin job with chromium trim, that a girl with wild hair and no visible clothing was laughing at him above the windshield. The girl climbed to her spray-damp foredeck, and he saw that it was Roz Borland, in a strapless *maillot*. The brown, barrel-chested god behind her was Jean Moreau—babying his wheel, now, as he throttled down to coast beside the *Lady Jane*.

Roz cupped her hands. "Can you hear me like this, captain, or shall I fetch my speaking trumpet?"

"I hope you couldn't hear *me* just now," Chris snapped. "You almost ran us down."

But Rosalie only waved to Karen. "Nonsense. Your mate is too good a sailor for that. What's your port of call, or am I intruding?"

Karen said, "We're picnicking on South Island, Roz. Want to come along?"

"We can't spare the gas. Besides, Jean has a date at East Point. Why don't you two lunch with us at the Officers' Club? We could swim at the pool afterward." The launch came alongside; Moreau leaned out expertly to fend the gunwales apart.

Roz put a bare foot aboard the *Lady Jane*, with the air of an explorer venturing into a new world. A brown, slim foot, Chris noted absently, with carmine toenails. He looked down automatically at Karen's toes—spread taut, now, on the cleated cockpit floor, as she held the yawl into the wind. It was an obscure relief to him to note that her toenails were untinted.

Roz said, "I'd even offer you a towline, Karen, if your skipper will stop scowling."

"Maybe we'd better enjoy our holiday and let you enjoy yours," said Chris, a bit surprised, even now, that the choked fury in his voice could be his own.

Roz said, unperturbed, "We could go dancing afterward at the Miramar. Maybe we'd fight, but I'm sure we'd enjoy it."

"Can you pack that much into a Sunday?"

"I have to, now I'm a working girl. Remember, you're responsible for that. Jean is still furious when he thinks how you've reformed me."

Moreau said, "She is teasing both of us, Doctor. Naturally

I am delighted that she is useful at last. May I congratulate you on the—miracle?"

"Never mind your miracles," said Rosalie, with her eyes on Chris. "What I want is the miracle man. Is the answer still no?"

Chris spoke crisply. "Sorry. Your psychoanalyst is on a holiday."

This time he knew that he had won the battle of looks. Watching the slim, red-nailed foot spurn his deck, watching Rosalie take the wheel from Moreau and put her motors in reverse, he felt no sense of triumph. Instead he had a sudden, insane desire to call her back; to follow her into the round of cocktails and dancing and flirtations in two languages that would make up her day ashore. Watching Jean Moreau settle like a benign sultan among the cushions in the stern, he wondered what rich patient the man was stalking today—and how much he relied on Rosalie for ground bait.

Of course that was her affair now. He could hardly leap aboard her launch and beat up the Frenchman a second time.

But Roz had cut down her motors and cupped her hands again. "Don't forget you're both coming to my war-bond party on Saturday, at Slave Hill. Invitations are in the mail now. You'll have to dance with me again, Chris—for your country's sake."

Then she was gone in a smother of foam, cutting a great white circle around the yawl, wallowing in her own wake as she set an arrow-straight course for East Point.

Karen said mildly, "Did you want to go back, Chris?"

He reached the cockpit in one long stride; with a hand at either elbow, he lifted Karen from the tiller and swept her into his arms. The violence of his kiss left them both gasping. Yet something in her face told him that the kiss had shocked her much less than him. He found that he was laughing, from sheer nervous release.

"Will that do for an answer?"

"Nicely," said Karen.

"You know, of course——"

"Of course."

"—what I've brought you out of sight of land to ask you——" He was floundering and pulled his thoughts taut. "With no help from Roz Borland—or from anyone?"

Karen said, "I know perfectly. Do you mind if we don't put it in words just yet?"

"Not at all," he said. "Not if you understand."

Once again she settled into the curve of his arm as they sailed before a following wind. Once again he knew that this holiday was all his, to do with as he liked. The knowledge stilled desire—for a time. Desire, and the need for words.

The breeze faded with afternoon; it was almost two when they skirted the green wall of mangrove on the island and the narrow brown beach below it. Chris could sail by instinct here, rather than memory. Even though he was nursing the yawl along on capfuls of wind, he could find the point that masked the bay he was seeking.

"It's really a lagoon, between two sandspits," he said. "Did you find it when you came out alone?"

Karen was straddling the bowsprit with the anchor beside her. She shook her head without taking her eyes from the shoals that showed on either side through the pellucid green of the ground swell.

"I anchored right here, Chris. Hadn't you better——"

He whooped a negative, happy that he could outsail her in this corner, at least. "Watch that dead mangrove to the right—and that clump of bay grape on the dune beyond."

The channel opened magically between the two sandspits, revealing a small lagoon ringed by dunes and beach. Once inside, it was as though they were floating in a private green lake of their own. Karen dropped the anchor a hundred yards from shore as Chris brought the yawl directly up into the dying wind. The *Lady Jane* shivered slightly, and her sails slapped in the last of the breeze. Karen loosened and lowered the jib sheet while Chris furled his mainsail.

"Will you swim now, or eat?"

"Not until you've fed me," he said, and ducked into the tiny cabin.

When he came up again in his swimming trunks she had spread their repast on the folding table beside the mainmast. An incredible lobster salad, garnished with stuffed eggs and an army of gleaming pink shrimps. Two ice-cold martinis were already beading their glasses beside a tall Thermos.

Chris rubbed his hands. "Why do you always offer me just what I want—at just the right time?"

He had expected to be increasingly nervous as the day moved on toward the inevitable question he was determined to ask her now. Instead it seemed only natural—and restful—

to be with her like this. To tease her a little, after the second martini, because three small freckles, on the bridge of her fine viking's nose, spoiled an otherwise perfect tan. To relax, lazily, shamelessly, in the cushions of the cockpit while she did the dishes afterward. Even to close his eyes for a moment and plan just how he would phrase the question she had accepted in advance. . . .

A blonde feather duster, strangely damp at the ends, was teasing his cheek. He opened guilty eyes to look up at Karen. Her face was just above him as she knelt in the cockpit; the salt-damp ends of her long bob tickled his cheek again as he rose on an elbow.

"Do you know it's almost dark?" she said. "When are you coming in? I've been swimming for an hour."

He sat up just as the first star showed above the dense wall of mangrove—a dark brown wall, now that the light was changing. Above him the pennant on his mainmast hung limp in the windless air. The hush was broken only by the call of a gull, circling low above the water in pursuit of a racing school of minnow.

"You should have wakened me, Karen." He knew that he ought to be furious with himself; a man in love simply did not fall asleep on the brink of his first proposal.

"Why?" she said. "You needed that nap."

"I need a swim now," he said.

"Race you to shore."

She had already plunged before he could rise. From the gunwale he saw her long body, like a white pencil of light tracing the ribbed sand of the bottom. He plunged after her, into the tepid lagoon, raced hard to catch her in the shallows. They stumbled to the beach hand in hand. The sand was still hot underfoot, though the mangroves were beginning to cast amorphous shadows as the last light faded. In the half gloom of the first tree they paused, as by common consent, for a long kiss.

"I needed that too," he said, and wondered why he did not follow the words with the question he had taken with him into the deep well of slumber. Perhaps he would have spoken if she had paused. Instead she walked quietly up the beach with his hand in hers.

"Here's a ready-made campfire, Chris. Who left it, do you suppose?"

"Probably the Greeks. The sponge fisherman. They put

in here for water now and then, on their way to Tarpon Springs."

"Could we light it? I love a beach fire at dusk."

"What'll we use for matches?"

She pointed to a matchbook beside the stones of the impromptu driftwood campfire. "I swam ashore with that in my teeth. Would the Coast Guard arrest us if we dared?"

He was already kneeling among the stones. "This won't show from the sea. For your sake, I almost wish it would. We're going to need a tow if this calm doesn't lift."

"Why for my sake, Chris?"

He chuckled as he cupped a flame in his hands. "Think of the headlines if you're marooned with me till morning."

"I wouldn't mind—would you?"

"Not if you'll let me make you an honest woman."

He heard her low, throaty giggle in the dark. "So we're back at that again?"

"May I put it in words now?"

Karen said firmly, "You may not. For all I know, you haven't wakened from that nap. Maybe you're talking in your sleep, Chris. Maybe that isn't wise."

He cursed adequately as the flame touched his fingers from the exhausted match. Her eyes had held him, over the pile of driftwood; at the moment nothing was more important than reading the enigma there. . . .

Karen said lightly, "Such words, before a lady."

He muttered an apology and went back to the business of making a satisfactory beach fire. When he returned to her she was lying flat on her back, with her eyes on the eastern horizon. The dark had pounced on them while they talked, but the sea beyond was faintly silver now. Chris saw why, when the great full moon swung lazily out of the Gulf, like a jack-o'-lantern in Brobdingnag.

Karen said, "That alone is worth the trip, Chris. Thanks for bringing me."

He sat down beside her without speaking. Already the moon had made a magic silhouette of the *Lady Jane*. In that hushed moment, when sea and sky seemed to hold breath in unison, she was a dream boat, carved in ebony on a silver screen.

"We might have saved the fire," he said. "It can't compete with nature at this moment."

Karen's voice was quiet in the dark. "Have I made you angry?"

"Why won't you let me say I love you?"

"Because it's quite needless. Because I know just how you feel."

"When will you marry me?"

It was out at last—the hardest question for mere man to put into words. He waited breathlessly for her answer. When no words came, he turned resentfully to find her staring into the multicolored flames of their driftwood fire.

"I don't think I'll answer that yet awhile," she said. "I don't really think you want me to answer, Chris. I think it's just something you had to say. Do you feel better—now it's out?"

She laughed aloud at his shamefaced nod. "And will you please relax at last and enjoy your picnic—now you have *offered* to make me an honest woman?"

"I'll try," he said.

Again she laughed in the dark. "Maybe you won't have to try too hard—now you've stilled your conscience."

"My conscience is bothered about that breeze," he said. "Why doesn't it come?"

He felt her fingers stroke his cheek in the dark. "Poor Chris. You've taken the ills of Milton on your shoulders. Don't worry about nature too. When she tells you that you're becalmed awhile, accept her verdict. Even though you're becalmed with a lady."

He looked at her narrowly as the flame of the beach fire leaped. "At the moment I don't feel in the least becalmed."

"Nor do I," said Karen. "Since we're being honest."

She was already in his arms: he never knew if he had drawn her there or if she had merely moved closer, of her own accord. This time her lips parted sweetly under his kiss, answering him with a passion that matched his own.

"Darling, I——" It shocked him a little to realize that he had never called her that before. "You've got to say you'll——"

But her lips had already silenced his by time-honored means. He watched her, unstirring, as she drew slowly away from him, rose to her feet, and turned toward the soft lap of the lagoon.

"You say you love me, Chris. Don't tell me again. Just love me."

Still he did not stir as she dove cleanly and swam to the yawl in a sturdy racing stroke. He watched her sound just before she reached the gunwale, and knew she had plunged to come up on the far side. . . . The memory of their first meeting stirred his pulses now. She had been naked when she swam in the bay that night. The moonlight told him that she was naked now, when she came overside and stood for a long, heart-bursting moment on the foredeck, like a figurehead come vibrantly alive.

She did not glance back to the beach when she vanished into the tiny afterhouse.

He never remembered swimming to the yawl. As he came aboard his feet snarled in the white wisps of silk she had worn. For a moment he stood at the door of the afterhouse, swaying like a drunken man. The moonlight poured in floods about him now, but he had found her even before her whisper came out to him.

"Just love me, Chris. Love me . . ."

13

DRIVING OVER THE CAUSEWAY at breakneck speed in the staring gray light of morning, Chris blessed the phone that had wrenched him out of dreams. When Sam had called he had been fumbling through the cotton-wool limbo that separates sleep from waking. Another half hour, and he'd have been staring at his boathouse ceiling in the dawn, with unlimited time to think. To remember that last kiss as he'd stood with Karen on the dock, just after the *Lady Jane* had sneaked into her anchorage with the tardy breeze. To ask himself just what he'd say to Karen when they met again in the routine of the hospital day. . . .

She'd been unconcerned about it all, God knows, when she went up the path to her cottage. He'd heard her shower drumming across the lawn before he could drop on his bed for that ill-advised catnap. Probably she had preceded him to Bayshore, as a good assistant should; probably he'd find her deep in work in the lab, if he wished to have this marriage business out. Well, there'd be no chance of that yet awhile. Not while a broken neck awaited his attention in the emergency room.

Taking the hospital driveway on two wheels, he waved to the traffic cop who had followed him across half of Milton. It would have been ironic if he'd broken his own neck in this effort to outdistance his own personal problems. Not that he had really outdistanced them, of course; he had merely put them aside for an hour or so, thanks to the job ahead.

Sam was bending over the patient when Chris entered the emergency room, watching the last of a plasma ampule drip into the blood stream. "Pressure's ninety," he explained. "This is just insurance, in case."

The man on the table was breathing; it was obvious that nerve control from the spinal cord had not been completely interrupted. The pulse at the temple was fast but easily perceptible.

"Any nerve signs?"

"Numbness in both arms. Weakness too."

Chris nodded. That meant nerve pressure, of course, but not complete cutting of the nerve tracks.

Sam said, "The X ray's waiting for you."

They went into the darkroom together. Sam flicked a switch to illumine the viewbox. They could see the vertebrae of the neck now, in sharp outline, like a textbook illustration of the injury. A "broken neck"—the term ordinarily used to describe dislocation of the vertebrae in that region—could be fatal for a number of reasons. In most cases death came because of pressure, brought about by the shearing action of the bodies of the vertebrae; when their normal positions were disrupted, they were all too liable to block the great nerves controlling the muscles of respiration and the sympathetic fibers governing the heart.

In this case pressure was only partial, as the preliminary examination had shown. The offending vertebra stood out garishly on the film, like a bit of jigsaw puzzle gone askew. Studying its position, Chris wondered why the spinal cord itself had not been severed.

"Speaking of tough truck drivers," said Sam.

"Is that what we drew?"

"He was lying in the palmettos when they found him. My

201

guess is he fell asleep at the wheel and nose-dived when he missed a curve."

Chris was still bent over the X ray. "We'll need traction to reduce it. Tongs, I think." A continued gentle pull in the line of the vertebrae would usually correct the dislocation. Naturally it required care; any mishandling would increase the damage to the cord, perhaps cut off the respiratory function altogether.

Sam turned to the door. "Tongs it is. I figured nothing else would hold him for certain. We're setting up now. Want to write him up before you start?"

"Where did you say he was from?"

"Fruit truck out of Florida."

Chris frowned at his desk blotter as he sat down in his office. Transient crack-ups of this kind usually went to the County Hospital, where they were controlled by Dwight and his group. He wondered how this one had managed to stray into Bayshore.

The question answered itself via switchboard, while he was working on his examination sheet. "Will you talk to Mr. Byers, Doctor? He asked that you call him back about the emergency."

"Put him on." Byers was the director of a funeral home that specialized in ambulance service on the side. Chris felt his jaw tighten as the man's syrup-smooth voice stroked his eardrum. The professional mortician's manner had always made his flesh creep; it was particularly nauseous so early in the morning.

"How's our broken neck, Doctor?"

"Did you send me that case?"

"I did indeed. Thought you might like to work on him awhile before we took over." The undertaker's laugh was a cross between a cackle and a crow.

Chris spoke crisply. "I'm putting him in traction. It looks as though he'll make it."

"Good work, Dr. Land. Splendid work, in fact." Byers' enthusiasm was a bit too professional to ring true. "You see, I thought it was your turn since you're new in town."

So my guess was right, thought Chris. Aloud he said, "Thank you very much. I'm sure you're very kind."

Byers' laughter was jovial now. "Shall we let it go at that, until I'm better paid?"

"What is your usual pay, Mr. Byers?"

Apparently the directness of the question had slapped the mortician into silence. Chris waited patiently for the man's next cackle.

"Quite a wit, aren't you, Doctor? Whatever you think right *is* right of course. Good luck with the traction."

Chris banged up the receiver. It was the first time he had been approached by an ambulance operator for a definite kickback; Byers' utterly casual manner indicated that this was the accepted thing in Milton now.

Remembering the lawsuit that was impending, Chris got slowly to his feet. The mortician's phone call had sent his mind plunging back to his battles with a vengeance. When he thought of yesterday's holiday—and its aftermath—he could almost rejoice in that challenge. Hard work was waiting for him upstairs—after that, a date with his lawyer, who had certainly digested the Dawkins summons by now. So long as he kept his mind on those realities, he knew that he was free from the tyranny of his emotions, to say nothing of his conscience.

But he must keep moving to stay free. He walked briskly toward the elevator and the operating room.

Their patient had been transferred to the table with the utmost care; Sam was holding his head steady while an orderly shaved away the hair. The tongs were ready on the side table—ingenious instruments whereby traction was applied directly to the skull itself, insuring an even, steady pull.

As Chris moved up to the table a masked nurse handed him a syringe filled with novocain. He injected superficially over the right temple, then deeper as the needle struck bone and sent the drug piling up against the deep fascia layers of the galea.

When the scalpel had laid open the bone, and mastoid retractors had raked back the skin to expose the tiny rectangle, he held out his hand for a drill. Firm, gloved fingers slapped it home; he scarcely looked up as he bent to begin the ticklish part of the operation. The drill, he knew, must bite into the outer of the skull's two bony layers, creating an anchor for the pointed end of the traction tongs. He watched his hands perform the work with fluent disdain of his fears, watched Sam turn the head so that he could repeat the job on the opposite side. Sutures came into his hand; he placed several stitches to close the tissues he had incised, while leaving room to insert the tongs.

203

The job was over now. It was a matter of seconds to anchor the tongs, letting the points bite deep into the cupshaped depressions he had created. The skull was held firm now, exactly as though it were a medium cake of ice on its way to the refrigerator.

"May I adjust the pulley frame, Dr. Land?"

It was Karen's voice behind the mask. He laughed aloud. It was quite like her to walk in unheralded to assist in this type of emergency.

"Forgive my concentration, Dr. Agard," he said as stiffly as he could. "I should have wished you good morning." His eyes, meeting hers above their masks, added that they had said good night barely an hour ago—in a misty dawn, on the dock at St. Lucie Cay.

Sam caught the look and gave an elaborately discreet cough. "Come off it, you two. Are you still enjoying your picnic?"

Chris wondered if he was blushing; Karen, he noted with approval, had taken the question in her stride.

"We enjoyed it immensely, thank you," she said. "Look him over, Sam. Don't you think it did him good?"

Chris turned to the scrub room and found that he had recovered his aplomb. "How soon can I see you in my office, Dr. Agard?"

"Will a half hour do?"

"If you can't make it sooner."

Once more Sam Bernstein brought them back. "When you two stop flirting you might help me get our patient off the stretcher. Of course he isn't in bad trouble; only his *neck* is broken."

Luke Fraser was waiting when Chris came back to his office. The big redheaded lawyer was puffing a corncob; behind the smoke screen he looked as fresh as the new morning. Chris reminded himself that this was not necessarily a good omen. He had known Luke since college; he could not recall a moment when he hadn't been breezy—and cheerful.

For all that, it was good to relax for a moment and resign a problem to an expert.

"I just had an interesting proposition."

Luke's fiery brows lifted. "Does Dawkins want to settle?"

Chris shook his head. "This was another racketeer."

The lawyer listened carefully while Chris detailed the accident case and the call from Byers. "All he means to me is a name on a plate-glass window," Chris concluded. "Is the fellow new here?"

Luke Fraser grunted. "The town's full of new people, but Byers has been here for three years or more. Has a fleet of ambulances and handles damn near all the emergency work. To say nothing of a standard cut-rate funeral line that's a gold mine too."

"So that explains it. He was certainly bald enough."

"It's common practice to kick back on ambulance work. You can guess who's doing it by who gets the most cases."

"Not at Bayshore you can't."

Luke smiled. "Sorry, Chris. Can't I be cynical before drink time?"

"I'm asking you what to do about it. Of course I could play along until I got some evidence, then let him have both barrels."

"Haven't you found enough stone walls to test your brains on?"

"You mean Dwight and his gang are too well heeled to beat on this?"

"They bought Dawkins, didn't they? I'd say that was enough headache for one busy doctor."

Chris braced himself in his chair. "I'm listening, lawyer. Give it to me straight."

"It looks like a tough baby from any angle. The way I get it, Travers called you out to the Dawkins place."

"He telephoned Dr. Agard and asked her to come. I drove out with her, as an assistant. Naturally I took over when I saw the child needed surgery."

"Had Travers treated her before you arrived?"

"He'd given serum."

"That helps, then. We'll ring him in as a defendant too. A few more defendants might make my end easier."

Chris shook his head. "That's out, Luke. Paul is doing too valuable a job here in Milton. I won't black-list him by stirring up the old hue and cry about Public Health men doing treatment."

"Check on Travers, then. Can we prove that the child actually had diphtheria?"

"Karen and I both saw the membrane. Anyone but a quack would have recognized it at once."

"Check on that too," said Luke. "Who expects the average

205

juryman to know what a sore belly means—to say nothing of a sore throat? Naturally Bibb will pound away at the fact there's no proof of diphtheria——"

"Who's Bibb?"

"Stanley Bibb, the great champion of the underdog," said Luke. "I reckon you've been too busy to hear of him, Chris—but he's been hell on wheels in court here. Ever since he decided he preferred our climate to New Orleans. I might add that he's only missed twice this year—one of those was a mistrial."

Chris took a cigarette as steadily as he could. "You're giving it to me straight, all right."

"I'll tell you more. Bibb knows as well as I that this is a put-up job. He told me as much when we met in chambers this morning. Unfortunately it's a put-up job with copper plating and brass rivets. That's why he's taken the case."

"You think he'll win, then?"

"It's a bit more complicated than that. Dwight's paying him to put you in a bad light and smash your reputation here. Maybe even make you lose your license. By the way, when did you actually apply for one?"

"The next morning."

"Then you had no right to operate at the time."

"But with credentials like mine——" Chris steadied his tone. "I was an assistant in surgery at Lakeview before I enlisted. I'm certified as a specialist by the American Board of Surgery; I've been a fellow in the American College for years. Any state would admit me to practice immediately." He shrugged. "But you're right, of course. I'll admit that I was worried at the time; I know now just how it'll look to a crossroads juror."

"So does Bibb. If you ask me, he's being paid to separate you from your license. Win, lose, or draw in court—that's all Dwight is really after."

"What are you asking me to do?"

"I don't know, Chris. It's for you to decide, really. My opinion is that Dwight would prefer to stay out of court if he can; that this summons is a last warning, nothing more. If you can settle with him without going before a judge——"

Chris said grimly, "You don't settle with people like Dwight. You take their orders—or you smash them. I've been in a smashing mood ever since I saw Mary Ann Dawkins

206

die. Simply because he wouldn't take the time to examine her properly."

"Shall I sound Bibb out, just in case?"

"Don't you want me to fight, Luke?"

"From a strict business viewpoint, I think you should settle if you can, before the back-yard gossip starts. You know as well as I what that can do to you. The State Medical might well convict you before we got this on the calendar."

Chris considered. Luke was right, of course—from a business point of view. It was a hard decision to make alone. Everything his uncle had was invested in this hospital; if the Bayshore Clinic went under, he'd go under too. And then there was Karen—the woman he had asked to be his wife. No matter how he tried, Karen would be dragged into court with him on this. If he was convicted, she would be tarred with the same brush. . . .

And then he laughed aloud at his doubts. He knew in advance just what Karen's answer would be to that unspoken fear. Just as he knew what Uncle Jeff would say, without consulting him.

"Sorry, Luke," he said. "I'm fighting this out—in court."

The lawyer's grin re-emerged through the acerb haze of his corncob. "I knew you would, boy. Fact is, I hoped you would, but I had to warn you. We'll let 'em have everything we can find." He rubbed his chin. "If we could only get to that rat Dawkins. Rats have been known to see the light in time."

"I'm afraid he's too well bribed for that."

"Me too. But we can always hope, can't we?"

Karen came in as the big lawyer was shouldering his way through the crowded waiting room. Chris saw that she was carrying a test-tube rack, and noted that she had left the door open behind her, not too pointedly.

"Was that necessary?" he whispered.

Karen held up the test tubes. Her tone was light but definite. "If you don't mind, Doctor—we'll take this first."

"Granted. But I think we're more important than any agglutination."

"Not this time we aren't." She put the rack on the desk between them. "Will the doctor please be reasonable?"

"If you'll get back to us later."

"It's a promise. It just happens that my work's important. To both of us."

He yielded on that and sat down at the desk. Some of the tubes were clear, but near the middle of the rack the fluid began to cloud. The rest of the specimens were definitely more murky than white.

"What's the reading?"

"O.X. nineteen."

"Pretty positive, isn't it? Don't tell me this is the arthropod case?"

Karen shook her head. "My guess is that Mr. Pryzinsky will be even more positive. *This* young lady came through only an hour ago."

"Shipyard?"

"She lives in a trailer too. Says they kill rats under the wheels nearly every day."

"How many cases do you suppose are lying out there right now, undiagnosed?"

"Paul says there could be half a hundred. People too sick to come to work but not sick enough to call a doctor."

So she had already phoned Paul Travers. He wondered why he felt no jealousy at the mention of the Public Health man's name. "I hope he isn't too worried."

"He's lining up the facts now for the next medical meeting." Karen smiled wryly. "Of course they'll stand behind Dwight until the last moment. The one thing he won't dare face is an epidemic in the making."

"What about the vaccine?"

"At least another week." She picked up the test-tube rack and studied it thoughtfully against the light. "Paul tells me there's something on the grapevine about you. A lawsuit in the making."

Chris said softly, "They didn't lose much time, I see." Abruptly he got to his feet, took the rack away from her, and drew her close.

Karen listened without interruption while he told her of the summons and his conference with Luke Fraser. He did not gloss over the facts; after all, she would be brought to book along with him, if this thing got to court. There was no point in blinking that obvious threat.

When he had finished she said only, "You knew about this on Sunday, Chris. Why didn't you tell me?"

"And spoil our day on the Gulf?"

"Nothing could have spoiled that for me."

"Thanks, darling," he said, and remembered, just in time, to close the waiting-room door before he kissed her.

Karen said quite calmly, "So we're back to us."

"Back to us. And this time you'll damn well listen."

Karen was still quite calm. "I know I deserve this. So do go on."

"In a way I'm almost glad of this suit. We can fight it so much better together."

"Is this another proposal?"

"My third. It's high time you answered."

"Actually it's your fourth. The first was before our driftwood fire. The second was"—she wrinkled her nose at him, in another of those sly, incongruous chuckles—"aboard the yawl, a half hour later. When we were still becalmed——"

"You're right," he said. "The third was on my boathouse dock, after I'd brought you home at last. This side of dawn, if I may add a detail of my own."

"And you think you should marry me just because you've kept me out all night?"

"Will you stop teasing me? You know that isn't the only reason."

"Give me just one more reason that makes sense."

"You might let me say how much I love you and need you."

The playful light went out of her eyes. "Do you, Chris? Really?"

Now, if ever, was the time for a burst of pure poetry. Even a lady scientist, he reminded himself, was not to be swept off her feet by statistics. He could hardly tell her that she had inspired the clinic, for example. Nor could he admit that it was all of six months since he had held a girl in his arms. A sun-steeped meadow in Capri, and Deirdre. Strange that Deirdre should remind him of Karen, and vice versa. . . . He pulled his mind back to the business in hand. Good God, could he admit to himself that he had proposed to Karen to soothe his own conscience?

He brushed the craven thought aside furiously. Karen was all a man in his position could ask for. Karen was peace and fulfillment, the richly rounded companion who would make his life complete in every sense. He forced conviction into his voice as he spoke the words aloud.

Karen smiled. "Oddly enough, I think you mean that, Chris."

"You'd better, damn you," he said, still a little angry at his own hesitation. "Furthermore, you'd better give me a definite answer before I choke it out of you."

Karen said slowly, "I'll do my best, Chris. First, about the lawsuit——"

"To hell with the lawsuit. What about *us?*"

"But the lawsuit is us, my dear. That is, it may well decide our future. I don't agree that we could fight it better—if we married first. For all we know, it might give Dwight's shyster something to build on."

He took a turn of the office to digest that. He could imagine what a lawyer like Stanley Bibb would do to them both if he uncovered the details of their sail to South Island.

"They'd say you married me to protect me," Karen continued. "That's one thing I couldn't bear."

He turned on her, banging the desk with his fist. "Will you marry me when it's over?"

"You might ask me again when it's really over, Chris." She went to him impulsively, silencing his protest. "When the clinic's established and Dwight's out of our hair."

"Isn't that a bit long to wait?"

She kissed him, briefly but adequately. "I think we'll be too busy to notice, Chris. Even if the pressure gets us down. There's always the *Lady Jane,* you know—and South Island."

"*Karen!*"

"Have I shocked you, darling? I hoped I would. This just isn't a morning to be Victorian. Not with twenty patients in your waiting room and thirty howling brats in mine."

"Don't you love me at all?"

"I love you very much, Chris. I love you in ways I'd never dare put into words." She kissed him again, not at all briefly. "For example, I love you unselfishly. So unselfishly that I wouldn't dare marry you now. Not until I'm sure I wouldn't —cramp your style."

"*Karen!*"

She wrinkled her nose at him one last time and turned toward the door. "Don't be so gallant, dear. You know exactly what I mean. It's American slang, and it's exact." At the door she paused with a hand on the knob and dropped her voice to a whisper. "Remember, I'm neither a hussy nor a virgin."

He sat down at his desk without answering. For the moment he was beaten, and he knew it. Still, he couldn't give up without a parting argument.

"Is frankness an old Norwegian custom?"

"If you ask me, it's a healthy custom in any language. Being what I am, I can face you without shame—or embarrassment. I can tell you that I'm honored by your proposal of marriage. If you wish to repeat it—when you're really free—I'd be delighted to give you your answer."

"I'll repeat it, damn you!"

She gave him the ghost of a chuckle from the doorway. "That's the third time you've damned me this morning, Chris. I suppose it's woman's reward when she's honest. Just because I admitted I loved Sunday as much as you apparently did—every minute of it. Just because I insist there are no strings attached——"

"But, Karen——"

She faced him directly now, her eyes brilliant. "Besides, I live with myself. I know I've a nice figure. Naturally I knew what would happen when I climbed on that bowsprit."

He jumped to his feet to call her back, thought better of it, and settled at his desk again to begin sifting his morning mail. In another moment, now, he'd press his desk buzzer and summon his first patient from that crowded waiting room. He needed sixty seconds to adjust his thoughts to Karen—and Karen's point of view. To ask himself why the principal emotion he felt at this moment was relief.

Naturally he was no less bound because of her unselfishness. He would repeat his offer of marriage (his demand, he added sharply) at a better moment. A bustling clinic was no place to display the tender passion. Especially a clinic in the shadow of the ax. . . .

And yet—why had his heart leaped when she had said there were no strings to Sunday? Even hinted (no, damn it, insisted) that there might be other Sundays? He pushed his mail aside and took a long-legged turn of his office, fighting that one down to its essence. Certainly he respected her no less for that attitude (he was no prude, thank God). Certainly it made her no less desirable as a wife. This affair (only it wasn't an *affair,* he reminded himself) was not just a repeat of his last holiday in Capri. This time he was playing the game of love for keeps, for definite stakes. He wanted a wife, a reason to settle down; Karen was that wife and that reason.

And yet why must he keep assuring himself of a fact that needed no confirmation?

He glanced at the clock on the wall and cursed under his breath. A doctor had no right to wrestle with his personal problems, it seemed; certainly it was out of the question with patients in his anteroom. Settling once again at his desk, he flicked through his mail one last time before signaling his receptionist—and felt his heart leap in earnest for the first time that morning.

The square white envelope was addressed in a strange hand, but he knew it instantly; his fingers trembled a little as he sliced the flap with a paper cutter. Trust Roz Borland to snatch this one invitation from her father's secretary and address it personally.

His eye skimmed the fine engraving which informed him that a war-bond rally, and outdoor ball, was to be held at Slave Hill on Saturday—that the honor of his presence and a check were requested. Below Roz had crossed out the R.S.V.P. and added ten words, in that same impudent squiggle: *I know you're game—if I save you a rumba.*

Until his secretary opened the office door to remind him of his patients, he sat on at his desk, staring down at her challenge. The clear, cool kindness that was Karen had vanished from his mind as though it had never been. In its place there was no room for thought, no sound but the heavy thud of his heart.

14

UNCLE JEFF SAID, affably enough, "The moon's real, isn't it, son? I wouldn't bet on the rest."

"Not even the stars?" said Chris. They looked up at the electric transparency spread fanwise above them, in the branches of the live oak at the edge of the Borland terrace. A transparency that glowed with prismatic pin points, iridescent as a peacock's tail in the backdrop of the Southern night.

"It's pure technicolor," said the older man softly. "Not that I don't like technicolor when it's well done. Reckon you did right to drag me to this jamboree, Chris. An hour ago I'd have settled for bed."

"We can't afford to high-hat our best customer," said Chris. He gave a sly chuckle he was far from feeling. "I'd have made you come, even if it wasn't for charity."

His uncle glanced back at the house: both of the great wings blazed with light. The central colonnade was illumined like a Parthenon in some scenario writer's dream.

"D'you think the bourbon's free, boy? Or will they tag me for another bond if I go up those steps?"

Chris pushed his uncle firmly out to the lawn. "We can afford it, Uncle Jeff. *I'm* cutting in on the first girl I see—and that's a bond a dance, you know."

But he did not turn back to the terrace after his uncle had gone gingerly up the slope of Slave Hill. The great, flagged expanse was patterned with spotlights now, as a hundred couples whirled and stomped to the beat of an orchestra that had been flown from New Orleans for the occasion. Karen, he knew, was dancing there with Paul: a lovely, carefree Karen, a brown lily in a calyx of chiffon. In a moment he would make himself turn and cut in. It was time that he faced down the panic that had kept him from the dance floor: the knowledge that he might well make a fool of himself when he came face to face with Rosalie Borland. She was dancing out there now; he had caught a glimpse of her as he had approached the terrace with his party a moment ago. She had even waved to them before she whirled away in the arms of a glittering captain of Marines. He could half close his eyes, here in the doubtful sanctuary of the live oak, and remember every detail of her: the whip of copper curls above her bare tanned shoulders, the dusting of gold across the tight blue bodice of her gown. . . .

"Dr. Land?"

The square-shouldered man in a tail coat was vaguely familiar. Borland's bodyguard, he told himself. Doubling as assistant butler tonight.

"Gatehouse phoned you'd arrived, Doctor. Mr. Borland's just back from Washington. Could you see him for a minute, maybe?"

213

It was a relief to turn away from the dancers, to follow the man through the crush in the great foyer up the noble sweep of stairs. In the comparative hush of the upper hall the detective took out a key ring and let them into a side door that gave to a dressing room. Borland stalked in from the vastness of the bedroom beyond, with his chest thrust out and arms extended. A valet trailed him expertly, to tuck in the scarlet ends of a cummerbund; a mess jacket fitted snugly over the massive arms. It was a costume that would have been ridiculous on most men of Borland's build. Once again Chris saw that the man could rise above fashion. Like Napoleon, he reflected, Cal Borland would probably have been impressive in his bathtub too.

Borland dismissed both servants with one wordless look. He said, "Want to talk turkey for a quarter hour, Land? If you're trailing a girl, I can make it tomorrow."

"Do I look like a wolf on the prowl?" Already Chris found that he had relaxed slightly. He wondered what Borland would say if he confessed that he had been on the point of trailing his daughter—for a purpose he had not quite formulated, even though the prospect left him breathless.

Instead he said, "I should have brought my bookkeeper. We can prove we're saving you money."

Borland grunted. "To hell with money. I can say that and mean it now. Particularly when I'm in my Washington mood." He led the way to the operatic bedroom beyond: a Federal jewel, complete to the last tall column on the four-poster. The ship magnate sat down wearily on the bed, though there was nothing weary about his grin when he waved Chris to a chair. "Know what the Washington mood means to a man like me, Land? Know what it means to fight brass hats to a standstill and still hold trumps?"

Chris smiled cautiously. "Now that I'm a civilian again, may I say that I sympathize?"

"You may indeed. Want a drink before you sound off?"

"I can wait for that, sir." Chris felt his knuckles tighten on the chair arms. Had Borland summoned him informally to catch him off guard?

Borland said, "You look tired, but prosperous. I'd say you were still proud of your team and full of fight. Stop me if I'm wrong."

He's been with Seward, thought Chris. I wonder if Scan-

214

lon and Dwight have had time to sound off too? "Right so far," he said.

"Think you've got health at West Island in control, eh?"

"Barring an epidemic, yes. Give me time to open my annex, and I'll be ready for that too."

Borland frowned up at the elaborate valance of his bed. "I suppose you remember that last dogfight you attended downstairs. When I put you on the spot to watch your footwork." He chuckled behind a relaxed poker face. "Don't spare me, Land. You must have sized me up as a money-hogging blunderbuss."

Chris spoke out of a poker face of his own. "Since you insist——"

"And would you die laughing if I told you I feel responsible to my workers—and can't show it often, for business reasons?"

Chris let his eyes open wide. Coming from Borland, this was encouragement indeed. A tacit admission that a point of view was shared, even though they might differ on methods.

Borland said, "A few years ago I started to build ships. Now it seems I've built me a world too. Don't get me wrong; I've no yen to play God. I'd just feel better if that world could be healthy as well as nigger-rich."

Chris felt his pulse rise. He had been right, then. Unpredictable as ever, Cal Borland was asking for his credo. His reason for being, on a man-to-man basis. This was the sort of conference that would not come again—the chance to cement a profitable beginning.

Borland said, "Don't get me wrong, I say. I'm no Santa Claus and no blueprint boy. I want my shifts to be good citizens because they'll be better workers. That's why I jumped up to Washington this time. Believe me, the blueprint boys are running in circles. Even they can smell the fact the war's ending—most of them are scared pink about their jobs." He slapped the expensive counterpane with a flat palm. "To hell with that, I say. I'll give 'em jobs, if this problem of reconversion is handled right. I'll keep my plants going without a layoff, if they'll let me plan ahead. . . . This time I think I got somewhere. As I say, they're scared enough to listen now."

Chris leaned forward sharply, feeling a private nightmare dissolve in Borland's words. He had lost enough sleep, this past month, wondering how to keep the clinic moving in the

215

chaos of reconversion. Even if Milton didn't slip back to its small-city status again, he had foreseen a hard-scrabble year or two, at least. But if Borland planned to keep his yards in operation——

The shipbuilder said, "The Gulf Coast is a logical manufacturing center. Plenty of cheap power from the Tennessee Valley, a direct route to the South American market, fine living conditions for labor. If we can teach 'em to live like citizens, not Okies. Milton's got everything."

Chris smiled. "As a native son, I accept the compliment."

"Maybe it'll do for now if we can just teach 'em to be healthy. Maybe the rest will come in time. Anyhow, I'm with you on this group plan, if it keeps paying off. I think it's high time that people who live on wages started saving for their own security. God knows the government has gone far enough to help them."

"Too far, in my dictionary," said Chris. "If you're talking about basic medical care——"

"Think they'll push that current bill through Congress?"

"Not right now. The country's too prosperous for the average citizen to worry. My guess is it gets tabled—until the next depression."

"By which time you hope to sell your prepayment plan, on its merits."

Chris said evenly, "I have hopes for Milton, at least—with the head start you've given me."

"What about the opposition?" Borland's eyes narrowed. "I've heard rumors of a suit against you."

Chris nodded grimly. So Dwight got to you first, he thought. He wished now that he had been the first to mention that threat to his future; without proof, he could hardly charge Dwight with manipulation; still he did not wish to give the impression that he had been holding back.

But Borland listened without comment as he recited the facts. "You'll have to win that one, of course," he said at last. "Even with that legacy, it could close your clinic overnight."

Borland, it seemed, had checked thoroughly on his affairs; it showed a continuing interest, at least. "I'm not using any of Dr. Embree's money yet," Chris said stiffly. "I don't intend to, unless it's really needed."

"Want to fight this thing on your nerve, eh?"

Chris said slowly, "Frankly, I don't expect to go too far

216

in my generation. I started this clinic to fight a definite threat
—state medicine, pure and not so simple. I'm not offering a
stopgap, or even a different brand of social evolution. I'm
merely proving that the fee system, as doctors practice it today, needs overhauling."

"And just how long will your medical friends let you get
away with that?"

Chris grinned. "I'm courting tomahawks, of course. And I
know I'll have to move slowly. Obviously, a group-clinic
scheme won't work everywhere. I don't even think it'll take
among all classes of wage earners. Take the white-collar
groups, for instance."

Borland nodded. "The boys between the millstones. The
Horatio Alger boys who belong to correspondence schools and
think they can be President if they sit up late enough." Once
again his great, hard hand banged the counterpane. "Of
course they're the ones who need you. Why can't you get to
'em in time? They have hospitalization in the big-city areas
now—to say nothing of group insurance and burial funds."

"And most of them are proud of their family doctor. So
proud that they'll borrow money at five per cent to pay his
bills."

"Where does the G.P. fit into your scheme?"

"He doesn't. The general practitioner is dead now, even
if his loyal friends don't know it. Medicine has belonged to
the specialists for a long time; it'll belong to them completely
when the war ends and transportation really comes into its
own. When you can bring a patient and the right expert together in a matter of hours——" Chris did not complete the
sentence. "The point is, who'll bring patient and expert together? A volunteer group, like mine? Or an order from
Washington?"

Borland said, "Don't tout your specialist too highly. For my
money, he's the worst gouger of the lot. Just how will you
break him of that habit?"

"There are gougers in every profession, no matter how it's
organized; I'll be the last to deny that medicine has less than
its share. I still hope to prove that the best type of specialist
can team up for the public good and his own bank account
as well."

"So you hope to get rich at this too?"

"Moderately rich, if my strength holds out." Chris grinned.
"Maybe I haven't quite given up that Horatio Alger dream

myself, Mr. Borland. I still plan to keep my private practice. So do all my colleagues. The Bayshore Clinic is home plate, that's all."

"Aren't you eating your cake and having it too?"

"Not at all. At present we're caring for the group that really needs us—the industrial wage earner. The man who'll never save for doctors' bills, in good times or bad, unless it's subtracted at the source. The white-collar earner and the low-salaried employee need us too. Perhaps they'll come round in time, if we prove that we're a going concern. In the meantime we stay within the industrial pattern and make our livings on the side. . . . Don't think that I'm a radical who's planning to scrap the profit motive. My doctors have wives, and daughters at Vassar, the same as anyone. Eventually I hope they'll be able to earn those things right out of their clinic shares."

"How many doctors will find room in clinics like yours—assuming the system was nationwide?"

It was Chris's turn to slap the counterpane. "When I've expanded completely, I can use a dozen more right here in Milton. There'll never be enough doctors to keep the people really well."

Borland said, "Put that the right way, Land. There'll never be enough *good* doctors to keep the people well."

"Group-clinic practice can help develop them. I'm speaking as a scientist now, quite outside the profit motive."

"Granted—if enough of you will band together. How can you if you go on cutting each other's throats? How many of you will even stand up and fight state medicine together—when and if it comes?"

"I'll admit all that freely. Most of us are too busy getting rich to pay attention to politics in anything but the lowest form. We've let ourselves be governed by reactionaries. We work behind a screen called medical ethics: so far as I can see, it's created nothing but a chiseler's heaven—and a cave where our troubles gather dust. For all that, I think we'll pull together when the danger really comes—providing a workable countermeasure has been created in the meantime."

"Like the One-Per-Cent Plan, eh?"

Chris grinned. "We sold you, didn't we?"

"I'm still playing ball; I still like your talking points. I'm only asking how you'll beat state control to the gun."

"By establishing the group principle, by communities, before the next depression. By taking on any group that will co-operate. By accepting government aid up to a point—if it's locally administered, through existing agencies. Give me five years, and I'll make this the American answer to regimentation. I'll have figures to prove that I can supply better medical care, through my group, than any statist system—and at far less cost to the taxpayer." Chris slapped the counterpane one more time. "Will you talk to my bookkeeper tomorrow, and see how much I've saved you?"

Borland laughed aloud. "I believed you the first time, Land. That's why I let you prove yourself—up to now."

Chris held his breath. Had the man led him on this far only to deliver an ultimatum inspired by Dwight? But Borland's next words set his heart skyrocketing.

"The old systems die hard, you know. Maybe they'll knife you yet, before you're established. If your footwork's that bad, don't ask for my help. If you come out on top—well, I'd like to talk over your ideas on medicine again." He turned back from the windows and the throb of the drums. "Now shall we go, before Roz scalps us both?"

Chris knew that his heart was still hammering as they walked down the stairs together. Bond booths had been set up at both ends of the hall, and the crowd made a dense eddy below them. He was not surprised to pick out Dwight's sleek shoulders; the compensation doctor was the sort who would buy a thousand-dollar certificate at this time, as conspicuously as possible. Besides, he could guess that Dwight was waiting to waylay Borland: here, at least, was one doctor who would not need a royal summons to air his views.

Let him talk now; let him spread his lies. Chris almost shouted the thought aloud. Borland had given no concessions, but he knew now that Borland was on his side—that Dwight and his uneasy crew were fighting for their very existence in Milton. On a small scale he was proving that he could handle shipyard work more efficiently than any compensation doctor. Eventually—if he lasted—he felt sure that Borland would permit him to organize the main yard. Perhaps he could organize Borland yards all over America, make his plans a reality in a dozen states.

He clung fast to the hope as Dwight raised his cold blue eyes to the stair well. Riding the hope high, he even permitted himself to smile thinly as the compensation doctor bustled forward to take Borland's arm. . . . Dwight's stare was his reward. He knew that the man was still staring as he waved Borland a cheerful good-by and marched out resolutely toward the dancing.

For once he could afford to ignore the threat he had left behind him. He could even put his self-selected crusade from his mind for a while—providing he cut in on Roz Borland before he lost his nerve again.

But Roz was nowhere to be seen when he paused on the edge of the terrace. Karen, he noted, was dancing with the marine captain now; Travers had been captured by a tall orchid who made the Public Health man look almost scrubby. Even Uncle Jeff was fox-trotting sedately with a sweet young thing who had captured him for the bond.

Abruptly he decided there was a better way to be patriotic. He wondered if Rosalie Borland and Moreau were walking in the moon-dappled garden—and slapped down the pang that the question stirred in him. Turning into the hall again, he followed one of the major currents to the bar and paid for a highball with a bond. The place was jammed with officers from East Point and their girls, with Milton townsfolk who had come to gape at the Yankees and remained to enjoy Borland's bonded whisky—to say nothing of the caviar in the carved gargoyles of ice, the champagne that smoked coldly from a dozen magnums all around the room. . . .

He bought another bond, and a third. Feeling his head sing a little on the last drink, he walked steadily into the moonlight again and headed straight for the terrace. This time Rosalie was dancing with a colonel—who favored him with a most unmilitary scowl as he cut in.

"Isn't this permitted?"

Roz said, "Of course it's permitted, Doctor, if you'll buy a bond. Remember, I go with the house tonight."

So he could capture her in his arms as easily as that. He gave her a few breathless whirls to test the spell, and found that she responded perfectly. A born dancer who took your rhythm by instinct, giving you the illusion that you were more graceful than you really were. . . .

Roz said, "I didn't expect this from you, Doctor. Eight to the bar, and all the trimmings. When did you find time?"

He accepted the taunt in dignified silence, and whirled her once again, under the lash of a trombone famous on two continents.

"How did you kidnap the music?"

"Thanks for the reluctant compliment, partner. When the Borlands give parties they don't spare the horses." She waved to the trombone player over the dancers' heads: in the gesture Chris realized that she was champagne-bright and enjoying her own party enormously.

"How are the muscle twinges?"

"Non-existent, thank you. Can't you tell?"

He whirled her again, to cover his gaucherie. This wasn't at all the way he'd meant to begin. After all, she was having a night off from the shipyard as well as he. Why couldn't he pay her a graceful compliment or two—and whirl her off the dance floor before another bondholder cut in? If she'd walk with Jean Moreau (in the moonlight of this miniature Versailles), why wouldn't she walk with him?

But he found himself asking another question, in the same vein. "You're still at the shipyard, then?"

"Very much so. I told you I'd stick. I believe that I even thanked you for sending me there."

"Adequately," he said. "Besides, it was your idea, not mine."

"Don't be so modest," said Roz. "You know I owe it all to you. Of course the work has its drawbacks. I'm too healthy— so I play too hard on week ends. And like all good welders, I sometimes drink too much."

"I thought you were training to be a riveter."

"I've changed specialties. The foreman's going to let me ride with the crane any day now. He says I have the touch."

She did not speak for a moment after that. Instead she let her cheek rest frankly against his and gave herself to the enjoyment of the dance—of his dancing, he told himself with an unfamiliar thrill of pride. Swinging her back into the current of the floor, he glanced along the curve of a balustrade and saw that Jean Moreau was watching them from the steps that led to the garden. A slender spectator, dynamic as ever in a satin-faced white tuxedo with a carnation at the lapel. And then he realized that Moreau had not been watching them at all. Instead the Frenchman darted into the crowd to cut in on Karen, who had just whirled by in Paul Travers' arms.

He came back to Karen with a sudden, guilty start. Why could he watch Moreau claim her in perfect calm—and yet ache at the mere thought of his arm about Rosalie?

The magic of the moment snapped abruptly as the question

221

sang through his mind, a taut string breaking. He had been twenty again, shocked out of himself by the will-o'-the-wisp he was piloting down the terrace. Now he was back in his cosmos: a shell-hardened doctor, with a half fiancée. The memory of a night on South Island beside a driftwood fire smote him like a visible blow; the picture of a tall blonde Venus, rising like temptation out of a moonlit sea.

"Incidentally," said Rosalie, "I should apologize for crashing into your picnic last Sunday. Did you enjoy it?"

"Immensely, thank you."

"Are you in love with Karen, or vice versa?"

He said, stiffly enough, "The answer to both questions is no. Why do you ask?"

"Maybe it's because I'm an honest hunter," said Roz. "One of those rare females who don't enjoy poaching——"

"May I, please?"

Chris looked up as a cool hand touched his elbow. It was Gilbert Dwight, with a crisp new war bond in his free hand.

"You may have your revenge later, Doctor. Just step up to the nearest booth."

He stood in the crowd of dancers for a moment, trying to locate them as they whirled away. Staggering just a little as he worked his way to the steps and mopped his brow. But even at the moment he knew he was sober as a judge. Sober enough to force himself back to the terrace at once. To seek out Karen and cut in on her firmly.

Karen said happily, "I was wondering when I'd have this honor."

"You didn't seem to lack partners."

"Moreau dances beautifully, doesn't he?"

"I didn't look. To tell the truth, I couldn't bear it."

He wondered at the facility of his tongue. Was he covering up to atone for the appalling discovery he had just made about himself—and Roz?

Karen said, "Paul doesn't dance at all, but I made him come out. Now he's buying bonds right and left, and enjoying himself immensely. Does that prove anything about me?"

"Only that you're an angel in disguise."

An angel of thistledown would have been harder to pilot through the crowd. For a tall woman, she moved with incredible ease. Once again he found himself contrasting the cool, sure pleasure of this moment with the open warfare he had just waged.

He went to the bar after he had lost her to Sam, to buy another bond. Someone was making a speech in the hall beyond; for once it was a luxury to ignore synthetic patriotism and let the long, cool bourbon and soda invade his soul. In a moment, of course, he'd go out and find Rosalie again—of that much he was certain. At the moment he could even admit it to himself, almost without shame. Tomorrow would be another story, of course. Tomorrow his only pride would rest in the fact that he had hidden the truth from Karen so expertly.

"May I have this dance?"

He blinked and looked again, but it was still Roz, with all that remembered challenge in her eyes.

"Who told you I'd be here?"

"Must I admit that I've hunted everywhere?"

He faced her squarely. "Why?"

"Because our argument was interrupted. I want to carry on. Besides, I'm the hostess. I've a right to pick my partners."

At the terrace's edge he bought a bond at the first booth. Rosalie waited calmly on the waxed flagstones beyond, her silver slippers already tapping. This time she didn't even look up when he put his arm around her; her cheek turned, as though by instinct, to meet his as he swung her into the familiar, aching rhythm of "Stardust."

"This is really my vintage," he said. "If you're at all interested, of course."

"Don't talk," she said. "Just dance. I was rude just now. Rude, and a little tight. But not too tight to know my right name."

For once he found himself saying exactly what was in his mind. "Good. I'm not too sober either."

Roz said, "Then we're starting even."

She did not speak again or look up as he spun her to the far side of the dance floor, where a great, lush sweep of magnolia leaves arched the steps that led to the lower lawns and the swan lake. She did not protest as he dropped his arm from her waist, took her hand instead, and led her down —toward the sheen of tree-drowned water.

"Have you fed the swans tonight?"

"If you're asking me about Jean, the answer is no. We *did* walk in the moonlight, true enough." She gave a little sigh. "Straight down the driveway, to welcome Admiral Rider's

223

party to the ball. Did you know that the admiral's ship put in at East Point yesterday?"

He started to ask about the admiral's gallstones, remembered that the gallstones had been the property of a general, and laughed aloud. At least the hiatus in his wits proved that he was twenty again, and reasonably careless of tomorrow.

Rosalie turned toward him slowly. Even in the deep shade of the magnolia the ghost of moonlight seemed to halo her copper hair. Her bare brown shoulders gleamed faintly too. He watched his hands, without conscious volition, as they moved forward to fasten hard upon the curve of her arms.

Roz said, "This is my first walk in the moonlight tonight. As a rule I don't go walking with strange men. Don't ask me why you're an exception."

He did not speak. Instead he bent to claim her lips in a long, heart-bursting kiss.

Roz said, "I've been waiting a long time for that. Did you have to get tight to risk it?"

Even then the spell did not break. He kissed her again, feeling his senses spin—and knowing that he was as sober as a judge about to read his own death warrant. It wasn't in the least reassuring to find that he loved her; to admit that he had loved her from the moment he'd glimpsed her from his train window that first night in Milton.

Roz said, "At least you're human when you're tight. It was worth a war-bond rally to find that out."

This time it was she who kissed—a long, hard kiss that made him unleash desires he had never known. But it was she who broke from his arms and ran toward the dancers.

He made himself walk twice around the little lake before he went back to the terrace. On the steps again, in the deep gloom of the magnolias, he let his eyes search for her in the crowd. . . . Karen and Paul danced by, and he blessed the dark that concealed him and the disturbing discovery he had made. Perhaps he'd get by after all, if he kept it to himself a little longer.

Across the floor the famous trumpeter brayed derision and retired as the orchestra glided into waltz time. Rosalie came spinning toward Chris like an inspired top, with Jean Moreau's arm around her.

For a moment Chris stood there in the dark, watching the crowd part in admiration to let the couple spin and reverse and spin again, giving them the terrace to themselves. He knew that Roz could not see him, but he found that he had stepped back to the garden long before she had danced to that side. Watching her from a distance, he told himself that this could not go on. After all, he had fought Moreau once; he could not fight him again, particularly when he was waltzing so beautifully.

On that note he found himself skirting the party like a fugitive, following the back alleys of the great garden until he had reached the drive where his car was parked. The old coupé had never looked shabbier or more welcome. He knew that he was still a fugitive as he drove away from the Borland bond rally, but he was beyond that now. He had kept his secret from Roz Borland: for the time being, that was solace enough.

15

THE PHONE was already ringing when Chris walked into his office that Monday only a few minutes later than usual. When he recognized Paul Travers' voice he regretted the bark he had just thrown at the receiver.

Paul said, jovially enough, "What's up? Still got a hangover from Slave Hill?"

"Sorry, Paul. I'm afraid I had a hard night."

"I phoned you at the boathouse yesterday and got no answer. Out on a case?"

"You might call it that." He could hardly admit that he had gone straight from Roz Borland's party to his dock and sailed the *Lady Jane* into the Gulf. That he had stayed out in the yawl all through Sunday, fighting a losing battle with his thoughts. . . . Well, he was calm enough now, with his personal future neatly arranged in his mind. In another hour he'd be in the groove again.

Paul said, "I've been out since dawn—with Sam. In the trailer camp."

"Fever cases?"

"Two kids from the same home. Looks like typhus."

Chris found himself nodding solemnly at the phone. He had returned to his groove sooner than he'd expected. "This is your line, Paul. I'll take orders."

"Pudge Carrol is meeting me now. I want to go through the workers and make up a real sick list. Hospitalize where needed——"

"Where are you now?"

The Public Health man chuckled wanly. "At the garbage dump, cursing my peers. Steal a half hour and drive out. We can curse together."

Chris hung up and walked over to his window. Across the flower beds on the hospital lawn he could see a phalanx of workmen ringing the old Slade mansion. They had been working for a week now, to remodel the place as an annex to the clinic. It would almost double their capacity, but he knew that they could use every bed. . . . The cheerful ring of the hammers made up his mind: if Paul Travers needed him for a conference, that was enough.

Driving across the flats to trailer town, he made himself face the threat of an epidemic. Naturally it would mean a killing load on the clinic. He could hardly refuse hospitalization to patients with typhus. Mortality from the murine type was low, but it was equally true that the cases dragged on for a long time. Fifty or more admissions, using a bed for a month or more, would be all the load they could carry without help. He forced his mind to grapple with those sober statistics for a while. This morning he preferred statistics to a renewal of his exhausted ego.

Travers was waiting for him where the cinder road forked to the coal tipples; on the slight rise beyond, Chris saw the union leader standing at the fence that masked the dump itself, staring down into the acrid depths with arms akimbo. Carrol was in street clothes this morning, the easy gift of laughter gone from his lips.

"Bad business, Doc—to put it mildly."

Chris felt his heart sink. Trouble must be moving in fast if Pudge had begun to check on his flock.

"I gather the absentee rate's been rising."

Pudge Carrol nodded grimly. "From what Paul says, I almost hope they're gold-bricking. Only I know they ain't. Not when they complain of chills and fever."

Travers said, "It could be malaria, of course. Officially it's extinct here, but Chris knows that some of it is still endemic in the back country."

"We can differentiate it by smears," Chris put in. "Providing we can line up our patients. Are they all West Island people, Pudge?"

"There's main-yard cases too. Right on these Flats."

"Dwight has reported two dozen malaria cases in the past fortnight," said Paul. "If you ask me, they're cases of typhus he doesn't want Borland to hear about."

Pudge already had Chris by the arm. "What say we freshen up your geography?"

They followed the cinder road to a bridge that spanned a small tidal creek—all that was left of the swamp that had been reclaimed as a foundation for trailer town. Following the contour of the land, Chris saw that Borland's engineers had scooped out a drainage channel here, while raising the actual site of the shipyard to a level with the solid mainland to the north. In this way the steam shovels had created dikes which kept the tide from flowing between the area covered by the coal piles, the artificial hollow of the dump, and the sprawl of trailer town to left and right.

Crossing the creek, Pudge left the bridge to walk along a narrow dike formed by nothing stronger than the soil scooped out of the creek bottom. He jerked a thumb toward the dump and the row of steel oil drums ranged beside the coal piles.

"Do I have to repeat that Paul's been studying out ways to burn out that stinking crater?"

The Public Health man said, "You admitted yourself it would make a swell fire."

"Sure it would. 'Specially if someone dumped a tank of that Diesel juice beforehand." Pudge spat into the creek and watched the mournful suck of the tide below them. "Even so, the rats would just scram across the road—unless the dike happened to break down too, and flooded 'em in."

Chris turned sharply. "Just what are you two hatching?"

"Keep your shirt on, Doc. We're just dreaming aloud. Course we know that Borland will never allow that sort of festival unless he has Scanlon's okay. Paul went to the main yard to ask for that again today—it's no soap."

"If you like, I'll go to Borland direct," said Chris.

"You can't. He's back in Washington, making someone's fur fly. Scanlon is the head bull while he's gone."

Chris glanced at Travers, who echoed the union leader's shrug. "Then all we can do now is pick up walking cases and go after the arthropods. Could you get every family on the West Island list to come in for an examination?"

Pudge nodded. "I've started working on that angle now. They'll begin comin' to you today, Doc—or else."

"What about the cases that Paul uncovered? Could I look at that home for a starter? I'm curious to see how the infection got in."

"Easy does it. It's a mile to the east, on a little hill of its own. Can't miss it: a prewar trailer with window boxes."

Chris was already heading toward his car, with Travers in his wake. "Want to come along, Pudge?"

"Not me, Doc. These folks are scared already: they'll do what you want, and no arguments. I've got to scare the ones who are well—or think they are."

As they backed into the cinder road Paul Travers leaned forward to light a cigarette at the dashboard. His face was tired but calm. Crises like this were part of Paul's daily routine, Chris reflected. He could even steal time for a cigarette and a discussion of other things.

"What about this shyster lawsuit against us, Chris?"

"Luke's answering the complaint now. We still hope to scare it off the calendar."

"Dwight doesn't scare easily," said Paul. "In fact, if you ask me, this is one hell of a time for us to uncover an epidemic."

Chris dropped a hand on the Public Health man's arm. "Leave out that 'we,' Paul. I'm fighting this on my own."

"But I'm just as responsible as you are."

"I'm using you as a witness to prove the Dawkins child had diphtheria. That's enough." He cut in quickly as Travers started to speak. "Isn't that the trailer, on the right?"

The top-heavy house on wheels was debonaire—and a bit down-at-heel. A leftover from the Florida land booms, Chris told himself—with the chromium stripped away long ago for scrap, the absurd afterthought of a front porch sagging crazily. The woman who opened the door was tight-mouthed with fear. There had been too many doctors on that sagging doorstep today; another could only mean bad news.

Paul said quietly, "Both children are doing nicely, Mrs.

Holmes. This is Dr. Land, the clinic head. We'd like to determine the cause of the fever, if we may."

The mother stepped aside, her face relaxing. Chris saw that the trailer was neat as a new pin: the palmettos had been hacked away on all sides, to make a rough yard; there was no sign of trash, until he let his eye rove down the slope and saw the nest of squalid trailers at the next bend of the road.

"Have you been troubled much by rats, Mrs. Holmes?"

"Now and then, thanks to those Okies in the hollow." The woman's voice was bitter as she looked down the slope. "Only yesterday my husband killed a big one right in our kitchen."

Chris glanced over her shoulder into the boxlike space that served as a bedroom; for the first time he noticed the heavy figure of a man sprawled on a couch.

"Isn't your husband working today?"

"He came home sick an hour ago."

They moved into the cubicle to look down at the sleeping man. There was a high flush on his cheeks; Chris touched his pulse slightly and noted the rapid beat. The man shook his head and moaned; his eyes opened to stare up at the stranger.

The woman said, "This is Dr. Land, Jack. He's come to see how you are."

The man rubbed his forehead. "My head. It throbs like it would burst."

"May I take your temperature?"

Chris glanced at Paul Travers as the Public Health man read the thermometer. The column stood at one hundred and three degrees; there was little doubt of the diagnosis now.

The woman walked out to the car with the two doctors. "Is it what the children have?"

"I'm afraid so, Mrs. Holmes. Brill's disease, or typhus fever. I'll send the ambulance out."

She wiped her eyes with her apron. "And me with two other little ones."

"At least you won't have to worry about doctors' bills."

"No, thank God. The insurance will take care of that."

Back on the road to Milton, Chris opened his motor wide. Paul did not speak for a while, but Chris guessed that he felt the same sense of urgency. "Speaking of war casualties," he said at last, "I'm going to Deavers and ask for a meeting of the Medical Society."

"Dwight is the president. He'll turn you down."

"Deavers heads the executive committee, and he's the oldest practitioner in Milton. If I work through him, we'll get results. Not even Dwight can keep this mess hidden much longer."

"I'll back you to the limit, of course."

"You'll be busy enough for the next few days, Chris. Wait till those examinations start piling up."

Paul's prediction had already come true when Chris reached the hospital. Under Pudge Carrol's urging, the workers had begun to arrive in family groups: all waiting rooms were filled, and there was an overflow on the hospital lawn. Karen and Sam, he found, had already worked out a routine for the examinations. In most cases a temperature check and a few questions were enough to separate the sick from the well. Those with symptoms passed on from an examining nurse to a member of the clinic staff.

He had time for only a nod to Karen before he slipped on a white coat and pitched in with the rest. It was late afternoon before the waiting rooms were cleared, but the results had been instructive. Ten fever cases had been discovered; blood tests had shown four positive Weil-Felix reactions of typhus. These four had been hospitalized immediately; the others had been instructed to return for daily checks.

At four MacLean—the business manager who was Chris's bookkeeper, checkrein, and comforter in times like these—came in with his balance sheets. Today MacLean's words were balm in Gilead. Despite the typhus threat, the clinic could count on staying in the black for the time being. Chris was still crouched over his office desk, rejoicing in the figures, when Karen came in. This time, he noted, she closed the door behind her, as definitely as possible.

"How's the head, darling?"

"If you're referring to the Borland party . . ." He managed a convincing grin. "When I left I was sober as a judge."

"Why did you leave so early—or is that a secret?"

He pulled her down into his lap, forcing his tone a little. "Not at all. I couldn't get near you for uniforms. I wanted to be alone and brood."

Karen smiled and rubbed her cheek against his. "Were you brooding all of yesterday aboard the *Lady Jane?*"

230

"Definitely. If you must know, I'm still upset." He hoped it sounded convincing. "Just a week ago I asked you to make an honest man of me. I'm still waiting for your answer."

"But I did answer you." If she was hurt that he had gone sailing alone, she did not show it. Perhaps she even believes me, he thought. God knows I'm going to work hard to be convincing from now on.

Karen said, "If you ask me, we've been very honest with each other. Let's not spoil it now, Chris. Were you *really* hurt because I asked you to—well, to wait with your proposal?"

He kissed her hard on the mouth, and knew that he had made his point when he felt her lips respond. Karen got up from his lap a little breathlessly. "Maybe we'd better have no more of this in working hours."

"Maybe you're right," he said solemnly. "I just wanted you to know I'm still on file. Don't let me gather dust too long, please."

He watched her go and permitted himself an inward smile. Their meeting had gone off much better than he had hoped. A perfect start, in fact, for the insulation he meant to build up against Rosalie Borland.

And then, perversely, he found that he could think of nothing but Roz during all the fag end of his hospital day. She was still in his mind when he dismissed his last patient and got into his car again; she rode with him through Duval Square to the chain store, where he loaded his rumble with groceries; she whispered beside him in the dark as he took the road to trailer town and the Holmes family. . . . *"This is my first walk in the moonlight. . . ."* Her lips, then, warm and vibrant on his own. *"I've been waiting a long time for that."*

Thinking of her still as he parked in the rough yard before the Holmes trailer, it seemed only natural to him that she should open the door in answer to his knock. She was in slacks and windbreaker now, her shipyard uniform. For a moment she stared at him blankly before her lips framed the familiar smile that had mocked him so long.

"Thanks, Doctor, but we've had our groceries today."

"Might I ask what you're doing here?"

"Jack Holmes is on my shift. I stopped by to see how he was."

231

He remembered himself in time. "That was kind of you, Miss Ogilvie. May I?"

Roz stood aside as he walked into the tiny kitchen to put down his bundles. The two remaining children were fast asleep in a double-decker; beside them, in a folding camp chair, the gangling Negro girl who was acting as "sitter" gave him a friendly grin. Mrs. Holmes was not in evidence.

Roz said, "She's on the swing shift tonight. I'm going back myself in a moment, to fill in for Jack."

"Time and a half, eh?"

She smiled at him impishly over the sitter's head. "Why not, Doctor? I can use it. Now that you're here, you might drive me to the gate. That'll save me a bus ticket."

He looked at her narrowly as they walked out together into the close, hot dark. Had she guessed that he was coming here and timed her visit deliberately? He put the thought aside firmly and opened his car door. Roz Borland stood for a moment with a foot on the running board. There was no moon tonight; the sky overhead was heavy with the threat of rain. For all that, he could guess that she was still laughing at him in the dark. . . . And then her hand brushed his as she felt for the door handle. He no longer minded her laughter; his whole being was consumed in the desire to take her in his arms, in the iron discipline that made him stand aside without even touching her and let her get into the car.

Roz switched on his lights as he walked around to get under the wheel. "I brought groceries, too, you know," she said. "So did several of the neighbors. You didn't have to play Lady Bountiful."

He did not look at her as he kicked the starter. "I hope they'll still be welcome, Miss Ogilvie."

She leaned forward, quite casually, and turned off the ignition. "We're alone now, Chris, let's use our right names."

He knew that he would be lost if he turned to her. Instead he spoke with his eyes on the vague curve of road ahead. "All right, Roz. May I apologize now for running out on your dance?"

Her voice was cool and still faintly mocking. "What was it, an emergency?"

"If you'll accept that as an excuse, yes."

"You mean you didn't enjoy my party?"

"On the contrary, I enjoyed it too well."

"Including our dance together?"

232

Still without turning, he knew that her eyes were daring him. He said carefully, flatly, "Our dance was the high point of my evening."

"I wanted another," said Roz. "Does that prove I enjoyed it too, Chris?"

One of her hands spread fanwise on the wheel between them, the long fingers curling. He watched the lure with a sidelong glance, aching to kiss those fingers, one by one.

Roz said, "Of course it wasn't cricket for either of us. You're going to marry Karen."

"Who told you that?"

"You, for one—merely because you denied it so solemnly. May I wish you luck, Chris? She's exactly what you need— and I mean that in a nice way, too. Even if she wasn't a good friend, I know I did wrong to poach."

His voice was still flat as he fought for control. "I think you're a little premature, but—"

"The champagne helped, of course," said Roz. "Maybe I couldn't have lured you under the magnolias without it. Maybe I wouldn't even have tried."

He turned to her at last, now that he had mastered his emotions. What do you want me to say? he all but shouted. That I've tortured myself with your memory for weeks? That I'll go on wanting you even now—when I've put Karen between us deliberately?

But he said none of this aloud. He only murmured, "I'm glad you know why I ran away."

"I almost ran too," said Roz. "Funny, isn't it, how we're either tearing into one another—or running away?"

"What have you to escape?"

"Jean. Only I don't want to escape him, really. I suppose Jean Moreau is what *I* need, Chris—if I may put it that way."

"Why shouldn't you—put it that way?"

"Now the war's making sense, he's back with bells on and singing 'Madelon.' Last week a silly woman in Chicago paid him ten thousand dollars to take out her stomach, of all things. . . . That rounds out the nest egg he's been building; he could restore his estates in Normandy tomorrow if the de Gaullists will let him back."

"Are you going too?"

"Dad's pulling wires in Washington now to get him a visa," said Roz. "It should include an American wife."

This time she made no move to restrain him when he started

233

his motor. The coupé rolled down the slight hill in high and picked up speed as it took the curve to the Bayshore Road.

Roz said, "Just to complete the story, Jean asked me to marry him last night, and I said I would. If you and I aren't a pair of two-timers, what *are* we?"

He ignored the stress she put on the verb. "I wish I could congratulate you."

"I'll be a countess. Madame la Comtesse de Moreau. Dad can't pronounce it now, but he'll learn in time." Her hand covered Chris's on the wheel; he was startled to notice that the fingers were ice cold. "Why won't you congratulate me?"

"Frankly, I think you'd be happier as a riveter. Or is it a welder?"

"You aren't being too gallant, Chris. Especially as I was so nice about Karen."

He might have lashed out at her, then, for teasing him with her nearness. For reminding him, so graphically, of the kiss she had stolen when she was all but promised to Moreau. Or he might merely have stopped the car and taken her in his arms. For the moment it seemed simpler to clamp down hard on his anger—and drive on in silence. To praise heaven that the floodlights on the West Island gate were already cutting through the murk ahead.

Roz said at last, "I suppose I should be complimented by your sulks. I might add that I intend to stay at the shipyard until the war's over. No matter how or when I marry. Jean understands that perfectly. In a way, he prefers it. Says it'll give him time to put his estate in order."

"The way you've rebuilt Slave Hill?" He had a sudden grotesque image of a poplar-bordered road leading to a gay château choked in weeds, its walls crumbled by Allied bombs. A swastika banner moldering above the mantel, where a Comte de Moreau by David had once hung. . . . The present Comte de Moreau would rip down the banner and restore his ancestor. Velvet lawns would replace the weeds. A brand-new mansard roof would rise among the poplars, thanks to his skill with American dowagers—and with Rosalie.

He forced the picture out of his mind and worked hard to make his voice affable. "Of course, if it's what you really want——"

"Do you *still* think I'm too stupid to know what I want?"

The sudden heat in her voice amazed him. He was still staring at her when he stopped the car at the gate. Rosalie tossed

234

one long leg over the car door and jumped out to the cleated company walk without looking back. For a moment he thought she meant to leave him without another word, but it was not like her to go without a parting shot. She delivered it just as her slender form merged with the gray mass of workers pouring into the yard.

"If there was a prize for dogs in the manger, Doctor, you'd win hands down."

He sat for five minutes under his wheel before he weakened. The gateman jumped up automatically at the sight of street clothes and settled back with a cheery wave as he recognized the clinic doctor; the crowd streaming down the West Island midway parted incuriously to let the doctor through. Doctors in a hurry were a commonplace in these men's lives; they did not even raise their eyes to take note of the stricken look in this doctor's face.

His poise came back before he turned into the great assembly shed where Rosalie worked—and with it enough common sense to steer his footsteps toward the catwalk, away from the deadly sputter of a hundred welders' torches. Her bright bandanna stood out in the fire-shot cave below him, like a twentieth-century improvement on Doré. . . . Yes, the scene below him was pure Doré—with streamlining. He let his mind dwell on the comparison for a moment, while he asked himself why he was here at all. Certainly they had said their final words to one another; certainly he had no intention of apologizing for his churlish attitude where Moreau was concerned.

High on the catwalk he watched a giant traveling crane seize curved shapes of metal in its magnetized jaws and distribute them with the competence of a robot in a nightmare. He saw Rosalie waiting in the welding line, watched her drop her mask and attack an aide plate with her torch. For a long moment she was only a silhouette in a cone of brilliance as the torch sputtered. Then the crane swooped back and picked up her piece-work, to add it to the flying bridge that was taking shape before his eyes.

His eyes had been blinded by the torch. When he looked back she had pushed her mask aside for a moment's breather and was chatting gaily with a colossus beside her—a muscle-bound Atlas of a man, stripped to the waist and gleaming like wet copper in the flame-lit line of workmen. No doubt about it, she had fitted herself to this routine like a glove;

235

no one who watched her could doubt that she had the temperament for the work and the touch. It was simply incredible that such a girl would permit herself to be called the Countess de Moreau. . . . He wondered if she had made up the whole story on the spur of the moment, and knew that it was true enough. Just as he knew he was torturing himself needlessly by standing here. The Rosalie Borlands of this world, he reminded himself, had the right to buy their titles where they would.

The thunder of the assembly shed seemed to follow him to the road outside, along with the blaze of the torches. When rain stung his face he realized that nature was putting on a show of her own, there to the west. Great spikes of lightning were splitting the sky as he drove back down the causeway; the rain was beating a devil's tattoo on his windshield now in the freshening wind. He cursed briefly as his lights picked out the St. Lucie gate and he saw that the caretaker had locked it for once. . . . Fumbling with his key in the downpour, he began to take a certain savage pleasure in the needling rain, in the fact that he was returning to his boathouse without dinner, with an empty evening ahead. Perhaps, if the wind built, he would swim awhile in the Gulf; these freak storms could build up quite a surf along the cay. Perhaps he would even bang on Karen's door and ask her to join him. By God, he'd earned a little solace after the last hour he'd put in.

Through the tossing windbreak of pines he saw that the lights in her cottage were on; letting the car's wheels find the ruts that led to her veranda steps, he cut his motor and stepped out into the lash of the rain a second time. The wind whipped the words away as he shouted her name. He cupped his hands to bellow it a second time, remembered that he might startle her in this wild moment, and went softly up the stairs instead.

A great clap of thunder seemed to shake the screen door even before he could push his way in. Karen, her shoulders trembling, was lying on the old wicker sofa with her head deep in cushions; in the white play suit she was wearing she looked like a frightened child.

Chris hurried to the sofa and sat beside her; here, at last, was something he could understand—and comfort. She clung to him, almost without raising her head; in that brief glimpse he saw that her eyes were blank with fear.

"Don't tell me you're scared of lightning?"

236

She nodded mutely, and burrowed her face into the fabric of his coat as a fresh crash came. Her arms had already crept round his body, seeking the comfort of his nearness, the solidity of his strength.

"Ever since I was a child," she whispered. "I can't help myself."

This was a new Karen, a viking with feet of clay. He didn't quite know why the discovery was so heart-warming. He had pictured her as a woman without weakness, sure of herself in every emergency. It was oddly reassuring to his vanity tonight to know that *he* could offer her protection, even from a childish fear.

"Why didn't you stay in town?"

"I usually do, with a storm coming. But this one burst so suddenly——" Her eyes had lost their haunted look as she lifted her face to his at last; they were trustful now and tender. "I suppose I half expected you, my dear."

He chuckled and kissed her gently. "Sorry if I'm late. Shall we have a drink and play Ajax together?"

The lightning flared again, and she clung even closer. The rain was a white sheet of metal now, even in the darkness; when the thunder came he could tell by the sound that the storm was whirling seaward. In a few moments it would be over, and Karen could be herself again. He smiled as he thought how short his little triumph would be, after all. . . .

"What about that drink? I'll settle for aquavit."

She did not speak: instead she lifted her lips to his. "Don't leave me, please."

"But you aren't frightened now."

"No, Chris. But I still want you close." She gave a rueful laugh. "You see, I thought I didn't need anyone, any time. I was wrong; I forgot all about thunderstorms."

It was quite like her to admit her weakness openly—even as she traded on it, just as openly, with the weapon of sex. He felt the familiar thud of his heart against hers as he cupped her chin and returned her kiss—this time in full measure.

"Am I close enough now?"

This, then, was his escape from Rosalie and the memories she stirred. He faced the fact, wondering why he wasn't more ashamed. At least Karen had asked for it; he could take some solace in that when he reproached himself tomorrow. He had only to close his eyes and kiss her one more time.

Perhaps it would even blot out that most recent memory of a tense, arched silhouette against a cone of brilliance. . . .

The phone shrilled, almost at his elbow, blasting away his prowling mood as though it had never been. Karen sat up on the sofa, with another of those small, rueful laughs. She seemed quite calm as she picked up the receiver.

Chris spoke solemnly. "They say it's dangerous to talk on a phone at this time."

"I'm not afraid, darling. *You're* here now."

He walked to the veranda as she began talking, and offered his face to the lash of the rain. The room behind him had a dreamlike, timeless quality when he turned back to it again. Karen, in the same white play suit she had worn the night they met. . . . The same aquavit bottle stood on her impromptu bookcase bar. In a moment he'd go in and pour them both a drink. Perhaps he'd even pick up their other mood again—even if she was talking to Paul Travers now.

He came forward in earnest as she put down the phone and turned toward her bedroom, unbuttoning the top of her play suit as she went. He remembered she had made *that* move, too, on their first night together. Right after she had talked to Travers on the telephone. They'd gone on from there, to fight for a girl's life, and lose. . . .

Karen spoke as she went through the door. "Is your car outside? There's been an accident at the West Island yards."

"Is Paul still on the phone?"

"He wants to talk to you. I'll get into my uniform."

Travers' voice on the phone was taut but calm. "I'm lucky to catch you two together, Chris."

You're luckier than you know, thought Chris. His mind had not quite adjusted to the present. Aloud he said calmly, "What happened?"

"A traveling crane crashed in the assembly shed. Another broken ratchet."

Chris caught his breath. Roz had been working under that same traveling monster a bare half hour ago. Working on an overtime schedule, to help a sick friend in the welders' line. . . .

"How many were hurt?"

"Just one welder. A big section boss named Joe Gaites. He tried to grab the cable and got a caved chest for his pains."

So he could let out his breath again after all. At least it

wasn't Rosalie. Even so, he knew that the injury had been due, in a way, to his own negligence. He should have followed through on that last accident in the assembly shed. Made certain that Scanlon had the ratchet fixed, even if it meant going to Borland. . . . He came back to the present in dead earnest and spoke crisply into the phone.

"Just what will you need, Paul?"

"Plasma and large dressings. I've an emergency pad working now."

"I'm on my way. Much blood lost?"

"Plenty."

"Karen will drop off at the hospital. Will you send on some workers to be matched?"

Paul said, "They're matching now. Will you hurry?"

Chris ran into the rain to back up his coupé, pointing his front wheels toward town. Behind him, in the lighted bungalow, he saw Karen's shadow cross the window as she swept her uniform cape around her shoulders. She had moved like this that first night, when they set out on their first battle. Time was a dream indeed. He sounded a summons on his horn—and wondered, just for a moment, if they would lose this battle as well.

16

THE AMBULANCE roared up the hospital driveway in the lessening downpour; Chris felt the crunch of wet gravel under his feet almost before the wheels had slowed. He watched his interns carefully as they eased the wheeled stretcher from ambulance to curb. The huge man on the stretcher did not stir, but Chris noted with satisfaction that his breathing was still steady.

Paul ran around the ambulance mudguard in the rain. "If those donors are only waiting . . ."

Chris grinned as they followed the stretcher into the lift.

"We can trust Karen for that, I think. Sam's off duty tonight; can you handle the transfusions?"

Paul Travers nodded. They both held their breath while the stretcher rolled out on the operating-room floor without a tremor. Even now there was a chance that the great, sucking wound in the patient's chest might open and throw a sudden pressure on a collapsed lung.

In the instrument room Chris made a quick check of the tray he had ordered. Closing an open wound in the chest was a ticklish job at best. Often the jagged ribs tore into lung tissue, causing hemorrhage that was difficult if not impossible to control. Pressure, while essential in the pre-operative period, sometimes closed tears in the larger vessels, which opened with fatal results when the patient was on the table.

He looked up gratefully, feeling his nerves steady as Karen came in. As always, she was crisply efficient; only her eyes betrayed the fact that she remembered what had all but happened between them a scant hour before.

"Transfusions starting now, Doctor. We've two Type O's in reserve."

"What about Sam?"

"I've already called him. He was at a movie."

Chris smiled grimly. "Poor Sam—I think that was his first movie since he came to Milton." It would probably be Sam's last for some time. They would all be rushed off their feet until the threat of typhus was in control again. Sam, at least, had deserved a breathing spell tonight.

Karen said, "We're set up for an intratracheal anesthesia, Doctor. I'm afraid I haven't given too much of it."

"I'll put in the tubes for you."

"What are we using?"

"Cyclopropane."

Neither of them said anything as they walked into the scrub room; both of them knew that cyclopropane was a highly explosive gas. From the patient's standpoint it was also the safest anesthesia, since it could be administered with an eighty-per-cent mix of oxygen.

When he came into the operating room their patient was already on the table. Karen had tripped a valve to fill the breathing bag; he saw, with approval, that she had slipped over her wrist the small metal bracelet that connected to a resistance unit known as an intercoupler. The device would reduce the danger of explosion.

He stood by for a few moments, to mark the even flow of the anesthesia. Here—in the early stages of the induction—they would have trouble, if trouble was in the offing. If the patient strained from the feel of oxygen lack they were trying to combat by using cyclopropane, he might well disturb the precarious pressure relationships still maintained by the dressing on his chest.

Karen controlled the flow of the gas with practiced fingers, increasing it slightly as the man's breathing deepened with the beginning of anesthesia. There was no sound in the room for long minutes, except the slither of the breathing bag in its wire frame, the click of valves in the mask, as the gas continued its two-way flow via the soda-lime tank that filtered out carbon dioxide, keeping the supply of oxygen fresh.

When anesthesia was moderately deep, Karen nodded at the side table and the compact apparatus that was now ready to be introduced into the trachea. It consisted of a metal flashlight tube containing batteries to furnish light and attached to a long, flat instrument grooved along the center for the passage of the actual sheath to be used in anesthesia. At its tip this instrument carried a brilliant lamp no larger than a grain of wheat. For all that, it gave a light through which internal passages and cavities could be thoroughly visualized.

Karen slipped the patient's head off the end of the table and lowered it until pharynx and larynx made a straight line. Chris lifted the patient's lower jaw and let the instrument glide between his teeth. Looking through the half tube formed by the grooved sides, he eased it past the soft palate and down to the glottis, the V-shaped opening to the voice box itself. He could see the vocal cords now—and, through the opening between, the wall of the windpipe itself. It was through this pipe that they must pass the tube. Then—even with an open wound in the chest wall—pressure could be maintained to inflate the lungs.

"A little lower, please."

Karen dropped the man's head a trifle. The passage straightened.

"Tracheal tube."

Paul handed him a soft rubber tubing about eighteen inches in length and almost the size of one's thumb. Near the end was a small, thin rubber cuff, which could be inflated from a second, smaller tube which paralleled the larger one. Chris inched the apparatus through the groove of the laryngoscope until its end was all but touching the vocal cords. Then, watching the opening of the glottis for any spasmodic movement of the vocal cords, he waited. As the glottis opened with the patient's next deep breath, he whisked the tube forward and into the trachea. The laryngoscope came out with a quick twisting motion of the wrist.

"He's yours now, Karen." Chris was already fitting a syringe to the smaller tubing. A little air, pumped into this sheath, would inflate the cuff, making an airtight connection between tube and lungs, insuring that the anesthetist could instantly inflate a lung that threatened collapse.

Karen was just turning on the gas valves again when Sam Bernstein appeared in the penumbra of the table, his coat over his arm.

"What's cooking now, folks?"

Chris pointed toward the scrub room. "Open wound, if you want to assist. I'm doing an exploratory thoracotomy."

"Brother, how you get around. I hope this is a nice, juicy compensation job."

"Right—if you must be mercenary." He knew that Karen was smiling behind her mask as Sam popped into the scrub room. Easy good humor of this sort, while not in the book, always relieved the tension of an emergency.

So far they had ridden their luck. Paul's transfusions were working smoothly, and the patient was obviously better. There was an excellent chance of saving him, if the wound could be closed promptly.

Chris removed the emergency dressing that Paul had applied at the shipyard and saw that the Public Health man had not exaggerated the seriousness of the injury. A jagged flap of chest wall had caved in just outside the heart: it bubbled now, with blood and air, each time the patient drew breath. Chris nodded to Karen, and she stepped up the pressure in the machine. Almost instantly the bubbling ceased as the lung expanded artificially to fill the wound.

Sam came under the lights as he finished draping the operative area and took his place across the table. Sponge and clamp ready, he waited while Chris cleared away the blood clot that half filled the depression in the chest wall. It was now obvious that a great force had struck the ribs, shearing off their inner ends. Farther back a corresponding

242

fracture had immobilized a section of chest wall perhaps six inches square.

Sam whistled gently through his teeth. "Brother, you sure can pick 'em."

It was the last bit of levity before their job began, and Chris accepted it as such. Even if Scanlon's criminal neglect was responsible for the accident, he could not absolve himself from blame. He knew now that he should have gone directly to Borland and reported the broken ratchet. Now, of course, the foreman would scramble to cover his tracks.

Sam said, "What about bone splinter?"

"We're going to have a look."

That, of course, was the first imponderable. The jagged rib ends lying against the lungs could mean almost anything; some of the splinters must certainly have penetrated the tissue itself. Chris began to trim the edges of the wound carefully, removing only loose and crushed skin. Then he went deeper, to sponge muscle fibers, trimming away all tissue too injured to recover its normal viability. In a way this preliminary was the most important part of the operation. It was devitalized muscle which formed an almost pure culture medium for the dreaded gas-bacillus infection.

Sam said, "Did you have much of this in Italy?"

"Too much." He cut away a section of loose muscle attached to a rib just above the cave-in. Blood spurted across the table.

Paul said, "That's where the bleeding was. I thought it was an intercostal——"

Chris had already gone into the chest cavity with exploring fingers to catch the artery that lay just beneath the bone.

"Lucky it wasn't deeper, Paul," he said. "That emergency pressure saved the day."

The bleeding was quickly controlled by suture. With a moist sponge he cleared away the fresh blood clot that had attached to the lung itself. He noted several lacerations in that spongy tissue, but they were quiet now, and slight enough to ignore. His job was to lever up the chest wall and attach it in normal position. Halfway through the process a faint, warning signal was transmitted to his hand via the broad-bladed elevator. He recognized it for what it was—the pulsation of the heart, relayed along a rib.

He exchanged glances with Sam. The warning was not necessarily serious; it might be merely the vibration of a rib pressed a trifle too close to the heart as a result of the injury. But Chris remembered the jagged bone spicules of the broken ribs too clearly. He stepped back from the table to consider.

"It's possible that the lower rib has penetrated the ventricle."

The effect around the table was electric. Even Karen's brows tensed as she glanced up from her machine. All of them knew that the end of the operation could come at any moment now, with blood spurting uncontrollably from a gash in the thick muscular ventricle of the heart.

Sam said, "We can't leave it there—if it *is* there."

Chris turned to Paul. "I'm going to explore, and hope I'm wrong. In the meantime let's get those Type O's working. We may need them in a hurry."

Sam asked in a whisper, "How will you tackle it?"

"By resecting a rib, freeing it entirely. Then, if there is a tear, we can get to it easily. It may be that the bone is merely on the heart."

Sam picked up a sponge. "Here's praying."

The scalpel laid open the rib below the one that had relayed the pulsation. Chris moved aside the periosteum, the delicate lining membrane of the bone, and slipped a curved instrument, like a miniature guillotine, beneath his objective. Pushing aside the periosteum beneath, he moved this small but efficient chopper six inches from the center of the wound, let it crush through the tough bony tissue—and repeated the process at the other end of the cleared area. So long as the periosteum remained, he knew that a new rib would regenerate later. At this moment removal of the rigid structure allowed him to cut along the lower edge of the injured area, freeing its third side. The flap of the cave-in was held in place now only by the rib in close contact with the heart.

Paul came in with the transfusion flask before he had quite completed the resection. A glance across the table told him that stitches were ready: slender needles, strong enough to close an actual wound without damaging the muscle of the heart.

"Sit tight, everyone. This is it."

He moved the rib backward. Something was holding it, offering definite resistance to the pull of his fingers. Thanks to the resection he had just made, however, he was able to get beneath the bone and ease it forward, toward the point of contact. His fingers tested the smooth undersurface of the rib as they moved inward. . . . Here, at last, was the obstruction. As he had feared, it was muscular, activated by a rhythmic, contractile impulse.

"Ventricle perforated," he said. "Ready, Sam?"

His assistant nodded, with his eyes on the incision. There were beads of sweat on his forehead: Chris paused for a second while a nurse came forward to wipe the drops away.

Increasing his tug on the rib, Chris knew that there would be a moment between the time it came away from the muscle (assuming it would come away at all, with this type of persuasion) and the time he'd be able to reach the heart wall and strive to close the tear by pressure. Blood would pump forth in that moment, tending to obscure the whole field. But it was a chance he must take; there was no way to suture the heart muscle before the bony plug was removed.

He felt the bone loosen and slide away. Shoving hard against the heart muscle with a free hand, he lifted the bone-and-muscle flap to study the injured ventricle. Sam's hands came into the enlarged opening, to cover the muscle with wet gauze and insert a metal retractor beneath the edge. His sponge moved quickly, removing the pool of blood which covered Chris's fingers as they pressed against the ventricle.

The picture was clear now. Spicules of bone from the injured rib had penetrated the heart wall. Without that warning pulsation down the bone itself, Chris saw that he might well have blundered into this situation without a suitable idea of the involved area—the most difficult position in which a surgeon can be placed, and the worst from the standpoint of the patient.

Sam said, "Can you suture?"

But Chris had already thrust a needle deep into the muscle of the heart, bringing the point out beyond the edge of the plainly visible tear. He repeated the pattern of the first stitch, until four sutures had been placed—a neat quarter inch apart, completely covering the laceration.

"You'll have to tie, Sam."

The pudgy doctor's hands were shaking a trifle, but he tied the sutures snugly—not tightly enough to cut through the muscle itself, but just enough to hold the edges of the tear. They breathed deep in unison—and knew that their relaxation had been premature when Karen's voice cut through the operating room.

"The heart has changed its beat, Doctor!"

Even as she spoke Chris noted the change in the organ under his hands. The ventricle, its tear closed, had suddenly gone berserk. Instead of its regular, throbbing beat—which had contracted and relaxed the muscle during the suture—the heart was seized with sudden delirium. It was beating and failing now—wildly and without cadence.

Paul spoke in a strangled whisper. "What is it, Chris?"

"Delirium cordis," Chris admitted. This sudden change in the function of the heart muscle was a rare complication—and one that was almost always fatal.

"Circulation failing," said Karen. "Blood pressure down."

The reason was in plain view. The beats were coming now in crazy succession—some large, some small. Many beats failed to build up pressure enough to open the heart valves themselves. It was glaringly obvious that not even the colossus on the table could live long in this condition.

Chris doused the heart with warm saline while his brain raced. There had been an article on delirium cordis recently—and a successful treatment. A heroic treatment, in which a surgeon had exposed the heart in a matter of minutes and bathed it in a solution designed to decrease that sudden build-up in hyperirritability. That much he remembered, but the solution which had been used escaped him.

He found himself speaking his dilemma aloud. "There was an article on this recently. They applied a solution directly to the heart, and got away with it."

Karen's voice was a sudden, glad cry. "Novocain. It was novocain. I remember now."

A nurse on the team, reacting instantly to the word, had already gone to the wall cabinet and returned with the proper flask. Chris emptied the bowl of saline and held it out. The novocain was ready in a matter of seconds. He began to drip the anesthetic solution over the heart itself, letting it flow freely over the irritable muscle.

"Pressure still dropping?" He had counted while he worked, forcing himself to wait a full two minutes before he dared to ask.

Karen's whisper was a thanksgiving. "Pressure going up, Doctor."

Once again his eyes corroborated her reading of the gauge. The rate of the heart was slowing at last; the beats were more distinct, more nearly normal in strength, if not in

246

rhythm. He heard a long sigh go round the circle at the table. Then, as suddenly as it had taken on the complete disorder of delirium, the ventricle again resumed its normal beat.

"Wipe my face, nurse," said Sam. "I think I'm going to drip." He added, *soto voce,* "And faint."

Paul was still shaking his head in disbelief as Chris reached for the sutures to close the chest wall. "I never saw that one before. I hope I never do again."

The operation was all but over now. It remained to place sutures in the chest wall to bring the muscle edges together, and lift the ribs. Chris placed a small tube in a puncture wound between two of the lower ribs; it would serve as a pop-off valve in case of air leak in the chest. When he had completed the closure he strapped a pad of gauze to the chest and stepped back from the table.

Sam said, "Don't tell me you weren't scared."

"Of course I was scared. I didn't have time to shake."

He turned to Karen, who was closing the valves of her machine, and tried to speak. Without her skill, they all knew what would have happened. To say nothing of the aftermath, if her smooth-working brain had not remembered the novocain.

For once he could not speak as he stripped off his mask; he could manage only a grateful smile as he went into the scrub room. He had asked her to be his wife before, and he would ask her again. She possessed everything that he could ever need. Even now it was hard to realize that he could never love her.

17

TWO MORE TYPHUS PATIENTS were admitted to the hospital in the night; when Karen, as admitting doctor for the day, canvassed the crowd that jammed the waiting room of the clinic in the early morning, she found three more cases of fever, presumably of the same origin. All came from trailer town, and all gave a history of contact with rats. Paul Travers was already waiting in Chris's office when he came downstairs after two morning operations.

"At this rate it looks like a full house for you by the weekend."

"Fair enough. I'll be about ready to expand into the Slade house by then."

"I wish I could face an epidemic that calmly," said Paul. Chris grinned. He was dog-tired at the moment, and strangely contented. Life was in the groove again, and the groove was of his own choosing.

"Epidemics are your business, Paul. I'm trusting you to handle this one. Any new orders?"

"I suggest a huddle with your bookkeeper. This business might easily wipe out the clinic before it's really rolling."

"MacLean says we've begun to build up a war chest. We've sold these people health insurance: we've got to deliver, if it takes everything. Any new cases on the outside?"

"Several at County Hospital; I think they're getting jittery in that pasture. Dwight is reporting cases as typhus now. Before they were mostly listed as malaria."

"If the vaccine would come, I'd ask Pudge to send in all the workers for immunization."

Paul opened his eyes wide. "Main yard and all?"

"Pudge was generous with his contribution. I ordered enough to take care of both plants."

"Speaking of idealism——"

"Remember the old Egyptian god of medicine, Imhotep? He came before Hippocrates—and the name meant 'he who cometh in peace.' Well, when it comes to vaccine, I'm fighting for lives—not against enemies." Chris opened his billfold and tossed a check across the desk. "A thing like this is another story."

Paul studied the check. "Twenty-five bucks, from the Acme Surgical Supply Company, made out in your name. What goes?"

"It goes back to a compression fracture a month ago—our second accident case. When the man left the hospital I sent him to this outfit to have a brace made. It seems that the compensation kickback in Milton is now twenty-five per cent. When I checked with the patient, he said his bill was a hundred dollars."

The Public Health man whistled. "Why did they send it to you? They must have known you wouldn't take it."

"Some clerk made a mistake, I imagine. At first I thought I'd send it back." Chris smiled grimly. "Now I'm keeping it in my files. A photostat is already on its way to the Capitol."

"Haven't you enough fights on your hands now?"

"Too many. But I won't be tarred with Dwight's brush— even if it was an error. Here's hoping the State Compensation Commission is interested." He got up from his chair. "Want to stop by the lab? Maybe Karen has some dope on that pig we injected."

On the way down the hall Paul said, "The exec committee of the Medical Society is having a huddle this evening. Will you represent the medical setup at West Island?"

"Definitely. Is Dwight coming?"

"He'll have to be there, as head man. Scanlon is representing Borland."

"Expect to get anywhere?"

"If I can scare them a little, I'll be lucky. I doubt if any positive action will be taken yet. Deavers and the old guard won't want it bruited about that there's an epidemic in the city. Bad for business."

They pushed through the swinging door to the lab. Karen was still in her clinic, but Jim Reynolds got down from his high stool to welcome them. With the air of a professor offering a Q.E.D., he swept his hand toward the guinea pig stretched on a board with a clean autopsy wound revealing his internal organs.

"Dead when I came in this morning, Doctors. Isn't it a beaut?"

Chris and Paul stared down at the evidence without speaking. Nothing expressed what they might have said more graphically than the inflamed nodules easily visible in the tiny, furry body.

"The Pryzinsky special," said Jim. "Positive as all hell. Now tell me that typhus can't step up from flea to louse—to put it bluntly."

"A brand-new reservoir," said Paul. "For all we know, it's building infection right now. Yet we can't be positive that any of the present cases are louse-borne. Not while we're fighting that nest of rats in trailer town."

Chris said, "Can we afford to wait for a real epidemic? If this thing *does* step up by vectors, the mortality picture

can change overnight." He let the thought ride; after all, it **was** the Public Health man's job to give orders now.

Paul said, "Rat-killing is in order. Lots of rat-killing. Of course that means burning the garbage dump. If Scanlon won't agree, I'll ask for a court order."

They all looked up as Karen came into the room. "When Paul starts talking of court orders," she said, "I'm glad we're on the same side."

"What about delousing?" asked Jim.

"That will have to wait. Our little friends, the arthropods, are potential transmitters. We can say that now." Paul stared down at the dead guinea pig before he turned toward the door. "But one case isn't proof. We know that the rats are the first enemies, so we go after them first. Delousing comes last—if we don't break this epidemic by other means."

Karen smiled. "Can't I even preach bathing at my clinic?"

Paul turned as he looked at his watch. His absorption in the task at hand, it seemed, had dulled his sense of humor. "Of course you can," he said, unsmiling. "Every precaution helps, at a time like this. I'm wiring Washington now. Just in case I have to get really tough."

He went out on that note, still unsmiling. Jim was already back on his spindly throne, the eternal scientist who could afford to disdain mortal woes. At a nod from Chris, Karen came back to the office.

"Paul's really worried this time," she said. "That's why he hurried out. He doesn't like to inflict his feelings on other people."

Chris nodded soberly. "He has a right to be upset. Have you ever fought an epidemic of typhus?"

"Twice," said Karen calmly. "Once in Poland, when I was still a student nurse. Once right here in America—in a migrant workers' camp. Paul was in on that last fight. I needn't add that we won it."

"I hope we're as lucky this time. You think a great deal of Paul, don't you?"

Karen raised her face to his. "There may be one other person who comes first. I'm not sure yet."

Chris turned away. He knew who that other person was. He had learned how much she cared for him that night on the Bayshore Road, when she had given him her lips—and again beside a driftwood fire on South Island. Last night, when she had cowered in his arms during the storm, he had learned how vulnerable this tall, poised girl could be. Now, of course, was the time to press his advantage—and he could only turn away.

At that moment he did not want her to see his eyes. She had given of herself too freely for that. He could not let her guess that his only emotion was gratitude.

In a wall booth at the deSoto Grill, Luke Fraser's hairy red fist banged the table for attention. "Why aren't you stewing, Chris? *I* am, God knows."

Chris shook his head. "Lunch is my hour to relax, Luke— if I get time for lunch. I refuse to run a temperature, even for you."

"If you won't worry about this suit—who will?"

"You will," said Chris calmly. "I've a budding epidemic on my hands. That's my specialty." For no apparent reason he found he was laughing aloud. "Think of it, Luke. Less than two months ago I was leaving the Army—hunting for peace and quiet."

"The way things are going, you may have plenty of both soon."

"In jail, perhaps?"

"Could be. If Dawkins wins the case, the Commonwealth's attorney may bring criminal action against you."

"When the whole thing's a frame-up? What about justice?"

"What about politics, you mean. This is election time in the back country. A good crusade might bring in the votes he needs."

Chris sighed. "You win, fellow. When do we begin fighting?"

"Not for another month. That'll give the evidence time to cool. Maybe we can manage to trip someone along the line."

"What about Scanlon?"

"He lays too low, I'm afraid. It's the old compensation tie-up between him and Dwight's crowd; but try and pin him down—just try."

"You'd think Borland would find out."

"Borland has too many irons in the fire right now. He's so busy preparing for postwar headaches that he leaves day-by-day fights to his local men. That puts Scanlon in the driver's seat, so long as he delivers the production." Luke blinked at Chris through a haze of pipe smoke. "What about Scanlon? I'll knife him, if you'll show me the jujitsu."

251

Chris mentioned Paul's plans for the garbage dump. Luke shook his head. "I'll grant you that Travers is a streamlined crusader, but he'll never put through a court order in this county. Not when it bruises so many toes."

"Borland would say yes if he were here."

"But he isn't here, and Scanlon is his legal no-man. He'll cover Dwight till the bitter end, so long as he gets his cut. From what you say, Dwight's whole campaign is based on keeping things just as they are in Milton—except that you'll be included out."

"It's too involved for me. I'd like to go after that status quo with an ax."

"And spill your own brains in the process. . . . No soap, gladiator; this lunch check is on me."

They walked into the afternoon sunshine together. At the entrance to the parking lot Luke paused to tamp in a fresh load of rough-cut. "Speaking of jujitsu—have you thought of going to Dawkins?"

"Dawkins is bringing the suit. How could I——"

"Easiest thing in the world. I've checked on him already, of course. He's a jerk with a few World War I medals. My guess is that Dwight hasn't laid too much on the line to suck him into this. We might up the ante and see what happens."

"Are you asking me to go in for bribery?"

"Why not, if it's in a good cause? In the long run it could be cheaper than defending the suit. To say nothing of the scandal."

Chris put a fist on Luke Fraser's jaw. "We've always been friends, Luke," he said. "Don't make me hang one on you now."

The lawyer grinned. "As your attorney, it's my duty to think of ways out. Sorry if I forgot you were a crusader."

Driving across town again, Chris knew that he had every right to be depressed by the forces that were gathering against him. Yet he still felt lighthearted when he swung his car recklessly down the bay shore, whisked past the hospital driveway, and roared on to trailer town. When he parked on the bridge and looked down the dike beyond, he was still smiling, even as his nose flared at the acrid aroma beyond. Only when he was a mile away—and driving down the road to town again—did he feel the impact of his mounting troubles sink home. To his right the pillars of the old

252

King place rose proudly on Slave Hill. It seemed an eon since he had danced there with Roz Borland in his arms—and only yesterday since he had put Roz Borland out of mind—forever, if not too firmly.

Even the Medical Society, Chris observed, had taken new offices on Duval Square: the small auditorium he entered that evening in Paul Travers' wake was a symphony in chromium and steel gray, a cinematic touch that bore little relation to the easygoing town he remembered. But he saw instantly that most of the doctors were the same: only the younger faces were absent. Dwight was present on the rostrum, but he had been careful to keep his assistants under wraps this evening.

The executive committee of the society—over which old Jerry Deavers had ridden herd since the days of Chris's father—had always managed the medical politics of Milton, with a benign nod from the actual president. Functioning between the regular monthly meetings and during the summer recess, it took most of its votes by proxy from the full membership—who, if they attended meetings at all, came for the papers and the back-scratching.

Tonight the committee was grouped informally around the table on the rostrum. As he came up to shake hands with Deavers, Chris was aware of a sudden tension and knew that he had been up for off-the-record discussion. The coldness of the older doctor's greeting confirmed this. Deavers had been dean of Milton's medical system since Cato Embree's retirement; it was a shock to realize that he, too, was sitting in judgment on the Bayshore Clinic tonight—and its embattled head.

Chris felt his lips tighten as he took his seat. Scanlon, he saw, had lumbered into the auditorium below them to slump into a seat in the front row—an uncomfortable, bulky figure in his blue serge. Dwight, who had scarcely bothered to nod, turned away from a whispered colloquy with Deavers.

"It's a hot night—shall we get this over?"

Paul Travers moved to the head of the table with his notes. For five minutes he outlined the findings at the Bayshore Clinic: the sudden, alarming increase in typhus cases, the positive results in the lab. Chris saw that he was addressing his remarks directly at Dwight and ignoring the testy coughing and fidgeting of the others.

Deavers cleared his throat as the Public Health man sat

253

down. The old doctor had an orotund delivery. Chris knew that he had used a slightly Byronic manner for years to impress his lady patients; he knew, too, that Jerry Deavers was an excellent doctor under that elaborate front.

"Dr. Travers, if I may make so bold, sir. Are you by any chance insinuating that cases of typhus are being covered up at County Hospital?"

"I'm stating a fact, Doctor," Paul said hotly. "Dr. Land treats only patients at the smaller West Island yard. Why should he report many more cases than the main plant?"

Dwight's voice was utterly calm as he answered the question without prompting. "West Island is a later development in the Borland system: living conditions among its workers are the worst on the Flats."

"I question that," said Paul. "West Island workers are not segregated. Many of your own people live as close to the garbage dump"—he bowed to Deavers—"if I may bring in the dump on such a warm evening."

Scanlon rumbled from row A below them. "Dr. Dwight has looked into all this. We find nothin' at present to slow down our job."

"What's your sickness rate today?" snapped Paul.

"No dice on that, Doc. It's restricted information—and well you know it."

"Can you assure this committee that it is not unusually high?"

"I'm production boss, and I'm not complainin'. Isn't that enough?"

Paul ignored the foreman and turned back to Deavers. "I have no wish to carry this outside the committee, Doctor. But Mr. Scanlon fails to realize that I represent the Government of the United States. I shall ask Mr. Borland for those figures immediately."

Dwight cut in. "Mr. Scanlon has a natural desire to protect important information. From the enemy, of course."

"What enemy?"

"You know as well as I that figures are always distorted by propaganda abroad. However, since you insist, I am sure we can get the figures for you tomorrow."

"That's better. Now may I offer concrete suggestions for controlling this epidemic?"

"If one exists."

"We'll prove it exists, from the Borland books," said Paul.

"We'll prove it's high time to make the people rat-conscious." He lingered on the word, with his eyes on Dwight. "We must exterminate as many of the pests as we can. I suggest a bounty system——"

Scanlon was leaning on the rostrum with both elbows now. "Who pays for your rats, Doc?"

"The Borland Company should."

"Not while I'm givin' orders it won't."

"Then the city should organize it."

Deavers held up his hand. "I'm afraid the city commission would not wish such a campaign made public. Certainly it would never finance it with public funds."

"Then I'll go to Carrol. The union will help us."

Deavers said flatly, "I am not a reactionary, Doctor; but I do not seek help from labor unions."

"Not even to save life?"

"Not until you prove an epidemic exists," said Dwight. "I'm with Dr. Deavers there completely. Frankly, Doctor, I see no reason to rob the taxpayer—or even the union funds—simply to spare Dr. Land expense."

The compensation doctor shot a quick look at Chris, and went on coolly in the sudden silence. "Naturally I am willing to co-operate completely if the epidemic comes. I am unwilling to offer support beforehand to a system of medicine I considered unsound from its inception." He made a well-timed pause, with his eyes on Deavers. "Occurrences such as this only show its weakness. A few extra cases, and the scheme falls through financially—simply because no one can predict sickness or prescribe for it in advance."

There was a small ripple of applause around the table; incredible as it was, Chris realized that these trained minds had accepted Dwight's obscurantism as gospel. He cut in quietly:

"Is my clinic under discussion?"

Paul said quickly, "Of course it isn't."

But Dwight went on regardless. "I contend that these two gentlemen are making capital of a danger that does not exist. I believe that Dr. Land expects to lose money soon—and plans to recoup from the city on the grounds of an epidemic."

Chris said, as quietly as he could, "Suppose you're wrong? Suppose I come through the epidemic in the black?"

"Then you will claim a triumph for contract practice," said Dwight. Abruptly he changed his tone. "I may be wrong, of

255

course. If so, I shall be the first to apologize. It just happens I don't like this raid tonight."

Deavers held up a hand for silence. "Personalities are not up for discussion either, gentlemen. Do you have any more evidence, Dr. Travers?"

"Only Dr. Land's report from his clinic."

Chris got up slowly in the hostile silence. He had an urge to do something dramatic; actually he could only read the reports on the examinations he had made. He went through them quietly, refusing to scamp as more than one portly posterior scraped a chair around the table. . . . When he had finished he turned to Deavers. "I've ordered vaccine enough to protect all the workers. It should be here within forty-eight hours."

The old doctor nodded, and his eyes met Chris's warmly for the first time. "Always a useful precaution, I'm sure. Have you considered the use of vaccine, Dr. Dwight?"

"We are prepared, of course, if need arises."

Chris knew that this was falsehood, pure and simple; but he was in no position to challenge it. He folded his notes and looked inquiringly at Paul. The Public Health man spoke promptly.

"We don't usually recommend vaccination for murine typhus. However, as we've pointed out, we've a strong suspicion that this epidemic—which Dr. Dwight so studiously ignores—may step up rapidly into the more virulent form. In any case, immunization is the best method of keeping trouble in control."

Deavers said patiently, and a shade too paternally: "What other measures do you recommend, Dr. Travers?"

"First and foremost, destruction of the dump at trailer town."

Scanlon got up heavily and lumbered into the aisle. "Here's where I came in, folks. I got work to do."

"Just a moment, Mr. Scanlon," Dwight soothed. "I'm sure we all stand ready to protect the health of Milton if the demands are reasonable."

"Then tell the U.S.P.H.S. to stop shootin' the moon."

Dwight nodded to Deavers, who took the cue. "You will confine your remarks to the subject in question, Dr. Travers."

Paul was on his feet again. "But this *is* the subject in question. That dump is a volcano of typhus at this moment. Until it goes, we'll get nowhere."

Deavers shrugged and glanced around the table. No one spoke. Dwight smiled in the silence, and Chris realized, with a sinking heart, that the battle had gone against them. The old doctor and his committee, in a bumbling way, were honestly attempting to fulfill their function. Tonight they were no match for Dwight and Scanlon. Even without that expert smoke screen, it was unlikely that they would have taken positive action. Tying their hands always was the fear of the Milton merchants—who would howl to heaven if they suggested that the health picture in town was anything less than perfect.

Dwight said, "May we take this under advisement, gentlemen?"

The motion was made and seconded, without a murmur. Deavers spoke politely. "If necessary, we will call a special meeting later."

"And meanwhile let the epidemic get ahead of us," said Paul.

"A thorough case study is still needed to prove that there is an epidemic. Rest assured, Dr. Travers, the medical profession will be behind you if the danger is real."

Paul jammed on his uniform cap and marched out the exit without a word. Chris followed him quickly, without pausing to shake hands a second time. His position as the medical outcast of Milton had not helped Paul's case. He saw that now, much too clearly. Perhaps it would have been better if he had stayed away.

Breakfast was the time least likely to interfere with the operation of the Bayshore Clinic: for that reason Chris had chosen the hospital dining room as the scene of the staff's monthly business meetings. The next morning, when he walked into the conference, he found that Sam, Karen, and Uncle Jeff had preceded him. MacLean came in through the office door as he was giving his order. Chris noted with satisfaction that their business manager still looked like an adding machine on a holiday.

Sam said, "I always thought bookkeepers wore a scowl to breakfast. This one looks like he gave away nickels for fun."

MacLean smiled. "Keep on giving me a surplus, and I stay happy. Start milking me, and you'll see how near a Scotsman can be."

Chris settled down at the head of the long table. This, he

reflected, was quite different from the meeting he had attended the night before. It was not merely that energy had replaced a kind of tired boredom. This morning he felt himself the member of a team.

MacLean was reading the figures now—with all the care that a poet might bestow upon a compact lyric. They totaled a respectable sum. Chris realized, perhaps for the first time, that Bayshore was already a sizable property, even when judged from the strictest of business viewpoints.

"Any trouble with collections, Mac?"

"Very little, thank you. I've got a double-check on the yard. Scanlon is crooked enough, God knows; but Borland hires honest auditors."

"What about minimums? Has Borland had to kick in anything for subsidies?"

"Not with full shifts and overtime. Nobody we've insured has fallen to less than two dollars per month." He flipped a page in his ledger. "What's more, every West Island family is now included in the clinic."

Karen said, "That's your proof, Chris. They've seen your value in a few weeks' time."

"*Our* value, you mean. None of us could get along without the others."

"And the rest of us couldn't get along without you, son," said Uncle Jeff quietly. "This is your show—we all know that."

"Take a bow, Chris," said Sam. "God knows you've earned it."

Chris grinned. "I didn't mean to start a mutual-admiration society. Still, I'd like to vote that we all take a bonus. Can we stand it, Mac?"

Karen said quickly, "Expenses will go up fast with the epidemic on top of us. Shouldn't we save for that?" And Sam added: "She's right, Chris. I can't spend what I make now."

"Only because I've kept you too busy with emergencies," said Chris. "What's your thought, Uncle Jeff?"

"Everyone has worked hard, son. I think the laborer is worthy of his hire—if Mac will forgive me for quoting Scripture before noon."

The business manager leveled a needle-sharp pencil at the tablecloth. "I've calculated expected expenses for the next few months—epidemic and all. Even if we go into the Slade place as an annex next week, and run full blast—there'll still be about fifteen hundred left over."

Chris said, "We'll split that."

"Check. That's three hundred and seventy-five for each of you."

"Three hundred, Mac: you're in on this too." Chris let his glance stray down the table. "And now we're all budding plutocrats, I've another proposition. We're beginning to get a great deal of outside practice, all of us. What say we open our clinic books for insurance groups outside the yard?"

Sam whistled. "You *are* riding high this morning, fellow. Doesn't group arithmetic mean a thing to you?"

"Naturally it does—if the groups are large enough."

"Scare him, Mac," pleaded Sam. "I know he doesn't scare easily, but do your best."

The Scotsman held up his hand. "The fact is, Dr. Bernstein, I put this bee in his bonnet."

"What about the risk?"

"There's risk in all expansion. The thing is, we've got to advertise. Prove we can function outside a simon-pure industrial setup. Of course we can't take individuals yet—not unless they organize themselves first and come to us with a ready-made treasury. . . . Don't talk to me about risks, if we can get that far with John Public. Even the West Island group is too small for the income to absorb the risk completely."

"The typhus bug may prove that for us," said Chris.

"Then I'd vote against expansion now. Why can't we advertise ourselves when things are quieter?"

"I'm still for it," said Chris. "Still, it's Uncle Jeff's money, as well as mine. If I'm wrong, hit me, Dr. Land."

The old doctor's eyes did not waver. "I'm with you down the line. You know that."

The vote was taken. Chris smiled inwardly when Sam raised his hand in an affirmative. He knew that the little obstetrician had objected only for his friend's sake.

MacLean said, "Very sensible, gentlemen, going after the contracts while you're being talked about. The fact is, I've already been approached by employees of the Public Service Company. In time I think we can draw in all city employees."

Sam whistled softly. "Brother, will they be out for our throats when that news gets around. What about extra doctors? We'll need 'em now, all right."

"I'm working on that now, Sam," said Chris. "Remember

259

Jake Fleming, when we were at the Station Hospital together?"

"Do I not."

"Jake has a new job now. He's helping young doctors who are discharged for medical reasons after a year or so in the services. I'm glad to say we're high on his list when it comes to placements. I hope we'll stay high."

The table was silent, and Chris knew why. If Dwight's lawsuit succeeded in smearing him, all of these high plans might go awry overnight. He might find himself without a license to practice in the state. Inevitably that meant placing his hospital on the official blacklist. Once that happened, they'd be on Jake Fleming's blacklist as well, when it came to finding new personnel.

Chris spoke against his mood. "You should all know where we stand with the suit," he said. "Luke's rounding up witnesses for me now—character and otherwise. He tells me that this Dawkins has a pretty strong case."

"Based on Dawkins' phony testimony," snapped Sam.

"It may be phony, but it's organized—I needn't add by whom. Luke's putting off the courtroom part as long as he can. With luck, it won't come up now until the new year."

Sam said darkly, "Maybe Dawkins will get typhus. Lend me a few infected fleas, and I'll manage that myself." Then he got up briskly, with a grin that belied his words. "Is the meeting adjourned? I'd like to walk across the lawn for five minutes and look at my baby."

All of them turned with the little doctor to look through the dining-room window at the workmen swarming over the scaffoldings that now ringed the old Slade place across the way. The foreman had promised Chris that they would be open for business on Monday—earlier, if they skipped the painting. . . . Chris got up and put an arm across his friend's shoulder. He knew that Sam was looking beyond lawsuits and epidemics, to the day when that annex would be a flourishing maternity clinic. Sam, he reflected, was a wise dreamer. If only he could keep his eye on their objective, he might step over the dwarfs that tormented his progress. . . .

This morning it was his turn to handle admissions. His nurse was busy with a case when he went through his office anteroom, and he did not pause to check on his appointment schedule. When he saw that someone was waiting in his office, it did not surprise him. Miss Ross frequently admitted a special case if the need was urgent. Chris had seated himself at his desk before he saw that his visitor was Gilbert Dwight.

The compensation doctor looked cool as the morning in a poplin lounge suit. His voice matched his dress.

"I'm afraid I walked in, Land. Am I keeping you from your patients?"

Chris recovered his wits if not his aplomb. "Not at all. What can I do for you?"

"I came to ask permission to take a tour of your clinic and learned you were busy with admissions. Fortunately your receptionist was courteous enough to show me around on her own."

"Any criticisms?"

"Believe me, none. In fact, my tour was more than an agreeable surprise. It was a revelation."

Chris did not ask himself what was coming. He knew by now that Dwight would play his hand in his own way.

Dwight said, "The Slade mansion will double your capacity, I believe. Of course I can't approve your plan to use it as an obstetrical clinic." He spread his fingers in that characteristic gesture of elegance that Chris had learned to hate. "Someday, Land, I'm going to ask you a confidential question. Why are you always so eager to dig traps for yourself?"

"Is that all you came to tell me?"

"That's only my opening gun, designed to get your back up." Dwight smiled, and Chris remembered that he hated the man's smile even more. "Will you confirm the rumor that you're about to open your insurance lists to groups outside the yard?"

Chris said, "We decided to do just that at a meeting this morning. May I congratulate you on your grapevine?"

"Then it's true that MacLean has been dickering with the city workers."

"And vice versa."

"As it happens, my organization handles all the city compensation."

"I'm not angling for compensation work. Is that what worries you?"

Dwight said, "I'm not in the least worried. In fact, Land, I give you only a few more months in Milton."

"If you refer to the suit against me——"

"That, and other things. Are you aware of what will happen when you lose that suit?"

" 'If' is a nicer word."

Dwight said, "I'm not here to trade nice words. I'm here to bargain. Let's begin by agreeing on whatever we can. For example, what you'll be facing—when you lose this pending lawsuit."

"The lawsuit you are financing."

Dwight did not deny the accusation. "Dawkins is claiming that you operated illegally and caused the child's death."

"Which is untrue, as you know."

"Fortunately I'm not on the witness stand today."

"Supposing you were. Would you testify that the Dawkins child did not have diphtheria when you saw her the day before?"

"I fully expect to do so."

Chris set his jaw. He knew what weight Dwight's smooth manner would have with a jury. "But you know the whole thing is a frame-up," he said slowly. "That's just for our personal record, of course."

"How do I know it? My examination showed no evidence of diphtheria. Twenty-four hours later you operate for diphtheria—and the child dies. Your mistake caused her death: any jury will agree to that. You'll get five years for manslaughter, even before the State Medical takes your license."

Chris pounded the desk for silence. He could feel the throb of blood at his temples, and fought to keep temper out of his voice. "Isn't it time you told me why you really came?"

"High time," said Dwight.

Chris let his voice ride on. "You must be getting desperate. Any day now a check on Borland's absentee records will show that there's an actual epidemic of typhus on the Flats. Why didn't you warn him? It's a question he'll want answered. When he finds that you let it ride, to make illness for your rotten crew to treat, he'll kick you out. Your compensation work will go to someone else."

"To you?"

"I don't know. Whoever should handle it will get it, this time—which is all right with me. The main thing is, your racket will be blown apart at last. I'll ride out a few lawsuits to wait for that."

Dwight did not stir. "You're building up a nice case of libel for me if you ever repeat that in public."

"I'll be public enough when the time comes. Shall I go on, or will you tell me why you really came?"

The compensation doctor spoke softly, as though he were thinking aloud. "Your father had a fine reputation in Milton, Land. What will people think when his son is found guilty of manslaughter?"

"Haven't you made enough threats?"

"What of your uncle? Do you want him to lose everything, and be branded in the bargain?" He made a light, skillful pause. "You see, I'm not in the least impressed by this martyr pose of yours. I think you'll back down if I'm generous."

"Just how generous?"

"What would you say if I offered you a hundred thousand for your clinic as it stands?"

Chris opened his eyes wide. "Last night at the meeting you were telling your fellow doctors that I was on the skids."

"Last night we had certain lame intellects to impress. This morning we are alone. I think we can be honest. I need this outfit almost as badly as you need my promise to call off Dawkins. How much did you pay for the Slade house?"

"Twelve thousand."

"I'll make that up in the total, then. What do you say?"

Chris smiled. "Only that I was wrong about you. It seems you *can* be generous."

"I can afford to be. Borland is staying here after the war; he's in Washington now to perfect his reconversion plans. I needn't tell you that this hospital would come in handy for my work; the County is already too small."

"Would you keep the insurance plan?"

"Certainly not. I'm paying you now to nip that in the bud."

"What about my staff?"

"They'd have to go, of course. All but Dr. Jeff. This is his home; with his share of the money, he could give up practice altogether."

Chris lit a cigarette with none-too-steady hands. Should he astonish Dwight by accepting his offer? Luke Fraser would have advised it, he knew; Dwight had not exaggerated the effects of a decision against him. He'd be crucified—to forward a political campaign, with all the finesse that a small-time lawyer can show when he is climbing too fast. . . . He found that he had made up his mind, quite easily, before flame touched his cigarette. He knew that Uncle Jeff would support that decision as well as the others.

"The answer is no."

"Wouldn't you like a little time? I can give you a day or so."

"I made up my mind about you the day we met. I decided it was you or me in Milton. That decision goes double now."

"You are worse than foolish. I won't warn you again."

Chris rose to his full height, but the compensation doctor did not stir. "Did you think that anything would change my mind? Have I got to tell you that I'm working overtime to smash you, too?"

"You'll find me quite invulnerable."

"The State Compensation Commission may have a different view. I've already put evidence in their hands to start an inquiry in Milton. If it doesn't center on you, it won't be my fault."

It was heartening to find that Dwight was human after all. To watch him bounce to his feet with a faint red stain on his cheeks. "So our back hair is down. You're forcing me to fight."

"For your life. I promised you that the day we met."

The flash of rage passed as quickly as it had come. Dwight's voice was calm again as he turned toward the door. "I wouldn't advise any counter-measures. You might force me to delve a bit into your private life."

"Meaning?"

"Even the Compensation Commission might be interested to learn that one of the doctors in your clinic is your mistress."

The compensation doctor did not quite reach the door. Vaulting across the desk to collar him, Chris found that his senses were wonderfuly sharp. He heard the whine of saws in the annex across the lawn; he saw Roy, up and about again after his operation, whistling mournfully as he watered the hydrangea bed outside the office windows. All this time he was propelling Dwight toward that same window. Now—with one hand knotted at the man's neck, another at the seat of his cream-white trousers—he swung him clear of the sill.

There was no real anger in his action. Only a sudden knowledge of what he had to do—and the rightness of it.

"The short way out—if you don't mind."

For a second he stood in the wide-open casement, watching Dwight spread-eagle into the flower bed. The hydrangeas would be ruined, he knew: somehow he felt that the gesture was worth it.

Roy came forward—not too hurriedly—to help the visitor to his feet. Dwight's eyes lifted briefly to the window, snake-bright with hatred. Then he stalked down the driveway without even pausing to brush the damp sod from his clothes.

Chris had hoped for a fight, but he felt no sense of letdown as he settled at his desk again. In fact, he was grinning as his receptionist put her head in at the door.

"Ready for your first patient, Doctor?"

"As ready as I'll ever be, Miss Ross."

Paul Travers came in at lunch time. One glance at his face told Chris the kind of news he brought.

"No luck at the bar of justice, eh?"

"Not a chance. Local politics are too jittery."

Chris closed his eyes on that thought for a moment. He wondered how his own suit would go, if a Public Health representative could not buck the system.

Paul said, "Of course I rather expected this. Local judges are never anxious to give court orders to outsiders. Especially outsiders from Washington. I still had to put on a front with the committee."

"They've a pretty big stake in this downtown, Paul. I learned that much this morning, when Dwight tried to buy me out."

"Is our friend that jittery? That's my best news today. How much did he offer?"

"One hundred and twelve thousand." Chris grinned. "I think I could have upped the ante after I told him about my report to the Compensation Commission. Unfortunately, we were too busy barking by that time."

Paul shook his head mournfully. "I wish you hadn't tipped your hand on that. He'll throw the book at you now."

"He promised as much before I tossed him out on his ear."

"Figuratively?"

"Literally. Take a look at Roy's prize flower bed."

Paul stared out the window a moment before he let out his breath in a whistle. "Why didn't you wait for me? We could have tossed him farther."

"Save your strength for your own battles, Paul. Are you trying another court?"

"There isn't time now. Besides, I think I have a better way."

Their eyes met; Chris knew that they understood one another without words.

"Officially?"

"Highly personal. They'd have my hide if they knew what

I have in mind. Of course I'm acting strictly as an individual."

"Want to make that two?"

"Speaking of your own battleground——"

"This is my battleground as much as yours. Besides, what can I lose now?"

They shook hands solemnly on that note. "Meet me at Karen's, then," said Paul. "Eight sharp. And wear old clothes."

Chris smiled in earnest. "I'm way ahead of you, Doctor. Mind if I bring along a few ideas of my own?"

18

DRIVING ACROSS THE BRIDGE to St. Lucie that evening, Chris saw that Karen's cottage was lighted as though for a party. Dance music beat through the screen as he parked his car. Paul was crouched over the dials when he entered, with a tall glass in his hand. Sam Bernstein, nursing another highball in the depths of an armchair, looked anything but cheerful.

Chris banged on the screen for attention. "Where's our hostess?"

"Headed for Bayshore, on my orders," said Paul. "She took it like a soldier, too."

"We could have used Karen tonight," said Sam. "Someone had to stand by at the hospital. Just in case, you know."

Chris came into the room and mixed himself a drink at the impromptu bar. It was strange how the three of them accepted their job without even mentioning it. Karen too: it would be no picnic for her, sitting at night admissions while she waited for news from the Flats.

"Why'd you pick this place to meet, Paul?"

"I wanted it to look like a party. Just in case anyone is snooping." The Public Health man stalked to the veranda to stare off into the dark. His voice had betrayed his edgy nerves.

266

Chris said, "Sam and I can handle this. You should stay clear. The Service would drop you like a shot if it knew."

"It's too late to argue about that. We're in this up to our necks."

Chris shrugged. The three of them knew that he had spoken only to ease his mind. "Talk, Sam. I can guess you lured Paul into this."

"Forgive me for planning this much without you?"

"We'll get to that later. Right now I want to know how well you've planned. Maybe I'll add a contribution of my own."

Sam hugged his knees and stared regretfully at his empty glass. "In just twenty minutes we move in on rat heaven— my pet phrase for the garbage dump. Pudge and certain friends of his will be watching for us in the yards. They've fixed it with the men at the gate. When they're sure we're waiting at the other side of the objective, they'll chop into a few of those Diesel drums under the coal tipples and dump 'em. If you ask me, we'll have a nice bonfire in no time."

"Who's going to start it?"

"Paul and I—with kerosene balls. Ever throw a kerosene ball when you were a kid?"

"And what'll the rats do when the dump gets hot?"

"Most of them will roast, I hope."

"You'll still lose some, unless they're penned in—or drowned." Chris had already begun to sketch the layout on the back of a prescription blank. His pencil paused on the tidal creek, with its high, flimsy dike. "Don't think you're the only conspirators on this job. I drove over that bridge yesterday and planned to do the whole job with dynamite. Of course dynamite and fire are a foolproof blend—so far as the rats are concerned."

Paul shook his head and poured a fresh drink. "Trust an amateur to show me up in my own business," he said. "Where'll we steal the dynamite?"

"I've stolen it now, from the work shed on the Bayshore grounds. Don't forget to take care of that foreman tomorrow, Sam. He might ask questions."

The little doctor started for the liquor and thought better of the move. "Since I'll be attaching the fuses, I'd better stay sober. You would remember that I worked with a construction gang one summer at college."

They found that they were moving out to the parked car,

as though by common impulse. It would take time to place a dynamite charge correctly—even with Sam's help. The car jolted just a little as Chris threw in the clutch; he laughed aloud as Sam gasped in fright.

"Dynamite doesn't explode on ordinary jars. At least that's what the book says."

"Maybe this dynamite doesn't read books."

The house still blazed like a store window behind them. As the car left St. Lucie, Chris turned back to watch Paul come down the steps and get into his own battered roadster. Somehow these precautions seemed a bit ridiculous now that they were actually rolling in the night; yet he knew that Paul Travers would be the last to bow to melodrama.

It seemed a remarkably short drive to the Flats. At the bridge Chris drew up on the shoulder and smiled at Sam in the dark.

"Are you as nervous as that silence sounds?"

Sam picked up the package of dynamite from the rear seat by way of answer. They walked down the top of the dike beyond the bridge, hearing the suck of the tidal creek below. Even in the darkness Chris knew that they were silhouetted against the skyline whenever a battery of torches in the yard went into action. They walked gingerly—and pancaked in the mud when the lights of a passing car all but picked them out. Borland's steel mesh was too close for comfort; Chris knew that there were guards posted there at intervals. Patrolmen with full police power, who might not be friendly to Pudge Carrol—or a pair of dark shapes skulking outside.

The car parked beside their own, and they sat up rather foolishly, realizing that it was only Paul. The Public Health man's voice was an odd anticlimax in the dark.

"Picked your spot yet?"

"Just about. I'm playing safe and planting two charges. One on either side of the dike."

Chris took a small shovel from the sack he had carried from the car. He had dug a foxhole with such an instrument many times before; somehow he had never bored for cover faster. Sam, he saw, was already unrolling a fuse from the package of explosive.

"How much time do you want?"

"Ten minutes should do." He watched Sam measure as he finished his first hole and scrambled to the other side of the dike. The little doctor measured a cap in his fingers and fitted it to the cut end of a fuse. Paul watched, too, as he squatted on his heels beside him, soaking fat wads of lint in kerosene.

"How will you clamp the fuse?"

"Dynamiters use a metal pincers," said Sam. "Amateurs use teeth."

No one spoke as he put the cap into his mouth and bit down sharply. In his second pit Chris was making the dirt fly; Paul went on with his homemade incendiary bombs as calmly as though he were working in his New York laboratory. We're in to our necks now, thought Chris. We're in so deep we haven't time to be afraid.

Sam spoke from the edge of the first hole. "Want me to plant the charge on this side, Chris?"

"Go ahead. I'm about ready here."

The job was done when he hoisted himself to the top of the dike again. Sam passed him, crabwise, and repeated the planting on the other side. He came back with his face smudged and waved Chris and Paul toward the bridge. The two fuses unreeled after them as they worked back toward their starting point.

Paul said, "Who'll touch 'em off?"

"I'm the expert," said Sam.

Chris shook his head. "This is my idea. Let me have some of the fun."

Sam put the fuse ends in his hands a little reluctantly. "Sure you can spot the signal from here?"

They turned in unison as a muffled clanking sounded from behind the steel-mesh fence beyond and above them. An eerie sound in the dark, which seemed to come half from the yards, half from the great, reeking pit just below the fence itself.

"Pudge is on time too," said Chris. "I won't need a signal, even if I miss it. My end of the job can wait until the dump is actually afire."

He lay quite still while Paul and Sam moved away in the dark. In a moment he saw their silhouettes against a sputter of white sparks in the yard, lost them again as the welding stopped. He knew that they were carrying the kerosene bucket between them, and prayed that no cars would use that short cut across the bridge. A curious intruder could play havoc with their plans, even now.

The metallic crunch of an ax on an oil drum told him that

Pudge and his cohorts were moving fast within the yards. Again the torches flared, and he held his breath as the gates below the coal tipples swung outward. He had just time to see a scurry of dark shapes before the light faded, but he guessed that they had already tipped the huge metal container toward the lip of the excavation below them. In another moment the acrid odor of the oil confirmed his suspicions—even before he heard another ax crunch home and the clatter of a second drum catapulting down the side of the dump.

Already he guessed that the inflammable Diesel fuel had spread into the malodorous pit. But Pudge was doing a thorough job, it seemed: four more drums rattled down the slope before his flashlight winked its summons to Sam and Paul. The union had done its part: the rest was up to the doctors. . . .

The doctors went into action when Sam Bernstein lit the first kerosene ball. There was no mistaking the roly-poly obstetrician against the flare. Paul Travers stood out in turn now, when a second match took hold farther along the lip of the dump. . . . Chris felt his own fingers itch for action; he stilled the impulse by testing the flame of his lighter. There'd be no time for fumbling when he went into his own routine.

In another moment Chris counted eight fireballs blazing in the gravel. Now, he knew, came the real trick: it needed a quick hand to swing these blazing missiles by their strings and arch them away toward the objective. Sam made the first throw, like an outfielder pegging home. Paul, a gaunt scarecrow in the flares, pitched almost in unison. The flaming wads of kerosene rocketed downward, like meteors bound the wrong way. The two doctors were already sprinting down the line to send the others in their wake.

Watching the fireballs form their graceful arcs, Chris all but forgot the important presence of the oil beneath: the multicolored tongues of flame that leaped up from the heart of the great dump reminded him abruptly of his own job. He must move fast now if he meant to cut off the escape of the rodents they were seeking to destroy.

He held the outer fuse to the lighter flame, forcing himself to keep the small blaze steady until he was sure that the fire had begun to run down the line. An overpowering impulse urged him to backtrack for the bridge, to trust that first charge of dynamite to do the job; he crushed it firmly and vaulted over the crest of the dike to lay the second fuse along the inner side.

Wet mud sucked at his foot and released it, to send him pitching toward the water. He went in above his chin and came up with his mouth full of the tidal backwash. By a miracle he had remembered to thrust his right hand skyward and save the lighter. For a heartbreaking moment he thought that the second fuse had fouled. Then, as the lighter blazed, he was watching a second train of sparks dance toward the deep-planted charge beyond.

He breathed again as he swung a leg over the bridge railing. The lights of an approaching car bathed him in brilliance, but he was beyond caring, now that the dump was spouting fire like a volcano gone berserk. The car roared down the slight dip in the road, ignoring the flames in its race to gain the drive a scant hundred yards to the north. Chris, his clothes flapping, spread his arms wide to snub it off.

"Put on your brakes! Can't you see the dump's burning?"

The headlights flicked this wet scarecrow disdainfully before the car sighed to a stop. A long white convertible with familiar lines. Chris remembered it perfectly, even before he heard the burst of French behind the windshield. Jean Moreau, he gathered, reverted to his native tongue in moments of stress. He cursed his luck as he moved toward the car door. Including Dwight himself, he could think of no other person he wanted to meet less at that moment.

"What are you doing here?"

White teeth flashed in the gloom of the tonneau. "I might ask the same question, Dr. Land. If you must know, we were cutting across the Flats to the Miramar."

They both turned when the car door opened on the far side. Chris gasped a warning, but Roz Borland had already run down the bridge for a nearer view of the fire. The flames etched her figure clearly against the night: Chris saw that she was in her shipyard garb, the bright bandanna knotted at her throat now to free her copper curls.

He tried to call to her again, but the words stuck in his throat. As a man watches his dearest possession vanish in a dream, he saw her slide down the side of the dike and point ahead in the dark.

"Look, Jean! The creek's burning too."

Chris saw that she was reeling just a little, and guessed

271

that she had had more than one drink before this projected trip to the roadhouse across the Flats. His mind had not adjusted to the reality of her presence. Then he heard Moreau shout behind him, and knew that the Frenchman was backing his car off the bridge. The purr of the motor stabbed at his brain, snapping him back to reality. Rosalie, he saw, was climbing farther down the bank, to point at the sputtering fuse. Already she had moved perhaps twenty feet along the dike, straight toward the cache of dynamite.

"Come back, Roz!"

He slithered down the bank as he saw her pause at the water's edge. The sparks raced down the fuse, and he scrambled forward frantically to outdistance them. Measurements meant nothing to him now: in the darkness he had no way of knowing how close she had come to the explosive. There was no time to shout another warning—no time for anything but a flying tackle that sent them both sprawling, half in the ooze of the dike, half in the brackish creek below.

Even as he spread-eagled his body to protect Rosalie, he was conscious of a great force pressing them even deeper in the mud. Thunder shook the ground beneath them and pounded in their eardrums. Almost instantly he felt the water pour over his shoulders in a cool, rushing torrent as the creek siphoned off through the gap in the dike. He staggered to his knees and pulled Roz up beside him. The water sucked cruelly at his legs, threatening to trip them both into the miniature waterfall he had created. Beyond he heard the hiss of flames as the creek roared into the gulley beside the coal tipples, sealing off the only escape from the blazing dump.

When he had dragged Rosalie to the top of the dike again, he saw that she had fainted. He pushed back the mass of wet hair from her face to make sure she was breathing; then, scarcely conscious of the act, he bent to kiss her lips.

The crunch of Moreau's feet on the dike brought him back to sanity. He did not even look at the Frenchman as he got to his feet and carried Rosalie back to the bridge. There was a tear in her slacks and a gash on the inner side of her leg, just below the knee. He found no other sign of injury.

Moreau said, "How did it happen?"

"Nothing's happened. She's just fainted. If you'll put on your headlights, I'll have a go at this cut."

He had started the emergency bandage before the Frenchman came back from his instrument board. The cut seemed only superficial, now that he could examine it in a perfect light. Moreau nodded a silent agreement as he knelt beside him.

"She was lucky, *non?*"

"We were both lucky. Will you take her to town and dress this properly?"

Roz opened her eyes and smiled up at them both. "Don't tell me that was dynamite!"

Chris wondered if she had faked that brief collapse. It was quite in character, he told himself grimly, now the danger had passed. He made himself step back, letting Moreau lift the girl into the car.

Roz said dreamily, "Dynamite, or Dr. Christopher Land. Maybe they're synonyms." Moreau was already offering her a flask of brandy; she took a long sip and smiled again at them both. "Am I being too original? Should I just say, 'Where am I?' or 'What happened?' "

The Frenchman was already getting into the car. "I'll explain on the way home, *chérie.*" He nodded crisply to Chris. "With your permission, Doctor."

"No one's taking me home," said Rosalie. "We were headed for the Miramar. That still goes."

"As you will," said Moreau. "In fact, the suggestion is excellent. Dutch Charlie has a medical kit in his office." He winked at Chris across the steering wheel. "I had occasion to use it on a former visit."

Roz fluttered a groggy hand as the long white car gathered speed. Chris still stood mutely at the roadside, watching the apparition vanish in the night as suddenly as it had come. It was easy to think he had dreamed it all—including the kiss he had pressed upon those cold, wet lips. And yet, as he fumbled with the memory, he wondered if Roz Borland's lips had been so cold after all—or so unresponsive. . . .

His fellow conspirators were running down the bridge— two grotesque gnomes against a scarlet backdrop. He shook himself into awareness as Sam pounded his back.

"Who's a hundred-per-center now? Did you ever see such a rat roast?"

"D'you suppose any got through?"

"Not with that dynamite right on cue. Come down to the cutoff and watch them float out to sea."

Paul was a trifle quieter. "Wasn't that a car I saw on the bridge just now?"

Chris described what had happened as briefly as he could. The fact that Roz had entered his life, and his plans, again seemed no less fantastic, now that he had put it into words.

Sam put the intrusion into words of his own. "Of all the breaks—having that steel-plated frog recognize you. To say nothing of the Borland brat. Boy, we'll get fireworks from both sides now." He walked to the bridge rail and stared back at the fire. "I suppose we can play three-handed rummy in jail."

"You two are in the clear," Chris said. "Remember, I'm the only one they saw."

"Stop leading with your chin, brother. We're in this as a gang."

It was a situation that must be faced now or not at all. Chris accepted that much as he turned toward his car. If the Frenchman reported this to Dwight, he would be stopped in his tracks. If Borland withdrew his contract now . . . He did not finish the thought as he slid in under his wheel.

"We mustn't be seen together, Sam. Will you drive back to town with Paul and drop off at the hospital?"

The little obstetrician gave him a puzzled glance. "Where are you bound?"

"Believe it or not, I'm getting a drink at the Miramar. Somehow I think I've earned it."

He waved to the two figures on the bridge as he backed into the cinder road that led to higher ground. There was simply no time to explain that he must see Roz again and learn the worst. No time to pause for one last look at the job they had done. Swinging up to macadam again where the shipyard fence ended, he saw that hoses were already playing along the sooty face of the coal tipples. Pudge, it seemed, had thought of everything; as a saboteur in reverse, Pudge was practically perfect. He would take time to square himself with the union leader—in the morning. The clinic's future was more important at the moment.

He felt curiously calm when he parked outside the roadhouse. The trouble he'd started tonight was only a vague red sheen now across the bay; if the flap of his wet trouser legs reminded him that he was a strange figure, even for the Miramar, Roz Borland was in the same boat too.

He found her in a wall booth, just as he expected, with a tall glass before her. Moreau was nowhere in evidence. He saw at a glance that her leg had been skillfully treated and

274

freshly bandaged. Dutch Charlie was behind the bar: he gave Chris a gimlet-eyed stare before his face cracked in a toothy smile. Nothing disturbed Dutch Charlie once he recognized a customer.

"Sit down, Doctor," said Roz. "What's your pleasure?"

"You'll excuse me if I'm intruding?"

"We expected you." She smiled up at the hovering waiter. "Bring the gentleman bourbon, Joe. Where's your memory?"

Chris stayed on his feet. "How's the leg?"

"Don't give it a second thought. Maybe *I* should apologize for intruding, out on the Flats. Jean would take a short cut to a drink."

So far their meeting had gone exactly on schedule. He wondered how long she would dare hold him at arm's length with this teasing line. To cover the tug of that question he sat beside her in the wall booth and pushed back the slashed fabric of her slacks to examine the dressing in detail.

Roz said, "Maybe you should ask Jean for a consultation before you go into that. I can assure you he won't split the fee."

"Where is he, by the way?"

"Telephoning."

Chris felt his jaw tighten. Apparently Moreau had lost no time reporting to Dwight.

Roz said, "He isn't turning you in, if that's what you're thinking. If you must know, he's calling to check on a patient."

"Believe me, you needn't explain."

"Isn't that why you're here, Chris?"

"I'm here to explain what I was doing on the Flats, if you'd care to listen. After that you may draw your own conclusions."

Roz said, "If you'll stop being righteous for a moment, I'll thank you for saving my life. I'm glad you thought it was worth saving."

"Never mind that now," he said, keeping his voice tight. "The point is, you've got me at your mercy. What are you going to do about it?"

She did not interrupt as he retold the story of the raid on the garbage dump, holding back no detail save the names of his accomplices. When he had finished she looked at him for a long, wide-eyed moment without speaking. He felt his heart thump madly; when the waiter brought his drink, he downed it in two swallows without even tasting it.

Roz said evenly, "Did you think I'd run to Dad with this?"

"You have every right to tell him."

"If you ask me, he was a mule not to listen to you."

Chris let out his breath softly. "Does this mean I'm reprieved?"

"It's Scanlon's fault, of course. Dad simply takes his word for things. But that's no excuse." Watching her face harden, Chris thought again how much she resembled her father from certain angles. Both of them were alike in their stubbornness —and their integrity.

Roz said, "Why didn't you ask me to join the party? I'd have jumped at it."

He smiled despite himself. "I'm afraid your fiancé would have objected."

"I've broken dates with my fiancé before, when the fun was selling."

"This wasn't a bit of fun. In fact, it was damned dangerous."

"Especially the dynamite," said Roz. "Last time it took a half pint of bourbon to make you kiss me."

He knew that he was blushing to the roots of his hair. It had been quite like her to feign collapse. "I thought you'd fainted," he said. "You're quite a good performer."

Roz said easily, "I didn't have time to be frightened. Besides, I had an edge on you. Remember, you were cold sober."

"Not at that precise moment," he said.

"Relax, Chris. I'm not saying a word about tonight. Not to anyone. I won't even tell Jean that you made love to me when you thought I was unconscious."

He let his hand cover hers. "Thank you, Roz."

"The pleasure was all mine. What you allowed me, at least. Of course I wouldn't admit that if I weren't a trifle tight."

You aren't in the least tight now, he told himself. In fact, I think you were shamming back there on the Flats. Trying to shock me—for what? If there was a reasonable answer to that question, he had no right to ask it now. Instead he got up carefully from the booth—found he was still holding her hand, and put it down, just as carefully, on the table.

Roz said, "Sometime soon we're going to say what we really think. Out loud. I can hardly wait for that day—can you?"

He had meant to make his exit as dignified as he could; he knew that he had already spoiled it by lingering. "I've tried to be frank with you," he said stiffly. "Sorry if I've given another impression."

"You aren't in the least sorry," said Roz. "What's more, you know I've my reasons for being tight this evening. Or any evening when I come off the shift."

She's acting even now, he thought. Even though I steered her into the first honest job she ever had. Even though her life was beginning to make sense again, until this Frenchman spoiled everything by proposing. . . . He reminded himself sharply that he had no right to criticize her engagement to Moreau. Or even to complain too strenuously if her talent for self-dramatization died hard. After all, he owed his professional future to her silence.

He said only, "Good night, Rosalie. And thanks again." And remembered Moreau when he stalked into the lobby again and met the Frenchman face to face beside the phone booths.

Moreau said, "A pleasure, Doctor. Won't you join us in a drink?"

"I've had one, thanks. What are you going to do?"

The words rasped out, despite his judgment. At that moment he knew that he had been insane to come this far. He had just escaped opening his heart to Rosalie: the sight of Moreau was a visible door slamming between them.

Moreau shrugged. "Do? Right now I am making sure that my fiancée's nerves are rested. Then, with luck, I shall persuade her to go home."

Chris said carefully, "I wanted to make sure she was unhurt."

"So you knew of her accident. A walk down the East Point jetty to look for the moon. . . . She might have picked a worse place to trip. She was drenched to the waist."

"Is that what you told Dutch Charlie?"

"And everyone, Dr. Land. Why not—since she desires it?"

Chris looked at the Frenchman narrowly. The man's eyes were utterly candid. If this was a game, it was not apparent on the surface.

He spoke carefully. "I don't think I get your drift."

"Rosalie has said she would marry me, Doctor. We face the world as one, when it comes to the reports we make. Especially on our evenings out."

"You know damned well I placed that dynamite."

Moreau ignored the statement with his usual show of manners. "Already Dutch Charlie gets reports from trailer town. It seems that someone has had the courage to burn out the dump at last. To drown the rats in the bargain. A magnificent job, Dr. Land."

"D'you mean that?"

"Of course I mean it. Long ago I told Dwight that he should make Scanlon do it. Dwight is a genius at money-making; he is also a stubborn fool."

"If you think that, why are you on his side?"

"One's temporary ally is not always one's friend," said Moreau. "That, I fear, is something Americans will not understand." He held up a soothing finger. "But I forget. The last time we discussed America we came to blows. Change your mind about that drink?"

"Thank you, no. I'm expecting an epidemic tomorrow."

"In that case, may I once more wish you *bonne chance?*"

Moreau went into the roadhouse with a negligent flick of his hand. He crossed the nearly empty dance floor and entered the booth where Roz Borland sat with the easy gesture of a man who knew his place and enjoyed that place thoroughly. For a moment Chris stood on irresolutely in the lobby, watching the man's sleek blond head close to Rosalie's copper curls. Then he walked slowly out to his car, consumed by the greatest letdown he had ever known.

19

THE LONG LINE outside the shack hitched forward a pace as the girl stepped up to the examining table. Chris had already noted the unnatural brightness of her eyes; now, as she parted the low-cut blouse she wore for his inspection, he noted the spattering of tiny red patches just above the swell of her breasts. He pressed upon one of the spots and watched it blanch but not disappear. The red color was replaced now by a rusty brownish hue. The rash was typical enough to end the checkup here. Only typhus gave that characteristic skin eruption.

He kept his voice quiet. "I'm afraid you have typhus." The girl swayed a little at the news, and he touched her elbow lightly to steady her. Despite his low tone, the line behind her had scuffed its collective feet and backed away. He raised his voice to give it authority. "There is no danger of contagion here—absolutely no danger."

Ten times in the past hour, while the inhabitants of trailer town moved through this impromptu immunization mill, he had used that same phrase. It had stopped the scuffing feet for a while, though the haunted look remained in many eyes down that long, waiting line. Now, as a nurse led the new patient toward the ambulance, he bent over his notebook to add her name to the admissions list. Tomorrow, as he well knew, that list would be filled to capacity. Already patients were beginning to crowd the Slade mansion, even before its formal opening as an annex.

Sam Bernstein touched his elbow, and he got up gratefully. They had been spelling each other on two-hour shifts like this ever since early afternoon. When he walked out into the palmetto scrub for a cigarette, he saw that the dusk was beginning to thicken in this man-made wilderness of jalopy and tar paper. He leaned against a pine bole and tried to forget how tired he was. Even as he watched he saw Karen switch on the lights in the big Public Health trailer parked on the shoulder of the road. The same long line he had been examining was moving toward that mecca now, arms already bared and ready for one of Paul's syringes.

The day just gone, he reminded himself, had not moved on such a precise schedule. There was the council of war he'd found waiting for him in the hospital dining room that morning. Sam and Paul, and a rather amused Karen, waiting doggedly to face the sheriff—and rather incredulous when Chris had told them that no sheriff was coming, so far as their raid on the dump was concerned. *He* had gone to his morning work with the certainty that the sheriff would call with Gilbert Dwight's complaint for assault and battery; but it seemed that the compensation doctor had taken that bounce in the flower bed as a personal matter. Chris was sure of that much when Sam had put his head in the office around noon and confirmed a rumor that Dwight had taken an early plane to Washington.

Now, standing relaxed in the heavy dark, he drew deep on his cigarette and considered his enemy's reasons for departure. Certainly it was to Dwight's advantage to be out from under, with this epidemic in the making. . . . He corrected the phrase sharply. The typhus epidemic was already in full swing, with a peak nowhere in sight. He had sensed that much as he'd faced his tense waiting room and read the terror in those haunted eyes. He had read that same message three minutes ago, when he saw a frightened girl walk toward the Bayshore ambulance. . . .

Dwight, it seemed, had pulled out in the nick of time, leaving Kornmann in charge. And yet when Karen came in from the express office with the fat package of vaccine, he had ordered the major share sent on to the Austrian without pausing to weigh the consequences. After all, the health of the main shipyard was the concern of every doctor in Milton; he could not believe that Kornmann would fail to use the vaccine if he could demonstrate the need.

Later that day, when he had gone over the charts from his own contagious ward, he had obeyed a sudden impulse and phoned Dr. Deavers. The older physician had accepted with alacrity when he had invited him to stop by and examine his patients. When he hung up Chris realized that Deavers must have seen Scanlon's absentee list at long last. There was no other logical reason for the man's change of pace. He had not been too startled to find that Deavers had brought two other visitors to his ward: Victor Baskin, the rickety diagnostician who happened to belong to one of Milton's oldest families—a fact which had given Dwight's office a cozy hometown aura from the start; and Kornmann himself, wheezing this afternoon from nerves rather than from a shortness of breath.

Deavers had been at his most orotund as he picked up the first fever chart. "The rash here is diagnostic, gentlemen. Definitely diagnostic."

Kornmann had said, "I haf observed often such a rash, with simple pyrexia."

"Not with a positive agglutination test in a six-forty dilution."

"How can we be sure the test iss authentic?"

Deavers had spoken ahead of Chris, with a sudden whiplash in his tone. "That will be enough, Dr. Kornmann. My opinion is that I've been deceived as to the number of typhus cases in Milton. Deliberately deceived."

"Are these tests run by the Board of Health Laboratory?" Chris had spoken then, for the first time. "We run our own determinations to facilitate early diagnosis."

"Then they are not—how you say?—authentic."

"There are twenty other cases in this ward." Chris's voice had the quiet edge of a man who is sitting at a poker table behind a royal flush. "All of their tests had been checked, and confirmed, by the State Lab. Would you care to see those reports as well, Dr. Deavers?"

He had led them down the line on that. Case after case lay in the rows of white-painted beds, each with the same jagged silhouette on its fever chart. In each case the report of the State Health Laboratory was attached, indicating a high positive reaction for typhus fever.

When they had seen ten cases, Deavers had spoken to Kornmann without turning. "It's evident that you owe Dr. Land an apology, Dr. Kornmann. How many cases of malaria has your group hospitalized at the County?"

"About ten, I think." The porcine refugee had turned on Baskin then, with the air of a master addressing a mongrel dog. "You will confirm that, please?"

But Baskin had refused to play the mongrel at that moment. Baskin, in fact, had apparently remembered that he had descended from at least one brigadier in the War of the Secession. "We've twenty-one malaria cases on our books as of now, Jerry," he had said softly, with a smile that was meant for Deavers alone. "Perhaps it's gone higher since we left the office."

Deavers had snapped at Kornmann in earnest then. "You will have agglutination tests run immediately, and notify me of the results."

"But Dr. Dwight——"

"Dr. Dwight is very fortunate to be out of town at this moment. In my opinion he has made a grave error in judgment. I shall so inform Mr. Borland."

"Borland's out of town too."

"Then I shall wire him at once and suggest he fly back to confer with me."

They had marched out on that note, as solemnly as they had come. But Chris had had little chance to rejoice at this unexpected victory. Paul Travers had phoned almost immediately, to lay the ground plan for his immunization of the West Island workers.

They had set up shop on the Flats at the break of the shifts, leaving Pudge Carrol to frighten his cohorts into line. Chris had stood by while Paul mounted the steps of the Public Health trailer to explain their danger—and his cure. He had watched Carrol pound a lone heckler into silence as Paul had spoken of last night's rat roast, of the union's bounty for each rat killed on the Flats, of the need of insecticides and spray guns and steam sterilizers. The tension in the crowd pressed tight around the medical trailer was a tangible thing; Chris had seen that it had frightened Paul a little, too, as he wound up his exposition. Somewhat to his own surprise, he had found himself mounting the steps at Paul's side, to remind them that a prepaid hospital bed would be waiting for all their sick. . . .

Now he threw away his cigarette and turned back to the tar-paper lean-to they had fitted out as an examining room. The waiting line looked as long as ever, but he made himself face it with a smile. Certainly they would be writing off the last of those terrified faces in an hour now. Perhaps, with complete immunization, they would see the number of new cases decline tomorrow. If Kornmann and Baskin were doing a similar job for their own flock, they might even nip terror in the bud.

Seating himself beside Sam, making that professional smile foolproof, he knew that he was only wallowing in false optimism. He had worked at this business too long for that. Tomorrow, and the day after, would prove that this was only an overture to the main nightmare.

Three days later—in the sanctuary of his office, making out his reports in another heavy dusk—he might have wondered if nightmare was too mild a word. Fortunately for his peace of mind, he had been working too fast to wonder. In a time like this you placed hospital beds in halls and sun porches—even in spare offices—when the last foot of ward space ran out. You wrote down a list of private homes on the side streets, and arranged to move your non-contagious cases there. Above all, you weren't in the least surprised when the town's doctors came to you one by one and asked leave to work for you on special shifts. Doctors are like that when crises come to the world they serve. The Dwights—and the Kornmanns—are only the exception that tests the rule.

Three nights ago, if anyone had told Chris that he was about to see the last of the Austrian refugee, he would have pronounced that person fit for the strait jacket. Yet he was not even ruffled tonight when Victor Baskin walked into his office without knocking and said just that. Three days and nights on one's feet in a contagious ward can numb any nervous system.

"When did he decide to leave, Victor?"

Baskin wavered to a chair and rocked his head in his hands. "I think it's being decided for him. That is, I—felt you should be the first to know. So I—slipped out the back way when they came."

"What are you talking about, man?" Chris looked at the diagnostician for the first time, noticing his rumpled shirt front and the smudge down the bridge of his too-well-chiseled nose.

"It's the workers, Chris. They came to—to protest."

Paul Travers entered, also without knocking, and slammed the door behind him. "So you beat me here, Doctor. I hoped you would."

Baskin said, "I'm afraid I ran on ahead, Travers. Will you tell Chris what happened? I'm a bit too—mixed up to breathe."

The Public Health man sat down in the open window frame and looked down the street outside. Then, before Chris could move or speak, he reached for the wall switch and snapped out the lights.

"Tell *me* something first, Chris. You did send Kornmann his share of that vaccine when it came?"

Chris got up slowly: a light was dawning in the darkness. "Karen knows the amount. More than enough to immunize the whole main yard."

"You delivered it three whole days ago?"

"He's had it longer than that now."

"Will you believe me when I say he hasn't used it?"

"Could even Kornmann be that dumb?"

Baskin's voice quavered. "The ampules are still in our icebox, Chris. I looked just before I——"

"So the union held a meeting tonight," said Paul. His voice raced as he snatched the story away from the other doctor. "It wasn't a formal meeting, but it was well attended. For-

283

tunately Pudge got to me in time, so I was able to put in a word. The men thought that you'd been vaccinating the West Island workers and deliberately keeping the serum from the others. That's the story Scanlon and his stooges have been spreading. . . . They said you needed all of it to protect the people you'd insured.

"God knows why they believed me when I told them the truth. Maybe they really think I'm impartial; maybe Pudge had enough of *his* stooges on hand to howl the hecklers down. Anyhow, they went to call on Kornmann before they called on you." He smiled briefly at the huddled form in the chair between them. "That's when Baskin decided to change sides. In other words, to run to cover before they escorted *him* to the city limits."

The diagnostician took up the tale in earnest now. "The crowd stormed round to the County, but Kornmann was out. Someone said he was at his office downtown, so they went there. Maybe two hundred of them—in jalopies and trucks— thick as flies on every mudguard. I warned Kornmann to go easy; I know how things can move in this town when trouble is selling. But he wouldn't listen. He just sat there, with that bull neck of his swelling above his collar. . . . They didn't break in, you understand; they weren't that sure of their anger at the time. Instead they sent three section foremen into the office to talk."

Again Paul took back the story. "Kornmann threw the first man out—or tried to. That's when Baskin hared it across town to you. As you see, I wasn't far behind."

Outside in the dark a great ball of a fist banged the window sill for attention. Pudge Carrol hoisted his bulk into the frame and said quietly, "None of us are far behind, Doc. What say we all think fast, while there's time?"

Chris felt his spine curl in the dark. Like Victor Baskin, he knew the temper of this town once it was aroused. It hardly mattered if he were innocent or guilty; thanks to his trust in Kornmann, the main yard workers had been deprived of their vaccine. Deavers had told him only today that the County Hospital was overflowing with patients now too. . . . He braced himself against the desk and blessed the chance that had sent Karen and Uncle Jeff to the other end of town to arrange for the use of a dozen beds in a nursing home. They, at least, would be spared the battle now in the making.

Pudge said, "When they come, I'll try to get 'em to send in

some deputies to talk to you. Just like they did with Kornmann. Don't talk back too hard, Doc, for God's sake. There's times when I can't make these lugs of mine see the light. Too many of your own fire-eaters on the roll, I guess."

Chris said, "I can see that now. Or is hear a better word?"

The roar that swept toward them in the dark was too synthetic to be ominous at first. A mélange of shouted words and screeching tires, of fists banged on mudguards, of a voice raised in drunken song—the one noisy drunk that is swept up in every crowd and comes along for the ride. . . . Then, as the first torches flared, Chris saw the reason for the shouts—and the hard rhythm of fists on metal.

He didn't recognize Kornmann at first when the grotesque procession swept across the corner of the hospital lawn, paused for a moment, and then clopped on, in rhythm to the fists beating a tattoo on a dozen mudguards and car doors. The Austrian was a two-hundred-pounder, so it took four huskies to handle the rail he straddled; four others flanked the rail with croker sacks, tossing fistfuls of chicken feathers at the rider. Kornmann was daubed with tar from head to foot; from the distance he looked like a surrealist's idea of a white turkey on the way to market. The torches did not show his face, but Chris could tell, from the way he clutched at his perch, that the man was paralyzed with fear.

Pudge Carrol spoke softly. "People can move awful fast when it comes to driving out a skunk. That's one thing I like about people."

Chris knew that he should feel angry at the savage ritual outside; at the moment he felt nothing but a deep exultation as he watched the Austrian vanish into the night. This was the payment he deserved for his crime against the Sanders girl—a payment he might even remember in the future.

"They're taking him to the railroad station," said Baskin. "I'll see that his baggage is sent after him. . . . Someone should tell Borland, of course."

"Borland's still away."

"His plane got in an hour ago," said Pudge. "I asked the airport to tip me off. Too bad he didn't get in sooner. If you ask me, he'd have enjoyed seeing this too."

He broke off as a rock crashed against a pillar of the hospital porch. Some of the crowd had streamed off after Kornmann, but the others had lingered, seeking another victim.

No one in the office spoke while the workers' cars jockeyed in the street outside, focusing a half-moon of headlights on the porch and the grounds.

"Thought of anything yet, Doc?" asked Pudge quietly.

"I'm ready," said Chris just as quietly. "Can you cool them off a little first?"

"I can try."

A shower of rocks banged on the porch, and Pudge vaulted down to the lawn. The crazy murmur of voices stilled as he walked into the headlights with both arms spread wide.

"What are you monkeys doin' here? Don't you know your friends?"

Scattered voices cut through the silence.

"Where's Land?"

"Ask him why he don't stop the sickness."

"He's got serum. Kornmann said——"

Pudge roared, "Does anyone here believe Kornmann?"

The same voice barked back, out of darkness. "He says Land hid the serum. That he only gave him a few shots."

"Whose pay roll are you on—Kornmann's or mine?"

There was a sound of blows in the dark, and the voice stilled. Chris realized that he had some friends in the crowd, at least. But the hubbub still continued.

"Land must of still known we weren't getting shots."

"He coulda done something."

Again Pudge spread his hands for silence. "Will you let Dr. Land explain this himself, you lunkheads?"

Chris had already walked out beside him, his white coat a target for the headlights. Pudge, it seemed, had gauged the temper of this crowd accurately when he threw him his cue. They were in no mood to send in a delegation now. Only a gesture of sheer drama would keep them from overrunning the hospital itself.

"Will you men listen? I trusted Kornmann to immunize all of you. He has more than enough vaccine at his office now."

A strangled voice rose from the crowd. "He said he'd have to charge us for the shots."

"That was a lie. The money for that vaccine came from your emergency fund. It was Kornmann's duty to administer it at once."

The crowd still rumbled, only half attentive. Chris knew that he had not reached them yet. In their hearts they still

286

lumped him with the Austrian, a threat to all they held precious.

"I can still help you, if you'll let me!" he shouted. "That vaccine is in Kornmann's office now. How many of you start the night shift?"

Pudge was with him, he saw. "Put up your hands," he bellowed. "Don't forget I know you."

There was a show of hands in the crowd—and only a few catcalls. Chris said quickly, "I can be at the main yard with that vaccine in thirty minutes. We'll immunize you men as you go in, and take the outgoing shift at the same time. Anyone on the swing shift is at liberty to join the line."

"What about our families?"

"The Public Health trailer will finish the job on the Flats in the morning."

"I got a sick kid at home," another voice cried. "What'll you do for her?"

"Leave your name, and the ambulance will call for her at once."

"But I'm not on your list."

"We aren't keeping lists of that kind. Just lists of sick people. I'll guarantee all hospital bills and make sure she has a bed."

He took a step forward, trying to reach the speaker with his eyes—and he knew he had made his point at last, as there was a faint scattering of applause. Pudge took full advantage of the wavering moment as he charged down into the dark melee of bodies below him.

"You heard the doc. Our folks get cared for, and we all get the shots. What else d'you want—a signed testimonial?"

The fight in the inchoate mass dissolved as abruptly as it had come. Chris knew that he was accepted when the backs began to turn. They were following Pudge now, seeping slowly off his lawn to find their cars again, laughing a little among themselves as they kicked at their starters. Pudge, in the vanguard, shouldered his way into a jalopy that already groaned with occupants. Then he cupped his hands to shout back at Chris.

"See you at the main gate, Doc." He slapped the driver's shoulder. "Take the lead out, Gus. We got a shift to make."

Chris leaned against a pillar on the hospital porch and watched them go. It had all happened so suddenly he had had no time to be afraid. Pudge, the bellwether, had saved him at just the right moment; he had won their confidence, though he must move fast to keep it. He turned abruptly and almost collided with Dr. Baskin, who was standing ramrod-straight on the steps.

"How long have you been here, Victor?"

"From the start. I thought we should stand together." Baskin had not relaxed. Perhaps he was still remembering that ancestor who had once ridden on Joe Johnston's staff. He looked for Paul—and realized that the Public Health man had gone into the hospital to rout out Sam Bernstein from ward call and line up equipment for the job ahead.

"You'll help with the vaccine, Victor?"

"If you'll permit me."

"Permit you? Who else is giving orders at the main yard until Dwight gets back?"

The diagnostician met his eyes. "If you put it that way, Chris——"

"What about Scanlon? Will he let us in?"

Baskin set his jaw firmly. "I can handle Scanlon, now that Borland's back."

They walked into the hospital side by side.

Looking back, he knew that this had been both the high and the low moment in the typhus battle. Of course the next ten days left him little time for reflection of any sort. He had been through these sieges before, at Lakeview and in the Army; he had taught himself to be an automaton as the need arose, and like it. This time it was not the heroic battle that most laymen visualize when the doctor goes out to beat down an epidemic. Rather it was dreary slogging from ward to trailer town, from fever-haunted shack to the jammed corridors of a clinic that was no less haunted. . . .

And yet from that taut moment in the glare of headlights he had known that the battle would go his way, so far as the typhus was concerned. It had been a hunch, with no backing of science, but he had felt it working from then on. When he could sleep for three whole hours, on an office cot, without an interruption, he felt all the quiet triumph of a general who has taken a city; when beds began to ebb from hall and sun porch, and a whole morning went by without the report of a new case, he knew that he could let down in earnest— and go out for a haircut again.

Paul Travers made it official when he came into the office the next afternoon with a chart under his arm. One glance told him that their all-out immunization had begun to pay dividends in earnest.

"Looks like a Dow-Jones average, doesn't it?"

"The price of human life has gone up pretty sharply these past few days." Paul traced the irregular peaked line before them. "This is the case-incidence record."

"Falling off as sharply as that?"

"It'll really plummet now that the Flats are a hundred per cent immune."

Chris put his finger over several short black columns at the bottom of the chart. "I wish we could have prevented these." They were the deaths—twenty in all, including one of the refugee physicians who had dropped of coronary while working on a vaccine line. He stared down at the man's name for a moment. Dr. Helmut Sacher, of Vienna. In a way it was a grisly atonement for Kornmann.

Paul said bitterly, "We could have kept that record clear if it wasn't for Dwight."

"Don't remind me of that now. Incidentally, I hear he got back from Washington yesterday."

"Check. Isn't that the surest sign the epidemic is licked?"

Chris fished a document from his desk drawer and handed it over. "Here's a sign that my troubles are just beginning."

"Don't tell me this is a notice of trial?"

"To Christopher Land, M.D., for malpractice and damages, brought by one S. L. Dawkins. That means it's on the docket now for the coming session. . . . No, Luke couldn't postpone it after all. Not with an election coming on He's checking now to see who pulled the wires."

"Friends of Dwight's, you can be sure of that." Paul dropped his chart into his briefcase and cursed adequately. "If only there were some way to get at Dawkins. I'm sure he'd sing for our side if we paid him more."

"So far I've managed this scrap inside the law."

"Except for the dynamite," said Paul with a grin. "Why can't we dynamite Dawkins too?"

"Because the defendant in this case is a stiff-necked Puritan, I guess."

"Okay, Puritan, it's still your war. I've got to leave you now and start my Washington report. They're barking at me to know if we've proved louse transmission in this show or not."

"I wouldn't swear to it in the epidemic. Dwight to Dawkins is something else again."

"Call me a few days before I'm to testify. I'll want Luke to streamline the truth your way."

The lawyer was ambushed behind a paper in the waiting room when Paul went out. Chris admitted him to his office with a sinking heart. Luke Fraser's jaws had never clamped down that hard on a cold corncob unless he had a reason.

Luke said, "We're not just on the docket, boy. We go to bat next week, at 10 A.M. What's more, Porter is on the bench. He always hated me, ever since my old man beat him out for the Senate twenty years ago."

"Are you taking bets on the verdict?"

"No one but a chump would bet on the average jury. The trouble is, our side is so damned negative. Even if you prove the defendant's a swell guy, what have you? Character witnesses aren't half the fun Dwight will be when he goes into his act." Luke sighed and lit his corncob at last. "Maybe we can get off with a small judgment. You were pretty hard hit by this epidemic, weren't you?"

"We're in to our eyes. Still, we haven't touched Doc Embree's money. And things should build steadily from now on."

"I'm surprised you didn't go under."

"Lots of young clinics have folded under a blow like this. They didn't have my staff, I guess."

"I'm using them too, of course. The jury is bound to be impressed by their loyalty."

Chris reddened. "Will you lay off those big words?"

"See what I mean?" said Luke dourly. "You're bored by praise, only in another way."

"When do I go on the stand?"

"At the end. I'm counting on the impression you'll make, too. Dr. Agard and Dr. Travers will be our main witnesses. They were on the scene."

"Paul is ready to swear the child had diphtheria."

"Dwight is just as ready to swear she didn't, and Dwight's better known around here than Travers."

"What about his record in the epidemic?"

"Kornmann's record, you mean. Dwight has already pussyfooted to Deavers and squared himself there."

"How does he do it?"

Luke laughed aloud. "Reckon that's a trade secret of Dwight's, boy. If *you* had the hang of it, you wouldn't be

Chris Land. The point is, Dwight's still got the heavy artillery on his side here in Milton. All Travers does is snoop for the Federal government—from their point of view. Or should I say for the Washington Yankees? I'm asking him just six questions, and letting him down. God knows what Stanley Bibb will do when I'm through with him. He's betting three to one that he'll get a conviction."

Chris said doggedly, "Dwight's a liar, and Paul will be telling the truth. A man's job should have no bearing on his testimony."

"Stick to doctoring, boy," said Luke. "You'd starve in my racket."

"At least they'll believe Karen."

"Maybe so. But she's a foreigner, don't forget that."

"I've forgotten it long ago."

"The jury won't, dammit. Those crackers are leery of anything that sounds its *r*s. Especially if it has an accent too. God forgive me for saying this, but they'll be thinking of Kornmann when she's on the stand, and lumping them——"

"They'd better not think aloud."

Luke gathered up his papers. "Well, we start playing ball the day after tomorrow. Come what may, I hope to get you off light."

"Thanks for the vote of confidence, but you don't mean it. If I lose this case, I lose everything."

"It won't be that bad."

"Dwight's planned on that too. If Dawkins gets a verdict, he promised a criminal charge would be brought against me."

"Did you have witnesses?"

"You know Dwight better than that."

"Wait till day after tomorrow—we'll both find out how little we really know."

When Luke had gone Chris stole the first free moment to seek out Karen. He found her alone in the lab, making order of her casebook. She pushed her work aside after one quick look at his face.

"Don't tell me, my dear—I can guess."

But he told her what Luke had said just the same, and she listened gravely. When he had finished she took his face between her hands and kissed his lips.

"I thought that wasn't allowed in office hours."

"Can't I wish you luck my own way, darling?"

He took up her hand and pressed it against his cheek. "Thanks, Karen. I rather needed that."

"It makes me furious—that people should turn against you after all you've done for them."

"Not people. Just the bandits who want to keep their hide-outs in order."

He put his arm about her waist and drew her close for a moment, letting his senses calm in her nearness. In the weeks gone by it had been easy to drown his longing for Rosalie in work. . . . He closed his eyes and did not even remind himself that this was Karen in his arms, not Rosalie. Karen was the woman he had chosen, with his eyes open wide—the antidote that would shut the torture of Rosalie away from his consciousness.

"Couldn't we run away from it—as of now?"

He saw them both aboard the *Lady Jane,* dropping South Island astern in a fresh morning wind. This time they'd set a straight south-by-southeast course, with the Ten Thousand Islands of the Florida coast pricked on their chart as the next landfall. They'd sail past Lostman's River and the great swamps of the Everglades. Down to the Straits and the purple wash of the Stream itself. On the Grand Cayman, suits and judgments would be forgotten. . . . He raised his eyes and saw she was laughing at him.

"Are we past Cuba by now—or am I taking you skiing in Canada?"

"It wouldn't work, of course."

"You wouldn't let it work. Remember what I called you the night we met?"

He grimaced. "Don't remind me, please."

"A Southern gentleman," she said gently. "I meant it as a compliment. I still do. Your good name will always mean more to you than any escape." It was her turn to smile wryly now. "Even with me. Thanks for the immoral proposal just the same."

"I'd make it as moral as you'd let me." He forced her to look at him. "If there were no other consideration, would you come?"

"I'd go anywhere—so long as you needed me. But you won't need me that way, Chris. You never will. Paul Travers, maybe. Not you."

She had spoken quietly, with no hint of transition. Once again he knew that he and Paul were somehow bracketed in her mind. As though they were two facets of a problem she was bent on smoothing away.

"What's this about Paul?" he asked, striving to keep his voice light.

There was no coquetry in her smile. "Paul means a great deal to me—I don't have to tell you that."

"As much as me—or more?"

She did not answer that directly. "You've seen us together, Chris. Did you ever wonder if Paul was my lover before you came?"

Paul Travers and Karen. . . . The picture was incredible, and yet the pattern fitted. A rush of impressions crowded into his mind: the unlocked door of her cottage, Paul's familiarity with every inch of it, the casual camaraderie between them. All of it added up to a picture of intimacy that was touching rather than grotesque.

Karen said, "Paul has needed me sometimes. There you have it."

"But I've been asking you to marry me!" His male ego had asserted itself in a rush, after that first moment of clarity. "Why must you tell me these things?"

"Did you think I'd accept your offer unless you understood me perfectly?"

He took her hands. "Believe me, I want you none the less for this."

"Only I haven't accepted—yet," she said. "When you yourself are quite certain of your wishes—and your future—then I'll be ready with my answer."

Chris sighed a deep reproach. "Haven't we been over all this before?"

"Too often," she said, laughing. "Now tell me just how I can help you with the trial."

Borland's phone call caught him between operations at the end of a busy morning. He was a bit startled to have the shipbuilder's voice bounce at him from the ward-room telephone, without even a secretary in between.

"How's chances of dining with us tonight, Land? Just Roz and me?"

Chris tried to keep the amazement out of his voice. A man in Borland's position simply didn't issue an invitation like that without a reason. "The chances are excellent. In fact, I'd be delighted. How's your daughter, by the way?" He recovered swiftly on that. "I'd heard she had a—a fall recently."

Borland's laugh rumbled over the phone. "Leg's still swollen," he said. "If you ask me, that's the only reason she's staying home nights. See you about eight."

In the operating room beyond, Sam was already draping their next case. Fortunately for his peace of mind, the hospital routine gave him no chance for introspection. Later Sam drove over with him to the boathouse to discuss plans for the baby clinic which would soon begin to operate in the annex. The little obstetrician sighed his admiration as Chris slipped into a white tuxedo coat.

"Strike a hard bargain, brother. I'm rooting for you."

"So you think something's in the air?"

"I'm sure of it. Cal Borland doesn't invite you to his house to talk baseball. Maybe he wants you to marry his daughter."

Chris kept his eyes on the mirror. "I'm afraid that's Moreau's assignment."

"Then he's going to make you medical director of both yards. I'll take odds on it."

"Borland is a businessman first. The heat's too close to my neck for that."

Swinging into the Bayshore Drive after he had dropped Sam at his corner, he found that he was humming to hide his nervousness, and switched on his car radio. The supercharged voice of a commentator invaded the darkness.

". . . Germany, reeling from the blows of the Allied juggernauts, could find no rest today. France is gone; Belgium and the French coast are gone; the Siegfried Line has been both pierced and flanked. The myth of Festung Europa vanishes in the din of war—and that sound can be heard tonight beyond the Rhine. Soon it will be heard in Berlin itself—and, for Adolf Hitler, that will be the music of Gotterdammerung——"

He cut off that staccato hymn of certainty. As an ex-soldier he still resented it—even if the radio was right. Over in Italy his friends were still working in the tent operating theaters, sometimes with portable operating lights, oftener by the gleam of a pocket flash screened from enemy machine-gun fire. Some of his outfit was far north now, he knew—moving into Germany itself after storming the beachheads of the Riviera. . . . In a way their life was simpler than his own—certainly it was more exciting than this rather prosaic victory over a typhus epidemic. Yet that threat of typhus was important too. Festung Europa would still stand firm tonight if American ships had not gone down the ways on schedule.

For want of a nail, the shoe was lost. . . .

It was a small comfort, but it was real.

On Borland's portico the black major-domo offered his familiar smile; in the hall the square-rigged detective in livery faded like a satisfied ghost. The shipbuilder was alone in the big drawing room, looking rather improbably relaxed with a newspaper and a cigar. Once more Chris noticed how easily he dominated the big, history-haunted room. History might frown down on the upstart, even as the King ancestors were bridling in their gilt frames. This particular upstart, knowing he belonged with the future, could afford to ignore them.

Borland threw the newspaper aside and shook hands cordially. The British butler, operating on a remote control that only butlers know, appeared by magic with decanters on a tray.

"Bourbon," said the shipbuilder. "Stop me if I'm wrong."

"Bourbon will do nicely."

"Roz is disappointing us after all. Her fiancé got in this evening from a big job in Florida." Borland studied Chris shrewdly above his glass. "I hope you don't mind fighting a steak with me? I didn't ask you for fun, you know."

Chris wondered if Sam could be right about the shipbuilder's motives after all. He kept his voice in control. "I'm glad she's well enough to go out."

"I'd say she wasn't—she's still limping a little. But Moreau must know his job. By the way, how did you know she'd had a fall?"

"Because I was responsible." Chris breathed deeply. "I was just about to blow up a dike on your land. Roz got too close for comfort, so I tackled her."

Borland's brows welded in a solid line; Chris braced himself for the blast that did not come. Instead the shipbuilder chuckled under his breath. "So you're the one who planned that party. I rather thought you were."

"I'd have told you sooner, but——" Chris smiled. "It was quite a show. I think you'd have enjoyed it."

"You've got what it takes, haven't you? Trying to burn me out, then coming to my house for dinner."

"The dinner was your idea."

"I suppose you'd reported that dump as a menace."

"Scanlon wouldn't budge. Or didn't you know that?"

Borland said, "He's budged now, all right. In fact, he's left Milton. I fired him yesterday. What say we eat? I'm hungry."

There was no further allusion to the fire; apparently the matter was settled, from Borland's point of view. Scanlon, it seemed, was only another item. Chris began to speak of the defective ratchet and thought better of the impulse. He guessed that Borland went into details on his own when he cleaned house.

Over the soup the shipbuilder said, "Is it true the epidemic's licked?"

"You'll have no more typhus on the Flats. The rats are gone; the workers are immunized."

"Is typhus a definite industrial menace in the South?"

"By no means. If communities will spend enough to insure good living conditions, we can ignore it completely. Malaria will be another story after the war. Here in Milton it's pretty well screened out in advance, thanks to Paul Travers—and you."

"Why me?"

"After all, you drained the swamps to build your empire."

Borland accepted the epithet without blinking. For a moment he stared up at the butler serving the burgundy, with the air of a man suspicious of his surroundings yet enjoying them too.

"I wanted to run up a low-cost housing project right outside my gate. The city fathers said no."

"Blame that on organized real estate. There's a group in every large Southern city that makes an excellent income renting the poorest kind of shacks to Negroes. Before the war they fought the FHA—they'll fight you to a standstill today, if they can. Once better housing comes to stay, they'll go out."

"Yet they lose in the long run. Trailer town moves into my land instead, and they make just nothing."

"Maybe you'll win the next round."

"I told you I was here to stay," said Borland. "I'm bringing steel from the Lakes by barge, and West Virginia coal down the Kanawha. Give me a year to assemble my machine tools, and I'll put in my own engineers on the spot. Yes, and bulldozers for that Pan-American highway you're reading about. And tractors to bite into the Amazon muck. . . . That means permanent workers—and permanent housing. I just about sewed up the Washington end last week. Local capital will finance the rest, I think."

"Does that mean you're staying too?"

The shipbuilder pointed a fork at a uniformed ancestor on the far wall. "Would I sink all this in real estate if I didn't mean to stay? How's your clinic doing?"

"We're still in the black, in spite of the epidemic." Chris was not startled by the shift in emphasis. He had been waiting for Borland to include him in this blueprint of the future.

"Think you'll last, eh?"

"Financially, I'm sure of it."

"You did a good job on this epidemic, Land. I heard from Baskin about the vaccine. And how you guaranteed all hospital bills at the main yard. Of course I won't stand for that. That Scotch bookkeeper of yours has already been told to send me an accounting."

Chris did not protest. The burden of those extra cases was really Borland's; it was only fair that he should foot the bill.

"What about your own overtime?"

"Doctors don't charge overtime," said Chris.

"They'd be richer if they did."

Borland scowled at his butler, who retired discreetly to the kitchen. "How d'you stand with the local medicos now?"

"We've worked together as a unit while the typhus lasted. I believe a number of our Milton doctors would join the clinic tomorrow, if I opened it to them."

"Got any such plan on your books?"

"Why not, if business warrants it?"

"You mean—if I let you include both yards in your plan?"

So Sam was right, Chris thought. It's coming after all. The thing I've planned on, offered to me with just one string attached. Remembering his last talk with Borland the night of the party, he realized that this was only another of a series of tests. If he spoke the right answers firmly enough, Borland might even grant him his diploma.

"What's your ultimate idea—a medical co-operative?"

"Call it that if you like. I'd model this one on the Mayo Clinic and put the doctors themselves in control."

"With you as boss?"

"If I was voted in."

"What about the people you'd insure? Would they have a say?"

"Definitely. The medical co-operative would work both

ways. Patients and doctors would have equal votes in a governing council."

Borland shook his head. "Sounds like tough sledding. How'll you get around the profit motive?"

"I'd encourage it to function. The doctors would profit by better income—not dependent on collections and sickness. They'd have regular vacations, the right to keep on studying, even to take postgrad work on a sabbatical. Eventually we'd offer scholarships to promising youngsters and train them in our own wards."

"What of the people you'd be treating?"

"They'd benefit by having the kind of medicine they can't get nowadays—and having it all the time, at a fixed fee. And they'd have a share in the control, to keep that fee within reason."

Borland said, "A medical school built around such a scheme might be the answer. I might even take a piece of it." He scowled again at the butler, who waited dutifully at the sideboard after serving the dessert.

Chris said, "I'd thought of the school as a philanthropic project. I'd even planned to put Cato Embree's bequest into research."

"That's what *I* meant when I said I'd buy a piece." Borland jerked a thumb toward the living room. "Will you have your brandy out there?"

The butler served cognac in bell-shaped glasses and retired at last. Borland studied the glass as though he didn't quite know what it was, then drained it at a gulp.

"I'm planning to make a change at the main yard—to get back from the future to the present."

He's thinking of firing Dwight, thought Chris. He hasn't made up his mind. If he had, he wouldn't talk around the subject.

Borland said, "You sell a good brand of medicine; so far as I've seen, you practice what you preach. Prove you've got what it takes, and I'll make you my director."

Chris took a deep breath. "That's quite an idea."

"Think you could handle it?"

"I'm sure I could—if I can keep my license."

"How's chances there?"

"My case comes up on Monday. Right now the outlook isn't too rosy."

Would Borland offer his help? If he did, the picture would

change in a twinkling. With the Borland money behind him, a battery of metropolitan counsel, the political pull of the Borland name . . . He breathed deeply now, and in earnest. The indictment might be quashed tomorrow. And yet he knew that he could never accept such a magic wand to waft away his troubles. This was his fight, and he must win it his own way.

Borland said, "You'll want to fight it on your own, of course?"

"Of course."

"Shall we talk again when the verdict's in?"

"If you still want to talk to me." Chris took a deep sip of brandy. "Now tell me what you think of the Cardinals' chances."

Borland hitched forward in his chair and unbuttoned his vest. "As I see it, it depends on who starts the first game. If they take a chance on that young busher from Texas——"

Chris relaxed in his chair for the first time. Sam was wrong, he told himself; we're talking baseball after all. Maybe that's my best bet while I'm still on the griddle. Here's praying I keep my batting averages straight. . . .

He had parked his car well down the curve of the driveway. Walking back to it in the clear starlight, he knew that he had chosen the spot deliberately. Otherwise he would have had no excuse for the detour that took him across the great south terrace and across the lawn beyond. Only a fool would visit the spot where he had kissed the girl he loved. Only a sentimental fool, he added judiciously. God knows he'd had little enough time for sentiment lately.

A spark glowed, deep in the shadow of the magnolias— the spark of a cigarette, he saw as he paused with one foot on the steps, a spark that waxed and waned as the smoker inhaled in short, savage puffs. He saw the glimmer of a woman's white dress in the dark and paused again, certain that he had blundered on a lovers' tryst. Rosalie and Moreau, he told himself savagely—and turned away just as she called his name. When he looked again he saw that she was alone.

She said quite casually, "Jean just dropped me here, at my request. I didn't want to break in on your conference too soon."

He stared at her, wondering why she had taken the trouble to invent so transparent a falsehood. Now that he had gotten back his aplomb, he knew that he should say something. Instead he went on staring like a sixteen-year-old in his first transport. . . . She had never been lovelier than tonight, in a foaming gown of white chiffon that seemed even whiter in the shadows. A tiger lily in a swamp, he told himself—without smiling at his adolescent poetry. Even in the dark her deep-tanned shoulders, bare in the strapless gown, seemed to blend with the dim copper sheen of her hair.

For all the poetry in his mind, his first words were banal enough. "I hope your leg's better, Roz. Your father said——"

She took his tone, with a faint hint of mockery. "I've been off the shift for two days now. Jean thinks I've a deep hemorrhage."

So the adventure on the Flats had had an aftermath, even though she did not seem to regard it as serious. A deep gash, of the kind she had suffered, could have repercussions, of course. In this case he had resigned the treatment to Moreau, and the Frenchman knew his business.

He took an undecided step toward her. "It didn't keep you from going out tonight."

"Don't you approve, Doctor? Would you like to look at my leg—professionally?" She fluffed back the white foam of her skirts, wriggling her toes in their open-work sandals. "I feel fine, really. Just limp a little."

Chris said hastily, "I'm sure I'm not alarmed if Moreau——"

"Don't notice me," she said. "I'm talking about anything, to keep from speaking my mind. So, for that matter, are you. Shall I go on in, while we're still good friends?"

"Why are you out here alone in the first place?"

"Because I hoped you'd come this way. Is that brazen enough, or shall I go on?"

The abruptness of her attack threw him off balance. He spoke mechanically. "Did Moreau know?"

"I didn't go out with Jean tonight. That was a story I made up for Dad. I drove into town to have dinner alone. Then I found I wasn't interested. So I came back to ambush you."

"I'm afraid I don't understand."

"I couldn't face you in the light, Chris. Especially with Dad looking on. I was afraid I'd give myself away."

He took a quick step forward—and checked himself just as quickly. "Careful, Roz."

Roz said, "Don't be a dim-wit all your life. I'm in love with

300

you, and you're going to marry Karen. How can I sit quietly and think about that?"

"But you're to marry Jean Moreau."

"Naturally. I had to do something, didn't I?"

He stared at her for a while without speaking. "When did you——"

"The day I met you on Karen's porch," she said.

"I don't believe it."

"At first I wouldn't let myself believe it either," she said. "I thought you were just another stiff-necked Utopian with your head in the clouds. Stubborn and clever, and so sure of yourself it hurt to look. . . . Then I found that I was right— and I loved you just the same."

Chris thought, That makes us even, in a way. I thought you were stubborn too. Positive you could buy anything, and wild as a maverick. I was right about you too, Roz Borland. And I loved you none the less. In fact, I've loved you so deeply that I've run for my life ever since.

Aloud he said, "You've been in love before—and lived it down."

"I've *wanted* love before," she said. "This is different. I want things for you, not for me. Karen, for example. Who am I to get in the way of a perfect match?"

She had said it quite simply, with no hint of bitterness. Now she got up and moved toward the steps with a slight limp. Chris pulled himself together and came forward to take her arm.

"You're an idiot to walk on that leg."

"That's right," said Roz. "Concentrate on my game leg. It's safer than talking about us."

"I'd better carry you," he said.

"I'm no lightweight," she told him. "Maybe we'd best be practical."

"Perhaps I'm stronger than you think."

He proved it—in more ways than one—by lifting her in his arms and walking across the starlit terrace where they had danced a few weeks ago. In the shadow of the portico he paused and set her down gently on the apron of lawn. Neither of them had spoken since he picked her up. There had been no sound but her heart, matching the insistent thud of his own.

Roz said, "Are we that bad for each other, really?"

"We're going to be friends. We've got to be."

301

"We can't be. Not like this. I heard your heart beat too."

He tried hard to smile. "Maybe I was working after all."

"Maybe you aren't as strong as you thought," she said. "Maybe neither of us is really strong, Chris. If that's a double entendre, please ignore it."

He held out his hand. "Good night, Roz. This will look different by daylight."

"That's what I've told myself for nine weeks now," she said. "Nine weeks and three days, to be exact. I'm good on dates, when they're important." She still clung to his hand; her fingers were burning. "And please don't think I fell in love with you because I couldn't have you. I'll admit that'd be right in character for Roz Borland a year ago. That's something else you changed."

"Good night," he said.

"Believe it or not, I'll make a good countess, too," she told him. "Or should I say, a good wife for Jean? God knows I've had enough practice playing the games he enjoys."

Chris said, "Good night, Roz. I mean it."

"Couldn't you say 'good luck' too?"

"Good luck too," he said.

"And would I be a hussy if I asked for a kiss to tide me over?"

He took a long stride up to the portico and cupped her chin in his hand. And then, as their lips touched, his arms went around her hungrily. They stood thus for a moment, fused in the embrace—a moment of oneness that went beyond desire. It was Rosalie who broke free, with a small, rueful chuckle.

"See what I mean, Chris? About being friends?"

He stood unstirring in the dark as she went into the house. The tall french door that closed between them was more than a symbol now. A half hour ago he had seen his future open wide before him in that same house. Now that a door had closed between him and the girl he loved, he heard the clang of a larger portal shutting out the world.

This time he walked straight down the driveway to his car and drove back to the hospital with his mind held taut on the immediate problems of tomorrow. Clinic at ten, MacLean at ten-thirty, inspect the Slade annex with Sam at eleven. Old man Peters' pneumothorax at noon . . .

The antidote had served him well before when he had fought despair. Tonight he cursed old man Peters and the

302

Bayshore Clinic—and focused all his energies on the road ahead. At any moment now he knew that his will power would crack—whip the car round in traffic and send it roaring back to Slave Hill. He fought the impulse craftily, sounding an insistent tattoo on his horn as he passed one of the Borland trucks, letting the driver curse as he kept that same truck just two car lengths from his bumper. . . .

With that convoy on my taillight, he told himself, I'll drive straight into Milton. What's more, I'll chase Sam out to the last show at the movies and take on night admissions. It's high time I decided what I'll say to that jury when I look them in the eye next week—and dare them to think I'm not honest.

2 0

Peters said, "We've a challenge left, Luke. Want to kill the lady with the turtle neck? If you ask me, she looks like a fugitive from America First."

"I'm not asking you, Joel," said Luke Fraser equably. "I happen to know that the lady is both intelligent and virtuous. What's more, she supports her mother and believes in social evolution: if she'd been born a generation later, Social Security might have let 'em live apart." His eyes sought the judge's on the high bench above them, and he shook his head slightly in response to the unspoken query. . . .

Chris sat back in the hard courtroom chair and gripped the rungs with all his strength. In another moment their jury panel would be complete, with the choice of two alternates.

Joel Peters chuckled. "Look at the old bat give us the fish eye. He could go before the cameras right now, without make-up. The stern and upright judge. . . . Wonder if he still gets blind every Saturday on Dutch Charlie's corn?"

Luke's assistant was a young man of vast cynicism; it went with the thick lenses that had kept him out of the draft, the delft-blue ties he wore to clash with his burning tweeds. For all that, Joe was a Blackstone in embryo, under his flippant manner. . . . Chris let his eyes stray around the courtroom for the thousandth time. Why should the law make men put a mask between themselves and their fellows? Why should old Judge Porter sit there in his robes, like an effigy of justice, and long for his five-o'clock bourbon—the first drink he'd take in secret, behind the blinds of his study in town, the drink that would open the bottle he'd been using for twenty years as a substitute for sleep? Why should Stanley Bibb, the plaintiff's counsel, look like a retired minister, right down to the mild eyes and the benign part in his sparse brown hair?

Why, for that matter, should the plaintiff sit at his lawyer's side like a model citizen in blue serge, betrayed only by his restless eyes?

The courtroom made a fitting background for these masks. It had been packed the first day with the curious. People had been eager to glimpse the doctor whose picture had stared from their papers the night before, under a headline that did its sly best to convict him in advance. Now, as the dreary preliminaries hung fire, the benches were nearly empty. A place of ancient, unwashed windows and cuspidors like caricatures in brass. Above the bench a tarnished eagle with widespread wings; behind it a faded state flag. Brooding down on it all, the worn profile of the judge himself—a face like a sleepy bird of prey, with tired eyes. . . .

Luke had shown that he knew his business while the jury was being drawn. He had hoarded his challenges and weighed each juryman as he came forward. Some he had let pass without even a query—an old lawyer's dodge, to show trust in advance. Sometimes he had asked a few soft-voiced questions, testing the man's past to see if he would be quick to change an opinion. Letting the faded lady with the turtle neck pass with only a polite bow. Sounding out the wheezy lady with the too-high color, to make sure she nursed no grudges against doctors from some old unpaid bill.

Now, as the box filled at last, he tamped his corncob with every outward sign of relaxation. "Time to go eat, boys. Old Porter's itching for his shut-eye now. We'll start the real war after lunch."

Joel had already gathered up their papers. "That means we won the first round, Dr. Land. When the boss is hungry, it's a good sign."

"Isn't this all routine so far?"

"Look at that foreman. He's a type: wouldn't change his mind once a century."

"What if he's already decided I'm guilty?"

Luke spoke around his unlighted pipe. "Pudge Carrol's been doing a little gumshoe work for me. That foreman's child is just getting over typhus. At Bayshore. Her old man is tickled pink at the way you treated her."

Chris found he could still laugh. "Just for that the lunch is on me."

"You'll be sorry," said Luke. "Pudge is coming too, and he's a mean man with a menu."

At the deSoto the lawyer hurried his client toward the elevator and a private dining room. "We'll keep clear of the reporters while we can. Did you know that you'll be on the AP wires this time tomorrow? If there isn't too much cable news, you might even hit a front page in New York."

Chris grimaced. "It it's anything like the break I got in my home-town press——"

"Never mind the *Gazette*. The owner is on Dwight's pay roll. I knew from the start we'd lose this case in the local press. Still, if we can get a break in the big time, it may loosen people's minds a little."

Pudge was already waiting for them in the private dining room. Chris saw that the union boss had an angry glint in his eye even as he perused the menu.

Luke said, "Don't tell me you've been fighting before lunch."

"I just missed at that. Too many loose mouths around this town, if you ask me."

"Too much Dwight dough, you mean. What are they saying about our boy now?"

"Only that Bayshore caused the epidemic by holding out on vaccine until the last minute. Said it was your way of advertising——"

"Never mind the megaphones," said Luke. "Did you get anything on Dawkins?"

Chris studied their faces one by one and frowned at what he saw. "I've warned you about this, Luke."

"Easy does it, boy. Pudge is just playing boy scout for now. Hanging round the Miramar and hoping the rat will have an extra beer."

Pudge said, "I bought him plenty last night. But he's the

kind of tank that don't talk. If you ask me, he's dumb and sly both."

"They often go together—and add up to the worst kind of witness."

"He's got dough now. He admits that much, all right. Won't say where it came from, though. Only that he'd win this trial and be on easy street for fair."

"He may be, at that," said Chris.

"Not if I start working on him in earnest."

"Confession under duress," said Luke. "No can do."

"What about a confession in public—when the guy knows he'll spill his brains if he don't talk?"

Chris said, "It's no use, Pudge—and I mean it. You're trying to help me, but I won't take that sort of help."

The union leader spread his huge hands on the table. "Do I look like I thought with these, Doc? The people I boss are my people, and none of us like meatballs. I mark this guy lousy, no matter what he's done to you. And I'm playing him my way. Don't let it worry you."

Once more Chris found that he could smile. "Thanks, Pudge. It's a promise—if you don't use those." He leaned across the table to take one of Pudge's curling fists in a hard grip.

There was a photographer waiting at Luke's car when they came out of the hotel, and with him a hard young man with a Brooklyn accent who asked questions in a bored tone.

"What about a special on your clinic, Doctor?"

"My clinic has nothing to do with this case."

"I got a few facts on it now. Want to check me to see if they're right?"

"I'm afraid I haven't time."

"Anything to say on the way organized medicine is fighting you?"

"I hadn't heard of it."

"If you lose this case, you'll lose your license, won't you? Will your associates carry on the clinic, or will it fold up?"

Luke put his car in gear and edged into traffic. "Now d'you see why I picked a private dining room?"

Chris nodded gloomily. "The law has the right dope, all right. Whatever you say is bound to be used against you."

The benches were packed that afternoon; the pattern of staring faces was now a familiar, almost a malignant, thing.

306

The jury seemed reasonably alert in its box, now that the trial was opening. Chris let his eyes brush the foreman as he took his seat with Luke and Joel at the defense table. The man was chewing tobacco with all the relaxation of a cow in a summer meadow. He was too fat to be menacing—until you noticed the craggy eyebrows that overhung two pale, codfish eyes. . . .

Bibb got to his feet as the court settled, with an apologetic smile for Luke. His voice was mild as his manner. "If the court please, we will not drag out this case. I will dispense with an opening argument, since the guilt of the defendant seems obvious."

Luke banged to his feet with an objection; Porter sustained it in a voice that was little more than a live whisper. Bibb bowed to them both, his composure unruffled.

"Samuel L. Dawkins, take the stand."

The plaintiff kissed the Bible, his eyes still wary. Chris watched him like a hawk, praying that his veneer of confidence would break down at the start. Stanley Bibb was too old a hand to run that risk. He took his time on the routine questions, letting the witness adjust himself to the sound of his own voice in public.

"You were the father of Mary Ann Dawkins, deceased?"

"I was." The man was not acting now, Chris observed with a sinking heart. The slight quaver had sounded entirely natural.

"What was the cause of her death?"

"An operation—performed by Dr. Christopher Land."

Luke got up swiftly. "Objection! It has not been proved that the operation in question was the cause of death."

Porter nodded. "Sustained. Strike that from the record."

Bibb allowed himself the ghost of a smile. He had made his first point in the collective mind of the jury. "When did your daughter become sick, Mr. Dawkins?"

"About two days before she—before she died."

"You took her to a doctor?"

"To Dr. Dwight, the day she fell sick."

"What treatment did he prescribe?"

"He said she had a sore throat and gave her some tablets."

"Did he feel that her illness was serious?"

"He said the medicine would help her to get well."

"That's not my question, Mr. Dawkins. Did Dr. Dwight seem at all alarmed at your daughter's condition?"

"No sir. He didn't."

"And then what happened?"

"Well, the next night the girl was having some pain. We had nothin' in the place to give her, so I phoned Dr. Dwight —only he wasn't in. Then one of the neighbors said Dr. Travers could help her. *He* was workin' on the Flats that night, so I got him right away. He looked the girl over and got right excited. I kept sayin' I wanted Dr. Dwight, but he went to the phone as though he hadn't heard and called another number."

Dawkins had stumbled a little here and there, but his voice was clear. Obviously the account did not square with the truth, but it would do Paul little good to deny that later. The sorrowing father had already made his impression with the jury.

Bibb, still infinitely patient, said, "And then?"

"Then Travers gives her some kind of shot. Serum, he called it. But she don't get better. He keeps tellin' me not to worry, this other doc is on the way out now——"

"Do you think Dr. Travers may have given her the wrong——"

"Object!" Luke was at the bench now. "The question is irrelevant to the case in point."

Porter smoothed his robes and looked down his thin nose at Bibb. "What is the reason for such a question?"

"It's well known that Dr. Travers and Dr. Land are now close friends," said Bibb. "If Dr. Travers gave the wrong medicine in this case, it would be natural for Dr. Land to try to get him out of trouble."

Luke's voice was little short of a bellow. "You're trying to discredit Dr. Travers in advance, by prejudicing the jury!"

Porter said only, "Your question is out of order, Mr. Bibb. It will be stricken from the record."

"It is already withdrawn, your honor." He turned again to the witness box. "I gather you were surprised when the defendant arrived?"

"I still expected Dr. Dwight."

"Never mind who you expected, Mr. Dawkins," said Bibb gently. "Who was with Dr. Land?"

"A woman doctor. Dr. Agard."

"Did you ask for Dr. Agard?"

"Travers called her," said the witness doggedly. "I keep telling you I asked for Dr. Dwight."

"Did they tell you the child had diphtheria?"

"For a long time they didn't tell me anything. They just went in and examined the girl. She seemed to in pain."

"What did they give her for her pain?"

"Nothin'. Just more of that serum. Then Dr. Land comes out to me in the yard and says she has diphtheria. Next thing I know, he's back with that woman doctor, operatin' on the girl."

"Had they asked for written permission to do that?"

"Object," said Luke. "This was an emergency. There was no time to ask permission."

"Objection overruled," said the judge. "The witness may answer the question."

Dawkins said, "He didn't ask me about anything. He just went ahead."

"Would you have given permission?"

"I would not! What did I know about these doctors?"

"You are answering questions, Mr. Dawkins, not asking them. How soon after the operation did the child die?"

"She never got over it."

"Object," said Luke. "The child was already dying. Dr. Land operated to save her life."

"Sustained. The witness will answer questions without comment."

Dawkins said, "She died in about two hours." Again the break in his voice was completely real. Chris did not have to look toward the jury box to gauge the effect.

Bibb said, "Your witness, Mr. Fraser."

Luke put an elbow on the rail of the witness box. Pretending to relax while he thumbed his notes, he kept Dawkins under a narrow scrutiny—holding the moment for all it was worth, waiting for the witness to fidget. And then, just as the judge cleared his throat ominously, he shot his first question.

"How long did Dr. Dwight take to examine your daughter?"

Bibb was already on his feet, but Dawkins spoke before he could object. "A couple of minutes, maybe."

'Do you consider that an adequate examination?"

"Object! Dr. Dwight is not on trial."

The judge said wearily, "You will not make statements in the form of questions, Mr. Fraser. Save that for your closing argument. The question and answer are stricken from the record."

Luke said, "Your daughter was much worse the second night—that is, the night you called in Dr. Travers?"

"She looked like she was——"

"—going to die. Is that it?"

"Object!"

"Sustained. Be more careful, Mr. Fraser."

"When Dr. Travers came, did he make much of an examination?"

"No." Dawkins was cautious now and properly indignant. "He just got out the serum."

"Before he called the other doctors?"

"Yes. He said it was for diphtheria. I told him what Dr. Dwight had prescribed, but he didn't listen."

"Confine yourself to the questions, please. When Dr. Land and Dr. Agard arrived, did they also examine the child?"

"Yes. They gave her a kind of once-over. Then they got to work with more serum. After that Dr. Land came to me in the yard and said the girl's throat was closing up."

"Was she having any trouble breathing?"

"No sir."

"Think carefully. Wasn't she having trouble in getting her breath through?"

Dawkins shot a glance at his own counsel. "Well, maybe a little."

"What was the color of her lips?"

"They were—sort of bluish."

"Do you know the medical name for that color?"

"Object as irrelevent," said Bibb.

"If your honor pleases, the blueness of the lips which the witness has described was due to cyanosis—the medical term for oxygen lack. My client operated in an attempt to compensate for that symptom, which, as any doctor will testify, is often fatal."

Porter said wearily, "Objection overruled."

Bibb settled back in his chair. For the first time Chris saw that his lips had set in a thin line. The man's mildness had vanished in that twinkling. He looked contained but dangerous—like a sleepy cottonmouth that might strike at any moment.

Luke turned away from the witness with just the right blend of civility and contempt. "That's all, Dawkins."

The plaintiff hesitated, then stepped down from the box. Bibb said, "The next witness is the wife of Samuel L. Dawkins. The child's mother."

Watching the woman stalk toward the court clerk to be sworn, Chris fumbled in his memory to place her. Obviously she had been one of that amorphous group in the farmhouse kitchen. He remembered a blowzy figure in overalls, slumped in a chair and staring blankly. She had been sleeping when he came out from his first examination—the exhausted stupor that only the overtime war worker knows. . . . Bibb had dressed her well for this public appearance: she was wearing a trim black coat suit now, with a small tricorne hat and veil, and a suggestion of white lace at her throat. Just the right garb for a mother in mourning, Chris told himself bitterly. Her voice was muted but resonant. From the first question he guessed that she would be what lawyers term a "hostile witness."

"You saw Dr. Land and Dr. Agard enter your home that night?"

"I most certainly did."

" 'Yes' will be sufficient, Mrs. Dawkins. Did you, too, expect Dr. Dwight?"

"I did indeed."

Bibb ignored the emphasis patiently. "Did you object to the—change of doctors?"

"I should have—when I saw they'd been drinkin'."

It was a quiet enough bombshell. The woman did not even raise her voice or glance toward the jury. Chris wondered how carefully the exchange had been rehearsed in Bibb's office. Certainly there was little chance that the jury would realize the quality of Mrs. Samuel L. Dawkins' acting.

Porter listened gravely to Luke's objection and overruled. "The witness can give her own opinion."

Bibb said gently, "How did you know they'd been drinking, Mrs. Dawkins?"

"I could smell it on their breath. It was a funny, foreign smell, but it was liquor, all rightie."

"Would you say they were intoxicated?"

"They'd been drinkin'. I don't know how much they had."

"Very well. Now tell us what you can of the operation. Did you know they were about to perform it?"

"No sir. I did not!"

"You gave no permission, then?"

Luke said, "This point has already been established. Dr. Land operated in an emergency. There was no time to obtain permission."

Bibb shifted his attack. "Did you think your daughter was dying?"

"Not until after the operation, I didn't."

"What then?"

"Then I knew they'd killed her."

Again the judge waved aside Luke's objection. No one stirred in the courtroom as Bibb resigned the witness to the defense. Luke looked at the woman for a moment of silent contempt, then shook his head.

"No questions."

Chris leaned across the table to whisper. "That harpy was dead to the world when we operated. Can't you drag that much out of her?"

Luke shook his head. "Bibb will have supplied her with an answer to that, I'm afraid. I'd rather give him this round, Chris. The female's dynamite."

They both turned back to the court as Bibb called the next witness—a dapper man in a dark Palm Beach suit with a dark red carnation at the lapel. Mr. Harvey Byers, mortician: the same Mr. Byers who had asked Chris for a kickback on the telephone. The Byers Funeral Home, Chris gathered, had handled the Dawkins child on its cut-rate schedule. . . . Oddly enough, Mr. Byers' assistants had all been busy that day, so he had done the job himself. He described that job with admirable reticence, under Bibb's prompting.

"Were there any wounds on the body?"

"Only an operative one, sir."

"What kind of operation had been performed?"

"A tracheotomy."

"Did you see any evidence of diphtheria?"

"I found none, sir."

"Did you see any cause of death?"

"None, except the operation."

Porter sustained Luke's bellow of objection, and Bibb resigned the witness with his aplomb unshaken.

Luke said, "Are you a doctor, Mr. Byers, as well as an undertaker?"

"I hold a medical degree, sir. As it happens, I have never practiced."

"Are you versed in pathology?"

312

"I have studied the subject. Naturally it is not my specialty."

"We understand that, Mr. Byers. Embalming is your specialty." Luke ignored the titter that swept through the courtroom. "Is it necessary to examine the larynx while embalming a body?"

"Certainly not. Only the incision itself."

"Then you could not say whether or not she died of laryngeal diphtheria. That's correct, is it not?"

Byers said carefully, "I expressed my opinion as a trained layman, sir—not as a specialist."

Luke sighed and turned aside. "You may step down." But he was smiling as he settled beside Chris again. "We canceled that monkey out," he whispered. "Not that I can take much credit. A bodysnatcher's always a bad witness, for either side."

Court recessed for five minutes while the judge trailed his robes down the short aisle to his chambers. Watching the old man vanish, Chris wondered if he had gone for his first nip this early. A glance at the clock told him that the afternoon was far advanced: Bibb's stage management had made the session seem all too short. . . . He swiveled in his chair for a look at the spectators. Only a few of them were frankly dozing: most of the eyes stared back at him with a hard, bright interest. Already, he reflected, they're sizing me up as a potential murderer. His eyes paused on the rear row. Cal Borland was seated there with folded arms, waiting for the trial to resume. If the shipbuilder noticed Chris, he gave no sign.

Bibb had skipped down a side aisle for the brief recess. He skipped back now like an agile gnome, a scant second ahead of the judge's own return.

"Dr. Gilbert Dwight!"

So Bibb had slipped out to prepare an entrance for his star witness. Heads were already turning as the compensation doctor hurried down the center aisle. Today he was every inch the busy practitioner, pulling free of his schedule to come to court. The immaculate healer in white linen, with a chaste gray wool cravat to match his eyes. He looked cool and fresh and utterly serene. Watching him pause to speak to a bailiff, Chris was conscious of his own rumpled seersucker, limp after a long day in court.

Dwight settled into the witness box, crossing his legs and

pulling his trousers up gently at the knee. He answered the standard questions gravely, giving the name of a famous medical school as his place of graduation, acknowledging membership in several medical societies.

"What is your present position, Dr. Dwight?"

"I'm in private practice in Milton. I am also medical director of the Borland Shipyards."

There was a slight stir among the spectators. Apparently they looked upon the medical director of such an empire with more than respect. Chris wondered if the jury would feel the same way. There was little difference between those twelve good men and true and the onlookers. Obeying a sudden impulse, he turned to look over the benches, and saw that Borland was no longer present. The discovery pleased him, though he could not have said why.

Bibb said, "I believe you are also acting president of the County Medical Society, Dr. Dwight?"

And Luke countered, without rising, "We accept the witness as a qualified physician, Mr. Bibb."

Bibb made the defendant's table a small, ironic bow. "Dr. Dwight, did you ever examine a child called Mary Ann Dawkins?"

"I did."

"When was this?"

Dwight consulted a penciled memorandum before answering. "I jotted down the date from my office record," he said. The impression was obvious: a busy practitioner could not be expected to remember every patient. The diagnosis, it seemed, had been nasopharyngitis. Dwight explained to Bibb that this meant inflamed throat and nothing more.

"The child, then, was not seriously ill?"

"My notes do not state that she was."

"You would not state that she was in any danger of dying?"

Luke said, "It is not claimed that the child was in a critical condition at this date."

Bibb nodded as the judge sustained the objection. "What did you prescribe, Dr. Dwight?"

The compensation doctor's gold pencil danced down his notes. "I gave her father a prescription for a sulfadiazine tablet every four hours."

"Sulfadiazine is a drug commonly used for treating sore throat, isn't it?"

Dwight said that it was; he added that he had been surprised to learn of the child's death the following morning. Oddly enough, the information had come from Dr. Land. Dr. Land had operated during the night—and the child had died.

"From the operation?"

Once again the judge sustained Luke's instant objection.

"When you last saw the child, did you think an operation necessary?"

"Definitely not."

"Is tracheotomy a common treatment for ordinary sore throat?"

"No, it is not."

"That is all. Your witness, Mr. Fraser."

This time Luke put both an elbow and a foot on the witness box. "You say you found no sign of diphtheria, Dr. Dwight. Did you take swabs for culture?"

"Why, no. There seemed to be no indication for such procedure."

"Isn't it always a good idea to take cultures when you've a child patient?"

"Most of the children down here have been immunized."

"But this was a worker's child. Did you ask the mother if she had been immunized against diphtheria?"

"Object," said Bibb. "Dr. Dwight is not on trial."

Porter's tired hawk profile inclined a trifle above them. "What are you trying to establish, Mr. Fraser?"

"We contend that no attempt to diagnose was really made. Therefore it could not be stated if the child had the disease."

"Overruled," said Porter.

Dwight shrugged. "I did not ask the mother."

"Then how can you rule out diphtheria?"

"I am expressing a clinical opinion. That's usually accepted as evidence in court."

"Would you accept Dr. Land's clinical judgment in deciding on an operation?"

Porter waved aside Bibb's objection. "The witness has himself raised the point that a doctor's clinical judgment may be accepted as evidence."

"Well . . ." Dwight's pause was beautifully timed. For a moment even Chris felt that the man's embarrassment was genuine. The jury saw only the ethical doctor—loath to say anything which might reflect on another doctor and yet leaving the impression that Chris had acted hastily.

"Naturally I hesitate to cast aspersion on Dr. Land's judg-

315

ment," said Dwight at last. "But he has been in the Army for several years. I assume that he has examined few children in that interval. A streptococcus infection may often resemble diphtheria."

"And what is the only sure way to tell them apart?"

"By culture and smear."

Luke smiled toward the jury and stepped back from the box to look over his notes. Luke could make a pause serve him too, in times of stress. He turned sharply now as Dwight got up to go.

"Just a moment. I'm not quite finished with you. . . . Were you available the night the child died?"

"Naturally. I went to a medical meeting and came home rather late. But the doctors' exchange always locates me."

"You'd have driven out to the Dawkins place, then, if he had reached you?"

"Of course. The child was my patient."

Luke whirled on the witness box with his face thrust forward. "Did you finance this suit to discredit Dr. Land as a competitor?"

Bibb jumped to his feet as the judge banged for order. "Another question like that, Mr. Fraser, and you'll be held in contempt of court."

Luke did not budge. "I shall prove later, your honor, that this is precisely what happened."

"Then save your accusations until you have proof as well."

Dwight spoke, in the slight pause that followed. "Do you wish me to answer this question, Judge Porter?" His smile, Chris noted, was pathetic, eager—and entirely candid.

The judge said, "The question is already stricken from the record."

And Luke added, "That is all, Dr. Dwight."

Chris sat quietly at the defendant's table as the compensation doctor went down the aisle. Above the buzz of the courtroom he heard the gavel pound again for order.

"Five P.M.," said Joel. "The old man's thirsty. Still, he likes a quiet audience when he adjourns."

Though he had been absent from the hospital since early morning, Chris did not turn into the driveway that evening. Sam Bernstein was in charge during the trial, and Sam was competent in almost any emergency. . . . He wasn't quite sure why he had driven by: perhaps he needed a glimpse of

316

those lighted windows to restore his confidence. At least it was visible evidence of one battle he had fought and won.

Halfway down the causeway to St. Lucie, with the night breeze from the Gulf in his face, he began to breathe freely again. This had not been their day in court, but the trial had not yet ended. Until that final battle with Dwight was over, he would hold fast to his dream. The clinic was a reality, at least, and he would keep it so, thanks to Doc Embree's legacy. Even without him it could fulfill its purpose. Someday, if Borland's plans went through, that same clinic might represent all that was best in medicine: a team of doctors, working together without jealousy or greed for the good of the people they served. The words of old Paddy Ryan—repeated each year at graduation time in Lakeview—came back to him now like the deep notes of an organ:

". . . that none who may be salvaged should pass through life mutilated and wrecked; that under your devoted care none should die needlessly, wastefully . . ."

At the boathouse, after he had put his car in the lean-to garage, he hesitated in the deepening dusk, tortured by a sudden, irrational desire to telephone Rosalie. Or even Borland. . . . The shipbuilder had dropped into court that afternoon for a reason. Perhaps he would help the cause even now if—— Chris suppressed the impulse firmly. He was asking no favors of Borland or of anyone. As for Rosalie, she had said her good-bys as firmly as a woman could.

His shoes crunched in the beach sand as he walked to the water's edge and sat down to stare at the dim gray mirror of the Gulf. The one lazy wave made only a murmur at his feet; he could hear the tiny sounds of life about him—the coquinas burrowing in the damp, the faint wispy sound a conch made when it walked its shell, the louder rattle of a stone crab in search of food. The peace of such evenings had been part of him since memory began. Since his return he had assumed that it would go on forever, when his day's work ended. And yet if he lost that dingy battle at Judge Porter's dais, the picture would change overnight.

When he rose at last his shoulders were drooping with something more than fatigue. There was a light in Karen's bungalow, and he walked toward it as a thirsty man might approach an oasis, hoping it was not a mirage.

"Chris?"

He had opened the screen door to her veranda without

317

knocking. Now he hesitated on the threshold, realizing that the light had come from her bedroom beyond.

"Come in, dear. I'm quite alone. In fact, I've been expecting you."

She came out into the dusky living room on that, a tall white shape in the gloaming. As she stood with the light behind her he saw that she was wearing a gay house coat, with her pale hair upswept like a hostess on a holiday.

"Don't talk, if you'd rather not," she said. "We can talk later."

Even then he wondered how she had divined his mood so soon. Not that he paused long in wonder. She was in his arms now, with no sense of transition, her lips parted sweetly to give back his kiss.

He spoke at last. "If you knew how I needed you——"

"I do know, darling."

"How long I've needed you——"

Karen's words were the merest whisper in the dark. "That's why I'm here, Chris. That's why I'll always be here—if you need me."

"I'll always need you."

"Always is a big word," she said softly. "But we'll make it do for now."

He wondered why she moved quickly away from him as she spoke. Then he knew that she had only gone to put out her bedroom lights before she held out both hands to him in the darkness.

21

NEXT MORNING IN COURT the picture was completely unchanged, so far as Chris could observe. As before, the spectators' benches were packed to the aisles. The same frowzy bailiffs stood at bored attention before each door; the same fat woman spilled her purse as the court sighed to its feet to welcome the judge. . . . Porter looked even frowzier than his bailiffs this morning. Watching him intently as he fluffed out his robes to settle at his desk, Chris guessed that he was concentrating to avoid a belch.

The jury, too, seemed bent on smothering a collective yawn. Chris wondered if they had also frozen their collective mind into a verdict. Certainly they seemed eager to get home again—a sentiment with which he heartily concurred. Only the foreman looked up incuriously as Luke called Paul Travers to the stand as the first witness for the defense. Luke had stolen a leaf from Bibb's book and dispensed with an opening argument. It was a bold step, but he had already planned it that way after a huddle with Chris.

"What is your work here, Dr. Travers?"

"For the most part, I help the local authorities to keep up minimum health conditions in the trailer camps." Paul's voice was crisp and definite: he was obviously a veteran in this type of procedure. Chris watched the jury stir slowly from its lethargy. He hoped that Paul's confident manner would not antagonize them. As always, the Public Health man was a bit on the didactic side. If the jury felt that he was lecturing them, they would probably cancel him out in advance.

"You were, of course, active in controlling the recent typhus epidemic on the Flats?"

"Naturally."

Luke seemed to feel Bibb's glare as he switched his approach. "Why were you on the Flats the night Dawkins' daughter died?"

"I was checking for rats." Paul made a careful pause as the courtroom tittered. "I knew they were spreading typhus even then."

"Were you treating people for this disease?"

"No. Epidemiologists do not ordinarily treat disease."

"But you are familiar with the routines of diagnosis?"

Paul smiled. "It's part of our job to diagnose contagion from clinical reports—and our own observation."

"Did you make such a diagnosis when you saw the Dawkins child?"

"Definitely. I saw at once that the child was dying of neglect."

Bibb caught the judge's eye and smothered his objection. Luke said easily, "Neglect on the part of the parents, you mean?"

"Precisely. Both parents worked at the yards. Their other

319

children had been immunized only through my efforts. Aside from that, they'd been allowed to run wild while the parents——"

Bibb said furiously, "Mr. Dawkins is the plaintiff in this action, your honor. He is not on trial."

Luke took another line instantly. "We've established the fact that the child had been taken to Dr. Dwight two days previous to your visit. At the time he prescribed tablets for an inflamed throat. Did you find they had helped her?"

"Apparently not. When I examined her she was well into the beginning stages of suffocation."

"And the cause of that suffocation?"

"Laryngeal obstruction."

From this point Paul went on to paint the familiar and fearful picture of diphtheria in its closing stages. Chris studied the jury, hoping they were impressed.

Luke said carefully, "Then your diagnosis was diphtheria, Dr. Travers?"

"Without question."

"Was the patient suffering from that disease when she was examined by Dr. Dwight?"

"Undoubtedly."

Bibb cut in with an objection. The judge waved him aside wearily. "Dr. Travers is expressing a clinical judgment, Mr. Bibb. Your own witness has established its validity as evidence."

Luke had not even slowed his tempo. "What is the present treatment for diphtheria, Dr. Travers?"

"Serum. I administered an ampule immediately."

"Is sulfadiazine of value in treating the disease?"

"Sulfadiazine is always contraindicated in diphtheria. The bacillus does not respond to it in any way."

"Then Dr. Dwight's treatment had not helped the patient?"

"Dr. Dwight's treatment was worse than useless."

Luke walked down the space before the jury box with an eye on Bibb. The point he was building now would need careful nursing.

"When did you telephone Dr. Agard?"

"After I'd injected the serum. I asked her to bring more ampules and a tracheotomy set. It was apparent that the child would soon suffocate without it."

"Did you plan to operate yourself at the time?"

"No. Dr. Agard had already informed me that Dr. Land

320

was at her house. I knew he would take over the surgical end."

"Then you did not hesitate to turn the case over to Dr. Land?"

"Naturally not. I was familiar with his qualifications."

"Will you give the jury your estimate of his ability as a physician and surgeon?"

"He is easily the leading surgeon in this community. I might add that he's one of the finest all-around medical men I've ever worked with. Without his help in the typhus epidemic, it might easily have gotten out of hand—and ruined Milton."

Bibb said, "The typhus epidemic has no bearing on this case."

Luke turned to the bench. "Your honor, I am merely proving that Dr. Land is a good doctor. That his clinical opinion as to a diagnosis is of more value than that of any doctor who examined the patient."

Porter whispered an affirmative, but Luke only stepped back from the witness box.

"No further questions."

Bibb took his time in crossing to Travers. "May I ask you why you are wearing a uniform, Doctor?"

"The Public Health Service goes into uniform in wartime, sir."

"You refer, of course, to the Federal Health Service?"

"Of course." Paul's voice was wary now. He saw exactly what was coming.

"That makes you an employee of the Federal government, Dr. Travers. How do you happen to be in Milton? Is there an office of your Service here?"

"Milton is now a large shipbuilding center," said Paul patiently. "I was sent here to work out local health problems as they might arise."

"At whose order? The head office in Washington?"

Paul smiled. "The local health department put in a request. I'm the answer."

"But you make your reports to Washington, do you not?"

"Naturally."

"That is all."

Had the point gone down with the jury? Chris studied their faces and feared that Bibb had succeeded too well. Paul's slight aloofness had helped the enemy, of course. Now he would stick in the jury's mind as an intruder, a spy sent in by the Federal government to interfere with a purely state function. Resentment against Federal control had always been a potent factor in the South—the logical offspring of the "damn-Yankee" point of view. Chris did not doubt that several members of the jury had damned Yankees—and Washington —from childhood.

"Dr. Karen Agard!"

He heard the creak of the wicket as the bailiff admitted her—and the murmur that went through the courtroom as she came forward to be sworn. All morning he had guessed that she was waiting in the front row of the spectators' section. So far he had not dared to verify the conviction. . . . She had given herself too completely last night on the cay. He would not ask for more, not even for the encouragement of her nearness.

Daring to glance toward the jury box at last, he saw that she was wearing a simple tailleur with an open collar; her pale blonde hair was brushed back from her ears, making her both lovely and a trifle severe. He sensed that she had done her best to blunt the impact of her beauty on the jury, and blessed her for the stratagem. He had gone to the mat with Luke when his lawyer had insisted on calling her as a witness. Sensing the almost avid interest in the courtroom, he felt that he had been right in his protest. Right for Karen's sake—to say nothing of the outcome of the case.

She was already testifying, ignoring the stares. Fitting her voice to Luke's pattern, she seemed quite calm as she informed the jury that she was a doctor of medicine with two American degrees; that she was thirty, and a citizen of Norway; that she was licensed to practice in their state and had served for almost a year as a staff physician at the Bayshore Hospital. Chris watched the jury as she spoke. There was something taut in their faces, and their eyes were withdrawn, for all their pointed ogling. Evidently they did not believe that anyone with Karen Agard's looks could practice medicine—or any profession—for a moral purpose.

"Let us go back to the night the child died. Were you surprised when Dr. Travers phoned?"

"Not at all. At the time it was impossible for any of the Borland employees to get one of the regular medical staff out at night."

322

Bibb cut in sharply. "Objection, your honor. The statement cannot possibly be proved."

"Sustained," said Porter. He fixed Karen with a glassy eye. "Stay with the question, Dr. Agard."

"I was attempting to be specific. I've made dozens of night calls on the Flats to see sick children."

"You are a specialist in children's diseases?"

"To a certain extent. I am primarily a laboratory specialist."

Luke took back his witness. "When you asked Dr. Land to accompany you on this occasion, did you expect him to perform an operation?"

"I knew that someone would have to operate when Dr. Travers ordered a tracheotomy set."

"Where did you obtain these instruments?"

"At the Bayshore Clinic."

"What was the condition of the child when you arrived?"

Karen answered patiently, verifying the picture that Paul Travers had already given the jury, describing the injections of serum that she and Chris had given and the sudden change for the worse that had made operation imperative.

"What was your diagnosis, Dr. Agard?"

"Diphtheria."

"Your witness, Mr. Bibb."

Bibb took up his cross-examination with a courtly bow and a smile for the jury. His manner was a perfect blend of old-school politeness and impertinence—the kind of veiled flippancy that the native reserves for the foreigner.

"How long have you been in this country, Dr. Agard?"

"I have worked here constantly since 1936."

"Were you here when Norway was invaded?"

"Yes. In New York."

"Did you leave your country for political reasons?"

"No. I left Oslo because of embryos."

"Embryos?"

"I was doing some rather difficult work on the egg cell of the chicken. As it happened, the laboratory services in Oslo were inadequate. The New York Institute made me an offer —so I came."

"Were you ever a Nazi sympathizer?"

Luke banged to his feet. "If it please your honor——"

The judge stared down vaguely at Karen. "What are you driving at, Mr. Bibb?"

"I have evidence that Dr. Agard was once a member of a

socialist group at Columbia University. I was interested to learn if it was on the Nazi model—as of 1936."

Karen spoke ahead of Porter. "The answer is 'no,' your honor. The group at Columbia was formed for discussion only. I spoke just twice—on *Norwegian* socialism. Even Mr. Bibb should realize that it's different from the Nazi brand."

The judge said, "In any event, the question has no bearing on the case. Both question and answer are stricken from the record. Proceed, Mr. Bibb."

The plaintiff's lawyer turned to the jury with his smirk intact, throwing his next question with his back still turned to Karen.

"Is the group with which you are now working approved by organized medicine?"

"Object," snapped Luke. "The question is likewise immaterial."

"I'm inclined to agree," said Porter.

Bibb shrugged. "I'll withdraw the question, your honor. You say you are a laboratory specialist, Dr. Agard. Can you tell me the one certain way to diagnose diphtheria?"

Yesterday Dwight had answered that same question instantly. Karen glanced quickly at Chris before she spoke. "The organism is identified by smear and culture."

"Did you make such an examination on the Dawkins child?"

"Certainly not. There was no time."

"Why didn't you contact Dr. Dwight when you were called to the Dawkins home?"

"The father himself was unable to find him and asked for our help."

"Is it considered good medical ethics to steal another doctor's case?"

"Is it medical ethics to desert a sick patient who may die?"

"You're here to answer questions, not to ask them. Why did you let Dr. Land operate without a license?"

"There was no choice. The operation was imperative."

"You knew it was illegal, didn't you?"

Watching Karen on the stand, Chris realized that he had never seen her angry before. With high color in her cheeks, and her eyes an icy blue, she was even lovelier—a circumstance that would hardly improve their position with the jury.

Now she waited for the courtroom to quiet, then spoke crisply. "I knew we had to save a child's life—or try, at least."

324

Once more Bibb smirked openly at the jury. "What were your relations with Dr. Land at that time, Dr. Agard?"

"We'd met only that evening."

"I don't follow. Dr. Travers said he was dining with you."

"That is correct."

"Were other guests present?"

"We were alone."

"Is it your custom to dine alone with strange men, Dr. Agard?"

The judge pounded for order and spoke ahead of Luke. Here, at least, was a point where Southern chivalry could rise triumphant in a brain dimmed long since by alcohol.

"You will moderate your tone, Mr. Bibb. What is the purpose of this approach?"

Bibb said humbly, "I ask the court's pardon. But if Dr. Land and the witness were such recent friends—how could she judge his ability?"

Porter bowed gravely to Karen. "You may answer that question, Dr. Agard."

"I expected Dr. Land to work at Bayshore Hospital. Naturally I had checked thoroughly on his record."

Bibb put both fists on the witness-box rail and spoke softly, "You think he's a good doctor, then?"

"I admire and respect Dr. Land as the finest surgeon I have ever worked with."

"What is your present relationship?"

"We are fellow members of the Bayshore Clinic, which he organized."

"The socialistic—pardon me, the *social-minded*—group of doctors who——" Bibb bowed to the bench as Porter admonished him sharply. "How long has this association lasted?"

"Nearly three months."

"Have you been associated in any other capacity?"

"None."

"Think carefully, Dr. Agard. You have no wish to modify that answer?"

Chris felt his fists strain at his chair arms as Karen snapped another denial. Bibb was playing to the gallery now, with the jury in the palm of his hand. Once again he took a turn before the box, letting his eyes roam down the taut row of faces, whirling to shoot his next question at point-blank range.

"Where were you four Sundays ago?"

Chris half rose from his chair as Bibb named the date; on

325

that instant his whole being fused into a single burning desire—to seize the lawyer by the throat and choke down his next question. Luke's hard hand closed on his shoulder and forced him back.

Karen said carefully, "I don't think I remember."

"Allow me to refresh your memory. Were you sailing in the Gulf with Dr. Land?"

"Now that you mention it, I believe we did go on a sailing picnic that Sunday."

"Alone?"

"With Dr. Paul Travers."

"You dropped Dr. Travers at East Point, didn't you?"

"Dr. Travers had business at the cantonment."

"Tell this in your own words, Dr. Agard. Don't make me drag it out of you. You were alone with Dr. Land—after you dropped Dr. Travers at the East Point dock?"

Karen's chin went up. "We were quite alone. We had planned a picnic at South Island with Dr. Travers. When he couldn't accompany us, we saw no reason for postponing it."

"When did you reach South Island?"

"About two that afternoon."

"When did you leave?"

"Shortly after midnight."

Bibb roared his next question above the buzz in the courtroom. "When did you reach the dock in Milton?"

"Just before dawn. We were becalmed."

"Is 'becalmed' the right word, Dr. Agard? Are you sure you aren't Land's mistress?"

Chris did not hear the tumult in the courtroom or the banging of Porter's gavel. He was still trying to get up from the table and smash Bibb. Luke Fraser, with both hands on his client's shoulders now, was restraining him, just as firmly. Throughout, Chris was conscious only of Karen's proud white face—of the blaze of her eyes as she drove Bibb back from the witness box without a word.

There was no need of an objection. The old judge was already subjecting Bibb to a tongue-lashing which left him red-faced but unsubdued. Then, with a final bang of his gavel, Porter excused Karen from further questioning and adjourned the court till afternoon. Luke still held Chris in his chair as Bibb and Dawkins went out the side exit—as young Joel Peters whisked up to the box, took Karen firmly by an elbow, and steered her toward another door.

Luke said, "The front steps for us, boy. Joel will take her back to Bayshore while we draw the flies."

The crowd in the portico of the courthouse parted to let them through. Chris knew that necks were craning all around him: he'd have been the center of attention this noon, even without the popping of flashlight bulbs. The reporters who assailed him today were all cut on a metropolitan bias, though Chris did not notice the young man with the Brooklyn accent. Probably he was already on his way to the telegraph office, to file a story for his tabloid. . . . He hoped that Joel would get Karen under cover before she, too, was photographed.

"No comment," shouted Luke. "Can't you understand English?"

He slammed the door of Chris's coupé and held back the fourth estate from the running board with two flailing arms.

"Is it true you'll take the stand this afternoon, Dr. Land?"

Chris nodded as he drove off. They could print that, at least, and be damned. On the way to the hospital he kept his eyes straight ahead, sure that even the traffic policeman was staring. Mercifully no one was about when he went into the clinic by the emergency entrance and hurried straight down the corridor to Karen's office.

He had expected tears—or at least a strained quiet—when he entered. But Karen was composed as she looked up from the neatly stacked reports on her desk. It seemed incredible that this was the same woman who had glared Stanley Bibb into silence a scant half hour ago.

For all that, he drew her swiftly to her feet—and into his arms for a long kiss. It seemed the least he could do, after her lost battle in his behalf.

"I know it doesn't help to say I'm sorry——"

"What have you to be sorry for, darling?" She smiled up at him, her voice completely contained. "Can we help it if they've spied on us?"

"I could knock a few heads together," he said gloomily. "Of course that wouldn't help us now."

"Be honest with me, Chris. Didn't my testimony help you at all?"

He turned away, beating fist to palm as he paced her office carpet. "I wish I knew. Of course it'd have helped if you'd worn horn-rims and a squint. Those apple-knockers in the box might have believed *that* kind of lady doctor." He turned

327

in amazement to accept her kiss and saw that she was crying at last.

Karen said, "I rather needed that compliment, Chris. Thank you very much."

"Admit one thing," he said sternly. "I did ask you to marry me the day after South Island. If you'd accepted me then, we could have faced Bibb as a unit this morning."

Karen smiled. "They'd have ruled me off the stand altogether. A wife can't testify for her husband."

"So much the better. I wanted to keep you out of this mess. You know that."

"But I'm not ashamed, darling. Not if you aren't." Her eyes searched his face quickly. "Just one thing upsets me now. The fact that I lost my temper with that little shyster. It gave him an advantage, and I'm afraid he used it."

"Don't reproach yourself for that," said Chris. "Bibb had his questions cued in advance. He's a fit mouthpiece for the gang we're fighting."

"Surely they'll accept the fact the child had diphtheria."

"Perhaps. Nobody can tell how a jury will react. For all we know, Dwight may have mesmerized them yesterday. I'm sure they think that Paul is only a Yankee spy."

"And I, of course, am just a foreign hussy with communist leanings."

"I must say you're taking this calmly."

"How else can I take it? If our heads don't fall, theirs will." She handed him a letter from the stack on her desk. "This came for you this morning, after you went to court. Perhaps it'll cheer you up a little."

Chris's face lightened as he skimmed through the letter. It was from the State Compensation Commission, thanking him for the evidence he had placed in their hands and promising a prompt investigation of conditions in Milton. Here, then, was another reason why Dwight had moved to crush him so quickly. A discredited doctor would hardly make a good witness in that hearing. Dwight meant to smother the investigation in double-talk: he might well succeed if Dr. Christopher Land was on the blacklist at the time.

Karen's arm was linked in his as he read; Karen's lips whispered softly in his ear. "You see, Chris? We've got to win now."

"Say you'll marry me—win, lose, or draw."

This time she gave him back his kiss with interest. "If you really need me, darling."

He released her slowly, smiling in earnest now. "That's all the hypo I want for this afternoon. Any more unfinished business before I tangle again with Bibb?"

"Only Sam's clinic in the annex. Will you take a quick look before lunch?"

He sensed that she was anxious to lead him into routine again—if only to channel his mind from more pressing troubles. Following her gratefully across the brand-new covered bridge that led to the Slade mansion, he saw that the annex was already functioning smoothly as a combined maternity ward and extra wing. Through the glass wall of the nursery several lusty infants howled in their bassinets. Beyond, in the first of three emergency rooms, Sam was preparing for yet another delivery.

"I promised to assist," said Karen. "Want to see how well we function without you?"

He nodded wordlessly and paused at the small window that permitted him to observe Sam at work without advertising his presence. The little obstetrician was scrubbed and ready—a quiet gnome beside the bulk of the patient groaning on the table. He looked up as Karen came in through a side door, masked and gowned.

"You're just in time, gorgeous. She's already had morphia and scopolamine. Just enough for twilight sleep."

"Do you want anesthesia too?"

"Sure. Enough pentothal for analgesia."

They worked together smoothly above the patient, who had begun to relax now under the drug and talk her heart out. The delivery was uneventful, but Chris felt his eyes mist as he watched Sam slap breath into the small red body. . . . Karen, he reflected, had said just the right thing when she left him there in the hall. They *did* function without him, a well-knit team that could call its own signals now. Come what may, the clinic would go on; blacklisted or not, this small, loyal group would see his dream through to a reality.

He would face Bibb this afternoon with that much established. Dwight might smash his own career. He could not wreck the idea that he had put in motion at Bayshore.

On that note he turned away from the delivery room window before Sam or Karen could see his face. Striding quickly down the hall, he missed the look they exchanged. Sam's slow, meaning wink as he leaned forward above the squalling infant to whisper in Karen's ear. . . .

Luke said, "How long were you in the Army, Dr. Land?"

"Two years and six months."

"Were you overseas?"

"For a year I was at an Army Hospital in Algiers and at the Ospedale Maggiore in Naples. For six months I served with a portable unit at the front."

"How were you wounded?"

"The operating tent was machine-gunned and forced to evacuate. During the removal I was wounded by a sniper's bullet."

"You received your medical discharge thereafter?"

"After my convalescence, yes."

"What caused you to locate again in Milton?"

Chris hesitated. Watching the jury's faces, he felt it was safe to pause for thought. Why had he given up his plan to resume a teaching career and plunged instead into this certain dogfight? Was it to save Uncle Jeff? Had Karen's example swayed him? He knew that his reason went deeper. He had made up his mind that first night in Milton—when he stood at a child's bedside and fought vainly to stop a needless death. Now, it seemed, his own professional death would soon result from that gesture.

He spoke quietly. "I located here because it was apparent that Milton stood in need of honest doctors."

There was an audible stir in the courtroom. Porter leaned forward on the bench, forcing his eyes into focus. "That's a rather sweeping statement, Dr. Land. Will you be specific?"

"With pleasure, your honor. When I returned to civilian practice I found that conditions here summed up everything that is wrong with modern medicine. I found a mushroom city, and health at a low ebb. So low, in fact, that an epidemic of typhus was already in the making—a disease which only accompanies squalor and extreme poverty. In this instance the poverty was strangely absent. Every shipyard worker threatened with the disease could have paid for his protection, but protection was withheld for selfish reasons."

Bibb said, "May I ask if this sermon is necessary to the progress of the case?"

"What I'm saying is the case in essence. I'm telling the court how medicine can go to pieces when the motives are

330

wrong. How a crooked lawyer can crucify a doctor who is only trying to save life."

The prosecuting attorney's voice went out of control for the first time. "Retract that statement, or I'll sue you for libel!"

The judge's gavel smothered the rest. Porter said, "That's enough, Mr. Bibb. You asked a question, and you were answered."

Chris said, "When I speak of wrong motives, I refer to compensation practice and all its evils. I mean to show that the group which controls that practice in Milton has withheld elementary health protection from the shipyard workers until the last possible moment."

"Do you have that evidence in court, Dr. Land?"

"No, your honor. I realize it does not belong in this trial. It will be presented next month, when the State Compensation Board begins its inquiry into illegal activities in Milton."

From where he sat he watched the reporters' pencils scurry in the press box. The spectators beyond sat unstirring, waiting for more. Chris hoped that Dwight had heard that last threat, but the compensation doctor was nowhere to be seen. To his surprise, however, he noticed Jean Moreau far back in the gallery. For once the Frenchman seemed to be part of an audience, with all his aloofness gone. When Chris caught his eye, Moreau turned abruptly away.

Chris said, "I hoped to prove to Milton that adequate medical care could be brought to large groups and small, without cheapening medicine in any way; with that end in view, I founded the Bayshore Clinic."

"Were you following this plan when you went to the bedside of Mary Ann Dawkins?"

"Object," snapped Bibb. "That's a leading question."

"I'll rephrase it, your honor. Why did you accompany Dr. Agard to the Dawkins home?"

"I wanted to do what I could. A child was dying of criminal neglect, and——"

Bibb roared an objection. The judge gave Chris another owlish look. "Is that a clinical opinion, Dr. Land?"

"A clinical opinion, your honor? It's a matter of fact."

Luke took back his witness as order was restored. Once again he took Chris down the familiar treadmill, to describe the routine he and Karen had followed until the child's death.

"Did Dawkins seem to feel that you did wrong to operate?"

"On the contrary, both he and his wife were grateful. He said we'd done all we could." Chris glanced at Bibb, but there was no objection.

"Then why do you think Dawkins brought this suit?"

"I think he was paid by others to do so."

Bibb bounced up. "I move that that statement be stricken from the record. It's deliberate hearsay, without evidence."

"Do you have such evidence, Dr. Land?" asked Porter.

"Unfortunately, no."

"Question and answer will be stricken from the record. Confine your answers to things which you know to be the truth."

Luke said, "No further questions."

Bibb was already at the witness box. "D'you admit you operated on Mary Ann Dawkins without her father's consent?"

"Yes. As you've been told, there was no time."

" 'Yes' will do, Doctor. Is the type of medicine you practice approved by organized doctors?"

"Not generally."

"Did you have a state license that night?"

"No, I did not."

"You admit operating illegally, upon a minor, without the parents' permission?"

"I operated to save a life."

"But were you qualified at the time?"

"My qualifications have been stated in court."

"But were you qualified that night?"

"I felt that I was."

"Mrs. Dawkins has testified that you'd been drinking. Do you deny it?"

"No. I'd had a small amount of aquavit."

"As a cocktail?"

"With after-dinner coffee, at least an hour before."

"Don't qualify your statements, please. Did you have cocktails before dinner?"

"I had just one martini."

"With Dr. Agard?"

"Yes."

"Is it true she makes her martinis with absinthe, Dr. Land?"

"I believe so." Too late Chris realized that Bibb had somehow managed to raid Karen's bungalow and make a thorough check on her liquor cellar. Already he had built an exotic picture in the jury's mind, merely by naming these strange beverages.

Bibb said with deadly emphasis, "Then you admit you were intoxicated when you operated on the child?"

"Certainly not. I did not drink enough to be affected by it."

"Gin, absinthe, and Swedish punch," said Bibb. "I congratulate you on your head, Dr. Land. No more questions."

He turned away from the jury with a parting smirk and went back to his table. Chris stepped down from the box, ignoring the snicker that had swept through the courtroom. He had hoped to make this an affirmation of faith: somehow the affirmation had been snarled in red tape even before Bibb had pounced.

For the rest of the afternoon he slumped wearily in his chair, willing the ordeal to end. Luke was still a willing Trojan at the jury box as he put on a succession of character witnesses, including Deavers and several of Chris's ex-patients. The evidence was complimentary, but he could not keep down the conviction that the jury had already made up its mind—perhaps at the moment Bibb had flung his accusation at Karen, or when he had pounded home the damning fact that a doctor might take a drink a whole hour before an operation.

He was almost relieved when Porter began his five-o'clock fidgets on the high bench above them. Sam Bernstein had just come down the aisle; he was leaning across the wicket now, to whisper in Luke's ear. To his astonishment, Chris saw Luke's face lighten at the news.

Porter said testily, "If defense counsel has quite finished his conference?"

Luke came up to the bench, pulling Bibb beside him with a look. "Your honor, I have reason to believe that I have developed new evidence. Will the court grant a three days' delay?"

Chris watched the old judge blink and suppress a smile. A continuance would give him time for a week-end holiday on his launch: it was no mean temptation, now that the groupers were running.

"Do you have any objection, Mr. Bibb?"

The plaintiff's attorney hesitated, then shook his head. Evidently he felt that the case was already in his pocket. A delay would only give him a chance for more smearing on the side.

Outside Pudge Carrol was seated in Luke's car. Sam came out beside them and jumped into the rumble. "We'll drive you over to the boathouse, Chris. God knows you need fresh air."

"Couldn't you explain that continuance in the courtroom?"

"I had to move fast, before Bibb objected," said Luke. "To say nothing of my client."

Chris looked up, frowning. "If you fellows are planning to work on Dawkins——"

"Nothing so crude as that," said Sam. "Pudge has been snooping, that's all. He thinks he's uncovered something."

"Anything we can put our finger on?"

"Not unless we play it right," said Luke. "I couldn't go to court tomorrow until I'd checked, that's all."

Pudge Carrol spoke for the first time. Chris noticed that the labor leader looked remarkably cheerful, considering his first remark. "I got reason to believe Dwight didn't stop with Dawkins."

"You don't mean he's got to the jury?"

"Half of 'em, at any rate."

"What about that foreman? He's certainly our man."

"They've got the hot-foot on him too, Doc. By tomorrow he'll be told definitely that he's to go the right way or lose his job."

No one spoke for a moment but Sam, who filled the air with a blue haze of profanity. The car was already boring across the causeway. Chris leaned far out to catch the first whiff of sea air. For the past two days he had been hit too hard and too often. His senses simply would not absorb this last blow.

"How much of this can we prove?"

"Not a word, unless someone talks."

"You aren't getting to Dawkins. You promised me that."

Pudge said, "Maybe there's another way. We ain't doped out all the angles, but——"

Chris put an earnest hand on the labor leader's arm. "I know you fellows are trying to be loyal. But we can't win that way."

"Who says we can't?"

"I can still convince that jury I'm on the level. I want you to let me sum up for you, Luke. Can you arrange it?"

"It's rather unusual."

"It's legal, though."

Luke shrugged. "Maybe it's a good idea at that. I've a hunch old Porter is on our side, but he can't influence the jury. You might be able to get through to them in spite of everything."

"You mean it's our only chance?"

"As of now," said Luke.

Waving good-by to them at the bridge to St. Lucie Cay, Chris had time to wonder why Luke had given in so readily to his request. He had the conviction that they were making plans over his head. The sort of planning he would veto instantly, if he knew. Well, he was too tired at the moment to ponder the motives of anyone, including his friends.

There was still a half hour of sunlight when he walked down his dock—and jumped aboard the yawl. Obeying a sudden impulse, he cast off the mooring ropes and let the offshore breeze bell the mainsail. The *Lady Jane* ran away sweetly from the wind, across the broad reach of the harbor. He took her out a mile beyond the pier before he rounded an imaginary buoy and shifted sail for the next tack. He had sailed this triangular course in actual races, as a boy. It was good to let his hands remember it now—to cut round the second phantom buoy with the wind on the quarter and the sail like a drumhead.

Heeling in the freshening breeze, he let the yawl run toward the sea wall that separated Bayshore Drive from open water. The sun plunged behind the crest as he came about at last; the clinic, serene on its hilltop, winked a score of friendly windows in the gloaming. Once more he reminded himself of its solid reality there in the dark, of the loyal friends who would fight for him to the last ditch, and carry on his work for him, if they failed. That thought was enough to sustain him at the end of a dreary day. Even if he never lifted a scalpel again, that light on the hilltop was the only touch of glory he would ask.

The phone was ringing in his boathouse when he tied up the yawl again. He scrambled to answer it, and smiled as he felt tranquillity vanish even before he could touch the receiver. The voice at the far end was familiar; he spoke the name aloud, before its owner could identify himself.

"Yes, Mr. Borland?"

"Can you come right over?"

"Of course I can. What's up?"

"It's Roz," said Borland. "Dwight and Moreau are here now. But I want you too."

"You mean she's ill?"

"She's worse than that, Land. A half hour ago she collapsed on her way to work. I've been ringing you ever since. That's how long she's been asking for you."

22

ROSALIE'S MAID was a nut-brown Englishwoman with a quiet voice. Chris saw instantly that she had been crying, and judged that she had been in the Borland service a long time. The idea of a family retainer did not fit the newness of Slave Hill, but he accepted it gratefully now as he moved with Briggs down the upper hall.

"Believe me, sir, I begged her not to go out today."

"When did she collapse?"

"Just before she set out for the yards. She was tying her kerchief at the mirror when I saw her sway a little. If you ask me, it came from that bruise on her leg. For days, now, she's been feeling poorly. I ran straight across the room to her, but she'd fallen to the carpet before I——" Briggs blew her nose lustily and turned the handle of the bedroom door. "She's been lying here ever since, waiting for you."

"Why did you mention the bruise on her leg?"

"You'll see for yourself, sir, when you look at her."

Borland was standing by the big four-poster with an unlighted cigar in his teeth. Outwardly he seemed composed enough: the scowl on his forehead might have been caused by a snarled assembly line as well as by an only daughter's breakdown. But Chris remembered his voice on the phone; when he paused to shake hands he was not surprised to find the shipbuilder's palm dank with sweat.

Borland said, "Moreau gave her a quarter of morphia. She's dozed off for a time."

"Where are the doctors now?"

"On ice. I'll keep 'em there till you've looked her over."

Even now Chris could not help smiling faintly. "Dwight too?"

"Why not? They've argued about her ever since they came. I'd have sent for you even if she hadn't asked." He led Chris firmly toward the bed. "Never mind ethics now, Land. You both work for me, don't you?"

Rosalie was propped high on pillows. Her skin was marble pale, the lips drained of color until they seemed almost gray. Though her breathing was labored, there was little chest movement; Chris saw that the process was being carried out almost entirely by the diaphragm.

Briggs said, "I got her straight to bed, sir, before she came 'round. I asked if her leg hurt, and she said yes. But she complained rather more of a pain in her chest."

"Will you get me some nail-polish remover?"

The picture was complete when Briggs had removed the polish from one of Rosalie's hands. The nail beds were pallid too, but there was also the evidence of oxygen lack in the bluish tint they showed.

Rosalie's eyes opened as he came back to the bed with a stethoscope. Her pupils were small from the effect of the morphine, but there was a glassiness about her stare that went with shock. An incredulous stare that didn't quite believe in his presence. He was prepared for the slow smile of relief; for anything, in fact, but her first words.

"I didn't think you'd come, Chris."

"You know me better than that."

"I don't know you at all," she whispered. "Kiss me, to prove we're friends." She smiled vaguely. "Or did we prove that once?"

He saw that Borland had gone to the window to stare down into the garden, and bent quickly to kiss her cold lips while Briggs turned discreetly aside. "Now will you be good, while I see what's wrong?"

"I'm always good—when people let me be."

But she relaxed before he began percussing, outlining the position of heart in relation to lungs. "Where does it hurt most, Roz?"

Her hand moved to her right side, and he noted the dullness to percussion here; her skin was damp with a cold perspiration. At his nod Briggs folded back the sheets to expose Rosalie's leg. Chris frowned as he noted the bluish tint of the bruise below the knee.

"Any pain here, Rosalie?"

Her eyes were closed now, but she nodded as she touched her upper thigh. Chris was already comparing the size of her ankles: there was a definite swelling of the right, where the bruise was present. The skin of the right foot was pale, as compared with the left.

His fingers moved gently to the top of her foot, seeking the pulsation of the dorsalis pedis artery. There was a lessening of pulsation on the side of the bruise, as if something had decreased the flow of arterial blood to the leg. The picture was becoming clear now—for, if his diagnosis was correct, this lessening of flow through the arteries was to be expected.

"I'm going to move your foot, Roz. Tell me if it hurts."

With her left leg extended, he pushed up on the foot from the sole, flexing it at the ankle upon the lower leg. With his free hand he pressed along the posterior surface of the calf, over the deep veins which formed here to channel blood from extremity to heart. When he moved to the other side there was an instant reaction to his pressure. He repeated the test more gently—but Rosalie still winced and drew away. He forced his fingers to continue the examination, tracing the great veins where they formed into one channel in the popliteal space behind the knee, then coursed around on the inner side of the leg to continue upward. There was pain reaction all the way.

Roz spoke contentedly. "Will I die, Chris?"

"Not if I can help it."

He watched her settle back into the tropic languor of the drug with her smile intact. It had been hard enough for him to keep his words light. Once again he examined the lung carefully, hearing the friction rub as the two layers of the pleura whispered together. There was pleurisy there, all right —but not a simple irritation. The trouble was deep-seated and deadly. Unless he could remove it promptly, it might take Roz Borland's life at any moment.

Borland went out of the room without a word when he asked for Dwight and Moreau. Something in Chris's tone had made him hurry without asking questions.

The sequence was clear enough, but Chris went over to the window to check the high points while Briggs folded the covers about Rosalie once again. The leg bruise (for which he was responsible) had irritated the deep veins in the calf sufficiently to form clots, as they so easily did. The phenomenon was common after an operation, sometimes with no history of injury or infection. It was easy to see how it might happen with this type of trauma.

A clot had formed—and grown, filling the veins to a higher and higher level. Rosalie had worked steadily at the yard, ignoring the pain. Remembering how she had limped that night in the garden, he went on to visualize the crisis. A portion of the clot had broken free—traveling in the blood stream as a rider, or common embolus. It had traveled through the great vein trees, always by larger and larger channels, so that there was no point of blockage until it reached the heart.

In the muscular ventricular chamber the clot had swirled and moved onward to the pulmonary arteries, those great, thin-walled channels that carried blood to the lungs. Now it was moving in reverse position, of course, with its progression from trunk to branches that narrowed steadily in size. Somewhere the passageway had proved too small. It had not been a major vessel, for when clots filled those, death was instantaneous. In this case it was evident that providence had released only a small clot—and sent it pelleting through the circulation to block part of the lung. The block had occurred in a small vessel, just large enough to cause one of those wedge-shaped areas of sudden blood lack which were called infarcts.

Rosalie would recover from this infarct, he was certain. Her buoyant young strength was sufficient insurance of that. There would normally be pain for a while—a triangular shadow on the X ray that might last for weeks. After that the effects would rapidly disappear. But there was a false security in that picture, enough to lull an unwary doctor. The truth was backed by scientific reports as well as his own surgical experience. In seven cases out of ten other emboli came—other clots that might not be as small as this one, carrying with them an even greater danger of death.

He went back to the bed to appraise Rosalie's chances, and felt terror settle in his heart. He knew that he loved her more than he loved anything, or ever would. And he knew that she had already chosen Moreau—as deliberately as he, in his stub-

339

born blindness, had chosen Karen. But he would save her, for all of that, if he could. Borland had put her life in his hands, and he must see that no second embolus occurred. He glanced up quickly as the two other doctors approached the bedside. At the moment he did not recognize them as personalities.

Moreau said, "What do you think?"

"The diagnosis seems obvious. Perhaps we should discuss it outside."

Rosalie shook her head and whispered, forcing him to bend to hear her words. "Please, Chris. Don't leave me."

The Frenchman nodded an agreement. Perhaps it was better for her to know everything, Chris thought. The operation he planned would be done largely under local anesthetic, making her co-operation essential.

Dwight said, "You agree there is a pleurisy?"

Chris looked at him directly for the first time; the compensation doctor returned his stare with utter confidence. He was in tropical dinner clothes tonight, complete to a snug scarlet cummerbund. As always, he carried his clothes with a subtle air of drama, the intimation of a competence that went beyond self-esteem. If he was remembering his debacle in Chris's hydrangea bed, he gave no sign of it.

Moreau said, "It's more than pleurisy, Doctor."

"Definitely," Chris agreed. "In this case the pleurisy is overlying a pulmonary embolus."

"And what, may I ask, is the source of the embolus you find so readily?"

"An obvious thrombosis of the femoral vein."

Dwight's voice was still light and mocking. He was evidently speaking for Borland's benefit now. "That is hardly the picture of a phlebitis, Doctor. No redness, no fever——"

"Nobody mentioned phlebitis," said Chris. "This is a mechanical type of clot."

"Exactly," snapped Moreau. "Intravascular thrombosis, Dwight. My estimate, from the start."

In the background the shipbuilder said quietly, "What do you recommend, Land?"

"Rosalie must go to a hospital at once. An X ray of the veins is imperative."

Dwight's voice was on the edge of a sneer now. "Come, Doctor! If she has an embolus, it would be dangerous to move her."

340

"She must be moved in any case. A ligation and section of the femoral or iliac vein is indicated immediately."

Dwight spoke with quiet contempt. "I disagree completely."

"What do you recommend?"

"Bed rest. Perhaps some dicoumarin to cut down the clotting tendency."

"What about another embolus?"

"I have seen a number of these cases. They don't occur often."

Moreau spoke to Chris directly, as though Dwight had not intervened. "If you're going to ligate, why stop for a venogram?"

"We must be sure that this clot hasn't already extended."

"Beyond the femoral level, you mean?"

"From the femoral to the iliac veins."

Moreau pursed his lips; in that moment Chris sensed once again that the Frenchman, at least, knew his job. If this last estimate were true, the operation would be many times more dangerous. The dissection would extend to the pelvis and beyond, carrying with it the risk of dislodging the clot still more, sending a fatal embolus winging toward heart and lungs. Moreau looked down at the half-unconscious form on the great bed between them. Watching his eyes soften, Chris guessed what he was thinking and turned away.

"Will the X ray tell you much?" asked Borland.

"All we need to know. We can operate above the level of the clot and avoid the danger of dislodging a part of it."

"You feel this must be done at once?"

"There's no other choice."

Dwight said, "Moving her is both foolish and dangerous. I do not advise it."

The shipbuilder's eyes moved on to Moreau. The Frenchman did not hesitate; in fact, his own glance burned Dwight as he spoke.

"I agree with Dr. Land—completely. I also grant the risk. It is one any competent surgeon would take without question."

Dwight accepted the defection with a shrug. "It seems I'm outnumbered, Mr. Borland. Do I gather that Dr. Land will perform this operation"—the well-bred voice made a pause— "when and if he finds it necessary?"

341

Borland said, "It's been Land's case for the past hour, Dwight. You're slow on the uptake tonight."

"In that case, gentlemen——"

The compensation doctor exchanged an ironic bow with Jean Moreau. Chris turned toward the bed without even noticing his enemy's exit. Gilbert Dwight had hurt him already, as much as one man can hurt another. Tonight he could well afford to toss the fate of Dr. Christopher Land on the gods' knees and leave it there.

"Where are we taking her?" asked Moreau. His voice seemed easier, now that Dwight had gone.

Chris considered that dilemma briefly. He would have preferred to have Rosalie at the clinic, where he could keep her continually under his eye. But Bayshore was miles to the west, and he knew that the road between was bad in spots. Besides (he reminded himself of this firmly), Jean Moreau would be an equally competent observer if they pulled her through tonight.

"The County is nearer," he said. "Of course I'm not on the visiting list——"

"You are now," said the Frenchman quietly. "A half hour ago I telephoned to make arrangements—just in case."

"For *me?*"

"For you, Dr. Land."

Their eyes met across the bed with new understanding. Then Moreau bent swiftly to put a soothing hand on Rosalie's as she moaned faintly and tried to raise herself from the pillows.

At the County Hospital, Chris found that the operating-room supervisor was already waiting with an ampule of diodrast; an orderly stood by, ready to adjust a portable X-ray machine. Moreau, he gathered, had been both emphatic and definite on the telephone. He nodded his thanks briefly to the Frenchman as he left the wheeled stretcher on which Rosalie lay and drew a file across the neck of the ampule. From this point on he knew that he would be blessedly occupied. Too busy, in fact, to mind the terror that pounded dully at the back of his brain.

Injected directly, the solution of diodrast would spread rapidly through the entire venous tree of the leg, outlining it in a network of white patterns on the dark X-ray film. Chris nodded to the orderly; together they adjusted the portable machine above Rosalie. Success in this examination, he reminded himself, would require exact timing. If the picture were snapped too early, the solution would not yet have filled the veins. If taken too late, it might escape into the general circulation.

He took Rosalie's foot in his hand and selected a narrow blue channel, visible through the tan of her skin just in front of the ankle. Blood spurted back into the syringe as he thrust the needle home; at the end of a minute the injection was completed. The technician flicked the switch in response to his signal, sending the machine's rays through flesh, bone, and the veins filled with the contrast medium.

"Develop at once, please."

Once again he left his patient with Moreau and went into the operating room to check his tray with the supervisor. Again he saw that the Frenchman's instructions had been complete. He was still counting sutures when Moreau himself came through the swinging door.

"Rosalie is in a half-coma now, from that second shot," he said.

"Like to see the film?"

Chris did not speak again until they paused at the darkroom door. "You'll assist, of course."

Moreau looked more startled than embarrassed. "I should be honored."

They went into the darkroom together as the light above the door winked its summons. "Clinically," said Chris, "the clot has extended well into the iliac veins. The X ray should confirm it." He watched the attendant lift the dark rectangle of film from the developing solution and wondered how he had kept his voice so calm.

"Can you see all that?" asked Moreau. "I am not accustomed to these venograms."

The film was in the bright window of light in the view box now. Chris indicated the white outlines of the vessels where he had injected the radio-opaque liquid. "There's the superficial network."

"I see no deep veins."

"Exactly. They're filled with the thrombus."

"How do you know the embolus has extended higher?"

"By the fact that the superficial veins do not empty into the femoral where they normally should."

Moreau nodded solemnly. "I am familiar with that junction. You must search deeper, then."

They returned to the operating room without completing that thought. Here Chris gave his orders to the anesthetist. Automatically he rechecked the instruments he would use: the guy sutures to hold the vein while he extracted the clot; a glass suction tip, bent to pass easily into the vessel and remove any upward extension of the process which might be dislodged by operative procedure; stout twisted ligatures, and delicate blood-vessel clamps ready to head off any clots that might pass through en route to the lungs.

"We may need a transfusion when this is over," said Chris. He felt calm enough now—all but released from the personal tug of the operation ahead. In another few minutes, he knew, he could put on the insulation completely.

The Frenchman said, "I already asked them to match me."

"Perhaps I should match too. She won't need it, in any case, until we've finished here."

They went together to the laboratory: Moreau stood by while the technician took a sample of Chris's blood for matching. If the Frenchman was nervous, he did not show it noticeably. Only the rhythm of his puffs, as he dragged on a cigarette, betrayed his inner tension.

Back on the operating-room floor, they scrubbed for a few moments in silence. A familiar tempo had picked them both up, drawing their perceptions taut. Rosalie was in competent hands on the table beyond. There was no need to worry about details. No point in thinking of their patient as someone to love—or to fight over in the parking lot of a roadhouse. . . . No reason for words, beyond a few routine questions.

"What anesthetic are you using?"

"Spinal," said Chris. "Pontocaine glucose."

Moreau nodded—and stalked into the operating room to take his place at the table. Chris breathed deeply and followed. The patient was already draped and ready—a patient now, he reminded himself one last time, not Rosalie Borland. The anesthetist handed him a syringe, and he injected precisely, turning Rosalie on her back when he finished injecting. With a needle he picked out the level of anesthesia by jabbing the skin gently. When it had traveled well above the level where he intended to operate, he placed the table in a horizontal position.

"Oxygen, please."

344

He went to the basin to continue his scrubbing. Moreau had drawn on sterile gloves when he returned, and stood ready—just outside the circle of light which glared down on Rosalie's skin, still a dusky hue from the disturbance of her respiration. The lower abdomen was already covered with the familiar crimson antiseptic. He knew that he must make his incision here, to search out the artery and vein to the leg —pulsing vessels a scant few inches from the bifurcation of the great central trunks of the body.

One more deep breath, and the insulation of his job had enclosed him in a blessed zone of quiet. Moreau stepped up to the table with clamp and sponge, without waiting for his nod. The scalpel had already made a smooth stroke across Rosalie's skin, baring the rectus muscles in an eight-inch incision.

Skin towels were ready to his hand. He covered the area around the wound, draping its edges completely as Moreau tied off the last of the bleeding. With forceps he lifted the tissue in the depths of the wound, dissecting down to the fusion of the fascial layers.

Moreau said, "Are you going through the semilunar line?"

Chris nodded. The scalpel bit on grimly, exposing the layer of the peritoneum. He knew he must move cautiously now. If this thin membrane was injured, the organs of the abdomen would spill into the wound, making exposure difficult.

"Retractor, please."

He placed the blade carefully. Injudicious pressure at this point might squeeze out another clot and send it pelting away into the circulation, with fatal consequences. Instead he moved the peritoneum toward the midline, shoving the membrane gently away from the deeper structures. In a moment the whiter, thicker wall of the iliac artery appeared in the wound. Their work lay deeper, in the darker wall of the iliac vein, just visible now in the depths of the field.

Chris worked gently with a sponge, dissecting away the tissues around the vein—careful always not to exert pressure which might dislodge a clot. Here, of all times, was a moment for steady hands. The room faded; the whole world was centered in the tiny space under his fingers as he sought to free the vein he was seeking. Otherwise he might never locate the clot—and he knew that it might well have extended this far from its point of origin.

345

He heard his own voice at last, quiet with authority in the frozen tableau. "I have it now."

Moreau bent with him to look into the wound. He saw a dark section of vein, dull and soggy with the obstruction it contained. Beside it the companion artery pulsed with each beat of Rosalie's heart.

"Le caillot, n'est-ce pas?" In the tension Moreau had lapsed into his own tongue.

"It extends completely through the iliac, and perhaps into the vena cava."

"You will expose the vena cava?"

Chris shook his head. "We can extract the clot with suction."

"Can you open the vein?" Chris knew the vision he had— of blood gushing up through the narrow operative wound —filling it, leaving them groping helplessly to control the flood.

"I'll pass temporary ligatures first," he said. It was a ticklish job, for not more than an inch of vein was available. The carriers had already come into his hand: blunt, curved instruments like needles with handles attached. Streaming from the eye of each was a dark strand of braided silk. With a finger against the vein, Chris worked the first curved end beneath the vessel.

He was conscious of the tension in the room. All of them knew that a slip in the rigid control he maintained upon the instrument might end the operation in a flash. Once the vein was ruptured, with no temporary means to control the bleeding, the wound under his hand would be a geyser of blood.

Moreau sighed his relief as the carrier appeared on the far side of the vessel. Reaching with a clamp, he grasped the loop of silk in the needle's eye and pulled gently until there was enough slack to hold. Chris then took up the second carrier and repeated the maneuver. With both ligatures in place, he worked them gently apart, until almost an inch of vein was free between.

"We'll open here," he said. "Guy sutures, please."

These were incredibly tiny needles—small enough to penetrate the paper-thin veins without severing tissue. He inserted them carefully, and when the tiny strands of cotton were lifted, a section of the vein was tented up between them.

"Suction ready?"

At the nurse's nod Moreau lifted the upper ligature.

"When I am ready," Chris told him, "I will say 'tie.' You must then knot the ligature snugly—and quickly."

The Frenchman nodded. Both of them knew that the upper ligature was their chief worry. Once the clot was removed, blood from the great channel of the vena cava would pour toward the wound. The knot below was not so significant, since the clot would prevent any serious flow at that end.

Chris took up the scalpel with the small blade, devised for just such work as this. He glanced about him briefly, noting the sound of the suction machine, the even click of the valve in the mask as the anesthetist gave oxygen. Satisfied that everything was ready, he cut cleanly across the vein. The thin edges parted, revealing the damp red hue of the clot that obstructed it.

"Suction, please."

He placed the tip of the glass tube against the slit in the vein. Holding the clot attached by the negative pressure of the suction, he worked the tip backward, extracting the clot from the vessel as he did so. It emerged slowly, a dark reddish strand as thick as his finger and tapering toward the end. For anxious moments he worked it back slowly, knowing that a false move could still break the clot into the circulation. Finally the end of the thrombus came out through the vein, and he spoke quickly.

"Tie!"

Blood gushed back through the open vein as Moreau drew the knot tight, stopping the flow instantly. He held the strands taut while Chris sponged the wound clean, permitting the second tie of the knot to be put in place.

"Good work. Now we'll go after that lower segment."

Again he worked with the suction tip. There was no tension now, for no clot could pass into the circulation. When Chris had removed about two inches of obstruction, blood flowed freely into the lower end of the vessel, indicating that the next large branch below them had been cleared. He tied the second ligature snugly and completed the severing of the vein.

"Why do you cut it?" asked Moreau.

"To break the sympathetic chain and prevent spasm. I'll inject sympathetics later, when the anesthesia has worn off."

There was little more to the operation now. Tissues sutured, he completed the closure, feeling his voice loosen as he spoke again.

"What about types for a transfusion?"

Moreau said, "You're the one who matched, Doctor. Do you feel she needs it?"

Chris hesitated. He knew that Rosalie was safe now. Yet a transfusion was always good insurance, especially in an operation of this kind. It gave him a quixotic thrill to realize that he could offer her that extra safeguard too.

"I'll let them take my blood now," he said. "Will you see her off the table?"

Moreau took his place as he turned aside. After all, he reflected, this was also a fitting gesture. Give all your skill to save the girl you love—and then resign your place to another man.

The Frenchman spoke softly. "May I say it from the heart, Dr. Land—that operation was a *chef d'œuvre.*" His hands were already busy above the sheeted form on the table as he strapped a dressing in place.

"A farewell performance, you mean."

Chris bowed formally—it seemed odd that he should be bowing to Moreau—and left the room without another word. Following an orderly to the transfusion table, he didn't feel in the least quixotic; he felt lonelier than he had ever been, drained of the last scrap of emotional resilience. Perhaps, he reflected, that is the fate of all Quixotes, if they live too long. . . . On the way he glanced into a waiting room and saw Cal Borland's bulky frame hunched in an armchair. He hurried on before the shipbuilder looked up. Jean Moreau would give him the good news soon enough. At the moment Dr. Christopher Land had no craving for gratitude.

To CHRIS'S TIRED EYES that morning the two lawyers at the bar of justice resembled caricatures of their own dominant traits. Bibb a confident cockerel, bristling with assurance; Luke a patient St. Bernard, with a bumbling strength all his own, even as he fought the last lap of a losing case. . . . At the moment they were stating their sides of the continuance for Porter's benefit while the jury yawned and waited. Bibb, it seemed, was using the moment as an excuse to probe his opponent's integrity; Luke was insisting that he would justify himself the moment the plaintiff appeared in court.

Chris stirred from his lethargy as Joe Peters spoke at his elbow. Ever since he had operated on Rosalie it had been easy to slip into this mood of dull waiting. To yield to Sam Bernstein's insistence and stay incommunicado at the boathouse, leaving the clinic to the little obstetrician and Karen. To avoid all contact with the world outside St. Lucie Cay, including Borland and the newspapers. . . .

Joel said, "Looks like Dawkins missed his bus. I wonder why?"

But Chris did not rise to the overtone of mystery. Dawkins had been only a pawn in this case from the beginning. Even Bibb's obvious malaise, as the judge queried him sharply, seemed of little moment now.

"We have telephoned the Dawkins home, your honor. I assure you he is now on his way."

Joel whispered, "Maybe he hitched a ride and the car broke down. That'd explain a lot, wouldn't it?"

Sam Bernstein came down the aisle on quick tiptoe and took a seat just behind the wicket. The judge looked up, frowning.

"The bailiffs will admit no more spectators. This room is dangerously crowded now."

Luke said, "If it please your honor, Dr. Bernstein is here at my request. You may wish to question him later."

"Take a look, Dr. Land," said Joel. "Tell me if that isn't nice timing."

But Chris had already swiveled in his chair, in response to a murmur on the side aisle. Dawkins had just come into court, arm in arm with Pudge Carrol. The plaintiff looked disheveled and a trifle dazed, but his walk was quite steady. Pudge stopped at the wicket and shot an inquiring look at the bench.

Pudge said, "Here's your boy, Bibb. Late, but all in one piece."

Porter's gavel banged. "You are out of order, Mr. Carrol. What's the meaning of this?"

"We drove in from the Flats together, your honor. Tangled

349

mudguards with a truck on Duval Square. Your boy was feeling a little groggy, so I brought him in myself."

Again the judge pounded for silence. "The court is grateful, Mr. Carrol. Will you take a seat?"

"Sure thing, your honor—if you got room for one more."

Porter ignored the laughter as a group of workers on the front row shuffled over to make room for Pudge. Dawkins had come through the wicket now, walking steadily. Luke was already claiming the floor.

The judge said, "The floor is obviously yours, Mr. Fraser. You were examining when we closed."

"In that case, your honor, may I recall Mr. Dawkins to the stand?"

Bibb had bounced up by now, signaling frantically to the plaintiff across the clutter of tables. But Dawkins was looking at Luke with a strange intentness. . . . Chris leaned forward sharply to study the man's face. He did not seem drunk. There was none of the dullness in his eyes that goes with alcohol. Rather, they were brilliant, as if lighted by some fire not normally present in that stodgy body. Shaken from his lethargy, Chris wondered if Bibb was near enough to see that glow.

The judge said. "If Mr. Dawkins is quite recovered——"

"I feel fine," said the plaintiff. His tone was clear and contained, but he was still looking at Luke, not at his own table or the bench.

"Have you been drinking?"

"No sir. Ain't had a drop."

"You may take the stand."

Bibb raised his voice. "Is this part of the new evidence the defense counsel has promised us?"

"Definitely," said Luke. "Do you object?"

"I would like first to confer with my client. If it please the court, this is most irregular."

Porter said severely, "The only irregularity I can observe from here, Mr. Bibb, is your client's tardiness. He is obviously sober and in possession of his faculties. The court sees no reason for delay."

"Boy-oh-boy!" said Joel Peters. "How's *that* for timing, Dr. Land?"

The courtroom was curiously still as Dawkins settled in the witness box. Outwardly there had been nothing striking in his hurried entrance or in the lawyers' fireworks. Yet even the sleepiest time-killer on the back bench sensed climax in the making as the plaintiff was sworn.

Chris was aware of two things while Luke put the witness into the groove. Though Dawkins' manner was as shifty as ever, the timbre of his voice had changed. His eyes were part of that metamorphosis: try as they might, they never left Luke's. Chris turned to shoot a wordless question at Sam, but the little obstetrician had made a prayer book of his hands and refused to look up from it. . . . Pudge Carrol, too, had bowed his head. Even as he glanced that way Chris saw the union leader's lips murmur a prayer of his own.

"In God's name, Joel—what's up?"

But Luke's assistant only grinned. "Keep your fingers crossed, Dr. Land. It's coming any minute now."

It came as they turned back to the witness box. The sort of quiet bombshell that caught the whole jammed room napping—including Stanley Bibb.

Luke said, "You are aware, Mr. Dawkins, that you are under oath on this recall?"

"Yes sir. I sure know that."

"Then will you tell the court how much you were paid to bring this suit?"

"I was paid five hundred bucks, cash."

Porter leaned forward. Luke's eyes were still locked with the witness's own anchored stare; Luke's question had been as calm as Dawkins' answer.

Luke said, "Five hundred dollars. Isn't that rather a low price for——"

But Bibb was on his feet at last, shouting above the tumult. "Objection! This man is drunk."

The gavel crashed insistently for silence. "One more such outburst and I'll clear the courtroom," said the judge. "I repeat, Mr. Dawkins—have you been drinking?"

"No, your honor."

"Objection overruled. Take your seat, Mr. Bibb. Order in the courtroom."

Bibb's face was pea green as he sank back at his table. Chris turned his eyes away, certain that the man was about to be sick.

Luke said, "You have testified that you were paid five hundred dollars to bring this action against Dr. Land. Who paid you?"

"Bibb—and Dr. Dwight!"

351

Porter's gavel banged down the incipient murmur. "May I take charge, Mr. Fraser?"

Luke did not even smile as he stepped down. "Indeed yes, your honor. My point is made."

The judge focused his watery eyes on the witness. "You may tell this in your own words, Mr. Dawkins."

"Ain't much to tell, your honor. One day Dwight comes out and cases my place when I'm at work. Gives my old lady a talkin' to, you understand. Next night he and Bibb are both there waitin' for me."

"You say that money changed hands?"

"Sure did, your honor—that same night." Dawkins' voice had that same strange clarity. He was entirely nonchalant about it, as though he were discussing an honest debt. "Course I didn't want to drag Dr. Land into court, when he tried to save my girl. Leastways not unless they'd go above five hundred. Then they said Land was a bad doctor—and offered to split with me when we won."

"Who was to get the balance?"

"Bibb. He said he was gambling on the case—so why shouldn't I."

"And what induced you to confess this today?"

Dawkins looked vague for the first time. "Confess, your honor?"

"Why are you telling us the truth this morning?"

The witness threw back his head and brayed. Luke sat down at his own table and carefully avoided Chris's eyes. So did Sam Bernstein when Chris turned once again to scan the railing behind him. . . .

This time the spectators did not join in the laughter. There was something here that did not invite collaboration. A quality that suggested nightmare in the making.

Porter forgot his gavel for once and banged his desk blotter with a fist. "Answer my question instantly, or I'll fine you for contempt."

"Sorry, your honor," said Dawkins. "I don't know."

"You must know."

"It just seemed natural, that's all."

"To tell the truth, you mean?"

The witness passed a hand across his eyes. "I guess that's it."

"Do you have these impulses often?"

"No sir. I sure don't." Dawkins cracked his knuckles in

a sudden access of misery, aware of the roar of the court-room. There was nothing off-center about that collective bray, Chris reflected. Ananias in a corner has always been fair game for the herd.

The judge forgot his threat as he shouted against the silence. "Did someone bring pressure on you?"

"No, your honor."

"What about the man who drove you to court?"

"Pudge Carrol? We talked about baseball and the war. Didn't even mention the case."

Chris turned toward the union leader and saw that he was praying no longer. In fact, the light in Pudge's face, as he looked toward the judge, was righteous virtue in person. But the judge was still concentrating on the witness.

"Think hard, Dawkins. Something must have changed your mind."

"I don't know, your honor. Honest I don't." The familiar whine had come back into the plaintiff's tone; it deepened as his roving eyes picked out Sam Bernstein among the spectators. "Unless it was the shot he gave me."

"To whom do you refer now?"

"Him." Dawkins leveled a finger at Sam. Not at all dramatically. Not even angrily. It was a statement of fact by a man whose mind had begun to fumble again after one lucid moment.

The judge kept his temper with an effort. He said carefully, "Tell this in your own words, Mr. Dawkins. And try, please, to keep them coherent."

"I was waitin' by the main gate for the bus to bring me here, when Pudge Carrol offers me a lift. We made fine time till we got to the corner by Duval Square and the boulevard. Then one of Borland's assembly trucks sideswipes us and tears off a mudguard. We stepped out into an argument, and somebody socks me. Next thing I know, that doc is bringin' me around. Givin' me what he called first aid."

"Exactly what did he do?"

"He shot somethin' into my arm with a hypo. Said it'd make me feel fine—and it did. Right up to now, at any rate." Again Dawkins cracked his knuckles and dropped his eyes before the hooting courtroom.

Sam got to his feet without waiting for an invitation. "He's right, your honor. I gave him an injection of hyoscine."

"Hyoscine?"

"Truth serum, to the layman," said Sam. "If you ask me, it's earned the nickname."

The gavel banged furiously, but the judge's tone was anything but stern. "Do I gather that this was a—plot, Dr. Bernstein?"

Sam nodded owlishly. "Busted mudguard and all. The hypodermic was all my idea, though. It's been used in precinct basements—why not in court?"

Bibb found his voice at last. "If it please the court——"

Porter turned vaguely in his direction, as though he had forgotten the lawyer's existence. "Did you speak, Mr. Bibb?"

"This is barefaced collusion, your honor. I move that this preposterous testimony be stricken from the record in toto."

"Why?"

"Because it was obtained while my client was under the influence of a drug."

The old judge came back to realities at last, with a reluctant shrug. "I need no reminder from you on that score, Mr. Bibb." He looked across the courtroom at Luke, with a curious smile. "The testimony we have heard this morning will be removed from the record; the jury will disregard it in its entirety."

To Chris's amazement, Luke made no move of protest. Instead he put his hand across the table and took from Joel's briefcase a long manila envelope, sealed with the state arms of Louisiana. Chris sucked in his breath as his lawyer heaved deliberately to his feet, weighing the envelope in his hands.

"Do I understand, your honor, that the court is about to declare a mistrial?"

"Emphatically, Mr. Fraser."

"Before your honor so orders, may I offer an affidavit in evidence?"

"If the plaintiff's counsel does not object."

Chris watched incredulously while Bibb stormed up to the bench. The judge's weary courtesy was no less bewildering to him than Bibb's manner. Even when a lawyer is on his back, he thought, he'll fight back with teeth and toenails. Bibb's voice confirmed the thought; but it was rounded on the surface, for all its inner quaking.

"What is the source of this document?"

Luke said equably, "It is a signed statement, delivered into my hands this morning by Dr. Jean Moreau. Dr. Moreau's name is no doubt familiar to the court. So is the name of the New Orleans judge in whose chambers the deposition was taken."

He handed the envelope up to the bench without another word. Bibb did not protest. At that moment Bibb looked in real need of the hand Luke Fraser anchored under his elbow.

Luke said, "If the court will admit this affidavit in evidence, I'll offer it as support to the allegedly incompetent confession just made by the plaintiff." He made another of his masterly pauses as the sealing wax of the envelope cracked under Porter's paper cutter. "As your honor will observe, this second statement was signed freely in the judge's chambers. By a certain Dr. Kornmann, who left Milton rather suddenly three weeks ago."

The judge said, above the crisp rattle of foolscap, "There is no need for defense counsel to offer this new evidence."

"No need, your honor?"

"In my opinion it will expedite matters if it is saved for a later date—when it may prove more useful."

Luke bowed his head in a quiet triumph of his own. He stepped back from the bench, letting Bibb weave to the doubtful sanctuary of his chair. Above them the gavel gave a final thud.

"The case against Dr. Christopher Land is dismissed. The clerk will issue a bench warrant against Dr. Gilbert Dwight, S. L. Dawkins, and Stanley Bibb, for conspiracy to defraud. Court is adjourned."

Much later Chris remembered the glare of flash bulbs in his eyes and the hug that Uncle Jeff gave him when he had fought through the sea of handshaking, the sudden pang that cut through the delirium of release when he looked for Karen and remembered that she was in charge of the clinic that morning. When his emotions had simmered down to externals he was already in Pudge Carrol's car, driving away from the last reporter's question. From that moment nothing was more important than cornering Luke Fraser.

Luke, too, was a sought-after news story that morning. It seemed only natural that he should come into his office out of breath, that both Sam and Pudge should make an impromptu barricade in the anteroom before Chris could get out a word.

Luke said, "Just double-lock that door, gentlemen, before I start my own confession. This is for my client's ears alone."

He tamped his corncob with maddening slowness. "Incidentally, Sam, did I look too much like Svengali in court? You *said* I'd have to mesmerize him a little, while the hop was still on."

Sam said blissfully, "If my name was Sam Goldwyn, I'd give you a contract tomorrow."

Chris banged the table for attention, remembered the judge's gavel, and relaxed sheepishly in Luke's best armchair. "So you planned this without me. All of you——"

"From the word go," said Pudge. "Sorry we couldn't let you in, Doc; you're just too upright for *that* kinda medicine."

"Sam thought up the hyoscine?"

"Sam and Karen," said the little obstetrician. "I've used it a hundred times, to induce twilight sleep. Used it again in the new clinic, just three days ago. . . . It was Karen who called my attention to the patient telling her life story, with no details barred. Me, I've stopped listening to ladies in labor some time ago." Sam smiled at Luke. "That's when I hightailed it to Luke and suggested a continuance."

"Pudge did the rest," said Luke. "As you noticed in court, it took timing. But we swung it."

"Twenty minutes I waited on that street corner for the smash-up," said Sam. "I was so squirrely when it happened, I almost flubbed the injection. Just think where we'd be now if that needle had stopped."

Luke chuckled through the blue haze of his corncob. "It helped, knowing we could get by without Dawkins after all." He grinned at Chris. "After we'd gone to all that trouble I decided to use him regardless. If only to put over an act those monkeys in court would remember. Admit this much: it cleared you in a way no thrown-out case could match. It would have paid off, even if Porter had declared a mistrial."

Chris said, "I'll be grateful when I've caught my breath. What about that final flourish with the affidavit?"

"Here's a copy," said Luke. "Read it aloud, if you like. It's pure poetry."

Luke was right, Chris reflected as he skimmed through the onionskin carbon of the affidavit. Kornmann had told all, with trimmings; Kornmann had evidently had ample time, in New Orleans, to build up resentment against one Gilbert Dwight. His statement backed up Dawkins' own confession in every way. The Austrian, it seemed, had been in on the conspiracy from the beginning.

"How did Moreau get to him so easily?"

"That Frenchman has friends everywhere," said Luke. "He found out, via Washington, that Kornmann had put in for an exit visa. That he was sailing from New Orleans, with a lady of his acquaintance, in a week or so. The rest was just a question of spade work. We located him with time to spare."

"But I still don't see——"

"Why Kornmann should do us a favor, you mean? That's something else I left to Moreau. Naturally the Frenchman wasn't in on this Dawkins deal. But he had enough else on Kornmann to lock him up indefinitely." Luke was deep in his smoke screen now and enjoying it completely. "Don't look so confused, Chris. I know that a mere legal paper was an anticlimax, after Dawkins and Bernstein. It was also necessary—and highly moral. Porter could never have dismissed the case without it."

"Just when did Moreau come into the picture?"

Sam said quickly, "The night you pulled his girl through phlebothrombosis. He contacted Karen first, and she brought him in to us." Sam smiled quietly at Chris across Luke's cluttered desk. "Moreau's no knight-errant, you understand, but he's got enough sense to be grateful to the right people. When I suggested he go to work on the Austrian he joined our team at once."

"But you went through with the Dawkins inoculation just the same."

"Luke has told you why," said Sam patiently. "Must I draw another diagram?"

"What about Dwight? When he knows I'm free——"

"Dwight will stay put," said Pudge. "I got three of my best boys tailing him right now, to make sure of that. *He'll* be in Milton when they slap him with that bench warrant."

Chris tossed the copy of Kornmann's affidavit among the welter of Luke's papers. He tried to summon a picture of Gilbert Dwight, waiting for the ax of justice to fall. For the last time he realized that Dwight—as a symbol of evil—left a great deal to be desired. Now that he was definitely crossed off as a menace, he couldn't even hate the compensation doctor too industriously. At the moment the problem of Jean Moreau—and how to thank him adequately—seemed far more urgent.

Sam said, "Of course we don't expect a medal for this, brother. But aren't you even grateful?"

357

"Shut up," said Chris. "You know I'd choke if I tried to say what I'm thinking."

Pudge roared with laughter. "So help me, Luke, I think he still blames us for fighting their way——"

"Like hell he does," said Luke. "He's not that pure a crusader. If you ask me, he's still trying to catch up on the fact he's out of clink."

"And wondering who to thank first," said Sam. Chris didn't miss the wink they exchanged.

Luke was elaborately casual. "You might start with Karen, then. After all, she dreamed up the hyoscine——"

"And put the heat on Moreau," added Sam. "What's more, she's waiting right now at the clinic for your report."

"Hold everything!" shouted Luke as Chris made for the door. "We've got to have a drink on this."

But Chris shook his head from the doorway. "I'll take a rain check on that, Luke. Right now I'm going back to work."

Karen said, "I knew you'd win, Chris. Even without Sam's touch of opera."

"I don't believe it. You were just as depressed as I."

"Only because those dwarfs dared to threaten you." She pushed back her crown of bright hair and stretched luxuriously before she got down from her microscope stool. "Just the same, I'd have given a great deal to see Bibb's face when the judge opened that affidavit."

"Someday I'll thank you for that, as you deserve——"

"For persuading Moreau? But he was already persuaded when he came to me." She crossed the tiny laboratory and took his hands. "Congratulations, Chris. When *I'm* so happy about it, why aren't you?"

He stopped short on that—amazed, as always, by her insight. This morning he had every right to happiness. He had won the trial, and Karen was waiting for him to propose. Or rather, to remind her of her promise to marry him. It was the moment for which he'd worked all these weary months. Chris closed his eyes to pin the vision down—and saw only the remembered outline of a strange operating theater. The heart-stopping curve of Roz Borland's body on the table. The dusky hue of her skin as he and Moreau had fought to save her.

Karen was laughing at him when he opened his eyes. "Isn't it real even now?"

358

"Never mind that," he said. "You know this game is just beginning for all of us. Maybe I'm at first base now, but that's all. We've still to testify at Dwight's trial. Then the compensation hearing——"

But Karen's laughter surrounded his words. "You've had enough law to last you awhile, Chris. Why not ask me to marry you, instead?"

"Why not give me a chance?"

Karen climbed to her high stool again and folded her hands in her lap. "Am I solemn enough now?"

He put both arms around her. "Much too solemn. You know damned well you've no reason for refusing me."

"Only one," she said. "You don't need me now."

"How often must I say I'll always need you?"

"Say it as often as you like, my dear. I do enjoy hearing it. But it simply isn't true."

He made an inclusive gesture—and wondered why his heart leaped with such a strange sense of release. "We built all this together, Karen. We've got to finish it—share it——"

"You don't love me," she said. "If you did, you wouldn't woo me by offering me the clinic. You'd offer me yourself instead." He bent forward to kiss her, but she put soothing fingers between his lips and hers. "Don't be gallant, Chris. Don't even try. I can take my discovery quite calmly. Surely that proves neither of us is in love with the other."

"But you said——"

"—that I'd marry you if you needed me. I'll be honest, darling. At the time I did think Dwight could break you. I know better now. You're going on to the career you've always wanted—and you're not going alone. Why should I remind you of your chivalry—when you can do so well on your own?"

He did not grasp her meaning at once. "But that night at your cottage——"

"The night I wore my hair up," she said. "I hoped it would intrigue you."

The thought came out whole, despite him. "Good God, Karen. Less than a week ago—we were everything to each other!"

"I enjoyed it too. Very much indeed. Does that mean I must marry you—or vice versa?"

He was still staring, trying to find his voice. "You're a woman in a million. Or did I tell you that once?"

"It bears repeating," she said.

This time she offered no resistance when he kissed her. "Don't take that for good-by, either," he said sternly. "You'll have to invent a much more respectable reason for jilting me."

Karen said, "Paul doesn't know it yet, but I'm accepting him this afternoon."

So that was it. Chris took a quick turn of the room and made what he hoped was a rueful pause at the glass specimen rack. Staring hard at the ranked test tubes and reagents, he was able to release a genuine grin. Of course it would never do to let her guess—so soon—how happy he was for them both.

"Does Paul propose as regularly as that?"

"He will," said Karen cheerfully. "And you needn't look so dazed. You know you're delighted."

Still he did not turn. "When will you be—leaving us?"

"Sometime in the new year. Paul is slated to go to the Pacific on a mission. Capital M, this time: a long-term research job on *filiarisis*. That's another reason why he can use a good lab assistant." She wrinkled her nose at him as he faced her at last. "Will you give me a reference?"

"You mean that you—and he——"

"I don't mean that at all, Chris. The Public Health Service will let us go as man and wife. You see, Paul is also determined to make me honest."

Chris said, "I'll give you a reference, all right. I'll make it the best damned——" He broke off to kiss her. "You win, Dr. Agard."

"Thanks, Dr. Land."

"And I don't know which of you is the luckier."

She accepted the accolade as calmly as she had taken his kiss. "You won't mind, then, if I stay over for your own wedding?"

"I'm not planning to marry."

"Oh yes you are. She's waiting for you now. We had a heart-to-heart conference this morning and arranged everything. She's going to keep it quite simple. Not more than a hundred intimate friends. Her father will give her away in the garden at Slave Hill——"

"If you're speaking of Rosalie——"

"What's more," said Karen, "you'd better go straight to the County and do your part. I can't let you off for more than a half hour: your patients are piled up like cordwood——"

She watched him—and laughed at him out of those kind eyes of hers, as he steadied himself on the zinc apron of her worktable. "One thing more. Don't waste my time asking about Jean Moreau. *He* bowed out of our cosmos, with a ticket to Cherbourg, just before he flew to New Orleans." She put an envelope into Chris's unresponsive hand. "It's all in writing, if you don't believe me. Can you bear to read one more letter this morning?" She went on smiling as he ripped the single sheet from the envelope. "If you ask me, Dr. Land, the French can be wonderfully efficient at times."

Her lips still framed that easy smile as he kissed them quickly—and rocketed out of the laboratory without even a backward glance.

Newsboys were crying an extra as he drove through Duval Square. He bought a copy at the next light and stared at it blankly until he heeded the traffic officer's bellow. Later he would remember quite clearly the story of Allied victory on the Rhine. Another story—in a front-page box—breaking the news of his vindication in court. The proof of that verification, when Dr. Deavers stopped him in the lobby of the County Hospital to wring his hand. Even the way the old doctor stared when he broke free to run down the elevator.

Her room was only half lighted when he paused in the doorway. For a moment he thought she was sleeping in the dim-gold aureole of her hair. Then she opened her eyes and smiled down at Jean Moreau's letter, crumpled against the newspaper in his hand.

"Did you come to read me that?"

"I don't think I should," he said. "It's much too flattering."

"Most of the adjectives are mine," said Roz. "Jean wrote it in this room, just before we said good-by."

Chris stood in the doorway while she put out her hand and opened the Venetian blind at the window. Her face came alive in the bright patina of sunlight, and her hair took on its wild, new-copper sheen. He found that he was beside her, stroking her hair softly with no sense of transition.

Roz said, "Won't you make it official?"

His hand paused against her cheek, and she covered it with her own. "Look back carefully," he said. "This is important. Which of us was stupider?"

"You, of course. I knew from the first. I even told you so."

"I knew too," he said miserably.

361

"It was quite in character—keeping your feelings in safe deposit."

He wondered what Karen had said to her—and knew instantly that both women had a right to that secret. He wondered, too, what he could tell her now, to atone for these months of waiting. But Rosalie Borland saved him the trouble, after all.

"I happen to owe you my life, Dr. Land. Twice, to be exact. I'll scream if you don't collect the first instalment."

After he had bent to her lips he found he didn't regret the waiting.